CW01477037

Dancing Shadows

Maya Dawn

Published by Maya Dawn, 2024.

DANCING SHADOWS

First edition. October 21, 2024.

Copyright © 2024 Maya Dawn.

ISBN: 979-8227723208

Written by Maya Dawn.

Chapter 1: Unraveled Connections

The studio is an intimate space, the wooden floors polished to a gleam that reflects the faint glow of the overhead lights. Mirrors line the walls, capturing every angle of my nervous energy as I adjust my hair in a loose bun, fingers trembling slightly. It feels like stepping into a painting where colors dance and intertwine, a vivid reminder of the artistry of life that New Orleans embodies. The faint strains of a jazz saxophone drift in through the open window, wrapping around me like a warm embrace. Outside, tourists meander, their laughter a distant echo of the vibrant city pulse, and I take a moment to absorb the beauty that surrounds me—a beautiful chaos that mirrors my own emotions.

I remind myself that I am here to teach, to inspire, not to dwell on past heartbreaks. My heart aches a little less as I picture the students who will walk through the door. I imagine them, bright-eyed and eager to move, to connect through rhythm and grace. I want to be the kind of instructor who ignites a passion for dance in them, someone they can look up to.

Just as I settle into this comforting thought, Rylan enters, and the air shifts around me. He strides in with an effortless confidence that makes the room feel larger, his presence commanding without trying. His tousled dark hair falls into his eyes, but it only adds to his allure, a charming contrast to his serious demeanor. Rylan wears a fitted black T-shirt and sweatpants that hug his frame, and I find myself involuntarily comparing his physique to that of the statues that adorn Jackson Square—chiseled, sculptural, and undeniably captivating.

"Ready to dazzle the crowd?" he asks, his voice low and teasing as he leans casually against the doorframe, a playful smirk dancing on his lips.

"Only if you promise to keep up," I shoot back, trying to match his playful tone. Inside, I'm a bundle of nerves, but I'm determined not to show it.

"Challenge accepted." He winks, and for a moment, the world outside fades. The connection between us feels electric, crackling with an energy that leaves my heart racing and my mind racing faster.

As the clock ticks down to our first class, I set aside my doubts, focusing instead on the music—the rhythm that courses through my veins like a lifeline. With each note, I allow my body to sway and lose myself in the anticipation of sharing this art with others. When the students finally arrive, a lively group of aspiring dancers with wide eyes and eager smiles, I feel the atmosphere shift again, filled with potential and excitement.

"Welcome! I'm Elise, and this is Rylan," I introduce us, my voice steady despite the butterflies taking flight in my stomach. "We're thrilled to share this journey with you."

As the class unfolds, I lead them through warm-ups, guiding them with gentle encouragement. Rylan demonstrates a move with effortless grace, and I watch as the students become enamored, their attention riveted on him. I can't help but feel a pang of envy; he seems to possess an innate charisma that pulls people in like moths to a flame. Yet, with every laugh shared and every misstep corrected, a camaraderie begins to form—a bond that is equal parts exhilarating and terrifying.

After class, we gather our things, and Rylan leans against the wall, a satisfied grin on his face. "You were amazing out there," he says, genuine admiration lighting up his electric blue eyes. "The way you connect with the students, it's inspiring."

I flush at the compliment, the warmth spreading through me. "Thanks, but I couldn't have done it without your help. You make it look so easy."

"It's all about finding the right rhythm," he replies, a twinkle of mischief in his eyes. "Maybe you could help me find mine sometime?"

I feel a jolt of surprise, and laughter bubbles up. "I thought you were the one who had it all figured out."

"Trust me, there's always room for improvement." His tone is teasing, but beneath it lies something deeper—an invitation to explore, to discover.

As the evening light bathes the studio in a golden glow, I feel a connection with Rylan that goes beyond mere attraction. It's the beginning of something exciting and uncharted, a thread woven into the fabric of my new life here in New Orleans. Yet, as much as I want to lean into this budding relationship, shadows of my past tug at the edges of my mind. The memory of betrayal lingers like an unwanted ghost, whispering reminders of heartache.

"Are you from around here?" I ask, curious to peel back the layers of his enigmatic persona.

"Originally? No. Just a wandering spirit, I suppose," he replies, his gaze distant for a moment. "But this city... it has a way of drawing you in, doesn't it? Like a siren song."

"Exactly," I agree, my heart echoing his sentiment. "It feels alive here, doesn't it? Every corner has a story."

"Many stories," he adds, his voice softening. "Some are beautiful, and others... well, let's just say they leave scars."

The air grows heavy with unspoken words, and I sense a shift in him, a glimpse into the complexity of his past. It intrigues me, but before I can pry further, he flashes that charming smile again, and the moment dissolves like sugar in coffee.

"Let's grab some beignets after this," he suggests, and my stomach flips at the idea of sharing a plate, an intimate experience amid the lively chaos of the city.

"Sounds perfect," I reply, feeling an anticipation surge within me. The city pulses around us, and I know this is just the beginning—a new chapter filled with passion, rhythm, and perhaps even the unraveling of past wounds.

As we step out into the warm New Orleans evening, the streetlights flicker to life, illuminating the world with a golden hue. The sounds of jazz drift in the air, weaving through the laughter and chatter of the streets, wrapping around us like a promise. In that moment, I embrace the uncertainty, ready to dance through whatever comes next.

The beignets are an explosion of sweetness, powdered sugar dusting my fingers as I take a bite, the warm pastry melting in my mouth. Rylan and I settle at a quaint outdoor table at Café du Monde, a steady stream of jazz wafting through the night air. The sounds of the city wrap around us, vibrant and intoxicating, like the smell of chicory coffee that mingles with the scent of the nearby river. I watch as Rylan takes a sip of his coffee, the steam curling upwards, and I find myself lost in the depth of his blue eyes, wondering about the stories hidden behind them.

"So," he begins, leaning forward, a mischievous glint dancing in his gaze. "What's the real reason you decided to move to New Orleans? Was it the jazz? The food? Or maybe the irresistible charm of your handsome co-instructor?"

I can't help but laugh, a lightness filling my chest. "Definitely the beignets," I reply, waving a sugary finger for emphasis. "But honestly, I wanted a fresh start, a chance to dive into something new. Life was getting a little too... predictable back home."

"Predictable is overrated," he says, nodding thoughtfully. "I mean, look at this city. Every street tells a different story. Take that one over there." He gestures towards a nearby alley, where a street artist is painting a mural, colors splashing vibrantly against the weathered brick. "How many tales do you think that wall has witnessed?"

"A thousand, at least," I muse, captivated by the way he observes the world. "It's like a living history, isn't it?"

"Exactly! It's chaotic and beautiful. Much like dance." Rylan leans back, and I notice the way his smile reaches his eyes, making my stomach flutter. "So, what story do you want to tell?"

I hesitate, the weight of his question settling over me like a heavy shawl. What story do I want to tell? The truth is, I'm still figuring it out. "I suppose I want to share the joy of dance with others," I say finally, feeling a bit bolder. "To show them it's more than just movement; it's expression, a way to connect."

"Connection," he echoes, the word hanging between us. "That's what it's all about, isn't it? Finding those threads that tie us together."

As the conversation flows, we delve deeper into our lives—past and present—layering vulnerability atop the lighthearted banter. Rylan reveals snippets of his life, a patchwork of experiences woven through different cities, each place leaving its mark on him. He shares how dance became his sanctuary, a refuge from life's unpredictability.

"I always thought I could outrun my past," he admits, his voice dipping low as the laughter of nearby diners fades into the background. "But it has a way of catching up with you, doesn't it?"

I nod, understanding all too well the sensation of ghosts lingering just out of sight. "What did you think you could outrun?" I ask, hoping he'll trust me enough to let me in.

"Just some... mistakes," he says, his smile faltering slightly. "I thought if I moved around enough, I could escape who I used to be. But every city reminds me of something I tried to forget."

His vulnerability catches me off guard, and for a heartbeat, I wonder if he can sense the shadows in my own past. "We all have them," I say softly. "Those mistakes. It's what we do with them that matters."

He looks at me then, a flicker of something—curiosity, perhaps—lighting up his eyes. "So what about you? What are you running from?"

I hesitate, my heart racing as I consider how much to reveal. "It's less about running and more about rediscovering who I am. I had a... complicated relationship before this. I thought it was everything I wanted, but in the end, it was just an illusion. I want to reconnect with myself, to dance without the weight of that past."

His expression shifts, a mixture of empathy and understanding playing across his features. "You're brave for stepping into something new," he says, his tone sincere. "It's easy to get stuck in our own narratives."

"Bravery is just fear in disguise," I reply, feeling a connection spark between us. The air is charged with unspoken possibilities, and I'm acutely aware of how our fingers brush against the shared plate of beignets.

"Can we agree to help each other unravel our stories then?" he suggests, a hint of mischief returning to his eyes. "A dance partnership of sorts. I promise to keep it entertaining."

I can't help but laugh again, a lightness returning to the moment. "Deal. But only if you promise to share the embarrassing stories. You know, the ones that make you cringe."

"Oh, I've got a treasure trove of those," he replies, leaning back with a grin that makes my heart skip. "But you'll have to earn them."

As the night wears on, we continue our banter, the city buzzing around us. The moonlight bathes everything in a silvery glow, and the beignets vanish, leaving only laughter and the promise of what lies ahead. We share our dreams and fears, our voices mingling with the soft sounds of jazz, the world around us fading until it's just the two of us, wrapped in a cocoon of connection.

"Hey, what's your favorite dance style?" Rylan suddenly asks, tilting his head curiously.

"Contemporary, I think," I say, a smile spreading across my face as I recall the freedom it brings. "There's something magical about it—breaking the rules, pushing boundaries."

He raises an eyebrow, a playful challenge in his expression. "Breaking the rules, huh? I like the sound of that. Care to show me your moves sometime?"

"Only if you promise to keep up," I shoot back, mirroring his earlier challenge.

"Challenge accepted," he grins, and with that simple exchange, I feel the thrill of possibilities unfurling before me. As we finish our coffees, the city hums with life, and I know this journey is just beginning. Rylan and I, two dancers on the cusp of something extraordinary, a duet waiting to be choreographed against the backdrop of a city that thrives on stories yet to be told.

The night air wraps around us like a silk scarf as we rise from the table, laughter bubbling between us. I can't shake the feeling that whatever lies ahead is going to be as unpredictable as the city itself, filled with twists and turns, but somehow, it feels right. And for the first time in a long while, the prospect of the unknown feels like an open invitation rather than a weight on my shoulders.

The night air has a life of its own as Rylan and I stroll through the bustling streets of New Orleans, laughter bubbling up between us like the fizz of freshly opened champagne. The city, vibrant and alive, thrums with the rhythm of music, laughter, and the occasional shout from a street performer drawing in a captivated crowd. The way the streetlights cast a golden hue over everything makes it feel as though we're walking through a painting, the colors warm and inviting.

"So, where's our next adventure?" Rylan asks, his voice teasing as we dodge a group of tourists clamoring for the perfect photo by a local artist's stall.

"Adventure? I thought we were just here for the beignets," I quip, nudging him playfully. "Besides, I'm not ready to risk my life on the streets just yet. I need to keep my limbs intact for the dance studio."

Rylan chuckles, the sound rich and full, wrapping around me like a cozy blanket. "Fair point. But beignets can only take you so far. I happen to know a hidden jazz bar that plays music straight from the heart of the city. They say the vibe can knock your socks off, and it's not just the beignets talking."

My curiosity piqued, I raise an eyebrow. "Are you sure it's not just you? You seem to have a knack for enchanting places."

"Why, thank you," he replies with mock seriousness, placing a hand over his heart. "I do my best to enchant when the situation calls for it."

"Alright, lead the way, oh enchanted one." I roll my eyes, a smile tugging at my lips as he takes my arm and guides me through the streets.

We weave through narrow alleys that feel like secrets waiting to be discovered, the sound of jazz growing louder as we approach our destination. The bar is unassuming, a small wooden door nestled between two larger buildings, its entrance adorned with a neon sign that flickers intermittently. "The Blue Note," he announces proudly, and my anticipation swells.

Inside, the atmosphere is intoxicating. The low light creates an intimate setting, with mismatched furniture that whispers stories of past patrons. The sound of a trumpet slices through the air, soulful and raw, and I can feel the music vibrating in my chest, drawing me in like a moth to a flame.

Rylan guides us to a small table near the stage, and I can't help but admire how he seamlessly navigates the scene, greeting the bartender like an old friend. "Two drinks?" he asks, turning to me with an expectant grin.

"Surprise me," I reply, leaning back in my chair and taking in the ambiance. The band plays a slow, sultry tune that makes my heart race, and I find myself swaying in time with the music, the rhythm curling around me like a lover's embrace.

When Rylan returns with our drinks—a vibrant cocktail for me, a dark brew for him—he settles in, his eyes sparkling with mischief. "You'll love this one. It's a secret recipe."

I take a sip, the flavors exploding on my tongue—citrusy, sweet, with just a hint of something spicy that lingers, much like the city itself. "Wow, this is amazing! What's in it?"

"Ah, a magician never reveals his secrets," he quips, leaning closer, a playful challenge in his voice. "But I will say, it captures the essence of New Orleans—unexpected and full of life."

"Speaking of unexpected, how did you end up here?" I ask, genuinely curious about the man who seems to have an endless supply of charm and mystery.

Rylan takes a moment, the light shifting across his face as he considers his response. "Like many people, I was running from something," he finally says, his tone sobering. "But I found a home in the rhythm of the city, in the dance of life that pulses through its veins. It's liberating, really."

"Liberating or chaotic?" I counter, unable to resist a playful jab.

"Both," he admits, a grin breaking through. "Isn't that the beauty of it? Life is a series of contradictions. Just when you think you have it figured out, it throws you a curveball."

A comfortable silence settles between us, the music enveloping our conversation like a warm embrace. I glance around the bar, taking in the myriad of faces lost in the music, couples swaying to the rhythm, friends laughing over shared stories. This place is alive, and for the first time in a long while, I feel a spark of hope igniting within me.

"So, tell me about your dance style," he says, breaking the spell. "What's your secret ingredient?"

"Movement is like a language for me," I begin, feeling animated as I speak. "It's all about expressing emotion. I want people to feel something when they watch. Whether it's joy, sadness, or the thrill of connection, dance allows us to communicate in ways words can't."

"Beautifully put." Rylan leans in, his gaze steady. "You really believe that?"

"I do. It's like a form of alchemy, transforming raw emotion into something tangible," I reply, my heart racing at the intensity of his focus. "But I think it's a two-way street; you have to allow yourself to be vulnerable, to let the audience in."

"Vulnerability is terrifying, though," he murmurs, the depth of his voice sending shivers down my spine. "What if they don't get it? What if they judge you?"

"Then they don't deserve to be part of your story," I say, surprising myself with the strength in my conviction. "Art is subjective, just like life. You have to dance for yourself first."

Rylan's expression shifts, his eyes softening with understanding. "That's profound. I think you might be teaching me more than I expected."

Before I can respond, the music changes, shifting into a lively, infectious rhythm that sets the room ablaze with energy. Rylan's eyes light up, and he stands, extending a hand toward me. "Come on! Dance with me!"

My heart races as I take his hand, rising to my feet and allowing him to lead me onto the small dance floor. The moment our bodies are in sync, the worries and fears that had clung to me like shadows begin to fade. The world melts away; it's just us, two dancers weaving through the rhythm, hearts pulsing in time with the music.

As we move, I feel a connection deepen, a chemistry that is undeniable. He spins me, the motion dizzying and exhilarating, and laughter spills from my lips. It's as if we've entered our own world, a space where everything else ceases to exist.

But then, just as I lean in closer to catch his eye, I notice something in the corner of the bar—an all-too-familiar face watching us. My heart plummets as I recognize the shadow of my past, a figure I never expected to see here. It's him, the ghost of my previous life, and the weight of that history crashes down around me like a wave.

I stumble mid-step, the world spinning as Rylan's hand tightens around mine, concern etched across his features. "Elise? Are you alright?"

I glance back at Rylan, my thoughts racing, heart pounding. "I—" I stammer, my voice barely above a whisper, suddenly unsure if I can continue this dance or this newfound connection. The air feels charged with unspoken tension, and I realize this moment is teetering on the edge of something monumental.

As I look back at the figure in the bar, I know this night is far from over, and the echoes of my past are about to unravel everything I've fought to rebuild.

Chapter 2: Ghosts of the Past

The café was a riot of color, with bright yellow walls adorned with vintage photographs and plants that spilled from their pots like nature's confetti. The smell of freshly brewed coffee mingled with the sugary scent of pastries, wrapping around me like a comforting blanket as I took my usual corner seat. It was a safe haven, a little world of my own, where I could drown out the echoes of my past. Yet, today, those echoes threatened to drown me instead.

As I stirred my caramel macchiato, the metallic clink of my spoon against the ceramic mug felt intrusive, a reminder of how I'd been failing to drown out the noise. I watched as couples mingled and laughed, their hands brushing together in fleeting touches that felt like the ghosts of my memories reaching out to me. Each glance in Rylan's direction sent an electric jolt through me—he was seated at the bar, laughing with the barista as she handed him a steaming cup. The way he threw his head back, his laughter spilling into the air like music, made my heart race and my stomach twist. It was infuriating.

Why did he have to be so effortlessly charming? It was like he was crafted from sunshine, radiating warmth that drew people in. My insides felt like a knot, twisted tight with the weight of my memories, and the last thing I needed was to be reminded of what I had lost.

"Hey, you," he called over, his deep voice cutting through the ambient chatter. "You look like you could use a pick-me-up." He flashed me that smile, the one that could probably light up a darkened room, and I felt my resolve wobble. I forced a smile in return, hoping it didn't betray my inner turmoil.

"I'm fine, really," I replied, my voice a touch sharper than intended. The laughter around us seemed to freeze momentarily, the air thick with my discomfort. I immediately regretted my tone, but it was too late; I'd opened that door. Rylan raised an eyebrow, a playful challenge glimmering in his gaze.

"Fine? You're in here alone, stirring your drink like it owes you money. That's not fine, that's like a textbook definition of not fine." He slid into the seat across from me, unabashedly taking up space with an ease that both fascinated and frustrated me.

"Maybe I enjoy my own company?" I shot back, leaning back slightly, crossing my arms defensively. But as I said it, I knew it was a lie. There was nothing enjoyable about the isolation creeping in, the way it settled in the hollows of my heart, making it hard to breathe.

"Ah, a classic case of 'I'm fine' that actually means 'help me.'" His tone was teasing, yet there was something deeper in his eyes that suggested he understood more than he let on. "Let me help then. How about I show you my favorite pastry? You'll definitely need a little sugar rush if you're going to keep up that tough facade."

I couldn't help but chuckle, a genuine laugh bubbling up against my better judgment. "You're insufferable, you know that?"

"Only because I'm persistent," he grinned, and it was like the sun breaking through a gloomy sky. "And you're the most fascinating person in this whole café."

Fascinating? I wasn't sure if that was flattering or just a polite way of saying I was a train wreck. The compliment hung in the air, threading through my defenses, challenging me to let it in. A part of me ached to lean into that, to revel in the warmth of his attention. But another part—a darker, more cautious part—reminded me of the last time I'd let myself fall.

The weight of my memories crashed into me again, like waves against a fragile shore. I thought of Ethan, his face, the way he'd looked at me just before it all shattered. The whispered arguments we'd had, each one another crack in the veneer of our relationship. "You'll never be good enough," he'd said one night, voice laced with disdain. "You're just... you."

That sting had lingered long after the breakup, festering like an untreated wound. It was that feeling of inadequacy that haunted me, echoing in my head every time I caught Rylan's eye or felt the warmth of his laughter wash over me. I should have known better than to allow myself to feel anything for him.

"I, uh, actually have a lot on my mind," I stammered, my eyes darting away. I could feel Rylan's gaze, piercing through my façade.

"Hey," he said, his tone softening. "I'm not here to pry. But if you need to talk, I'm all ears. No judgment."

It was a simple offer, yet it unsettled me. Why was he being so kind? I was a mess, riddled with insecurities and uncertainties, and the last thing I wanted was to burden him with my past. "I just... need some space right now."

Rylan nodded slowly, the disappointment evident in his eyes. "Space is fine. Just know that I'm here when you're ready."

I watched him retreat into silence, the flicker of hurt crossing his face making me ache in a way I hadn't expected. He wasn't just a distraction; he was someone who genuinely seemed to care. The tension twisted in my chest, reminding me how tightly I was holding onto my ghosts. But in that moment, I wanted to take a risk, to embrace the possibility of a connection beyond my fears.

The barista placed a pastry in front of me, a lemon tart that sparkled under the light like a tiny sun. Rylan glanced at it with raised eyebrows. "You're going to need a fork for that," he pointed out.

I rolled my eyes but couldn't help but smile, the weight of my memories momentarily lifted. As I picked up the fork, my fingers brushed against his, a spark igniting between us. My heart skipped a beat, an unexpected thrill surging through me. Maybe, just maybe, I could trust myself to enjoy this moment without the ghosts looming over me.

The lemon tart sat tantalizingly before me, the bright yellow filling glistening under the café's soft lights. I speared it with my fork, bringing the first bite to my lips. The tangy sweetness exploded on my tongue, momentarily distracting me from the whirlwind of thoughts that threatened to consume me. It was absurd how something so small could offer such a burst of joy, yet as the flavors danced in my mouth, I felt a flicker of something I hadn't in a while: hope.

Rylan was watching me, his eyes twinkling with amusement as I savored the pastry. "So, what's the verdict? Is it worthy of your undivided attention?"

I swallowed, the taste still lingering as I met his gaze. "It's definitely better than wallowing in my own melodrama," I replied, attempting to lighten the mood. "But don't get too cocky. I'm not about to turn my entire life over to pastry."

"Yet," he countered with a smirk, leaning back in his chair. "Just you wait. Before you know it, you'll be a regular here, trading your secrets for baked goods."

The easy banter sparked something inside me, a flicker of warmth that threatened to push against the fortress I had carefully constructed around my heart. As much as I wanted to brush him off, Rylan had this way of breaking through my defenses, chipping away at the walls built from disappointment and fear.

I took another bite, pretending to focus on the tart, though my thoughts began to drift. It was impossible not to think of my past, of the way Ethan's words had seeped into my bones, filling me with a doubt that had settled in like an unwelcome guest. I wanted to push those thoughts aside, but they crept in, lingering just at the edges of my consciousness.

"So, what's your story?" Rylan asked, breaking my reverie. "You can't possibly be all work and no play. What do you do for fun when you're not busy avoiding eye contact with me?"

The directness of his question caught me off guard. I hesitated, my mind racing through the things I used to love before the shadows of my past loomed so large. "I like to paint," I finally admitted, surprising myself with the revelation. "It's a way to express what I can't say out loud."

"Really? I would have guessed you were secretly a rock star or a world-class chef," he replied, his eyes bright with intrigue. "But painting? That's unexpected. What do you paint?"

"Oh, you know, the usual—landscapes, still lifes, the occasional existential crisis rendered in oils," I quipped, trying to keep the conversation light. "But lately, it's just been a lot of blank canvases staring back at me."

"Blank canvases? Sounds like you need a muse." He leaned forward, a glint of mischief in his eyes. "How about me? I've been told I make a pretty decent subject. Classic, handsome, and a little mysterious."

I laughed, a genuine burst of sound that surprised even me. "Mysterious? More like a golden retriever in a denim jacket."

He feigned offense, placing a hand on his chest as if I had delivered a fatal blow. "How dare you insult my rugged charm! I'm a complex soul with layers. Like an onion. Or a parfait."

"A parfait? Now you're just trying to flatter yourself," I retorted, the warmth of our banter lifting the weight that had been pressing down on me. There was something liberating about the way he made me feel, as though he could see beneath the surface, peeling back the layers to reveal something worth exploring.

"Listen, I'll take any comparisons to desserts. It means I'm sweet and full of surprises," he grinned, clearly pleased with his metaphor.

As we exchanged playful jabs, I felt my heart fluttering. This was new territory, unfamiliar yet exhilarating. I could almost feel the tendrils of my past loosening their grip, and in that moment, I realized just how desperately I craved connection.

But that realization was swiftly accompanied by a sharp pang of guilt. How could I allow myself to feel this way when the ghosts of my past were still haunting me? Every laugh, every flirtatious quip with Rylan felt like betrayal to the memories of Ethan, memories that were still too raw to confront.

"What's your favorite color?" Rylan suddenly asked, his tone shifting to something more earnest.

I blinked, caught off guard by the simplicity of the question. "Why do you want to know?"

"Because it tells me something about you," he said, leaning closer. "Colors say a lot, you know? They reflect moods, emotions... sometimes even secrets."

I stared at him, a flicker of vulnerability sparking between us. "Blue, I guess. It reminds me of the ocean. Calm, yet unpredictable."

Rylan nodded, his expression thoughtful. "Blue. I like that. It suits you."

I felt my cheeks flush slightly at his compliment, the warmth spreading through me like the sun breaking through a cloudy day. "And you? What's your favorite color?"

"Red," he replied without hesitation. "Bold, vibrant, and unapologetic. Just like me." He winked, and I couldn't help but roll my eyes, but the truth was that I was captivated by his confidence.

Before I could respond, the café door swung open, and a gust of wind blew through, chilling the warmth of our moment. In walked a figure I recognized instantly—Ethan. My heart plummeted into my stomach, an icy chill washing over me as the reality of my past came crashing back like a tidal wave.

Rylan's attention shifted, and I watched as he caught sight of the man who had haunted my dreams. Ethan's presence felt like a dark cloud over the sunlit café, tainting the air with an uneasy tension. I froze, my pulse quickening, the laughter fading into an uncomfortable silence.

"Are you okay?" Rylan asked, his voice laced with concern as he sensed the shift in my demeanor.

I nodded, but the lie felt heavy on my tongue. I couldn't let the ghosts of my past dictate this moment. "Yeah, just... a surprise," I managed to say, though I felt anything but composed.

Ethan scanned the room, and for a brief moment, his eyes locked with mine. The familiar ache stirred within me, the memories rushing back uninvited. How had I thought I could escape this? How could I ever truly move on when the past could walk back into my life so easily?

Rylan's hand found mine on the table, his touch grounding and warm, a beacon in the storm brewing within me. I glanced at him, and the concern etched across his face made my heart ache. I was scared—scared of the past, scared of what it meant for my future. But as Ethan turned to approach, the choice lay before me: would I let my past define me, or would I finally find the strength to step forward into something new?

Ethan strolled into the café, exuding an unsettling mix of confidence and nonchalance, like a man who had just emerged from a storm and was determined to make his presence felt. The vibrant chatter around us dulled, the clinking of coffee cups faded into the background as I felt the heat of Rylan's hand tighten around mine, grounding me even as panic surged through me. Ethan's dark eyes swept the room, lingering on the familiar faces of patrons lost in their own worlds, before finally locking onto mine.

"Seraphina," he called, his voice slicing through the tension like a knife. It was a sound that had once filled me with warmth, now twisted with an edge of something more sinister. The way he said my name, like a spell he was trying to cast, sent a shiver down my spine.

I turned to Rylan, whose expression had shifted from playful to serious, concern etching deeper lines on his handsome face. "Do you want me to...?" he began, but I shook my head, not quite trusting my own voice. I was caught between the urge to flee and the stubbornness to stand my ground.

"Ethan," I managed, my voice barely above a whisper.

He approached our table, hands tucked casually into the pockets of his tailored jacket, exuding a charm that had once melted my resolve. "Fancy running into you here. I thought you'd been avoiding this place."

"I wasn't aware I needed to check in with you about my coffee habits," I shot back, the sharpness of my tone surprising even me.

Rylan cleared his throat, shifting slightly as if preparing for a confrontation. "We were just enjoying some pastries," he said, his tone polite yet tinged with a protective edge that was new and thrilling.

Ethan's gaze flickered to Rylan, assessing him like a hawk sizing up its prey. "And you are?"

"Someone who doesn't need to justify himself to you," Rylan replied, his voice steady, unwavering.

"Is that so?" Ethan leaned closer, a dangerous glint in his eyes. "Seraphina, you sure know how to pick them. What's next? A tattooed rock climber?"

The slight jab stung, not because it was true, but because it reminded me of how easy it had been for him to belittle my choices, to make me feel small. "I can choose whoever I want," I said defiantly, my heart pounding as I stood up to him. "Maybe you should focus on your own life instead of trying to dictate mine."

Rylan's hand slipped from mine, and I felt an empty space where warmth had just been. "Maybe it's time for you to leave, Ethan," he suggested, his tone now cool and measured.

Ethan straightened, the façade of casualness slipping for just a moment. "You think you can just come in here and play hero?" he shot back, directing his ire toward Rylan, who stood his ground with an air of confidence I had to admire.

"Let's not make this a scene," I interjected, desperately wanting to diffuse the tension hanging thick in the air. "I'm here to enjoy my day, not rehash old arguments."

Ethan regarded me with a mix of surprise and something deeper, as if he couldn't comprehend my refusal to submit to his presence. "Old arguments? Is that how you see it?" His voice lowered, taking on a softer, almost conspiratorial tone. "You're still dwelling on the past, Sera. You should know I'm willing to forgive."

My heart twisted painfully at his words. The idea of forgiveness sounded so appealing, so tempting. But deep down, I knew that forgiveness was often a ruse to trap someone in the past. "Forgiveness doesn't erase what happened, Ethan," I replied firmly. "It doesn't change the hurt or the doubts you planted in my head."

He straightened, a mask of indifference sliding over his features. "Well, I hope you find your way in this...new adventure." The sarcasm dripped from his words, sending an icy tendril of dread curling in my stomach.

"Funny you should mention adventure," Rylan chimed in, his voice filled with dry wit. "Because I think it's time for you to leave, and this adventure is ours to continue."

Ethan's smile hardened, and for a moment, I could see the storm brewing in his eyes, the anger barely concealed beneath a thin veneer of charm. "You think you can just sweep in and take my place? You don't know her like I do."

A chill settled in the space between us, heavy and suffocating. Rylan and I exchanged glances, and I felt the unspoken question hang in the air—could I truly trust him?

"Trust me," Rylan said, his voice low and serious. "I'm not trying to replace anyone. But you're not going to manipulate her again."

The challenge in Rylan's voice ignited something in me, a mixture of gratitude and something else entirely. This wasn't just a confrontation; it was a stand against the shadows of my past, a refusal to let them dictate my present.

"Don't fool yourself, Rylan," Ethan spat, turning his gaze back to me, dark and stormy. "She'll come back to me. They always do."

The implication sent shockwaves through me, and my pulse quickened. How could he still have that hold on me? The heat of Rylan's presence was comforting, yet the remnants of my past were clinging stubbornly. "No one is going back to you," I retorted, my voice firm. "You don't get to decide that."

"Ah, but don't you see?" Ethan's smile was slick, insidious. "You're still haunted by your choices. You're still playing with fire, and fire always burns."

With that, he turned on his heel and strode toward the exit, leaving a tension-filled silence in his wake. The café's chatter gradually resumed, the world outside continuing its mundane rhythm, but I felt suspended in a moment of realization.

Rylan remained silent, his eyes fixed on the door where Ethan had just exited, a storm of emotions swirling in his gaze. "Are you okay?" he finally asked, concern evident in his tone.

"I... I thought I was," I replied, my voice shaking slightly. "But now I'm not so sure."

"Look at me," he said gently, forcing me to meet his gaze. "Whatever that was, it doesn't define you. You're so much more than your past, Sera. Don't let him pull you back into that darkness."

His words were a balm, yet doubt clawed at me, whispering that I was still tethered to that darkness. Just as I opened my mouth to respond, my phone buzzed on the table, vibrating insistently. The sudden sound shattered the fragile moment, and I reached for it, my heart sinking as I saw the name on the screen.

It was Ethan.

With shaky hands, I pressed the button, and the message glowed ominously before me: "I know you think you can move on, but I'm not done with you yet. Meet me tonight at the old lighthouse."

Panic surged through me, a rush of fear and uncertainty. The lighthouse. A place where secrets had been buried, where past shadows had lurked, waiting to rise again. My heart raced as I glanced at Rylan, the unspoken question hanging thick in the air. Did I dare confront the ghosts of my past again, or would this be the moment that unraveled everything I had just begun to stitch together?

Chapter 3: Unexpected Encounters

The dimly lit jazz club hummed with a soft vibrato, the air rich with the scent of polished wood and faint smoke, mingled with the tantalizing aroma of something sweet from the kitchen. The band, a trio of skilled musicians, wove a melody that wrapped around the patrons like a warm embrace, inviting them to lean into the rhythm of the night. I nestled into my corner table, a safe distance from the throbbing pulse of the dance floor, my drink clutched tightly in my hand. The music spilled over me, and for a moment, I felt like an audience member in a grand performance of life, each note pulling at the strings of my heart.

It was on that fateful night, when the saxophonist's breathy notes painted stories of love and loss, that I found myself mesmerized by the swirling bodies on the dance floor. I watched couples sway, some lost in each other, others merely basking in the shared electricity of the music. My gaze drifted, and that's when I spotted him—Rylan. His movements were fluid and captivating, a testament to years of practice that danced on the fine line between passion and abandon. I had seen him before, lurking at the fringes of the dance scene, his magnetic aura a beacon that drew me in.

The moment seemed to stretch as I found myself leaning a little closer to catch a better view, my glass tipping dangerously close to the edge of the table. Just as the beat swelled, I turned to give my drink a celebratory lift, the ice clinking softly against the glass, and then—chaos. The sweet, vibrant liquid arched through the air like a comet, splattering across Rylan's impeccably tailored shirt. His eyes widened for the briefest second, shock morphing into surprise before erupting into laughter that rolled over the room like the very music that had entranced us both.

"Oh, dear, it seems I'm the victim of a flying cocktail," he quipped, shaking off the shock with an easy smile, his lips curving into a mischievous grin that sent a jolt of something warm through me. "I didn't know it was open bar night!"

I could feel the heat rising in my cheeks, a crimson blush blooming with each beat of my racing heart. "I'm so sorry! I thought you were part of the ambiance, like one of the performers," I stammered, trying to salvage the moment, though the laughter dancing in his eyes told me I was far from an irritable cocktail thrower. "I didn't mean to drench you in my drink. I was just—"

"Entranced? Lost in the music? Care to dance it off with me?" he suggested, his tone teasing yet sincere, as he gestured towards the floor. I blinked, my heart hammering against my ribcage. Dance? With him? This wasn't a simple spill; it was a full-fledged invitation wrapped in an unexpected twist of fate.

Without thinking, I rose to my feet, buoyed by a sense of adventure. The laughter of the crowd faded, replaced by the pulsating rhythm that beckoned us closer. As Rylan swept me onto the dance floor, the world around us faded into a blur of color and sound. His hand rested lightly on the small of my back, guiding me with an ease that made my nerves dissolve into a heady blend of excitement and fear.

We twirled together, the music wrapping around us like silk. I could feel the heat radiating from his body, our movements perfectly in sync despite the unpredictability of our earlier encounter. I surrendered to the moment, letting go of the thoughts that swirled in my mind. He spun me, and with each turn, I felt like I was shedding the weight of the week, the ghosts of my past swirling away in the night air.

As we danced, laughter spilled from our lips, a shared rhythm that punctuated the music. His eyes sparkled with mischief, a light that contrasted sharply with the brooding undertone I had sensed before. The energy around us shifted subtly, the jubilant atmosphere taking on a deeper, more intimate hue. Between the notes and the movement, he leaned in closer, his breath warm against my ear. "So, tell me about your drink-spilling skills. Is this a regular occurrence, or am I just special?"

I couldn't help but chuckle, the tension releasing in a burst of honesty. "You're definitely special, but I can't promise this isn't a hidden talent of mine. It could be my calling!" My playful retort drew a genuine laugh from him, rich and unguarded, and for a brief moment, I forgot about the worries that had clouded my mind.

"Maybe I should be flattered, then," he replied, spinning me again, our bodies moving in a rhythm that felt both exhilarating and safe. "Or maybe I should watch my back—who knows what other beverages might be thrown my way?"

The laughter faded, and in its place, something deeper lingered in the air. His expression shifted, and the teasing glint in his eyes softened. "You know, everyone has their burdens, their stories," he said, his voice dropping to a more serious tone. "Mine... well, it's not something I wear on my sleeve, but I've learned that sometimes the dance floor can be a good place to forget."

I met his gaze, feeling an invisible thread pulling us closer. "We all have something we're trying to escape," I replied, my heart unexpectedly heavy as I thought of my own shadows lurking at the edges of my mind. It was a delicate balance—vulnerability meeting the electrifying pulse of the night. "What led you to the dance floor?"

He paused, the rhythm of the music fading to the background as he considered his answer. "A family tragedy. It knocked the wind out of me. Dancing became my escape, a way to express what I couldn't put into words." The revelation hung between us, heavy and profound. In that moment, we were no longer just two strangers spinning on a dance floor but two souls intertwined by shared pain and unspoken understanding.

As he spoke, I glimpsed the vulnerability behind his charming façade, the flicker of emotions he typically shielded from the world. I could feel my own ghosts echoing in the shadows of his past, and I wanted to reach out, to connect, to mend the fractures that had marked our lives. Our laughter faded into a comfortable silence, replaced by a new kind of intimacy that made the air crackle with potential.

In the midst of the swirling dancers and the smooth notes of the saxophone, a connection began to form—fragile yet undeniable. The music swelled again, pulling us into its embrace, and for the first time in what felt like an eternity, I didn't feel so alone.

The music wrapped around us, a velvety cocoon of sound that made the world outside the club feel far away, as if it existed on another plane entirely. Rylan held me close, our bodies moving in sync, a beautiful choreography that seemed instinctive rather than practiced. Each spin and sway unearthed a deeper connection, the kind that felt like stumbling into an old, forgotten dream—one that was both thrilling and terrifying. My heart raced, not just from the dance, but from the intensity of the moment we were sharing, a delicate tapestry of laughter, vulnerability, and unspoken understanding.

I glanced up at him, his eyes glimmering like emeralds in the dim light, and for a fleeting second, I could almost see the layers of his story behind that charming exterior. There was a restlessness about him, a spark of passion that hinted at battles fought and lost. "What about you?" he asked suddenly, pulling me back from my thoughts. "What led you here tonight? Did you come to spill drinks on unsuspecting dancers?"

I laughed, the sound bright and carefree, buoyed by the rhythm of the music. "Not quite. I came to forget, like everyone else, I suppose. Just another ordinary Tuesday night turned extraordinary by... drink spills and footloose strangers." I emphasized the last part with a playful twirl that sent a few nearby dancers stumbling, eliciting chuckles and cheers from the crowd.

"Ah, the magic of chance encounters," Rylan mused, his voice low and inviting, as if he were sharing a secret. "Or should I say, the unpredictable nature of liquid refreshments?"

I leaned in closer, the intoxicating scent of his cologne—a mix of cedar and something almost citrus—invaded my senses, grounding me in the moment. "You know, for a guy who was just doused in a cocktail, you're remarkably charming," I teased, matching his playful tone. "Do you come here often to seek your revenge on unwitting drinkers?"

He chuckled, the sound rumbling in his chest, sending a delicious shiver down my spine. "Only when I'm feeling particularly brave. I can't resist the allure of dance and distraction. Besides," he continued, his expression turning thoughtful, "I've learned that sometimes it takes a little chaos to shake off the shadows of the past."

The warmth of his words settled between us, a comforting balm on the edges of our unspoken fears. "It's funny, isn't it?" I said, trying to navigate this emotional territory with the same lightness we had danced through. "How a simple spill can lead to a deep conversation about shadows and chaos? I could use a little more chaos in my life, honestly."

His gaze held mine, and for a heartbeat, the surrounding club melted away, leaving only the two of us suspended in this moment of understanding. "Chaos has its way of pushing us into the light," he replied, his voice dropping to a whisper. "But sometimes, it also reminds us of the darkness we try so hard to escape."

I felt a wave of recognition wash over me, a connection that echoed through the very marrow of my bones. "You've had your share of darkness, then?" I asked, my voice softening. "What haunts you, Rylan?"

He hesitated, a flicker of something profound crossing his features before he replied. "My family. They never understood my need for dance, my escape. When tragedy struck, it tore us apart. I found solace in the music, the movement, but the rest of my life was left in shambles." His words hung in the air, heavy with truth, and I could see the pain etched in the lines of his jaw.

"I'm sorry," I said, feeling the weight of his story settle between us. "It must have been incredibly hard."

He shrugged, the movement almost dismissive. "We all carry our burdens. You can't always choose how your story unfolds, but you can choose how you respond to it."

The honesty in his voice stirred something deep within me, and suddenly, I wanted to share my own burdens, my own dance with shadows. "I lost my brother a few years ago. An accident," I confessed, the words tumbling out before I could stop them. "He was my anchor, and when he was gone, I felt like I was adrift in a storm."

Rylan's expression softened, a deep empathy shining through. "That kind of loss leaves a mark, doesn't it? Like a shadow that never truly goes away."

"Exactly," I breathed, the truth of our shared pain creating a bond I had never anticipated. "It's as if you're constantly searching for pieces of yourself, but they're all scattered, like confetti after a celebration. You think you can gather them up, but some always slip through your fingers."

His hand tightened around mine, the connection between us sparking like electricity. "That's why we need moments like this—to remind us that we're not alone in the chaos. That we can dance through the pain."

I glanced around the room, where strangers continued to sway and twirl, blissfully unaware of the intimate dialogue unfolding amidst the melodies. "Or spill drinks on each other, right?" I quipped, hoping to lighten the mood, but the sincerity of our connection hung in the air, palpable and weighty.

"Exactly," he laughed, the sound rich and infectious, drawing me back into the moment. "Every spill, every dance step—it's all part of the journey."

Just as we seemed to be making sense of our worlds, the music shifted. The tempo quickened, the saxophone crying out with a frenetic energy that pulled us back into the thrumming heartbeat of the club. Rylan stepped back slightly, his eyes gleaming with mischief. "Ready for the real test? Let's see how well you can keep up."

Before I could respond, he spun me back into the throng, the dance floor a riot of color and movement. Laughter bubbled between us as we navigated through the crowd, my heart pounding not just from the exertion, but from the sheer thrill of being alive in that moment. The rhythm surged, vibrant and alive, filling the spaces between our words and fears with a joyful pulse that seemed to echo the very essence of life itself.

"Is this your secret weapon?" I shouted over the music, breathless as he twirled me again, the world blurring around us. "Dancing your way out of darkness?"

Rylan met my gaze, a wild light in his eyes. "Something like that! And it helps to have a partner who can keep up!"

With every turn, I felt more alive, the dance floor transforming into our shared sanctuary, where laughter drowned out the lingering shadows of our pasts. As the music crescendoed, it became clear that this moment—this spontaneous connection—was just the beginning of something that might help us both navigate the chaos, one dance step at a time.

The music pulsed around us, transforming the dance floor into a swirling tempest of movement and emotion. With each turn, I felt lighter, as if the burdens I carried were dissipating into the warm glow of the club. Rylan's laughter blended seamlessly with the rhythm, creating an intoxicating symphony that enveloped us. It was easy to get lost in this moment, to let the weight of reality slip away like the last notes of a fading song.

As we spun, his grip on my waist tightened, pulling me closer, our bodies moving in a harmonious dance that felt almost effortless. The warmth radiating from him ignited something deep within me, a flicker of hope that perhaps I could let go of my past, if only for tonight. I caught a glimpse of his carefree spirit, a stark contrast to the shadows that haunted him. "You know," I shouted over the music, "I think you're just trying to distract me from my drink-spilling skills!"

"Or maybe I'm hoping to teach you a few new moves!" Rylan shot back, his eyes sparkling with mischief. "Just wait until you see my secret weapon—it's called the 'avoid the drink.'"

We both laughed, the sound ringing out like a melody in its own right. Each spin and dip brought us closer, the connection between us becoming more tangible with every step. It felt as if we were rewriting the rules of our individual dances with darkness, creating a duet that was both thrilling and terrifying.

"Okay, show me this secret weapon!" I dared him, feeling an electric thrill run down my spine. He grinned, his confidence radiating like a beacon, and in that moment, I felt like the luckiest person in the room.

As the next song began, he led me into a series of quick footwork and spins, our bodies colliding and separating with a kind of playful abandon. I stumbled slightly, laughter spilling from my lips as I tried to keep up. "Is this part of your plan? Making me dizzy on the dance floor?"

"Absolutely!" Rylan replied, his voice laced with playful seriousness. "If I can't keep you on your toes, what's the point?" He leaned in closer, his breath warm against my ear, sending a shiver down my spine. "But I have to warn you—dizziness might come with the territory."

I returned his teasing smile, feeling a delightful rush of adrenaline. Each moment spent dancing with him felt like a stolen secret, an escape from the ordinary. Yet amidst the laughter and joy, I felt a thread of something deeper weaving between us, a recognition that went beyond our shared experiences.

"Do you dance often?" I asked, curious about this intriguing man who had unexpectedly stepped into my life like a breath of fresh air.

"Only when the music calls to me," he replied, his expression turning contemplative. "Sometimes, it's the only way to silence the chaos in my head. It's therapeutic, you know?"

I nodded, understanding all too well the way art and movement could serve as both refuge and release. "It seems like we both found our antidote tonight," I said, feeling a surge of connection between us. "Who knew a spilled drink could lead to this?"

The rhythm shifted again, drawing us deeper into the music's embrace. The saxophonist took center stage, pouring his soul into a haunting solo that wrapped around us, sending chills racing down my arms. I closed my eyes, losing myself in the sound, and for a moment, it was as if the world outside ceased to exist.

When I opened my eyes, I found Rylan watching me, his gaze intense and searching. "What are you thinking about?" he asked, genuine curiosity etched into his features.

I hesitated, my thoughts a swirling mix of vulnerability and hope. "Just how strange it is that we can connect like this in such a short amount of time. It feels... significant."

"Significant, huh?" He grinned, an inviting spark dancing in his eyes. "What if it's just the cocktails talking?"

"Or the jazz?" I countered playfully, raising an eyebrow. "Maybe it's the universe trying to tell us something."

"Or it could just be a coincidence," he replied, though there was a hint of intrigue in his voice that suggested he was more invested in this moment than he let on. "But I prefer to think that sometimes, chance encounters lead to unexpected connections."

The music slowed, and with it, the frenetic energy around us transformed into something more intimate. The laughter of fellow dancers faded into the background, leaving us cocooned in our own world. Rylan pulled me closer, and I could feel the warmth radiating from his body, the steady rhythm of his heartbeat matching my own.

"Tell me more about your brother," he prompted, his voice low and soothing, inviting me to peel back another layer.

I felt a lump form in my throat, a reminder of the sorrow I had buried beneath layers of humor and distraction. "He was... everything to me. My confidant, my cheerleader. Losing him was like losing a part of myself. I never thought I'd feel this lost, you know?"

Rylan's expression softened, a deep understanding reflected in his gaze. "I get that. The world doesn't prepare you for the sudden absence of someone who means everything."

As I spoke, I saw him open up just a little more, the walls he had carefully constructed starting to waver. "I often wonder how different things would be if he were still here. I think about all the conversations we'd have, the plans we'd make. But sometimes, I also think about how I can honor his memory by living fully, even when it's hard."

"Exactly," Rylan said, the words resonating deeply. "We can't change the past, but we can choose how to move forward. And sometimes, that means dancing through the pain."

As the final notes of the song faded into silence, I realized how profoundly connected I felt to him. It was as if we had both been caught in the same storm, finding shelter in each other's company. Just then, the lights flickered, casting a brief shadow over the dance floor. I noticed a flicker of unease in Rylan's eyes, the mask of lightness slipping for a moment.

"Is everything okay?" I asked, concern tinged with curiosity.

He hesitated, his gaze darting toward the entrance of the club, where a figure stood silhouetted against the dim light. The shadow shifted, revealing a tall man dressed in a dark leather jacket, his expression inscrutable. The energy in the room seemed to shift, an undercurrent of tension threading through the joyous atmosphere.

"Rylan," I whispered, sensing the change in his demeanor. "Who is that?"

He stiffened, his eyes narrowing, and the playful light that had danced between us dimmed. "It's... it's nothing. Just someone I thought I left behind."

I didn't miss the hint of worry in his voice, the way his body tensed as he watched the stranger approach. "Rylan," I pressed, an unease coiling in my stomach. "Are you sure?"

Before he could respond, the figure moved closer, the crowd around us parting as if sensing the gravity of the moment. I felt Rylan's hand slip from my waist, the warmth of his presence receding like a tide, leaving me standing at the edge of uncertainty.

"Hey, Rylan," the stranger called, a voice smooth but edged with menace. "Thought I'd find you here. We need to talk."

The words hung in the air like a thunderclap, the sudden shift in the atmosphere sending a chill down my spine. The dance floor, once a sanctuary of joy, now felt like a battleground. As Rylan's expression hardened, I realized that the chaos we had found refuge in had suddenly turned into something far more complex.

"Maybe we should go," I suggested, the urgency in my voice barely masking the rising dread.

But before Rylan could answer, the stranger stepped forward, a knowing smile creeping across his face. "Oh, I wouldn't leave just yet. This is going to be... interesting."

In that moment, with tension crackling like electricity between us, I understood that this was just the beginning. The night was about to unravel in ways none of us could have anticipated, and I wasn't sure whether we'd emerge unscathed or if the shadows of the past would engulf us both.

Chapter 4: Tides of Change

The soft buzz of my phone sliced through the stillness of the room, startling me from the comforting cocoon of thoughts I had been wrapping around Rylan and me. I glanced at the screen, my stomach twisting into knots as I saw my mother's name flashing. The excitement that had danced through my veins moments before evaporated, replaced by a cold rush of dread. I swiped to answer, bracing myself as her voice crackled through the line, shaky and strained.

"Catherine, I need you to come home. It's urgent."

Her words hit me like a punch, the kind that leaves you gasping for air, struggling to recover from the sudden shock. My heart thudded loudly in my chest, the idyllic vision of my life here—filled with Rylan's laughter and the warmth of our shared moments—shattered in an instant. The distance between us loomed larger than the ocean itself, an expanse filled with unanswered questions and fears.

"Mom, what happened? Are you okay?" I stammered, already knowing I wouldn't like the answer.

"I fell. It's just a sprain, but the doctor says I need help, and I can't manage alone."

The news clawed at my insides, leaving a hollow ache that gnawed at my resolve. I had finally begun to let Rylan peel away the layers of my guarded heart, and now I was being called back to a life that felt like a distant echo of who I used to be. The warmth of our stolen moments felt like it was slipping through my fingers, and I could hardly stand the thought of leaving it behind.

"I'll come home," I managed to say, my voice steadier than I felt. "I'll be there as soon as I can."

After hanging up, I paced the length of my room, glancing out at the sun-drenched horizon. The waves crashed rhythmically against the shore, their soothing sound now a cruel reminder of the distance that would soon separate me from Rylan. Each step echoed my turmoil—my longing to stay, my duty to leave.

I gathered my belongings, the mundane task transforming into a physical manifestation of my emotional struggle. Clothes, books, the small trinkets that had come to symbolize my life here, were tossed into my suitcase with little care. It was as though I was packing not just for a trip, but for a farewell. Each item seemed to whisper memories of Rylan: the way his laughter could lift the darkest of days, how his presence made the ordinary feel extraordinary.

As I zipped up the suitcase, I felt a familiar weight pressing down on my chest, a reminder of the promises I had made to myself—promises to be brave, to take chances. Would leaving mean breaking those promises? The thought made me pause, glancing at the door as if expecting Rylan to come bursting in, his presence grounding me against the storm of anxiety raging within.

Just then, a soft knock echoed through the stillness. My heart raced, and I opened the door, half-expecting a piece of my heart to walk through. Instead, it was Rylan, his face a mask of concern. "Catherine?" His eyes flicked to my suitcase, and the unspoken question hung heavily between us.

"I got a call from my mom," I said, the words spilling out in a rush, as if saying them quickly would make them less painful. "I have to go home."

Rylan's expression shifted, the warmth fading into something more serious. "Is she okay?"

"She fell. It's just a sprain, but she needs help." I took a breath, hoping to maintain some semblance of composure, but the tremor in my voice betrayed me.

"I'm sorry," he said, stepping closer, the heat of his body a comforting presence amidst my turmoil. "How long will you be gone?"

I shook my head, fighting the swell of emotions. "I don't know. A few days, maybe longer." I couldn't meet his gaze, afraid of what I might see reflected back—the disappointment, the understanding that sometimes distance can be the silent killer of budding love.

Rylan reached out, brushing a strand of hair behind my ear with a tenderness that sent a shiver down my spine. "You have to go, Catherine. Your mom needs you."

"I know, but..." My voice faltered, a mixture of guilt and longing welling up within me. "What if this... what if we don't make it through?"

He stepped back, giving me space but his eyes held mine, fierce and unwavering. "You're stronger than you think. We both are. If this is real, it will survive the distance."

The sincerity in his voice struck me deep, igniting a flicker of hope amidst my despair. "But what if it doesn't?"

"Then it wasn't meant to be," he said simply, his confidence wrapping around me like a warm blanket. "But I believe it will be. Just promise me you'll call."

The weight of those words hung in the air, heavy and profound. I wanted to argue, to voice all my fears, but something in the way he stood there, resolute and unwavering, made me reconsider. Perhaps love, like the tide, ebbed and flowed, but it was still a force to be reckoned with.

"I promise," I whispered, my heart aching with the bittersweet realization that the tide of our relationship was about to change, perhaps forever.

With a final, lingering glance, I stepped back into my room, the door closing between us like a curtain falling at the end of a show. The reality of my departure settled in, and I felt the absence of Rylan's presence like a wound freshly opened. The world outside continued to hum, oblivious to the storm within me, but I couldn't shake the feeling that this was a turning point—a crossroads where

I would have to decide if I would swim against the tide or allow the currents of fate to pull me away from the shore I had only just begun to explore.

The flight back to my childhood home was a blur of turbulence and thoughts spiraling like the clouds outside the window. I stared out at the gray sky, a mirror of my mood, while the cabin hummed around me, filled with people lost in their own worlds. I used to find comfort in the gentle sway of the plane, the sense of escape it offered. But today, it felt more like a cage, sealing me away from the warmth of Rylan and the life I had begun to build.

My thoughts drifted to our last moments together. Rylan's eyes held a mix of determination and vulnerability, as if he were daring me to believe in something more than the distance between us. I clung to that memory like a lifebuoy in a storm, even as uncertainty gnawed at the edges of my mind. What if my return home turned into an extended stay, a commitment I wasn't prepared for? I could almost hear the sigh of my own heart as it whispered reminders of past failures, of relationships lost to the relentless march of time and distance.

When the plane touched down, I took a deep breath, trying to shake off the weight of anxiety that had settled over me. The familiar landscape unfurled outside the terminal—patchy grass and weathered fences that lined the small airport's entrance. This was home, a place infused with the scent of childhood memories: fresh-baked cookies from the kitchen, the lingering warmth of my father's laughter echoing through the hallways, and the soothing hum of my mother's voice as she read stories that wrapped around me like a favorite blanket.

Yet, as I stepped outside, the crisp air hit me with the sharpness of reality. My mother needed me, and the momentary relief I had hoped for was quickly swallowed by the weight of responsibility. Climbing into the backseat of my sister's car, I was met with her concerned expression. "You look like you've seen a ghost," she said, her eyes scanning my face for clues.

"It's just... a lot," I replied, forcing a smile that felt more like a grimace. "Mom's waiting for me."

"She'll be okay. You know how she is."

Her words, meant to comfort, fell flat against the uncertainty that churned in my stomach. We drove through the familiar streets, my childhood home rising up like a fortress at the end of a long road, unchanged yet somehow different. As we pulled into the driveway, the sight of my mother's garden—once a riot of colors—now seemed muted, the flowers wilting under the weight of neglect.

I stepped inside, and the comforting scent of vanilla and lavender wrapped around me, mingling with the faint trace of antiseptic. My mother sat in her favorite armchair, a thick blanket draped over her legs, a hint of frustration flickering in her eyes as she looked up from her book. "Catherine, there you are! You look exhausted," she said, though her voice was laced with relief.

"I'm fine," I replied, though the tremor in my voice betrayed me. I rushed to her side, enveloping her in a hug that felt both familiar and distant, like reaching for a shadow. "How are you feeling?"

"Oh, it's just a little sprain. I can manage," she insisted, though the way she winced when she shifted told a different story. "But I do appreciate you coming home. I just didn't want to be alone."

As I settled in, I fought to keep my mind from drifting to Rylan. Conversations flitted between household chores, family gossip, and a string of mundane tasks that filled the air. It was comforting, yet I felt the gnawing emptiness of my own heart, a longing for the spark that had ignited with Rylan. The vibrancy of our moments together felt like a distant echo, drowning in the familiarity of this place.

Days slipped by in a haze of worry and care, the urgency of my mother's needs demanding my full attention. We shared meals that echoed laughter and stories, yet a part of me remained tethered to a world where my heart was learning to soar. Each night, I would find myself staring at my phone, the silence of the screen a reminder of what I had left behind. I could almost hear Rylan's voice in my mind, urging me to be brave, to trust in the bonds we had formed.

Then one evening, as I sat curled on the couch beside my mother, a sudden thought struck me. "Mom," I said, setting down my book, "what do you think about long-distance relationships?"

She glanced at me, her brow furrowed in contemplation. "Well, it depends. I think love can survive anything if it's strong enough. But it takes work. You have to communicate, trust each other, and make an effort to stay connected."

Her words felt like a gentle push from the universe, a reminder that perhaps love could be more than just a fleeting moment. "Have you ever had to do that?" I asked, curious to know how my parents had navigated their own challenges.

"Your father was away a lot for work when you were younger. It wasn't easy, but we made it work. Letters, phone calls, planning trips to see each other." She paused, her gaze drifting to the window, where the twilight deepened the shadows. "Love isn't always easy, but it can be worth it."

I couldn't help but smile, warmth blooming in my chest. "Do you think it's worth the risk?"

"Risk is part of love, my dear," she replied, her voice softening. "You have to decide what you're willing to fight for."

As her words settled in, a flicker of resolve ignited within me. I had to fight for Rylan. But how? Just then, my phone buzzed beside me, the screen lighting up with a familiar name. My heart raced as I picked it up, the tension coiling tighter in my chest. It was Rylan, and as I swiped to answer, I felt the weight of our distance pressing in once more.

"Hey, Catherine," he said, his voice wrapping around me like a warm embrace. "I've been thinking about you."

"I've been thinking about you too," I replied, my heart swelling at the sound of his voice.

"I miss you," he added, and the sincerity in his tone sent a shiver down my spine. "I wanted to see if you're okay."

"I'm managing," I said, though I could hear the wavering in my own voice. "It's tough here, but I'll be alright."

"Just remember, I'm here. I'm not going anywhere," he said, and there was a promise in his words, one that made the distance between us feel a little less daunting.

As we talked, the barriers I had built began to crumble, and I realized that our connection could endure. The tides of change didn't have to wash away what we had; instead, they could shape us into something even stronger.

Days turned into a blur of routines at home, where my mother's recovery became a delicate dance of care and chaos. I spent mornings making breakfast, my hands moving automatically as I stirred oatmeal and brewed coffee, while my mind flickered to thoughts of Rylan. Each moment of laughter shared with my mother felt like a bittersweet reminder of the joy I had left behind, punctuated by my phone buzzing with his texts—a lifeline connecting me to the life I craved.

"Hey, what are you wearing?" he texted one evening, his playful tone breaking through the weight of the day.

I smiled, imagining his mischievous grin as I responded, "Sweatpants and a tee. Fashion statement of the year."

"Wow, I'm amazed you could get any more chic," he replied. "But I'm sure you're rocking it. What's the scoop on the home front?"

I leaned against the kitchen counter, the familiar scent of my mother's lavender air freshener mingling with the aroma of simmering soup. "It's pretty mundane, actually. Lots of doctor visits and Netflix marathons. But you know what? I've realized I really can't stand that cooking show you love. Too much flambéing and not enough actual food."

He chuckled through the phone, and I could almost see him shaking his head. "Catherine, you're missing out. Just think about all the culinary skills you could acquire."

"I'm more of a cereal-for-dinner type," I shot back, feeling lighter, the laughter easing some of the tension in my chest.

"Don't worry, I still think you're fabulous," he replied, and his sincerity sent a warmth through me. I was grateful for these moments, where our connection felt real despite the distance, yet it only deepened the ache of longing.

As the days wore on, my mother's recovery progressed, and I started feeling the stirrings of restlessness. I missed the beach, the freedom of the waves lapping against the shore, and the invigorating scent of salt in the air. Most of all, I missed Rylan.

One evening, as I flipped through channels in search of something to distract me, I caught sight of a sunset painting the sky in hues of orange and pink. I turned to my mother, who was nestled in her blanket, a content smile on her face as she flipped through a magazine. "What do you think about me going back to the beach for a little while?" I asked, testing the waters.

Her expression shifted, a mix of surprise and concern clouding her features. "I thought you'd want to stay here until I'm fully recovered."

"I do want to help you, but I also need a break," I admitted, biting my lip. "It's hard being here and not feeling... like myself."

She nodded, her gaze softening. "You deserve to take care of yourself too. Maybe you should visit Rylan for a few days? You can't let life slip away while you're here."

The thought sent a rush of excitement through me, and I felt a flutter of hope. "I think I will," I said, a grin spreading across my face. "I'll call him tonight."

Later that evening, I finally dialed Rylan's number, my heart racing as it rang. When he answered, his voice washed over me like a warm tide. "Catherine! I was just thinking about you."

"Good thoughts, I hope?" I teased, and we fell into our easy banter, laughter bubbling up between us like champagne.

"Absolutely," he replied, his tone turning serious. "You sound... different. Are you okay?"

"I'm good, really. But I think I want to come back soon. I could use a dose of your questionable charm and all the terrible puns you've been saving for me."

His laughter filled the air, and I felt myself relax. "Well, I've got plenty of both waiting for you. When can I expect you?"

"I was thinking this weekend? My mom is getting better, and I could really use a break."

"Sounds perfect," he said, a warmth creeping into his voice. "I'll be counting down the hours."

After hanging up, I felt lighter, the weight of the past few weeks lifting just enough to let me breathe again. I spent the following days gathering my things, packing a small bag with clothes that held memories of sandy beaches and sunsets. Each piece felt like a promise—a promise of laughter, of joy, of the simple act of being together.

Friday arrived, and the day stretched out before me like an uncharted map. I said goodbye to my mother, who wished me well with a knowing smile, her eyes sparkling with understanding. "Just remember to call me when you land," she said, her tone half-playful, half-serious. "I want all the juicy details."

"Of course, I'll fill you in on everything," I promised, the excitement bubbling within me as I headed toward the door.

The flight felt shorter this time, the anticipation of reuniting with Rylan propelling me forward. The moment I stepped off the plane and into the familiar warmth of the seaside town, a rush of nostalgia enveloped me. I took a deep breath, the salty air filling my lungs, a reminder that I was back where I belonged.

Rylan was waiting for me at the airport, his broad shoulders silhouetted against the sun. As soon as he saw me, his face lit up, and in an instant, I was swept into his arms. The warmth of his embrace chased away the lingering shadows from my time away.

"I've missed you," he murmured, his breath warm against my ear.

"Missed you too," I replied, feeling a surge of joy. "How was your week?"

"Long," he said, pulling back to look at me. "But worth it now that you're here."

We made our way to his car, the banter flowing easily between us, a familiar dance that felt like home. As we drove along the coastal road, the sun dipping low on the horizon, everything felt right. The world was alive, bursting with colors and possibilities.

"Let's hit the beach," Rylan suggested, glancing at me with that infectious grin of his. "I've got a surprise waiting for you."

Curiosity piqued, I raised an eyebrow. "A surprise? You've got my attention."

When we arrived at the beach, the golden sand sparkled under the setting sun, and I could feel the magic in the air. Rylan led me to a cozy spot where a small fire pit flickered with flames, casting a warm glow over our faces. "I wanted to make tonight special," he said, pulling out a bottle of wine and two glasses.

"Wow, you really went all out," I laughed, feeling the weight of the world melt away.

He poured the wine, the rich red liquid swirling in the glass as he handed one to me. "To new beginnings," he toasted, our glasses clinking in the twilight.

We settled onto the sand, and as the stars began to twinkle above us, we shared stories, laughter, and a few hesitant touches that sent shivers down my spine. Every moment felt electric, the space between us pulsing with an undeniable tension.

"I've been thinking about you a lot," Rylan admitted, his voice low as he looked at me, the firelight dancing in his eyes. "And I really want to know where we stand. This thing between us... I want to explore it, but I need to know you feel the same."

I felt my heart skip a beat, the weight of his words settling into the air like the coming tide. "I do, Rylan. I want this too. But I'm scared. We've already faced so much distance."

"Maybe we can find a way to make it work," he suggested, his eyes steady and sincere. "I'm willing to put in the effort. I'll do whatever it takes."

Just as I opened my mouth to respond, a shout pierced the night air, a sudden disturbance that sliced through our moment like a knife. A group of people emerged from the shadows, laughter mingling with a hint of chaos as they stumbled closer, bottles in hand, oblivious to our intimate space.

"Hey, you two!" one of them called, a wild grin on his face. "You're just in time for the party! Join us!"

I exchanged a glance with Rylan, a mix of surprise and annoyance reflected in our eyes. But before we could respond, the group was upon us, their energy infectious, yet overwhelming.

As the laughter erupted around us, Rylan leaned closer, a glimmer of mischief in his eyes. "Looks like our moment just got hijacked."

I chuckled, the warmth of the fire and the vibrancy of the crowd making the night feel alive. But beneath the laughter, my heart raced with a new tension—what if the unexpected intrusion changed everything we had just begun to explore?

Before I could think it through, Rylan squeezed my hand, and I felt the connection we shared pulse beneath the noise. Whatever happened next, I knew I would have to decide whether to let this chaos pull us apart or bind us closer together.

And just as I began to lean into that thought, a figure stepped out from the shadows, someone I had never expected to see here, a ghost from my past with an unsettling smile that sent a shiver down my spine.

Chapter 5: Across the Miles

The old wooden floors creaked beneath my feet, echoing memories that clung to the walls like fading wallpaper. Each step I took through the narrow hallway felt as if I were walking through a time capsule, capturing snippets of my childhood. Sunlight streamed through the dusty windows, illuminating the motes that danced lazily in the air, and for a moment, I could almost hear the laughter of my younger self. But that laughter was a ghost now, drowned out by the tension that had wrapped itself around my family like a too-tight embrace.

My mother was sitting in the living room, her frail frame almost swallowed by the oversized armchair that had been hers since I could remember. The chair was a patchwork of colors, much like our family: bright moments stitched together with darker threads of worry and heartache. I caught her gaze, an amalgamation of warmth and sorrow that twisted my insides. She offered a smile, but it didn't reach her eyes, which had begun to shadow the vibrant light they once held. I wanted to comfort her, to tell her everything would be alright, but the words lodged themselves in my throat, heavy and unyielding.

"Have you heard from Rylan today?" she asked, breaking the silence that had settled like a thick fog between us.

I nodded, though my heart sank. His messages were like flickering fireflies in the dark—beautiful and bright but ultimately fleeting. Each ping of my phone stirred a mixture of joy and anxiety within me, the thrill of connection punctured by the fear of disconnection. I had tried to maintain the rhythm of our communication, but my words felt stilted, like a dancer forgetting the steps to a well-rehearsed routine.

"He's busy with work," I replied, choosing my words carefully, as if they were fragile glass. "He's been swamped with clients since the merger."

She nodded, her gaze drifting back to the window, where the garden I had once tended lay in a haphazard state, weeds mingling with the stubborn remnants of summer blooms. "You two will figure it out. Love conquers all, right?"

There was a tenderness in her voice that tugged at my heartstrings, yet it felt laced with a bitter irony. I wanted to believe her, to latch onto that age-old saying like a life raft in a stormy sea. But the distance between Rylan and me loomed larger every day, a silent chasm filled with unsaid words and unexpressed fears. I didn't just miss him; I missed the part of myself that felt whole when he was near.

That evening, the sun dipped low, painting the sky in hues of orange and pink, a breathtaking canvas that seemed to mock my turmoil. I stepped out onto the porch, the wood cool beneath my bare feet, and took a deep breath, inhaling the familiar scents of the earth awakening after a long summer's day. I loved this place, with its ancient oaks and wildflowers, yet the nostalgia that wrapped around me felt like chains rather than comfort.

My phone buzzed, the sound jolting me from my reverie. It was a text from Rylan. My heart fluttered, a nervous bird trapped in a cage, as I opened the message. "Hey, thinking of you. How's your mom?"

My fingers hovered over the screen as I crafted a response, knowing that no matter how I framed it, the truth was layered and messy. I wanted to share the reality of my day, the weight of my worry, but instead, I typed out a simple "She's okay. Trying to stay strong." The words felt like a façade, brittle and deceptive, but I hit send before I could change my mind.

"Let's video chat later?" His reply was immediate, the hope in his words sending a jolt through me. The thought of seeing his face—those deep, warm brown eyes that seemed to see straight through to my soul—sent a rush of adrenaline through my veins. Yet a nagging doubt whispered in the back of my mind, urging caution.

"Sure, I'd love that," I typed back, my heart fluttering with both excitement and anxiety.

As night fell, I prepared for our call, pacing the small room that had once been my sanctuary, now transformed into a cocoon of uncertainty. I fiddled with my hair, wishing I could summon the confidence I used to feel effortlessly. I caught my reflection in the mirror—my cheeks flushed, eyes wide with anticipation, but underneath it all, a deep-seated fear loomed large. What if Rylan looked at me and saw the shadows clinging to me, the uncertainty painted on my soul?

The screen lit up, and there he was. Rylan appeared on the other end, his familiar smile pulling me in like a tide. "Hey there," he said, his voice a warm embrace across the miles.

"Hi," I managed, a breathy whisper escaping my lips.

His eyes roamed over my face, and I could almost hear the gears turning in his mind. "You look beautiful, you know that?" The compliment hung in the air, a fragile balloon waiting to be popped by the weight of my reality.

"Thanks," I replied, but the warmth of his words felt overshadowed by the looming shadows of my worries. I knew he could sense the tension, the uncertainty that clung to my words like stubborn cobwebs.

"How's everything with your mom?" he asked, genuine concern etching lines on his forehead.

And there it was—the question that shattered my carefully constructed façade. I hesitated, weighing the truth against the desire to protect him from my burdens. "It's... complicated," I admitted finally, the word heavy on my tongue.

"Complicated how?"

The earnestness in his voice ignited a spark of frustration within me. "It's not something I can just sum up in a text, Rylan. I wish it were that simple."

He leaned closer to the screen, his expression serious, and for a fleeting moment, I could see the distance between us fade. "Then let's talk about it. Really talk."

As I looked into his eyes, I felt the weight of my insecurities start to lift, even if just for a moment. Here we were, two souls connected by threads of love and uncertainty, navigating the tangled web of life's complexities together.

The conversation with Rylan lingered in my mind long after the screen went dark, the silence of my room settling in like a thick fog. I hugged my knees to my chest, an anchor against the chaos swirling within me. There was something both comforting and disconcerting about our connection, a tether stretched taut over miles. His sincerity brushed against my fears, a warm caress that felt all too fragile. It reminded me of the way the sun broke through clouds after a storm, only to be swallowed again by impending gray.

I turned to the window, gazing out at the backyard that had once been my playground, my refuge. Moonlight spilled across the overgrown grass, casting ghostly shadows of the trees, which loomed like guardians of my childhood. Somewhere in the depths of that darkness lay the echoes of laughter, the bright memories that seemed so distant now. I wondered if those echoes were all that remained of my joy, fading whispers in the vastness of my adult worries.

The next morning arrived cloaked in a heavy mist that blurred the edges of the world outside. I made my way to the kitchen, the scent of brewed coffee wrapping around me like a well-worn shawl. My mother was already up, sitting at the table, her eyes glued to the news on the television. The screen flickered with images of a world I barely recognized—headlines flashing across the bottom like sirens demanding attention.

"Anything interesting?" I asked, pouring myself a cup of coffee that would likely remain lukewarm before I got a chance to finish it.

"Same old chaos," she replied, her voice a mixture of resignation and fatigue. "But you know how it is—better to focus on the small things, like our flowers. Did you see the daisies bloomed?"

"Not yet." I took a sip, letting the warmth seep into my bones. "But I'll go check later."

"Good. They're stubborn little things, just like us," she chuckled, though it was more of a sigh. I could see the way her hands trembled slightly as she reached for her mug, a subtle reminder of her fragility.

After breakfast, I donned my gardening gloves, a ritual that always calmed the storm inside me. The garden had been my sanctuary since I was a child, a place where I could lose myself among the petals and leaves. Each flower represented a piece of my history, from the vibrant marigolds that I had planted with my father to the sweet peas that my mother adored. I knelt in the soil, feeling the cool earth beneath my fingers, grounding me in a way that nothing else could.

As I tended to the daisies, my mind drifted to Rylan. I imagined him waking up in his sleek apartment, the sun streaming through tall windows, casting a warm glow over his workspace. I wondered if he thought of me as often as I thought of him or if the distance was slowly dulling the edges of our connection.

Just as I lost myself in those thoughts, my phone buzzed again, slicing through the stillness. I glanced at the screen, and my heart skipped a beat. A message from Rylan. "Hey, can we talk later? I have something important to share."

The words thrummed in my chest, a mix of excitement and anxiety. I wasn't sure if I was ready for another serious conversation. "Sure. Everything okay?"

"Yeah, just want to chat. Talk to you soon."

With that cryptic note hanging in the air, I resumed my weeding, each tug at the stubborn roots mimicking the restless pull in my stomach. I hoped it was good news, but a tiny voice in my head whispered that perhaps it was not.

The day dragged on, heavy with anticipation. I threw myself into chores and gardening, but my thoughts kept drifting back to Rylan. Would he tell me he had met someone? Or was he about to drop a bombshell about his work that could change everything? By the time evening rolled around, the sky had turned a deep indigo, stars peeking through the veil of night.

I positioned myself in front of the computer, the familiar light illuminating my face. My heart raced as the minutes ticked by. Finally, a ping echoed in the stillness, and I opened the video call. Rylan's face filled the screen, the hint of a smile dancing on his lips, but his eyes held a shadow of something deeper.

"Hey there," he greeted, and I could see the tension in his shoulders. "Thanks for being patient."

"What's up?" I leaned closer, trying to read his expression.

"I've been thinking about us a lot lately," he began, and my breath caught in my throat. "About how far apart we are, both physically and... emotionally."

My heart sank, a lead weight dropping into my stomach. "I've been feeling that too. It's hard, Rylan. I don't know how to bridge this distance."

He ran a hand through his hair, a gesture that always made my heart flutter. "I know. I want to make this work, but I also think we need to talk about what that really means for both of us."

"Are you saying we need to break up?" The words slipped out before I could stop them, raw and jagged like broken glass.

"No, no! Not at all," he hurried to reassure me. "I just think we need to be honest about how this distance is affecting us. I hate the idea of you feeling like I'm moving on without you."

The lump in my throat was almost unbearable. "I can't shake the feeling that you're out there living your life, and I'm stuck here, feeling like a ghost."

"You're not a ghost to me," he insisted, his voice soft yet firm. "I think about you every day. Every single day, I wish you were here, laughing with me over dinner, or just sitting in silence together. I miss you."

"I miss you too," I whispered, tears pooling in my eyes. "It's just hard to feel that connection when all we have are screens and miles between us."

His gaze turned serious, and I felt the weight of his sincerity in the air. "What if I told you I was considering coming back for a while? Just to see you, to figure this out together?"

The breath caught in my throat, and my heart soared with a hope I hadn't dared to nurture. "You would do that?"

"Of course I would," he said, a smile breaking through the tension. "But only if you want me to. I need to know you're still on this journey with me."

A wave of warmth flooded my chest, a flicker of light pushing back the shadows of doubt. "I want that more than anything."

As we continued to talk, the distance between us began to shrink, and I could almost feel his presence beside me, as though he were right there, reaching for my hand, pulling me from the depths of my uncertainties. I knew the road ahead wouldn't be easy, but for the first time in what felt like ages, I had a glimpse of hope—a spark of connection that promised to guide us through the murky waters of uncertainty.

Days turned into weeks, each one blending into the next like the muted colors of a watercolor painting. The morning fog lingered longer, the crisp air sharp against my skin as I made my way to the garden, where the daisies stood in stubborn defiance against the autumn chill. I often found myself lost in thought, reflecting on my conversations with Rylan, our plans intertwining like vines around the trellis of my heart.

When he announced his intention to visit, the exhilaration was quickly tempered by the weight of reality. My mother's condition fluctuated like the unpredictable weather. Some days, she seemed brighter, her laughter a sunny melody echoing through the house; on others, shadows cloaked her eyes, drawing out the worry that gnawed at my insides. I found myself questioning the timing of Rylan's visit—was it the right moment to stir up emotions that had long been buried beneath the surface?

One afternoon, I found myself seated at the kitchen table, a steaming cup of tea cradled in my hands. The autumn leaves danced outside the window, a vibrant tapestry of orange and gold, but my thoughts were entangled in a different kind of chaos. "Mom," I began, the words feeling heavy on my tongue, "what do you think about Rylan coming to visit?"

She glanced up, her eyes brightening at the mention of his name. "I think it's wonderful! You two have something special. But are you sure you're ready for that?"

A lump formed in my throat as I considered her question. "Ready? Maybe. But what if he sees how fragile things are here? What if he thinks this is too much?"

"Sweetheart, life is always messy," she said, a wise glint in her eye. "If he truly cares for you, he'll want to be a part of your world, not just the pretty parts. And if he doesn't, then maybe he's not the one you thought he was."

Her words hung in the air, ringing with a clarity I desperately needed. I felt a surge of determination; I would show Rylan my life, the good and the bad, and trust him to meet me there.

The day of Rylan's arrival dawned bright and clear, the sun breaking through the clouds like a promise fulfilled. My heart raced as I busied myself preparing the house. I fluffed pillows, set the table with mismatched plates that spoke of history and family, and even tried to coax a smile from my mother, who sat in the living room, her gaze distant.

When the doorbell finally rang, it felt like a crescendo of emotions crashing against my chest. I opened the door, and there he stood, a vision of warmth and familiarity wrapped in a snug jacket, his smile lighting up the cool autumn afternoon. "Hey, gorgeous," he greeted, his voice wrapping around me like a favorite song.

"Hey, you," I replied, unable to contain my own grin. He stepped inside, the scent of fresh air and him mingling in the cozy space of my childhood home.

The initial warmth of reunion faded quickly as I noticed the tension beneath the surface. He glanced around, his expression shifting from happiness to concern as he took in the room. "It's so... homey," he said, trying to lighten the mood.

"Homey? Is that your polite way of saying cluttered?" I teased, nudging him playfully.

"Not at all! It's charming. Very... lived-in."

I chuckled, appreciating his effort to make light of it. "Well, it's a work in progress."

As we settled into the living room, I introduced Rylan to my mother, who greeted him with an encouraging smile, though I could see the flicker of worry behind her eyes. The three of us shared stories and laughter, but a tension lingered in the air, unspoken and palpable.

Later that evening, after dinner, Rylan and I found ourselves on the porch, the cool breeze whispering through the trees, carrying with it the scents of pine and earth. I wrapped my arms around myself, fighting the urge to lean against him, craving his warmth. "How are you really feeling about everything?" he asked, his tone shifting to something more serious.

I sighed, the weight of my worries spilling forth. "It's just... complicated. I want you to see the good, but I also don't want you to think I'm stuck in a place of sadness. My mom's health is unpredictable, and I feel like I'm walking a tightrope."

Rylan leaned closer, his gaze steady and reassuring. "I'm here for all of it, you know? I want to be a part of your life, even the messy parts. You don't have to protect me."

His words wrapped around me like a lifeline, but doubt still curled in my stomach. "What if it's too much?" I whispered, the vulnerability slipping through the cracks I'd tried to patch.

"Then we'll figure it out together. That's what relationships are about, right?" He reached out, tucking a loose strand of hair behind my ear, his touch sending electric shivers down my spine.

Just as I opened my mouth to respond, the night was shattered by a loud thud from inside the house, a sound that echoed through the silence like a thunderclap. Rylan shot up, his expression shifting to one of concern. "What was that?"

I froze, fear coiling in my gut. "I don't know. Mom?" I called, my voice trembling as I rushed back inside, Rylan close behind.

The living room was empty, the remnants of our earlier laughter now tainted by an eerie silence. "Mom?" I shouted again, panic rising in my chest as I searched every corner, my heart pounding like a drum in my ears.

Then, I caught sight of her in the hallway, her frame hunched over, a broken glass scattered around her feet. "Mom!" I rushed to her side, kneeling beside her as my heart sank. "What happened?"

She looked up, her face pale, but her smile was steady. "Just a little mishap," she said, her voice soft but strained. "I didn't mean to startle you."

Rylan knelt beside me, his concern palpable. "Are you hurt?" he asked, his brow furrowing as he examined the shards of glass.

"No, no, I'm fine. Just a little clumsy," she insisted, though the tremor in her hands told a different story.

As I helped her to her feet, I couldn't shake the feeling of dread that hung in the air. Rylan's eyes darted between my mother and me, his expression shifting from worry to confusion. "Maybe we should get you checked out," he suggested gently, his voice a soothing balm.

"I said I'm fine," my mother replied, a hint of steel in her tone that surprised me.

"Mom, please," I implored, unable to hide the tremor in my voice.

But just as the tension peaked, the lights flickered, plunging us into darkness for a split second before they returned, more vibrant than before. We all exchanged glances, a palpable energy crackling in the air. Rylan's hand brushed against mine, a silent promise, while my heart raced with uncertainty.

Before I could speak, my phone buzzed on the table, an urgent message illuminating the darkness: "I need to talk to you. It's important. Meet me."

The message sent a chill racing down my spine. "Who is it?" Rylan asked, his brow furrowing in concern.

I held my breath, staring at the screen, the words blurring as a wave of dread washed over me. I glanced back at my mother, whose expression had shifted, the worry lines deepening.

"I... I don't know," I stammered, the sense of foreboding growing.

"Then let's figure it out together," Rylan said, his voice steady.

But just as I opened the message to reply, another thud resonated from the back of the house, shattering the fragile calm we'd tried to rebuild. My heart raced, and I knew, deep down, that nothing would ever be the same again.

Chapter 6: A Tenuous Thread

The afternoon sun filtered through the sheer curtains of my small living room, casting playful shadows on the walls, as if the universe itself was painting my day in soft pastels. I had returned to my cozy sanctuary after a long week, craving the silence that echoed within my four walls. Yet today, that quietude felt oppressive, weighed down by the enormity of what I had received in the mail.

As I unwrapped the brown paper package, the scent of aged paper and a hint of sandalwood wafted up, reminiscent of Rylan's cologne—a lingering memory of our last evening together, where laughter had mingled with stolen glances. A letter, neatly folded, nestled amid a collection of handmade CDs, each inscribed with song titles in his familiar scrawl. The sight made my heart flutter, a pang of affection mingling with trepidation. What had he poured into these songs? Were they echoes of our moments together or reflections of his own solitude?

I settled into my favorite armchair, the fabric soft against my skin. With trembling hands, I unfolded the letter, Rylan's neat handwriting spilling across the page like a cascade of thoughts. His words danced before me, each sentence pulling me deeper into his world. He spoke of his days, filled with coffee shops and quiet corners where he would jot down lyrics that had sprung from the very marrow of his being. Each line was laced with a mixture of nostalgia and hope, a reminder of the fleeting time we had spent in each other's orbit.

"I'm writing these songs for you," he wrote, "each one a reflection of what you mean to me. It's a strange world without you here, but the music keeps me company. I hope it brings you a little bit of me, wherever you are."

As I read his words, warmth enveloped me, but beneath it lay an icy tendril of doubt. Could our connection withstand the weight of distance? Every note I had ever played, every lyric I had ever sung in my mind, had woven a tapestry of longing and fear. The more I thought about it, the more I realized I had never really trusted myself to sustain the love we had kindled. I picked up the first CD, my fingers brushing over its surface like a whisper.

With a flick of a switch, the room filled with his music—a gentle melody that wrapped around me, a soothing balm against the chaos swirling in my heart. Each chord struck a familiar note, drawing me into the warmth of his presence. The melodies spiraled through the air, conjuring images of us: late-night conversations under starlit skies, his laughter mingling with the rustling leaves, the easy way he leaned in, as if the world outside had faded away.

But then, like a sudden gust of wind, the memories turned bittersweet. I could almost hear the echoes of our discussions—conversations that had twisted around our fears like a vine choking a fragile bloom. Could I rise above my insecurities, or was I destined to let them ensnare me once more?

The music shifted to a more upbeat track, a lively rhythm that made my toes tap involuntarily. I imagined Rylan grinning as he played, his eyes sparkling with mischief. The thought momentarily banished my worries, and I found myself swaying, letting the melody carry me away. Yet as the song wound to a close, a pang of reality crashed over me like an unexpected wave.

Would I be able to navigate this intricate dance of emotions? The patterns of my past loomed large, and I could almost hear the whispered doubts—echoes of relationships that had crumbled under the weight of similar longings. I sank deeper into my chair, the weight of uncertainty pressing down as I contemplated the delicate thread that tethered us.

Picking up the second CD, I hesitated, feeling as though I were peering into a mirror reflecting all my vulnerabilities. What if I listened and found a melody that echoed my fears? What if his songs carried an unspoken weight, the burden of our shared history? But Rylan's letter was a lifeline, a reminder that perhaps we could forge a new path, a fresh harmony that could drown out the cacophony of doubt.

I pressed play again, and the soft strumming of an acoustic guitar filled the room. The lyrics unfolded like petals of a flower, blooming with the promise of something beautiful yet fragile. "Let's take this step by step," the song urged, its message weaving through the air, wrapping around me like a comforting shawl. I closed my eyes, letting the sound wash over me, each note a tiny reminder that perhaps vulnerability could lead to strength.

Yet with every rising crescendo, my heart clenched with apprehension. I could see the shadow of old patterns lurking just beyond the door of my consciousness. I had spent so long crafting walls, each brick laid with the fear of vulnerability. Could I bear to dismantle those walls, to risk opening up to Rylan completely? The very thought made my stomach twist, a visceral reminder of all I had lost before.

As the final chords echoed into silence, I realized I was caught in a delicate web of desire and fear, the weight of longing pressing against my chest. But Rylan's voice, woven through those songs, seemed to pierce the darkness that had settled in my heart. He had always seen me, flaws and all, and perhaps that was the greatest gift of all.

I stood up, the urgency of my emotions compelling me to move. The music had ignited something deep within, a flicker of courage that dared me to face the fear that had kept me at bay. The sunlight glimmered on the floor, inviting me to step into its warmth. I could almost hear Rylan's laughter, a melody of encouragement whispering through the air, reminding me that love, however tenuous, was worth the risk.

A few days passed, each one punctuated by the haunting strains of Rylan's music drifting through my apartment, wrapping around me like a familiar blanket. I found myself slipping into the melodies during my morning coffee, letting the notes swirl in the air, their echoes mingling with the scent of roasted beans and cinnamon. Each time I pressed play, I was transported to the world we had built together, where laughter spilled over like the foam in my cup, and our dreams danced like fireflies in the dusky twilight.

But reality had a way of creeping in, with its unyielding questions and harsh reminders. I busied myself with work and friends, trying to drown out the part of me that longed for Rylan's presence. "You're unusually quiet today," Claire remarked one afternoon, her brow furrowed with concern as we sat at our usual café, the sound of clinking cups providing a comforting backdrop. "You look like you've seen a ghost. Or worse, someone who has forgotten how to smile."

I chuckled lightly, pushing a strand of hair behind my ear, knowing she could read me like a book. "Maybe I'm just contemplating the universe. You know, the typical existential crisis." I stirred my coffee, watching the swirl of cream dissolve into the dark liquid, a metaphor for my own muddled thoughts.

"Or maybe you're just pining over a certain musician," she teased, a smirk dancing on her lips. "Let me guess, he's tall, dark, and has the kind of smile that could probably solve world hunger."

"Something like that," I replied, unable to suppress a grin. Claire always had a way of nudging the truth out of me, her humor like a gentle poke that made the heaviness of my heart a little lighter.

"You know," she continued, her voice dropping to a conspiratorial whisper, "if he's writing songs about you, he's probably just as lost without you. Men can't help but put their feelings into music. It's practically in their DNA."

"Or in the coffee shop where they work," I shot back, recalling the countless hours Rylan had spent crafting lyrics while nursing a latte. The thought sent a warm shiver down my spine, but the familiar weight of doubt settled in again. What if those songs were just fleeting musings? What if he was out there, moving on while I was trapped in this whirlwind of emotion?

"You need to talk to him," Claire urged, her eyes sparkling with mischief. "Just shoot him a message. How hard can it be? You'll never know unless you ask."

"Sure, let me just whip out my trusty message and say, 'Hey, Rylan, I've been staring at your music like a lovesick puppy. What are you doing with your life?'" The sarcasm dripped from my voice, but inside, a flicker of hope ignited.

"Or maybe just say you love the songs!" Claire encouraged, her enthusiasm infectious. "You know, keep it casual. Maybe even a little flirty."

I rolled my eyes, a smile creeping onto my face. "Flirty? Me? I think you've mistaken me for someone who actually knows how to flirt. I might as well be a statue in a park, just standing there, looking awkward."

Claire laughed, her joy brightening the dim café. "You're so much more than that. Just think of it as you taking a leap into the abyss. Worst case scenario, he thinks you're a hopeless romantic, and you get to roll your eyes at him later."

Her encouragement lingered long after our coffee date had ended, making my heart race as I returned home. I paced my living room, the urge to reach out to Rylan clawing at me. Each note from his songs echoed in my mind, weaving an intricate tapestry of longing and anxiety. I could imagine his reaction—his smile that could light up even the darkest corners of my soul.

Finally, I sank onto my couch, the plush cushions enveloping me like a safety net. Taking a deep breath, I opened my phone and began typing, my fingers hovering over the screen, my heart pounding like a drum.

"Hey, Rylan. I've been listening to your songs, and they're incredible. They really got me thinking about us."

I hesitated, my fingers twitching as doubt flooded in. Was I really ready to cross this precarious bridge? What if he didn't feel the same? Just as my resolve began to falter, a notification popped up on my screen, illuminating the darkness in the room. A message from Rylan.

"Hey! I'm glad you're enjoying them. They're pretty much a reflection of everything swirling around in my head."

My heart raced, excitement flooding my veins as I typed back quickly, the conversation flowing between us like a river that had burst its banks. Words flew like sparks, lighting up the shadows that had clung to me for days. I found myself sharing little snippets of my day, my laughter spilling onto the screen, and his replies were equally vibrant, filled with witty banter that felt like dancing in the rain.

For a moment, the world outside ceased to exist. It was just us—two souls entwined in a digital embrace, where honesty reigned supreme.

"Do you think we could catch up soon?" I typed, my fingers trembling as I hit send. The vulnerability of asking felt like standing at the edge of a cliff, ready to leap.

A moment passed, and my heart thudded in my chest. "I'd love that," he replied, and a thrill coursed through me, igniting a warmth that spread from my chest to my fingertips. "How about I swing by this weekend? We could grab some coffee—though I can't promise I won't try to steal your drink again."

A laugh bubbled up, spilling out of me unbidden. "Only if you're prepared for me to steal yours in return. It's a deal."

With that simple exchange, a flicker of hope ignited within me, a flame kindling against the backdrop of uncertainty. The promise of seeing him again, of feeling the warmth of his presence, made my heart leap. Perhaps I was stronger than I had given myself credit for. Maybe, just maybe, this time I could navigate the labyrinth of my emotions without losing my way. The tenuous thread that held us together felt a little sturdier now, weaving a tapestry of new possibilities, a connection that, though delicate, shimmered with the potential of something extraordinary.

The weekend arrived with a bright, cheerful sun, casting golden rays across the streets and beckoning me outdoors. It was the kind of day that whispered promises of possibility, and I could hardly contain the fluttering excitement in my chest. Rylan was on his way, and the mere thought sent a cascade of butterflies dancing through my stomach. I stood before the mirror, scrutinizing my reflection. The casual t-shirt and jeans I had thrown on felt too plain, almost an affront to the vibrant anticipation brewing within me. After a few adjustments, I settled on a flowing sundress, one that swayed with every step I took, echoing the rhythm of my racing heart.

As I stood in my living room, fiddling with my hair and dabbing on a hint of perfume—citrusy and fresh, like a spring morning—I caught a glimpse of the clock. Time, it seemed, had decided to play tricks on me. The minutes dragged on, each second stretching into an eternity. I finally flopped down onto the couch, trying to channel my restlessness into something productive. My eyes flitted to the stack of books piled on the coffee table, remnants of a cozy reading spree that had fizzled out under the weight of anticipation.

Finally, the familiar sound of my doorbell sliced through the thick air of expectancy, making me jump to my feet. I smoothed my dress, taking a moment to breathe deeply and steady my racing heart before I opened the door. There he was, Rylan, standing on my doorstep with that effortless charm that always seemed to light up the space around him. His dark hair was slightly tousled, and the hint of a smile played on his lips, as if he carried secrets he was eager to share.

"Wow, you clean up nicely," he said, leaning against the doorframe in a way that made my heart race a little faster. "I was half expecting you to greet me in pajamas, which wouldn't have been too far off considering how you were the other night."

"Please, you know I reserve my pajama days for serious contemplation," I quipped, unable to hide my grin. "Can't let you think I'm always this put together. Wouldn't want to ruin my mystery."

He chuckled, a warm sound that filled the space between us. "Your mystery is safe with me. Shall we?" With a graceful gesture, he motioned toward the world outside, and I felt a rush of exhilaration as I stepped out into the sunlight.

We walked side by side, the city humming with life around us. Rylan kept up a light banter, his words flowing like the gentle breeze that tugged playfully at my hair. The vibrant colors of storefronts and the laughter of passersby created a backdrop that made the moment feel almost cinematic. Yet, beneath the surface of our playful exchanges, I felt the tension simmering just below, like an undercurrent in a river.

As we neared the café, I caught sight of a familiar face—an old friend of Rylan's, Jenna, sitting at a corner table. She waved enthusiastically, beckoning us over. "You two look adorable!" she exclaimed, her eyes sparkling with mischief. "What's this? A date? I can't believe I'm witnessing it first-hand!"

"Jenna," Rylan warned playfully, "let's not scare her off just yet."

I laughed, feeling my cheeks warm. "Is this where I declare that I'm merely his coffee buddy?" The joke hung in the air, but the truth lingered unspoken, heavy with meaning.

"Coffee buddy sounds like a lot of fun. I'd love to be part of that," Jenna replied with a wink, her enthusiasm palpable.

After we settled into our seats, I found myself slipping into a comfortable rhythm. Jenna shared tales of her recent escapades, interspersing them with laughter that echoed through the café. Rylan chimed in with his own stories, his eyes sparkling as he recounted misadventures from his coffee shop days. Each shared laugh bridged the space between us, but with every glance at Rylan, I felt the threads of our unspoken connection tightening, drawing me in closer.

As Jenna excused herself to grab another coffee, the atmosphere shifted. Rylan leaned forward, his expression turning serious. "I've missed this—just hanging out, being ourselves," he said, his voice low and steady. "And I've missed you."

My heart skipped a beat, the weight of his words pressing against my chest. "I've missed you too. The songs, the letters—it all felt like a lifeline."

"But I can't help but feel like we're tiptoeing around something," he continued, searching my eyes with an intensity that sent shivers down my spine. "What are we really doing here?"

The question hung heavy in the air, the buoyant mood shifting into something more profound. I opened my mouth, ready to reply, but the words tangled in my throat. The weight of my fears rose like a tide, threatening to pull me under. "I—I think we're trying to find our way," I finally managed, my voice trembling slightly. "But it feels like we're walking on a tightrope, Rylan. One misstep, and..."

"And what?" he pressed, leaning closer, his gaze unwavering. "We fall? Or we find a way to catch each other?"

His question sparked a tempest of emotions, and I knew I had to be honest. "I don't know if I'm strong enough to risk falling again. The last time I got too close, it hurt. It was hard to breathe under the weight of everything."

"I'm not asking you to jump in headfirst," he replied, his voice soothing, like the gentle strumming of his guitar. "Just take my hand. We can figure it out together."

The sincerity in his eyes was enough to make my heart race, but doubt twisted in my gut, whispering that it might be too late for us. Before I could respond, a shrill laugh erupted from behind me. I turned to see Jenna approaching, her arms full of steaming cups. "So, are you two going to sit here all day staring into each other's eyes, or can I join the conversation?"

I shot Rylan a grateful smile, grateful for the interruption that pulled me from the brink. We spent the next hour exchanging stories and laughter, but the weight of our earlier conversation lingered, the tension woven between us like an invisible thread.

When we finally stepped outside, the sun had begun its descent, painting the sky in hues of pink and orange. I breathed in the crisp evening air, the sweet scent of impending summer dancing around us. Rylan turned to me, the moment stretching, the world fading away, and I felt an electric current spark between us.

"Let's go to the park," he suggested, a hint of mischief in his eyes. "I hear the fireflies are out tonight, and I can't think of a better way to cap off our not-a-date."

"Fireflies?" I asked, intrigued. "You mean those little glowing bugs that make everything feel like a fairytale?"

"Exactly. And they can only enhance your already radiant charm," he replied, his smile disarming.

As we walked to the park, our shoulders brushed, and each moment felt like a thread weaving us closer together. The evening air crackled with potential, and my heart raced at the thought of what lay ahead. But just as we stepped onto the grassy expanse, the atmosphere shifted. A figure emerged from the shadows—a familiar silhouette that made my heart plummet.

It was Derek, my ex, lurking at the edge of the park, his expression a mix of anger and desperation. "What the hell are you doing here?" he spat, his voice cutting through the tranquility like glass shattering.

In that moment, my heart raced with panic, the safety I had felt moments before evaporating into thin air. Rylan's hand brushed against mine, a gentle reminder that I wasn't alone. But as Derek took a step forward, I could feel the fragile threads of our connection strain, ready to snap under the weight of my past.

Chapter 7: A Step Back

Returning to New Orleans felt like stepping into a faded painting, colors dulled and edges blurred. The streets were lined with the familiar creole cottages, their intricate ironwork glinting under the late afternoon sun, but the vibrant energy I once thrived on seemed muffled, as if the city had wrapped itself in a thin veil of fog. The sweet, spicy aroma of jambalaya wafted through the air, but even the smell felt muted, a ghost of the excitement it used to evoke. Each step I took echoed in the empty corners of my heart, reverberating with the absence of Rylan.

I had spent countless hours at the dance studio, the mirrors reflecting not just my movements but the laughter and camaraderie shared with Rylan. Now, as I stood alone in the dimly lit space, it felt like a shell of what it once was. The polished wooden floor, usually alive with the rhythm of our feet, was silent, save for the faint whisper of my shoes against the surface. I could almost hear Rylan's voice, teasing me about my tendency to overthink every pirouette, a playful smile dancing on his lips. Today, though, the studio seemed to absorb my sadness, holding it captive, the walls closing in around me like a slow exhale.

I attempted to immerse myself in my routine, hoping the familiar movements would bring solace. As I stretched, my muscles protested against the tension that knotted within me. Every plié and relevé felt foreign, like a language I had once spoken fluently but had now forgotten. I pushed through the pain, but the dance no longer felt like a release; it was an echo of the joy I once found in it, a bittersweet reminder of how intertwined my spirit was with Rylan's presence.

The air shifted when he walked in, cutting through the solitude with a presence that was at once comforting and electrifying. Rylan filled the space with a warm energy, his tousled hair catching the light like a halo. My heart raced, a fluttering bird seeking to escape its cage. He smiled, but there was an uncertainty behind it, a shadow that lingered just beneath the surface.

"Missed you, partner," he said, his voice a blend of sweetness and sincerity that wrapped around me like a favorite song.

"Missed you too," I replied, my voice softer than I intended, tinged with an ache that was both thrilling and daunting.

We began to move, our bodies instinctively falling into sync as if no time had passed. Each step was laden with unspoken words, the tension weaving through our movements like an intricate dance. The first notes of our favorite song filled the air, and I lost myself in the rhythm. The studio transformed around us, walls fading as we slipped into a world where nothing else mattered. Our bodies communicated in a language more profound than words, but as I twirled, I caught a glimpse of the uncertainty in his eyes.

It was an undercurrent of doubt that tainted the magic of the moment, a reminder that the passionate connection we shared was tangled in my unresolved feelings. As we spun together, I felt the weight of decisions pressing down on me, a heaviness I couldn't ignore. When our lips finally met, it was electric, igniting every nerve ending in my body. His kiss tasted of sweet urgency and lingering longing, but beneath that sweetness lay the sharp edge of uncertainty.

As we pulled away, the reality of the situation crashed over me. I could see the flicker of doubt in his gaze, the way his brow furrowed as if he were wrestling with thoughts he couldn't quite articulate. I reached for his hand, needing the connection to ground us both. "Rylan," I started, the words tasting bitter on my tongue. "There's something we need to talk about."

His expression shifted, concern etching lines across his face. "I know," he admitted, his voice steady yet cautious. "I felt it when you left."

The truth hung between us like a dense fog, threatening to suffocate the fragile thread of our connection. The thought of unraveling everything we had built together filled me with dread, but I also knew that avoiding the conversation would only deepen the chasm. "I wasn't just leaving the city, Rylan. I was leaving... us. I thought it was for the best."

"I thought we had something special, something worth fighting for." His voice was a whisper, yet it cut through the tension like a knife. "But it feels like I'm the only one still holding on."

His words struck a chord deep within me, a reminder of the choices I had made in my fear. "You don't understand," I said, frustration bubbling to the surface. "It's not that I don't care. It's just—"

"Just what? Just easier to run away?" he interrupted, his tone sharp but not unkind. "Because that's how it feels from where I stand."

A lump formed in my throat as I faced the truth. I had hoped that by distancing myself, I could eliminate the chaos swirling around my feelings. Instead, it only magnified them. "I don't want to lose you," I confessed, each word heavy with vulnerability. "But I'm scared. I'm scared that I can't give you what you need."

Silence enveloped us, thick and suffocating. The music faded into the background, replaced by the sound of our heavy breathing. I could see the weight of my confession settling over him, and in that moment, I realized that we were standing on the precipice of something monumental. The uncertainty that hung in the air felt like a challenge, beckoning us to confront the fear and doubt head-on, to either bridge the gap or let it swallow us whole.

The silence stretched between us like a taut wire, ready to snap at any moment. I could feel the pulse of my heartbeat thrumming in my ears, drowning out the soft whispers of the outside world. Rylan's expression was a mix of hurt and hope, a precarious balancing act that could tip either way. I wanted to reach out, to close the distance, but the fear of what lay beneath our unspoken words held me captive.

"Look," I said, my voice steadier than I felt, "maybe we should just—"

"Maybe we should just what?" he interjected, a challenge lacing his tone. "Ignore it? Pretend everything is fine? Because that's what I've been doing, and let me tell you, it's exhausting."

His frustration was palpable, and it pulled at my heart. We had once danced in sync, moving as one, but now it felt like we were stumbling through a chaotic routine, desperately trying to find our footing. "You're right," I admitted, running a hand through my hair. "It is exhausting. I thought that maybe if I came back, things would feel... normal again. But normal isn't what I need."

"What do you need then?" Rylan stepped closer, his eyes piercing through the fog of uncertainty. "Do you even know?"

I looked away, unable to meet his gaze. The truth danced just out of reach, a tantalizing whisper that beckoned me to confront the very heart of my fear. "I need to understand what I want, and I don't think I can figure that out if we keep pretending."

He took a breath, his frustration softening into something more vulnerable. "Then let's not pretend. But I need to know if you're still in this with me, or if you're just biding your time."

His words cut deeper than I anticipated. I could feel the heat rising in my cheeks, a blend of anger and fear. "Rylan, this isn't about you. It's about me trying to find my footing in a world that feels like it's spinning out of control. I don't want to hurt you."

"And I don't want to be the one left standing on the sidelines, watching you dance away," he replied, his voice low but filled with emotion. The vulnerability in his words wrapped around my heart, squeezing it tight.

In that moment, I recognized the weight of our situation, the delicate thread that tied us together. I wanted to bridge the gap, to bring us back to the warmth we once shared, but the uncertainty loomed like a storm cloud overhead. Just as I was about to respond, a loud crash echoed from the hallway, startling us both.

"What was that?" I jumped, my heart racing.

"Let's check it out," Rylan suggested, his tension momentarily forgotten as he moved toward the door.

We stepped into the hallway, where chaos had erupted. A group of students had knocked over a stack of practice mats, sending them sprawling across the floor like a tumble of oversized pancakes. Laughter bubbled up around us, the kind that made the heart lighter even in the face of disaster.

"Don't worry, I've got this!" a girl shouted, her ponytail swinging like a metronome as she hurried to help clean up the mess.

Rylan and I exchanged glances, the laughter breaking the tension that had woven itself tightly between us. "See? Normal," I said, a teasing smile creeping onto my lips.

"Normal, huh?" he chuckled, shaking his head as he helped the girl gather the mats. "I've never seen a dance studio that required such an extreme cleaning protocol."

I stepped in to help, the camaraderie of the moment distracting me from the weight of our earlier conversation. As we worked together, a warmth blossomed in my chest, the familiar rhythm of laughter and teamwork sparking a flicker of hope. "What do you think? Should we charge admission for the next round of mat wrestling?" I quipped, tossing a mat into a nearby pile.

Rylan laughed, the sound filling the air like music. "Only if you're willing to get on the floor and demonstrate your moves."

"Ha! I think my dance card is full for now," I replied, winking at him.

Once the chaos subsided, we retreated back to the sanctuary of the studio, the weight of the earlier conversation still lingering but momentarily forgotten. Rylan leaned against the mirrored wall, arms crossed, his playful demeanor masking an undercurrent of seriousness that I couldn't ignore. "So, are we back to square one? Or do we keep pretending we haven't just nearly shattered the very foundation we built?"

I hesitated, searching for the right words. "Maybe... maybe we need to stop pretending. Just for today."

"Okay, today it is," he replied, his eyes softening. "But tomorrow? Tomorrow we tackle the big stuff, all the mess we've been avoiding."

A sense of relief washed over me, mingling with the excitement of what could be. "I can handle that. Just as long as you promise to be gentle with the heavy lifting."

Rylan's grin returned, illuminating his face. "You know I've always been gentle with you."

"Gentle? Is that what you call that kiss?" I shot back, an impish glimmer in my eye.

"Touché," he laughed, his eyes sparkling. "But I promise, if we're going to dive deep, I'll keep the life raft handy."

The lightness hung between us, a thread woven through the fabric of our interaction, bridging the gap of uncertainty that had threatened to divide us. As we resumed our practice, the music filled the air again, a familiar comfort wrapping around us like a warm embrace.

We moved, the tension melting away with each turn and leap, our bodies flowing in tandem once more. And even though the weight of our unresolved feelings lingered like an uninvited guest, for now, I allowed myself to revel in the dance. There was a sense of renewal in the air, an unspoken promise that tomorrow would come with its own set of challenges, but today, we were alive, we were moving, and we were together.

The dance studio pulsed with life, the music swirling around us like a vibrant whirlpool, drawing me in with its magnetic force.

Each note ignited something deep within, but even as we spun and twirled, an undercurrent of unease tugged at my heart. The earlier lightness had not entirely banished the shadows of doubt lurking just beyond the surface. Rylan moved effortlessly beside me, his body a perfect counterpoint to my own, yet I sensed a wall between us, an invisible barrier that neither of us dared to breach.

As we reached the crescendo of our routine, I caught a glimpse of his face in the mirrored wall, the strain of our earlier conversation etched into his features. It was a reminder that while the dance might have temporarily soothed our worries, it couldn't erase them. "What are you thinking?" I asked, trying to keep my voice light, even as my heart raced.

Rylan hesitated, his gaze flicking away from the reflection. "Just wondering how we went from passionate kisses to this... complicated tango."

I felt my cheeks heat. "It's not all bad, right? We're still dancing, still here."

"But we're not really dancing, are we?" His voice was low, an edge of frustration surfacing. "We're just moving through the motions, pretending everything's fine when it's clearly not."

He was right, of course, and I hated that he had to say it. My heart sank with the weight of his words, but I pressed on, unwilling to let the moment slip away. "What do you want me to say? That I'm scared? That I wish everything felt as easy as it used to?"

"I want you to be honest with me," he said, stepping closer, his breath warm against my skin. "I don't want to be just a shadow in your past, a lingering thought when you're back in town. I want to be part of your future, too."

His vulnerability struck a chord within me, urging me to step out from behind my own walls. "I want that too," I admitted, my voice trembling. "But every time I think about it, I freeze. I keep picturing all the ways it could go wrong."

"What if we don't let it?" he countered, a spark of determination igniting in his eyes. "What if we just take a leap? One step at a time."

A leap. The word sent my mind racing. I was no stranger to risk, but this felt different. This was my heart on the line, my future dangling precariously. "And what if I jump and you're not there to catch me?"

Rylan reached for my hand, his touch igniting a warmth that traveled up my arm. "Then I'll jump too. We'll leap together, or not at all."

My heart thrummed in my chest, a fierce drumbeat of hope and fear battling for dominance. Just as I was about to respond, the studio door swung open, and a wave of exuberance rushed in. A troupe of dancers entered, laughter spilling from their lips like confetti, transforming the serious atmosphere into one of chaotic joy.

"Sorry we're late!" one of the newcomers shouted, bouncing on her toes. "You'll never believe what happened—"

I shot Rylan a look, our moment dissipating into the lively chatter that enveloped us. "Seems like the universe has other plans," I said, a hint of disappointment seeping into my tone.

"Or maybe it's a sign that we need to pause for a moment," he replied, a wry smile dancing on his lips. "You know, avoid jumping into the abyss just yet."

I laughed, the sound easing the tension in my chest, but the sense of urgency lingered. As the new dancers began to stretch and prepare for their own rehearsal, I found myself drifting to the back of the studio, an observer rather than a participant. Rylan moved among them, effortlessly slipping back into the role of leader, his charisma shining brightly as he guided the group through warm-up exercises.

And yet, in the midst of all this life and energy, a nagging doubt gnawed at my insides. I wanted to step forward, to reclaim the moment we had nearly grasped, but the swirl of laughter and movement felt suffocating. I leaned against the mirrored wall, watching Rylan as he interacted with the other dancers, his easy laughter drawing them in.

A pang of jealousy flickered through me, unexpected and unwelcome. He was so alive in this space, the way he always had been, and I felt like an outsider. The warmth between us seemed to flicker, battling against the shadows of my insecurities.

"Hey," Rylan said, his voice cutting through my thoughts as he approached. "You okay? You look like you just stepped into a cold shower."

"Just enjoying the show," I replied, attempting to feign nonchalance. "You're a natural up there."

"Thanks, but it's hard to shine when my partner's hiding in the wings."

The warmth of his words wrapped around me, and I realized then that he was right. I had been avoiding stepping into the light, paralyzed by my fears. "I'm trying to figure out how to join you out there without stumbling over my own feet."

He stepped closer, his expression shifting to one of understanding. "Then let's practice together. Right here. Right now. Just you and me."

With that, he pulled me back to the center of the studio, the laughter of the other dancers fading into the background. My heart raced with anticipation, the thrill of reclaiming our connection overwhelming any lingering hesitation. The music started again, filling the air with an irresistible rhythm, and as we began to move, something shifted between us.

With each step, I felt my confidence blossoming, the familiar ache of doubt retreating into the shadows. Rylan's presence was a steady anchor, grounding me as we navigated through the choreography, his eyes locking onto mine, igniting the unspoken words that hung in the air.

Then, just as I started to lose myself in the dance, a loud crash echoed through the studio, pulling us from our rhythm once more. We stopped mid-movement, hearts racing, as we turned toward the source of the noise.

The front door swung open violently, and a figure rushed in, breathless and wide-eyed. "You won't believe what just happened! There's a fire in the storage room!"

Panic spread through the studio like wildfire, dancers scrambling to grab their belongings, the earlier camaraderie replaced by urgent chaos. My stomach dropped, a knot of dread forming as I caught Rylan's gaze across the room. The moment we had just reclaimed felt like it was slipping away again, and all the unspoken words hung heavy in the air.

"Let's go," he shouted, his voice rising above the tumult. "We need to evacuate!"

In that instant, the world around us faded into a blur, the laughter, the music, and the warmth all extinguished in the face of this new reality. Rylan reached for my hand, the grip firm and reassuring, but even as we rushed toward the exit, a sense of dread settled over me.

What if this was it? What if the fire was just the beginning of a much darker storm? I glanced back one last time, the flickering light from the storage room casting ominous shadows that danced in the corners of my mind. A choice lay ahead, one that could either extinguish our connection or spark it anew, and I couldn't shake the feeling that the real battle was just beginning.

Chapter 8: The Fork in the Road

The flickering candlelight cast dancing shadows across the café's walls, creating a tapestry of movement that mirrored the tumult within me. I sat across from Rylan, the rich aroma of freshly brewed coffee swirling around us, but the warmth of the atmosphere couldn't penetrate the chill of our conversation. His hazel eyes, usually so bright and filled with mischief, now held a weight I had never seen before. It was as if the very air between us was laden with the echoes of unspoken fears and desires.

"I don't know if I can keep doing this," I said, the words slipping from my lips like a confession. My fingers toyed with the delicate edge of my ceramic cup, tracing the spiraled design as if searching for answers in its texture. "Every time I think I'm making progress, it feels like I'm just digging a deeper hole."

Rylan leaned back, his expression contemplative. The playful banter we often shared had evaporated, leaving behind a stark reality. "You're not the only one, you know. I've been trying to figure out what we are... what we could be." His voice was low, almost a whisper, but it cut through the ambient noise of the café like a knife.

I could see the flicker of vulnerability in his gaze. It was a rare sight, and yet, it filled me with a mixture of relief and dread. He wasn't just the charming, confident man I had been drawn to; he was human, flawed, and grappling with his own insecurities. "You mean you're confused too?"

He rubbed the back of his neck, the motion casual but the tension in his body palpable. "I've been hurt before. I don't want to get too close just to be left behind again. It scares me."

Those words wrapped around my heart like a vice. I understood that fear all too well, having danced with my own shadows for years. "But we could figure it out together," I pleaded, the desperation creeping into my voice. "I don't want to lose you, Rylan. You mean more to me than I've ever said."

His gaze softened momentarily, and I felt a flicker of hope, like sunlight breaking through heavy clouds. "It's not that simple. Sometimes stepping back is what we need. Maybe... maybe we should take some time apart. Just until you sort things out."

Time apart. The words echoed in my mind like a drumbeat, steady yet jarring. "You're suggesting we just... stop?" I was grasping for something solid, something to hold onto in this whirlpool of uncertainty.

"I'm suggesting that maybe it's for the best," he replied, his voice steady but edged with sadness. "I want you to be okay, really okay, before we dive into whatever this is."

My heart sank. The idea of separation felt like a gaping chasm opening beneath me, threatening to swallow everything I had come to cherish about our connection. I glanced around the café, my eyes landing on the cozy couple in the corner, their heads bent together in a conspiratorial whisper. A pang of jealousy shot through me. I wanted that. I wanted to lean into Rylan, to share secrets and dreams, not drift apart like ships lost in a fog.

"What if I never get there?" The words tumbled out before I could stop them, raw and unguarded. "What if I'm just stuck in this endless loop of confusion? You could be my way out."

He sighed, a sound heavy with unvoiced concerns. "You need to find your own way, and I can't be the crutch you lean on. It wouldn't be fair to either of us."

The truth of his words was like ice water thrown in my face. I took a shaky breath, forcing myself to meet his gaze. "And what if I need you? What if losing you means losing my chance at happiness?"

"Maybe happiness comes from within," he said softly, his eyes piercing into mine, searching for something that felt just out of reach. "It can't come from someone else."

We sat in silence, the ambient noise of the café fading into a dull roar, our thoughts swirling like the steam rising from our untouched coffees. My heart pounded in my chest, the rhythm of it echoing in my ears. The world around me felt suspended in time, the delicate clinks of cups and soft murmurings of conversation fading into the background.

"What are we doing?" I asked, the words escaping before I could rein them in. "It feels like we're at a crossroads, and I don't know which way to go."

"Maybe that's okay," he replied, his tone softening. "Maybe not knowing is part of the journey."

His words hung between us, a fragile bridge over the uncertainty. I longed to reach out and grasp his hand, to feel the warmth of his skin against mine, to anchor myself in the moment, but fear held me back. What if this was the last time we shared a space like this? What if the next time I looked into those eyes, they were filled with a distance I couldn't bear?

"I don't want to let go," I admitted, my voice barely above a whisper. "But maybe... maybe you're right. Maybe I need to find my own footing first."

The weight of that acceptance settled on me like a heavy blanket, both comforting and suffocating. I could feel the tears welling in my eyes, threatening to spill over. Rylan reached across the table, his fingers brushing against mine in a fleeting connection that sent a jolt through me.

"Promise me you'll be honest with yourself," he said, his voice low and steady, as if he were grounding me in a storm. "I want you to find what you need, even if it's not me."

With those words, the dam inside me broke. I squeezed his hand, desperately trying to convey everything I felt—fear, longing, and an unbearable weight of sadness that threatened to pull me under. The café faded away, and for that moment, it was just us, two souls tangled in an emotional web, unsure of the next step but unwilling to let go completely.

A single drop of wax slid down the side of the candle, a miniature waterfall captured in time. It reminded me of how quickly moments could solidify into memories, both sweet and painful. Rylan's fingers still lingered near mine, a tantalizing whisper of connection. I could feel the heat radiating from him, mixing with the aroma of espresso and warm pastries. Yet the warmth felt distant, as if the world outside our bubble pressed against us, demanding attention we were unwilling to give.

"I can't promise you anything," I said finally, the words catching in my throat. "But I can promise to try. To be honest with myself." Rylan's gaze bore into mine, searching for sincerity. It was as if he could unravel the chaos swirling inside me just by looking hard enough.

"Trying is a good start," he replied, his tone softening but still edged with the tension of uncharted territory. "Just don't be surprised if it leads you somewhere unexpected."

Unexpected. That word lingered in the air, an uninvited guest at our table. I didn't want unexpected; I wanted certainty. I wanted the easy comfort of his laughter, the way he threw his head back when something amused him, filling the air with joy. But the truth was, the harder I tried to hold onto those moments, the more they slipped through my fingers like grains of sand.

As I stared into my coffee, I felt a tightening in my chest, a familiar blend of dread and exhilaration. "So, what do we do now?" The question hung in the air like a suspended breath, waiting for release.

Rylan shrugged, his expression a mixture of reluctance and understanding. "We take it day by day. Maybe we start with a little distance—just a bit of space to breathe."

A lump formed in my throat. Space. It was such a clean, simple word, but its implications were messy and complicated. I imagined us drifting apart, like two stars that once shone brightly in the same sky, now hurtling away into the dark abyss. "How much space are we talking about?"

He let out a soft sigh. "Enough to let you figure out what you really want. Enough to give us both a chance to reflect."

Reflect. The word echoed in my mind like an unwanted refrain, conjuring images of late nights spent overthinking every decision I had ever made. "And if I decide I want you back?" I dared to ask, the vulnerability in my voice striking a chord in the dimly lit café.

"Then we cross that bridge when we get to it." He smiled, but there was a shadow behind it, a trace of longing that lingered like the last notes of a beautiful melody.

For a moment, I let the silence envelop us again. My heart raced, each beat a reminder of the stakes involved. I wanted to be brave. I wanted to leap into the unknown with him, to take his hand and forge a path through our fears together. But the specter of my insecurities loomed large, reminding me of all the times I had fallen short.

"I need to be alone for a while," I admitted, the weight of those words pressing against my chest. "I need to remember what it's like to be me without... all of this."

Rylan nodded slowly, his expression unreadable. "That's fair. Just promise me one thing: don't lose yourself in the process."

With a deep breath, I smiled through the ache in my heart, my mind swirling with uncertainties. "I'll try not to. I promise."

As the evening wore on, the café began to fill with laughter and chatter, couples leaning in close, sharing secrets over shared plates of pastries. A part of me longed to join them, to lose myself in their world of carefree joy. Yet here I was, caught in a whirlpool of what-ifs and maybes, with Rylan's presence still anchoring me despite the distance we were discussing.

"What do we do about our plans this weekend?" I ventured, my voice a mixture of hope and dread.

He ran a hand through his tousled hair, a nervous gesture I had come to recognize. "We can still keep them. It might be good to have some normalcy, right?"

Normalcy. The word struck me as both comforting and ironic. I had sought out normalcy for so long, yet it felt like a distant dream now. "Okay. A day in the park, then?" I suggested, picturing the sun-dappled grass and the laughter of children playing, a snapshot of happiness amid the uncertainty.

"Sure," he replied, the corners of his mouth lifting slightly. "We'll just keep it friendly, right?"

Friendly. The term felt like a double-edged sword. It was a lifeline, yet it also carried the weight of what we were leaving unsaid. "Right. Just friends," I echoed, my heart clenching at the thought.

As we settled the bill and made our way to the door, the air outside was cool and crisp, a welcome change from the stifling intimacy of the café. I glanced at Rylan, his silhouette framed by the streetlights, a beacon of warmth against the encroaching night. "Thanks for understanding," I said, the sincerity of my gratitude wrapping around my words. "I know this isn't easy."

"It's not," he admitted, his voice low as he looked away, almost as if he were battling his own emotions. "But I want what's best for you. Even if it means letting go for a while."

Letting go. The thought wrapped around my mind, swirling in dizzying circles. How could something so simple feel so monumental? I wanted to shout, to scream that this was the worst idea ever. But I knew he was right. I had to confront my own demons before I could be anything for him.

Just as we reached the crosswalk, I caught a glimpse of a couple in the distance, their fingers intertwined, laughter spilling from their lips. An ache pierced through my heart, bittersweet and sharp. I turned to Rylan, a smile breaking through my uncertainty. "We should probably go to that bakery you love after the park. The one with the chocolate croissants."

His eyes brightened at the mention of his favorite treat. "Now that's a solid plan. How can anyone resist warm chocolate wrapped in buttery goodness?"

"Exactly!" I chuckled, feeling a flicker of our familiar camaraderie spark to life, momentarily pushing aside the heavy clouds of uncertainty looming overhead. "Maybe we can treat it like a research trip—find out if they're truly as good as you claim."

"Challenge accepted," he replied, his playful tone easing the tension between us just a little. The moment felt electric, a reminder of all the laughter and connection we had built.

And in that brief exchange, as we stepped off the curb and into the rhythm of the night, I felt a flicker of hope amid the uncertainty. We might be treading on shaky ground, but at least we were still walking together, one tentative step at a time.

The air was crisp as we stepped out of the café, the remnants of twilight painting the horizon in shades of violet and gold. I felt a shiver run through me, not just from the cool breeze, but from the weight of the conversation we had just shared. The streetlights flickered on, their soft glow illuminating our path, but the shadows still clung to the corners of my mind, a reminder of the uncertainties that lay ahead.

"So, the park this weekend?" I ventured, attempting to ground myself in the familiar rhythm of our plans, hoping to divert the heaviness of our earlier discussion. "You still up for that?"

"Definitely," Rylan replied, his lips curving into that disarming smile that had first drawn me to him. "Just don't expect me to be all sunshine and rainbows while we keep things... friendly."

"Hey, I'm not a monster," I shot back, laughing lightly to ease the tension. "You might have to remind me not to let my guard down, though. Old habits die hard."

"Oh, I'll be sure to keep my eyes peeled," he teased, nudging my shoulder with his as we walked side by side, the banter creating a fragile but comforting bubble around us. But beneath the surface, I could feel the currents of our situation swirling.

As we made our way toward the park, the soft crunch of fallen leaves beneath our feet felt like the universe's way of reminding me that change was inevitable. The distant sounds of children laughing and the faint music from a street performer reached us, weaving through the air and pulling me deeper into the moment. Yet, the laughter felt almost foreign, a reminder of the innocence I once had—the ease of living without second-guessing every interaction, every look shared.

"What if the croissants don't live up to the hype?" Rylan mused, breaking my reverie.

"Then we'll simply have to take it upon ourselves to conduct further research," I replied, my tone mock-serious. "I mean, it's a tough job, but someone has to do it, right?"

Rylan chuckled, the sound warm and genuine, washing over me like a soothing balm. "You're right. We have a moral obligation to the croissant community."

"Exactly!" I laughed, feeling a weight lift, even if just for a moment. The path ahead was still uncertain, but the joy we found in the small things—a silly conversation, a shared laugh—seemed to forge an invisible thread between us, one that I desperately hoped wouldn't unravel too soon.

As we approached the park, the trees stretched above us, their branches forming a canopy against the night sky. A scattering of stars began to peek through the darkening blue, twinkling like tiny promises waiting to be fulfilled. The faint scent of caramel popcorn drifted through the air, mingling with the earthy smell of the damp grass.

"Have you ever had popcorn in the park at night?" Rylan asked, a hint of nostalgia in his voice.

"Is that a thing?" I raised an eyebrow, intrigued.

"It is now! I declare it an essential part of our outing," he insisted, his playful tone igniting a spark of excitement in me.

"Alright, Mr. Popcorn Advocate," I grinned, "if that's what it takes to convince you to keep things light, then so be it. Let's grab some popcorn."

He laughed, the sound brightening the atmosphere around us. It was a joy I yearned for, a sense of normalcy amid the swirling chaos of my thoughts. Just two friends enjoying a night out, dipping their toes into the waters of what could be—simple yet profound.

As we strolled deeper into the park, we found a cozy spot on a weathered bench overlooking a small pond. The moonlight shimmered on the water's surface, creating a silvery path that beckoned us closer. The night felt alive with possibilities, yet I could sense the tension lingering beneath the surface, a taut string waiting for the right moment to snap.

"You know," Rylan said, breaking the comfortable silence, "I'm really glad we're doing this. It feels... nice, just being here with you."

"It does," I agreed, watching as a group of children ran past us, their laughter echoing through the night. "Even if it feels like we're playing pretend."

"Playing pretend? How so?" His gaze fixed on me, curiosity igniting the depths of his hazel eyes.

"Like, we're acting like everything's fine," I admitted, the vulnerability creeping back into my voice. "Like we're just two friends enjoying a nice evening when, in reality, we're balancing on this tightrope of uncertainty."

Rylan's expression shifted, the mirth of the moment replaced by something deeper, something more serious. "You're right. But maybe that's okay, for now. We don't have to have everything figured out tonight."

"Maybe," I murmured, but the weight of my unconfessed feelings loomed large, casting a shadow over our lighthearted moments. The truth hung heavily between us, a secret yearning that both terrified and excited me.

Just then, the sound of laughter erupted nearby as a couple began a playful argument over who could toss a popcorn kernel the farthest. I watched them, caught in their joyful exchange, and my heart ached with a sudden intensity. They were so carefree, so blissfully unaware of the complexities that could twist love into something unrecognizable.

"Do you think we'll ever get to that point?" I blurted out, the words tumbling from my lips before I could catch them. "I mean, will we ever be able to joke about our issues like that couple?"

Rylan's brow furrowed for a moment, as if he were considering the question seriously. "I think that kind of connection comes from understanding and overcoming the tough stuff together. It's about weathering the storms, not just enjoying the sunshine."

His words hung between us, heavy with implication. I couldn't help but wonder if we had the strength to weather those storms, or if the winds would tear us apart before we could ever find our way back to the sun.

"Hey, look at that!" Rylan suddenly exclaimed, breaking the tension. He pointed toward the pond, where a pair of ducks glided across the water, their silhouettes smooth and graceful against the moonlight. "They look so peaceful, don't they?"

"Yeah," I replied, but my thoughts were still tangled in what lay beneath the surface of our conversation. "Maybe we should take a lesson from them—just float along, no matter what's happening around us."

"Or just enjoy the bread crumbs," Rylan quipped, his smile returning. "Life's too short to get bogged down by the details."

"True," I laughed, but the laughter felt hollow, a thin veneer over the deeper issues we were facing. As we settled back on the bench, I felt a flicker of hope mixed with uncertainty.

But just as I began to relax, a commotion erupted nearby. A group of teenagers had gathered, their voices rising in excitement as one of them pulled out a small drone, launching it into the night sky. The little machine whirred above us, cutting through the darkness like a comet, its bright lights flashing in vibrant colors.

"Looks like the night is about to get a little wilder," Rylan said, amusement dancing in his eyes.

"Should we join the chaos?" I suggested, a spark of spontaneity igniting within me.

"Why not? It could be fun!" Rylan replied, his enthusiasm infectious.

As we stood up, I felt a surge of adrenaline, as if we were leaping into a new adventure together. But before we could make our way over to the crowd, a sudden commotion caught my attention. A voice rose above the laughter, sharp and urgent.

"Stop! Don't touch that!" A woman shouted, her voice trembling with panic.

The joyous atmosphere shifted, confusion rippling through the air. I exchanged a glance with Rylan, our momentary excitement dashed by the unexpected tension. "What's happening?" I asked, my heart quickening.

"I don't know, but we should check it out," he said, a determined look crossing his face.

We moved toward the crowd, curiosity and concern mingling within me. As we got closer, I caught sight of the woman pointing frantically at the drone, her face pale and strained. "It's not safe! It's malfunctioning!"

My breath caught in my throat. The atmosphere shifted from light-hearted to electric with unease, and as I turned to Rylan, the air between us crackled with an impending sense of danger.

"What if something goes wrong?" I whispered, fear creeping into my voice.

Before he could respond, a sudden explosion of light erupted from the drone, blinding us for a split second.

The world froze, a sharp intake of breath, and in that moment, everything changed.

Chapter 9: The Unraveling

Driving home felt like navigating a labyrinth of emotions, each twist and turn evoking fresh waves of sorrow. The familiar landscape blurred through my tears—trees standing sentinel like silent witnesses to my heartache, their leaves whispering secrets I couldn't decipher. Each sob that escaped my lips felt like a release, but it was a release tinged with the suffocating weight of regret. I gripped the steering wheel, knuckles whitening, as I replayed the evening's events in my mind like a broken record.

Noah's voice echoed in my ears, playful and light. "You know, your fear of commitment could probably fill a novel. A very dramatic one, complete with plot twists and cliffhangers." His laughter had rolled over me, soft and teasing, but beneath the surface, it carried the undertones of a challenge. Maybe he was right. Maybe I was a character in my own story who refused to turn the page, too afraid of what came next. My heart ached, not just from the thought of losing him but from the crushing realization that I had built walls so high that even I struggled to see over them.

Pulling into my driveway, the glow of the porch light felt like a beacon, but instead of comfort, it filled me with dread. Home should have been my sanctuary, but it had morphed into a reminder of all the things I was running from. I wiped my cheeks dry with the back of my hand, taking a moment to gather myself. Each step toward the front door felt monumental, as if I were marching into battle rather than returning to a place filled with memories.

Inside, the air hung heavy with the scent of my mother's lavender candles, mingling with the faint echo of an old jazz record playing somewhere in the house. I paused, absorbing the familiarity of it all—the vibrant colors of the paintings she had collected over the years, the cozy throw blankets draped haphazardly across the couch, the mismatched cushions that told stories of laughter and late-night movies. My heart clenched at the thought that this could all change.

"Maggie?" My mother's voice floated down the hall, warm but laced with an urgency that sent a shiver down my spine.

"Yeah, Mom, it's me," I called back, forcing a smile that felt more like a grimace. I stepped into the living room, where she sat with her legs tucked beneath her, surrounded by a fortress of medical pamphlets and glossy magazines. She looked up, her brow furrowed, and in that moment, I saw something I hadn't seen in years—fear.

"Sweetheart, I've been trying to reach you," she said, the softness of her voice making my heart race. "We need to talk."

My stomach dropped, a free-fall sensation that threatened to consume me. "What's wrong?" I asked, every syllable weighed down by the dread that churned within me.

"It's about my doctor's appointment. The tests came back..." she trailed off, her gaze drifting toward the window where the moonlight cast a silvery glow across the room. I could see the struggle etched on her face, the tension in her shoulders as she fought to maintain composure. "I have some health issues. Nothing definitive yet, but... we need to prepare for what could happen."

The world tilted on its axis, the room swirling like a kaleidoscope of colors and sound. "What do you mean? What's wrong?" My voice trembled, thick with disbelief. This couldn't be real; I had just seen her last week, laughing over a pot of my famous chili, her face alight with joy.

"It's possible I'll need surgery," she replied, her voice steady but her eyes shimmering with unshed tears. "I didn't want to tell you until I had more information, but I thought you should know."

I staggered back, the wall of her words crashing over me like a wave. "Mom, you can't—" I choked on the words, grappling with the enormity of what she was saying. "You can't do this to me. I need you."

She reached out, her hand trembling as it touched mine. "Maggie, listen to me. I'm not going anywhere yet. We'll get through this together."

But I couldn't shake the cold grip of fear that wrapped around my heart. The thought of losing her felt like an anchor pulling me into the depths of despair. I had spent years building walls to protect myself from commitment, from connection, from love, only to find the very thing I feared most standing before me—fragility.

As the evening wore on, we spoke in hushed tones, the gravity of the conversation hanging heavily in the air. I felt like a child again, lost in the world of adult worries, and suddenly, the trivialities of my fears about relationships seemed so petty. My heart had been so consumed with my own insecurities that I had forgotten the weight of real loss.

"Promise me something," she said, her voice barely above a whisper. "Don't let fear stop you from living your life. Love fiercely, even when it scares you."

Her words settled like a warm blanket around my shoulders, offering comfort amid the chaos. Yet, a part of me felt like a fool for worrying about my own romantic missteps when my mother was facing something so monumental. I wanted to scream that I would fight for her, for our family, that I would not let fear dictate my choices any longer. But even as I promised her I would, I realized I needed to confront my past, to embrace whatever future awaited me, with all its uncertainties.

The night wore on, and as we spoke of her upcoming appointments, of possible treatments and hopeful outcomes, I felt the first stirrings of resolve. Perhaps it was time to let go of the past, to embrace not just the fear of commitment but also the thrill of possibility. Life was unpredictable, a wild, beautiful mess, and it was time I learned to dance in the chaos.

The following days unfurled like a series of uninvited guests—each one more unwelcome than the last. My mother's diagnosis hung over us like a persistent cloud, a damp blanket that stifled our laughter and dimmed our usual banter. The warmth of her lavender candles couldn't mask the chill of impending uncertainty that had settled into our home. We tiptoed around the topic, discussing it as if it were a fragile artifact, something precious that could shatter if handled too carelessly.

I spent my mornings wrapped in a cocoon of anxiety, working remotely while trying to focus on my tasks. My fingers danced over the keyboard, but my mind was a restless sea, churning with worries and what-ifs. Each email I sent felt like a hollow echo in a cavern, resonating but lacking substance. Meanwhile, my phone buzzed constantly, a barrage of messages from Noah that I struggled to respond to. His texts were a lifeline thrown into my stormy sea, but I was too overwhelmed to grab hold.

"Hey, Maggie! Are you alive? I haven't seen your face in a week!" Noah's message came in like a ray of sunshine breaking through a storm. I could almost hear his playful tone, the one that seemed to dance through the air with a lightness I desperately craved.

I hesitated, my fingers hovering over the screen. I wanted to tell him everything, to unravel the mess of emotions I was tangled in, but how could I burden him with my mother's health? A deep breath steadied me as I typed, "Just busy with work. Can we catch up soon?" It felt like a half-truth wrapped in a bow of avoidance, but I hit send anyway, almost immediately regretting it.

When the weekend rolled around, I decided to put my work aside and finally visit my mother. I gathered fresh flowers—vibrant sunflowers that seemed to defy the shadow hanging over us—and drove to her house, hoping the bright petals would lift her spirits. The familiar route felt different, each turn tinged with the weight of my worry. As I parked outside her little bungalow, the sun peeked through the clouds, casting warm rays across her garden, which was still bursting with color. It was a small comfort against the storm brewing in our lives.

As I walked in, the door creaked open to reveal my mother perched on her favorite armchair, a cozy, faded seat that had seen better days. She looked up, her face breaking into a smile that didn't quite reach her eyes. "You brought me flowers!" she exclaimed, her voice a sweet melody amidst the lingering tension.

"Of course! I thought they might brighten up the place a bit," I said, placing them in a vase on the kitchen counter. "And they do have that 'get well soon' vibe, don't you think?"

She chuckled, a sound that felt both foreign and familiar. "I suppose they do. But you know me; I've never been one for traditional get well cards. Flowers are more my style."

We settled into a routine of quiet conversation, dancing around the topic of her health. She asked about work, and I shared the latest gossip from the office, embellishing the stories to elicit laughter. Just as I was gaining momentum, her phone buzzed on the table, drawing her attention. The momentary distraction sent my heart racing; I had felt the air thicken, the unspoken truths hanging in the space between us.

"Sorry, just a quick text from Dr. McAllister," she said, her fingers brushing the screen as she read the message. I held my breath, fighting the urge to ask what it said, but the knot in my stomach was too tight. I watched her face fall, a mask of forced calm slipping away as she stared at the phone.

"What did he say?" I finally blurted out, the words bursting forth before I could rein them in.

She hesitated, her expression a storm of conflicting emotions. "It's just... we have to schedule a follow-up. It's standard procedure, but..." She paused, biting her lip. "I'll be fine. I promise."

"Mom," I said, my voice softening as I reached across the table to squeeze her hand. "It's okay to be scared. I'm scared too. We can talk about this."

She looked down at our hands, a gentle smile creeping back. "I don't want you to worry about me, sweet girl. You have your own life to live."

"But I want to be here for you! You're my everything," I insisted, a flare of frustration lighting my voice. "We're in this together, remember?"

Her eyes sparkled with unshed tears. "You have no idea how much that means to me. But you also need to focus on your life. You can't let my issues hold you back."

It was a sentiment that made my heart ache even more. "It's hard to think of my life when I'm worried about yours," I murmured, a softness settling over our conversation.

The afternoon slipped away in a haze of flowers, laughter, and unspoken fears. As the sun dipped low in the sky, casting golden light through the windows, I felt a shift within myself. It was as if the weight of my mother's diagnosis was slowly merging with my own worries about love and commitment, a confluence of emotions threatening to overflow.

"Can I ask you something?" I said, breaking the comfortable silence. She nodded, and I took a breath, gathering my thoughts. "What if we find a way to tackle this together? I mean, maybe it's time I stopped hiding behind my own fears."

Her eyes widened slightly, curiosity mingling with concern. "What do you mean?"

"I've been running from commitment for so long, thinking I'd protect myself. But if anything, it's made me miss out on real connections, like with you, and..." My voice trailed off, the fear of revealing my true feelings gnawing at me.

"Like with Noah?" she prodded gently, a knowing smile spreading across her face.

"Yes! I mean, maybe I should just let myself fall, rather than worry about where it lands me. It's just... so scary," I confessed, each word feeling like a small surrender.

"Love is always scary, Maggie. But it's also beautiful," she said, her voice steady and reassuring. "And you won't know until you take that leap."

We sat in a comfortable silence, the air between us thick with shared understanding. I looked around at the home that had always felt like a fortress and realized it was more than just walls; it was love, safety, and the potential for growth. If I could face the future, embrace the uncertainties, and be there for my mother, then perhaps I could do the same for myself.

As the evening darkened outside, I made a promise to myself—a promise that echoed my mother's words. I would confront my fears, take that leap, and embrace whatever came next. With the gentle hum of the jazz record in the background and the warm glow of the sunflowers illuminating the room, I felt a flicker of hope igniting within me, a quiet but unwavering determination to write my own story, one page at a time.

The week unfolded with a strange blend of anticipation and dread, a tightrope walk across the delicate balance of my mother's health and the murky waters of my own emotions. Each morning, I woke up determined to embrace my fears, armed with the resolve I had found in our heart-to-heart. Yet, as I moved through my days, life's little challenges conspired to pull me back into the shadows.

My phone buzzed incessantly, a reminder of the world that continued to spin around me, full of responsibilities and social invitations I had begun to ignore. Even Noah seemed to fade into the background, his lighthearted texts now replaced by a frustrating silence that echoed my own emotional turmoil. It wasn't that I didn't want to see him; it was that I didn't know how to face him without spilling the mess I was wading through. So, I steeled myself and focused on the task at hand: my mother.

The weekend arrived, bringing with it the promise of our regular brunch at the little café down the street, the one draped in fairy lights and overflowing with potted plants. I had always loved that place, a sanctuary of sorts where we could drown in mimosas and pastries while the world outside faded into a blur. But this time, the excitement felt muted, as if I were trying to tune into a radio station that was barely coming in.

I arrived at the café to find my mother already seated at our usual table, her hands wrapped around a steaming mug of chamomile tea. The smile that spread across her face was genuine, yet it didn't quite reach her eyes. "You look tired, darling," she said, concern lacing her voice as I slid into the chair across from her.

"I've just been a little busy," I replied, waving a dismissive hand. The truth was, I felt exhausted not just from work, but from the weight of unspoken fears hanging between us. "How did you sleep?"

"Better, thanks," she said, but the slight tremor in her voice hinted at the unease lurking beneath her words. We ordered our meals, the comforting familiarity of the café momentarily lifting the heavy atmosphere.

"I heard back from the doctor," she finally ventured after a long pause, stirring her tea as if it were a potion she could brew to ward off reality. My heart raced, anticipating news I wasn't sure I was ready to hear. "They want me to start some treatment next week."

I swallowed hard, a lump forming in my throat. "What kind of treatment?"

She hesitated, then replied, "It's a medication to help manage the symptoms. Nothing too drastic, but..." She sighed, her fingers tightening around the cup. "I'll need you to be strong for me, Maggie. It's going to be a long road."

"I'm here for you," I said, trying to infuse my voice with confidence. "Whatever you need, we'll face this together." But the words felt hollow, like a promise made under duress. Inside, I was terrified—not just for her, but for what this meant for me.

After we finished brunch, we strolled through the nearby park, the crisp air invigorating and yet hauntingly bittersweet. Children chased each other, laughter ringing out like music, a stark contrast to the quiet thoughts swirling in my head. I looked at my mother, her gait slower than I remembered, and felt a pang of guilt. She had given me everything, yet here I was, still grappling with my own hesitations, my own selfish fears.

"Isn't it beautiful?" she said, stopping to admire a cluster of bright flowers bursting through the ground. "Life always finds a way to bloom, doesn't it?"

"Yeah," I replied, forcing a smile. "Even in the toughest conditions."

We continued our walk, but my mind was elsewhere. Thoughts of Noah crept in uninvited. What would he think if he knew how I was feeling? Would he be the anchor I desperately needed, or would my own insecurities send him sailing away? The looming question nagged at me as we made our way back home, each step weighted with uncertainty.

That evening, I found myself staring at my phone, the screen lighting up with messages from Noah, each one a gentle nudge reminding me that life still moved forward. "Dinner tomorrow?" read one. "You owe me a laugh!" Another simply said, "Miss you."

My heart wavered, battling between the urge to reach out and my instinct to retreat. Finally, I gathered my courage and typed back, "Let's do it. Dinner sounds great."

The response came almost instantly, his enthusiasm palpable even through the screen. "Awesome! I'll pick you up at seven. Can't wait to see your beautiful face."

As the clock ticked down to our dinner, my stomach twisted with anticipation and nerves. I chose my outfit carefully, picking a soft sweater that hugged me just right and a pair of jeans that felt comfortable yet stylish. I looked in the mirror, searching for a spark of confidence. "You can do this," I whispered to myself. "You deserve this."

When the doorbell rang, a thrill shot through me, mixing excitement with a touch of fear. Opening the door, I was greeted by Noah's radiant smile, bright enough to cut through my anxiety like a warm knife through butter. "There she is!" he exclaimed, stepping forward to pull me into a tight embrace. I melted against him, inhaling his familiar scent—fresh linen and a hint of cedar.

"Hi," I managed, a shy smile breaking through my nervous exterior.

We walked to his car, the air crackling with an electric tension. As we drove through the city, I let myself relax, the rhythmic sound of his laughter and the music filling the space around us creating a cocoon of comfort. The restaurant was bustling, filled with laughter and the clinking of glasses. We found a small table in a corner, candles flickering softly, casting a warm glow.

"Okay, spill," Noah said, leaning in as we browsed the menu. "What's been going on? You've been quiet lately."

I hesitated, the weight of my thoughts pressing down on me. "Just... dealing with some stuff at home," I said, choosing my words carefully.

He studied me, those perceptive eyes of his reading between the lines. "Maggie, you know you can tell me anything, right? I'm here for you."

"I know," I replied, feeling the warmth of his sincerity seep into my heart. But just as I was about to unveil the truth of my fears and my mother's health, a loud crash echoed through the restaurant, cutting through the soft chatter.

Everyone turned toward the source of the noise—a man had stumbled, his chair toppling over as he collided with a nearby table. Gasps rippled through the crowd, but it wasn't the crash that had my heart racing. It was the sudden flash of recognition I felt as I locked eyes with the man on the floor.

His gaze met mine, and time seemed to freeze. It was a face I hadn't seen in years—a face that haunted my past and dredged up memories I had tried to bury.

"Charlie?" I breathed, the name escaping my lips before I could stop it, my voice barely a whisper against the backdrop of chaos.

Noah turned to me, confusion flickering across his features. "Do you know him?"

I barely heard his question, the world narrowing down to that one moment, that one face. My heart pounded in my chest, a relentless drumbeat echoing the unsteady rhythm of my breath. Everything I thought I had buried beneath layers of time and distance suddenly resurfaced, and I knew, in that instant, that nothing would ever be the same again.

Chapter 10: Fractured Bonds

The hospital room felt too sterile, an artificial cocoon that contrasted starkly with the warmth I'd always associated with my mother. The rhythmic beep of the machines punctuated the air, a constant reminder that life was precarious, teetering on a delicate edge. My mother lay there, framed by stark white sheets, her face pallid and drawn. The once vibrant woman who had spun tales of magic and mischief now resembled a fragile doll, propped up by a tangle of IV tubes and wires. I leaned closer, inhaling the scent of antiseptic mingling with the faintest trace of her familiar lavender perfume, a comforting ghost of what she used to be.

"Hey, Mom," I murmured, my voice barely a whisper. "How are you feeling?"

Her eyes fluttered open, revealing a glimmer of recognition before the shadow of worry clouded them. "Oh, honey, I'm just fine. You know how these hospitals are—always looking for an excuse to keep us longer than necessary." She attempted a smile, but it faltered, revealing a vulnerability that twisted my heart. I wanted to believe her, to cling to the hope that this was merely a temporary setback, but the pit in my stomach told a different story.

I glanced at my phone, its screen lighting up with Rylan's name. A rush of warmth spread through me, a stark contrast to the chill that had settled in my bones. We had shared so much laughter, so many dreams of what could be, and here I was, tethered to a hospital bed while he thrived in the vibrant streets of New Orleans. I hesitated, torn between the two worlds that felt increasingly at odds with one another. The weight of my mother's illness anchored me here, yet my heart tugged me toward the jazz-laced nights, the bewitching allure of a city alive with possibility.

"Is that Rylan?" My mother's voice cut through my thoughts, sharp and knowing. She always had a way of seeing through my carefully constructed façades. I nodded, unable to hide the flush that crept up my cheeks.

"He sent a message," I admitted, swallowing hard. "He's been really supportive."

"Supportive? Or just convenient?" Her tone was teasing, but her eyes searched mine, digging deeper into my emotions. I couldn't help but let out a laugh, the sound ringing hollow against the sterile backdrop.

"Mom, it's not like that," I protested, feeling the heat of her scrutiny. "He genuinely cares."

"Does he?" The question hung in the air, heavy with unspoken concern. I shifted uncomfortably in my chair, suddenly feeling the weight of my choices settle on my shoulders like a leaden cloak. I had kept Rylan at arm's length, always a step away from fully embracing what we could be. Did I dare explore that path now, with my mother's future hanging in the balance?

"Maybe you should go to him," she said softly, her gaze shifting to the window where clouds floated lazily, masking the sun. "You could use some time away from here, sweetheart."

The thought sent a thrill of guilt racing through me. "Mom, I can't just leave you. What if...?" I trailed off, unable to voice the fear that lingered in the corners of my mind.

"What if I get better?" she countered, her voice steady yet laced with an underlying fragility. "What if this is just a hiccup? I've fought through tougher things than this, you know. You shouldn't have to put your life on hold because of me."

As she spoke, I felt a rush of emotions collide—love, anger, sorrow, and frustration swirling together in a tempest of conflict. I wanted to be her anchor, but I also longed for the winds of change that Rylan represented. I had spent so much of my life putting others first, ensuring my mother was taken care of, and yet, now, I stood at a crossroads, unsure of which path to take.

My phone buzzed again, and this time, I pulled it out, the screen lighting up with a new message. Rylan's words spilled across the display: Thinking of you. Wish you were here to share a beignet with me. A bittersweet smile tugged at my lips as I imagined the café, the air rich with the scent of powdered sugar and coffee.

"I should reply," I said, more to myself than to her, feeling a sense of urgency rise within me. She nodded, her smile returning, albeit feebly.

"Go on then, sweetheart. Don't let me hold you back. Life's too short to let opportunities slip through your fingers."

Her words, so simple yet profound, resonated within me. I hesitated, hovering between sending a playful response and the weight of reality pressing down. My fingers danced over the keys, crafting a message that was light, casual, yet filled with an undercurrent of longing. Save me a beignet for when I can join you? I hit send, my heart racing as if I had just opened a door to a world I had been afraid to step into.

As I looked up from my phone, I caught my mother's gaze, her expression unreadable yet somehow hopeful. "You're going to make a decision, aren't you?" she asked, her voice steady, like the gentle lap of waves against the shore.

"I don't know, Mom. I feel torn."

"You need to follow your heart. I won't be here forever, but I want you to live. Really live."

With those words, I felt the first flicker of resolve ignite within me. The tension that had coiled in my chest began to ease, replaced by a burgeoning sense of possibility. Perhaps it was time to acknowledge that the world was still turning outside these sterile walls, that love and life were waiting for me beyond the hospital's grim facade.

The walls of the hospital room closed in around me, a suffocating reminder of reality's harshness. My mother's breaths were shallow, each rise and fall of her chest a fragile testament to her strength, yet they struck me like a drumbeat marking time—time I wished I could pause, rewind, or fast-forward to brighter days. I focused on the delicate blue floral pattern of the wallpaper, each petal a ghost of the comfort I craved. The harshness of the fluorescent lights seemed to exaggerate the shadows under my mother's eyes, casting doubt on the woman who had once been my unwavering rock.

As I wrestled with my emotions, a sharp knock on the door startled me. In walked Dr. Wells, her white coat a stark contrast to the warm hues of the room. She carried an air of authority, her expression a mix of professionalism and genuine concern. "Good evening, Ms. Mercer," she greeted, her voice smooth but laced with gravity. "How's your mother holding up?"

My mother offered a weak smile, attempting to mask the truth. "Just peachy," she replied, though the quiver in her voice betrayed her. I wanted to reach out, to take her hand and squeeze it, to assure her that she was more than fine. But I stayed still, caught in a web of worry.

Dr. Wells shifted her gaze to me, her eyes piercing yet empathetic. "We've run some tests, and I'd like to discuss the results with you both if that's alright." I felt my heart race, a primal response to the unknown.

"Sure," I managed to say, my voice barely more than a whisper.

As she began to explain the findings, I grasped the implications, each word sinking like stones into the ocean of my thoughts. My mother's condition was serious, yet there remained a flicker of hope—a possibility of recovery if we acted swiftly. Dr. Wells detailed the options available, the treatments that could help, and I nodded along, though each piece of information felt like a heavy stone added to my already burdensome load.

"You're both strong women," Dr. Wells concluded, a note of encouragement creeping into her tone. "You'll navigate this together. Just remember to take care of yourselves too."

When she left, the silence settled between my mother and me, thick and weighted. I wanted to break it, to inject some levity into the atmosphere. "What do you think? Should we start a band? You could play the tambourine, and I'll do all the singing. We could go on tour!"

My mother chuckled softly, the sound strained but genuine. "I think I'd prefer knitting over your off-key serenades."

"Oh, come on, I'm not that bad," I retorted playfully, feeling the familiar warmth of her laughter wrap around us. "It's called creative expression."

"More like creative torture," she teased, her smile fading as fatigue washed over her.

I watched her, the fleeting moments of joy replaced by a deep-rooted sadness. The notion of losing her, of saying goodbye to our shared memories, sent a wave of nausea crashing over me. But in that moment, an idea sparked—a resolve to honor her spirit by seeking joy, even in the darkest corners. I had to hold on to the belief that laughter could bridge the chasm between our fears.

As the evening wore on, I slipped outside for a moment of fresh air, needing to breathe, to think beyond the sterile walls that felt like a prison. The cool night wrapped around me like a balm, and I closed my eyes, imagining the vibrant streets of New Orleans, the distant sound of jazz drifting through the humid air. Rylan's laughter echoed in my mind, an alluring siren call that pulled me away from the despair of this moment.

A sudden buzz from my pocket yanked me back. It was another message from him, a playful photo of a beignet, half devoured, dusted with powdered sugar. The caption read, You're missing out. Come join the fun! My heart swelled with warmth and a flicker of longing. I wanted to be there, to lose myself in the magic of the city, to immerse myself in laughter and love, even if it felt like a betrayal to my mother.

With a sigh, I replied, crafting my words carefully, the weight of my choices heavy in the air. Save me a bite? I'll be there soon. It was a promise and a prayer, a flicker of hope amid the darkness.

When I returned to my mother's room, I found her resting, her breathing more even now. I settled back into the chair, my heart lighter. As I watched her sleep, the shadows under her eyes seemed less daunting, the lines on her forehead less harsh. For the first time that day, I allowed myself to breathe deeply, filling my lungs with the scent of antiseptic mixed with a hint of lavender.

Hours passed, or perhaps only moments; time twisted strangely in that place. The door creaked open again, and in walked my younger brother, Ben, a whirlwind of energy and chaos. He was the family's wild card, with tousled hair and an irreverent smile that could lighten the heaviest of hearts. "Hey, sunshine! How's the most fabulous lady in this hospital?" he announced, plopping down onto the edge of the bed with all the grace of a cat falling from a tree.

"Just fine, Ben," my mother replied, her voice stronger now, a hint of warmth creeping back.

He launched into a series of stories, punctuated with exaggerated gestures, recounting his day filled with clumsy mishaps. Each word he spoke felt like a balm, healing the fractures in our hearts, stitching us together with laughter.

"Remember the time I tripped over my own feet during the family barbecue?" he laughed, slapping his knee. "You thought I was performing some kind of interpretative dance!"

"I still say it was avant-garde," I chimed in, and the three of us erupted in a chorus of laughter, the kind that rang through the sterile halls, echoing with life amid the beeping machines.

But just as the laughter faded, a shadow crept back into my mind. I glanced at my mother, her eyes shining with a mixture of joy and pain. Beneath the surface of our laughter, a current of reality surged, reminding me of the precarious balance we walked. My phone buzzed again, but this time I ignored it, choosing to embrace the moment instead. In this fleeting time together, I felt the bonds of our family strengthen, a collective armor against the darkness that threatened to engulf us.

As the night deepened, the sense of unity we forged offered a glimmer of hope, a promise that we would face the unknown together. The road ahead was uncertain, but in this moment, surrounded by love and laughter, I allowed myself to believe in the possibility of brighter days.

The night deepened outside the hospital, stars cloaked in clouds, creating a heavy blanket that muffled the world beyond. Within this small room, laughter still danced like fireflies, but the shadows loomed larger now, creeping back into my mind. Ben, with his infectious energy, had just recounted yet another story of his latest mishap, and I had momentarily forgotten the weight pressing on my chest. But as the laughter faded, the air grew thick again, each silent moment reminding me of my mother's fragility.

"Hey, I brought snacks," Ben announced with the bravado of a magician unveiling his greatest trick. He rummaged through his backpack and pulled out a bag of chips, the crinkling sound punctuating the heavy atmosphere like a balloon popping. "Don't tell Mom, but these are definitely not hospital-approved."

I snorted at his audacity. "What kind of son brings his mother snacks that could double as a surgical tool? You know what those chips do to your arteries, right?"

My mother chuckled, shaking her head as she reached for a chip, the act itself a small victory against her circumstances. "You know, they say laughter is the best medicine. I'll take a handful of that, please."

As we munched on chips and shared stories, I felt the familiar pang of guilt weave through me like a thread. Here we were, embracing life's absurdities, yet outside those walls loomed uncertainty. Would we still find moments of joy in the coming days? Could we continue to hold on to laughter when the specter of illness cast a long shadow over our family?

"Do you think I should start taking up interpretative dance?" Ben joked, an eyebrow raised. "That way, I can embarrass myself professionally. Think of the family legacy!"

"Oh, God, no!" I laughed, the sound bursting forth despite my reservations. "You already have a legacy of pratfalls; no need to add a tutu to the mix."

Just then, my phone buzzed again, an urgent vibration that felt strangely out of place in this cocoon of familial warmth. I glanced down to see Rylan's name flashing on the screen. I hesitated before unlocking it, my heart pounding with both excitement and trepidation.

Can I call?

The simplicity of his request sent a cascade of emotions rushing through me. I felt a wave of longing, the way a cool breeze can stir the stillness of a hot summer day. Yet, the guilt returned, wrapping around me like a heavy quilt. Should I invite him into this chaos?

"Everything alright?" Ben asked, his keen gaze flicking to my face. "You look like you've seen a ghost."

"Just a message from Rylan," I replied, keeping my voice steady. "He wants to call."

My mother raised an eyebrow, a knowing smile creeping across her lips. "That sounds promising. Why not?"

"Because..." I trailed off, lost in thought. Because I didn't want to disrupt the fragile balance we'd forged in this hospital room. I didn't want to invite someone into our moment who didn't understand the weight of our reality. Yet, the pull of Rylan's voice, the promise of comfort it offered, tugged at me fiercely.

"Just say yes," Ben urged, his patience waning. "You deserve a little something good. I'll even pretend to ignore your entire conversation, like a good little brother."

I exhaled sharply, my decision crystallizing in the air between us. "Okay, I'll call him," I said, my heart racing at the thought. I dialed Rylan's number, each ring echoing like a countdown, and when he answered, his voice spilled through the phone like honey—rich, warm, and reassuring.

"Hey, you," he said, a hint of a smile evident in his tone. "How's your mom?"

I felt my heart soften at the sound of his voice, a gentle balm against my fears. "She's... hanging in there," I replied, stealing a glance at my mother, who was listening intently. "We're managing, I guess. Ben's here, so that's a plus."

"Just a plus?" Rylan teased. "I thought you'd say he's the highlight of your day. What kind of brother would bring you chips?"

"Clearly not the kind that's concerned about my health," I shot back, my heart lifting with our banter.

"Hey, I have to keep my reputation as the 'fun brother,'" Ben chimed in, attempting to interject humor. "Without me, she'd be drowning in hospital gloom."

"True, but that doesn't mean you can't manage your snack choices," I teased back, laughter bubbling between us.

Rylan's laughter echoed through the line, and for a moment, the hospital room faded into the background. "Tell your brother I approve of his snack selection," he said, amusement dancing in his voice. "But maybe add some fruit next time, just for balance?"

"Great, now he's trying to be the health coach," I joked, but a lightness filled the air, an electricity that made me feel alive amid the chaos.

As the conversation flowed, we shared snippets of our lives, the distance between us shrinking with each word. Rylan described the vibrant colors of the French Quarter, the way the sun set like a painter spilling its palette across the sky. I closed my eyes, imagining the scene, wishing I could be there, tasting the beignets, soaking up the music, dancing beneath the stars.

"Why don't you come visit me?" he asked suddenly, a hint of hope threading through his voice. "I know this is a lot to deal with, but I want you to be happy too. You deserve it."

I hesitated, a wave of guilt crashing over me. "Rylan, I can't just leave Mom. What if something happens while I'm gone?"

"I get it. But you can't carry the weight of the world on your shoulders. She's strong, and she'd want you to be happy," he urged, his tone earnest.

In that moment, I felt an unexpected swell of determination, the words igniting something within me. Perhaps he was right; perhaps I had been so focused on the storm that I'd forgotten to look for the rainbows.

As I opened my mouth to respond, my mother shifted, her breathing suddenly erratic. My heart raced as I turned to her, the color draining from her face. "Mom?" I called out, panic lacing my voice.

"Mom, what's happening?" Ben's voice turned serious, the laughter fading into an anxious silence.

Rylan's voice became muffled through the phone, his laughter replaced with concern. "Is everything okay?"

I could barely hear him over the sound of the monitors beeping furiously, my mother's face contorting in pain. I rushed to her side, my hand grasping hers tightly, searching her eyes for answers. The chaos of the hospital surged around me as I pressed the nurse call button, a piercing sound shattering the stillness.

"Mom, stay with me! Please!" My voice broke, fear choking me as I felt the coldness of her hand.

Just then, the door swung open, and a flurry of medical personnel rushed in, their expressions a whirlwind of urgency. As they surrounded my mother, I was shoved back, the reality of the moment slamming into me like a freight train.

"Get back!" a nurse barked, her tone leaving no room for defiance.

I stumbled backward, my heart pounding, each beat echoing the silent prayer that I would not lose her. Rylan's voice echoed from the phone, but I couldn't focus on his words. All I could see was the frantic motion of medical staff, the chaos closing in around me like a vice.

In that moment, as the world spun out of control, I was left dangling on the precipice of uncertainty, torn between two worlds—one filled with laughter and love, the other darkened by fear and loss. I reached for my mother, desperate to pull her back from the edge, but the chaos swallowed my pleas whole.

Chapter 11: The Dance of Despair

The afternoon sun filtered through the half-drawn curtains, casting a patchwork of light and shadow across the living room, where I sat curled on the faded couch, surrounded by the scent of chamomile and the muted sounds of the world outside. My mother, a mere shadow of her former self, reclined in her armchair, her thinning hair spilling over the cushions like autumn leaves. I could almost convince myself that this was a scene from a play—a bittersweet tableau vivant that trapped us both in a time loop, endlessly repeating the same lines. "Are you ready for your tea, Mom?" I called, my voice bright and cheerful, but it lacked the usual buoyancy. I could feel my smile stretching too tightly across my face, a mask barely held together by my fraying resolve.

She blinked slowly, her once-vibrant blue eyes dulled by fatigue and treatment, and offered a feeble nod. As I poured the steaming water over the herbal tea bag, the delicate fragrance curled into the air, but it couldn't mask the acrid scent of antiseptic that clung to the room. I added a spoonful of honey, stirring it slowly, as if I could somehow sweeten our reality with each swirl. The kettle's soft whistle was a reminder of how fragile our lives had become—one moment of boiling water, and everything could change.

Mom sipped her tea, the porcelain cup shaking slightly in her trembling hands. "It's lovely, sweetheart. Just right," she murmured, her voice rasping with the effort. I offered her a reassuring smile, the kind I'd perfected over the last few months, but it felt like a brittle thing, liable to shatter at the slightest touch. I knew I should feel gratitude for these quiet moments, but instead, a pang of frustration twisted in my chest. I glanced at my phone, willing it to vibrate with a message from Rylan, each second stretching into an eternity, amplifying the hollow ache of his absence.

The days had blurred into a haze of appointments and medications, punctuated only by my increasingly desperate attempts to hold onto the threads of my life. I could feel Rylan's texts hovering in the back of my mind, ghostly reminders of everything I was trying to avoid. Each time my phone buzzed, my heart leapt, only to plummet when I saw the name of another well-meaning friend checking in or a family member offering their support. I longed for Rylan's voice, his teasing banter, the way he could make the world outside seem less daunting. Instead, I replayed the last conversation we had like a well-worn record, each crack and pop echoing with the unresolved tension that stretched between us.

"Why do you keep pushing me away?" Rylan had asked, his brow furrowed with concern, his eyes searching mine for answers I wasn't ready to give. I remembered how his words hung in the air like a thick fog, suffocating and unyielding. I could have confessed everything then—my fears, my hopes, the way my heart raced at the mere thought of him—but instead, I had buried my feelings beneath a pile of responsibilities and the specter of my mother's illness.

"I'm just... dealing with a lot right now," I had said, the words tasting bitter on my tongue. "It's not the right time." I watched as the light dimmed in his eyes, a flicker of understanding mingled with disappointment, and in that moment, I knew I had built a wall too high to climb over. He had stepped back, and the distance between us had widened, becoming a chasm I was terrified to cross.

Now, as I took a deep breath and tried to focus on the task at hand, I felt resentment simmering beneath the surface. It wasn't just the burden of my mother's illness; it was the gnawing feeling that I was losing a part of myself in the process. I was a daughter, a caretaker, but what about the woman I used to be? The one who could dream and laugh and love without hesitation? I missed her fiercely, as if she were a phantom from a life I once led, but that seemed like a world away, lost in the shuffle of syringes and hospital gowns.

Just as I settled back into the rhythm of our afternoon routine, my phone buzzed again, this time vibrating with a sense of urgency that sent my heart racing. I snatched it up, my breath catching in my throat as I saw Rylan's name flash across the screen. "Can we talk?" it read, simple yet loaded with meaning. I hesitated, my thumb hovering over the screen as a surge of conflicting emotions roiled within me—desire, fear, hope.

"Can we talk?" It felt like a lifeline thrown into turbulent waters, and yet, the weight of everything else held me back. I glanced at my mother, who was now staring out the window, lost in thought. Was it fair to pull Rylan into my chaos? Would he even want to enter this fractured world, or would he slip away like so many others? The thought made my heart ache anew, sharp and insistent.

With trembling fingers, I typed back, "Yes, let's." The response was immediate, and I could almost hear the sound of his heartbeat echoing across the miles that separated us. As I awaited his reply, a tension hung in the air, thick and electric, crackling with unspoken possibilities.

The dance of despair was winding down, and perhaps, just perhaps, a new melody was beginning to play, one that might lead us back to a rhythm we could both understand.

The afternoon light dipped lower, bathing the room in a warm, golden hue as I settled into the familiar weight of the couch, the upholstery slightly scratchy against my bare legs. My phone lay on the coffee table, glowing faintly like a beacon amidst the quiet chaos of our lives. Rylan's message echoed in my mind, a siren call that tugged at the edges of my resolve. I took a deep breath, summoning the courage to confront the emotions that had simmered beneath the surface for too long.

"Mom," I said, turning my gaze toward her. She was dozing lightly, her thin fingers cradling the tea cup like a precious artifact. "Do you need anything?" I could feel the weight of the world pressing down on my chest, but I pushed it aside, focusing on her needs.

"Just some quiet, honey. The world outside can keep spinning without me for a little while," she murmured, her voice a gentle rasp. I watched her closely, tracing the lines etched into her skin, a roadmap of battles fought and stories lived. In this moment, she appeared at peace, lost somewhere between consciousness and dreams.

With a nod, I slipped away from the couch, heart pounding in time with my restless thoughts. The kitchen beckoned with its promise of warmth, and I busied myself with pouring another cup of tea—an excuse to buy time, to gather my thoughts before diving headlong into the conversation that loomed ahead. The kettle whistled, steam curling up like tiny ghosts, and as I poured the hot water over the tea bag, the familiar scent filled the air, grounding me in the present.

When I returned to the living room, my phone buzzed once more, breaking the stillness. I glanced at the screen. Rylan had replied. "How about tonight? I need to see you."

My heart raced, an inexplicable mix of excitement and dread surging through me. I didn't respond immediately, instead allowing the words to linger like a fine wine, swirling in my mind. Tonight. The notion both thrilled and terrified me. The prospect of Rylan's presence was intoxicating, yet the fear of facing the truth loomed larger.

"Is something wrong?" my mother's voice broke through my reverie. I looked over to find her watching me, concern etched in the furrow of her brow.

"No, Mom. Just... thinking," I replied, forcing a smile. "Rylan wants to talk tonight."

"Ah," she said softly, a knowing smile creeping onto her lips. "That's good, isn't it?"

"I guess," I mumbled, swirling the tea in my cup as if it might unveil some cosmic answer to the turmoil inside me. The truth was, I didn't know what was good anymore. "I mean, it's complicated."

"Love rarely isn't," she replied, her gaze steady and wise. "Don't forget, sweetheart, you deserve happiness too."

The words struck me with unexpected force, a reminder that my desires weren't trivial in the face of my mother's struggles. I sank into the couch, warmth creeping over me as her understanding wrapped around me like a comforting shawl.

Just as I opened my mouth to respond, my phone chimed again. "Meet me at the café on Maple at seven?" Rylan's message appeared, and I felt a flutter of panic. A simple question, yet it felt monumental. What if I went and everything spiraled out of control? What if we couldn't bridge the gap that had formed between us?

I glanced at my mother, who was now scrolling through a magazine, momentarily distracted from her reality. "Mom, what do you think?" I asked, the words spilling out before I could catch them. "Should I meet him?"

She paused, looking up from the glossy pages with a twinkle in her eye. "I think you should. Nothing worthwhile ever comes from hiding."

Her encouragement warmed me more than the cup in my hands. I took a moment, gathering my courage. Rylan had been a steady presence, an anchor amidst the chaos of my life. But was I strong enough to confront the feelings I had kept hidden?

After a moment's contemplation, I typed back: "Okay, I'll be there."

As the sun dipped below the horizon, casting shadows that danced across the walls, I found myself frantically throwing on clothes—a carefully curated outfit that struck the perfect balance between casual and put-together. It felt absurd that choosing a top could evoke so much anxiety, but every choice felt like a declaration of intent, a silent admission of my hopes and fears.

The café on Maple was a quaint little place with chalkboard menus and the aroma of fresh pastries wafting through the air, mingling with the sound of laughter and the clinking of cups. As I stepped inside, the warm glow enveloped me like a familiar embrace, but my stomach twisted with nerves. The world around me buzzed with life, yet I felt like I was moving in slow motion, each heartbeat echoing in my ears.

Rylan was already there, seated at a small table near the window, his tall frame hunched over his phone. As I approached, his head snapped up, and for a moment, everything else faded away. There was a moment of recognition, that spark that always ignited between us, but it was laced with an undeniable tension.

"Hey," he greeted, a tentative smile breaking through his initial surprise. "You made it."

"Of course," I replied, sliding into the chair opposite him. "You didn't think I'd bail, did you?"

"Honestly? Part of me was prepared for it," he admitted, his tone wry, eyes dancing with an unspoken challenge. "You've been good at avoiding me lately."

"I've had a lot on my plate," I countered, not wanting to reveal the depths of my struggle.

"I get that," he said, leaning forward, his elbows resting on the table, eyes earnest and searching. "But I'm not just here to talk about your plate. I want to know about you—about us."

The air grew thick with the weight of his words, my pulse quickening. I could feel the walls I had built around my heart start to crack, revealing a glimpse of the truth I had tried so desperately to hide. The tension in the air shimmered like heat above asphalt, and as I opened my mouth to respond, I felt the power of that moment—a pivotal crossroads where I could either retreat or step forward into the unknown.

"Then let's talk," I said, summoning a confidence I didn't fully feel.

The atmosphere in the café hummed with energy, laughter mingling with the soft strains of music that filled the air. Rylan leaned in, his attention unwavering, and I felt a rush of warmth at the intensity of his gaze. I hadn't anticipated the way my pulse quickened simply by being in his presence, and it made the decision to engage all the more daunting. The world around us faded into a blur, the chatter of other patrons dissolving like sugar in hot tea, leaving just the two of us suspended in a moment that felt ripe with possibilities.

"Let's not pretend this isn't a little awkward," I began, trying to find a tone that blended sincerity with humor. "I mean, here we are, about to have a heart-to-heart over overpriced coffee and pastries. It's practically a rom-com cliché."

Rylan chuckled, his shoulders relaxing slightly. "You're right. I should've brought popcorn. But you know what? Sometimes clichés are clichés for a reason. They tend to have the most genuine moments."

I raised an eyebrow, amused by his earnestness. "So, you're saying our love story is going to be one for the ages? Should I expect a montage of us sharing pastries and laughing in slow motion?"

"Only if you promise to wear a beret and a scarf," he teased, the familiar banter sparking something deep within me—a reminder of who I used to be before the weight of the world pressed down so heavily on my shoulders.

"Deal. Now, let's get to the heart of the matter. I've been avoiding you, Rylan. And you know why," I confessed, unable to hold back the honesty that bubbled to the surface. "Things at home are complicated, and I guess I thought distancing myself would keep you safe from all this."

"Safe from what?" he pressed, his voice low and steady, yet tinged with concern. "Safe from you? From how you feel? That's not a safe place at all."

The truth in his words struck me, slicing through the fog of my insecurities. "But it is a safe place for you. If I keep my distance, I'm protecting you from—"

"From what? My inability to handle a little emotional chaos?" he interrupted, a spark of frustration flaring in his eyes. "Because if you think I'm afraid of a little mess, you don't know me at all. I've been in the trenches, Mia. I can handle the storm, but I need to know you're in the fight with me, not standing on the sidelines."

His words ignited a fire within me, an urge to step out from the shadows of fear that had clouded my judgment for far too long. "You don't get it," I countered, my voice rising slightly as I grappled with the weight of my emotions. "This isn't just about us. It's about my mom, and the uncertainty that comes with her illness. I'm terrified that if I lean into what we have, I'll lose everything. I can't afford to lose you too."

Rylan's expression softened, a mixture of empathy and determination painting his features. "What if I told you that you don't have to carry that burden alone? I'm here, Mia. Not just for the fun parts, but for the messy, complicated ones, too. But you have to let me in. You have to trust me."

The weight of his words pressed on me like a tangible force, and for a fleeting moment, I considered the possibility of surrendering—of letting him bear the weight with me. I opened my mouth to respond, but just then, the café door swung open with a jingle, and a rush of cold air swept through the room. My heart skipped a beat as I turned to see a figure silhouetted against the dimming light.

It was my brother, Alex, his tall frame unmistakable. The moment our eyes met, a sense of unease washed over me. He rarely ventured into this part of town, and his expression was one I had come to dread—a mixture of urgency and worry. I felt my stomach knot as he strode toward us, his brow furrowed deeply.

"Mia, can we talk?" he said, his voice low and intense, cutting through the cozy ambiance of the café like a knife.

Rylan's gaze flickered between us, the easy banter replaced by an awkward tension that hovered like an unwelcome guest. "Is everything okay?" he asked, concern lacing his tone.

"I'm not sure," Alex replied, his eyes never leaving mine. "It's Mom. There's something you need to know."

My heart dropped into my stomach, panic clawing at my throat. The carefree moment I had been sharing with Rylan disintegrated into a cloud of dread. I stood up, the chair scraping harshly against the floor as I felt a whirlwind of emotions collide within me. "What do you mean? Is she okay?"

"Just come outside," Alex urged, his voice low but insistent. The weight of his urgency crushed the air between us, and I felt a churning sense of dread clawing at my insides.

Rylan reached for my hand, grounding me with his presence. "Mia, wait—" he started, but I shook my head, my heart racing as I glanced back at him.

"I have to know what's going on," I said, my voice trembling as I stepped away from the table. "I'll be right back."

As I followed Alex outside, the chill of the evening air hit me like a wave, sharp and biting. My mind raced, fear gnawing at my insides like a hungry beast. What could possibly be wrong? My heart thundered in my chest, each beat a painful reminder of the uncertainty we were living under.

Once we reached the sidewalk, Alex turned to face me, his expression grim. "Mia, it's about Mom's treatment. The doctor called. There's been a change."

The world seemed to tilt on its axis, and I felt my breath hitch in my throat. "What kind of change?"

"Her latest tests... they didn't come back as we hoped. There's a new complication," he said, his voice barely above a whisper.

The ground beneath me felt as if it were crumbling away, leaving me teetering on the edge of an abyss. My mind raced, thoughts spiraling out of control. I couldn't breathe. I couldn't think. "No. No. This isn't happening. She was getting better!"

"Mom is strong, Mia," Alex said, his voice firm but laced with concern. "But we need to prepare for what's next."

"Prepare? How do we prepare for this?" My voice rose, trembling with fear. "What does that even mean?"

"I'm not sure yet," he said, his expression unreadable. "But we need to talk to her, and we need to do it now."

Suddenly, the café door swung open again, and I caught a glimpse of Rylan standing there, watching us with a mix of confusion and concern. A question burned in his eyes, but I felt the chasm of uncertainty widening between us as my brother's words echoed in my mind.

As I turned back to Alex, I could feel my world shifting, everything unraveling into a chaos I couldn't control. "Okay," I finally managed, steeling myself. "Let's go inside."

The air was thick with tension as we moved back toward the café, each step feeling heavier than the last. Rylan met my gaze, and for a moment, I saw the understanding flicker in his eyes—an acknowledgment of the storm brewing inside me. But as the door swung shut behind us, sealing us off from the world outside, I couldn't shake the feeling that everything was about to change.

"Mom needs us," I whispered, feeling a chill creep into my bones. And as I stepped forward, a sense of dread loomed, threatening to engulf us all. Little did I know, the night had only begun to reveal its secrets, and what lay ahead would test not only my resolve but the very fabric of my family.

Chapter 12: Strings Attached

The moment I step into the dance studio, the familiar scent of polished wood and aged mirrors envelops me like a warm embrace. It's a sweet nostalgia that tickles the back of my mind, wrapping around memories of endless rehearsals, laughter echoing against the walls, and the rush of adrenaline that used to course through my veins before every performance. It's here, among the wooden barre and the sun-drenched floor, that I feel most alive.

Rylan is leaning against the wall, his figure silhouetted by the light streaming in from the tall windows, creating a halo around his messy curls. The instant our eyes meet, the air crackles with an intensity that sends shivers down my spine. His relief is evident, but so is the concern etched on his brow, a silent acknowledgment of the turbulence I've navigated since my last time here. I swallow hard, feeling the weight of the past week pressing down on my shoulders.

"Hey," he says, his voice a low rumble that fills the space between us. It's a simple greeting, but it carries the weight of everything unsaid.

"Hey," I reply, my heart thudding in my chest. I can't tell if it's the thrill of being back or the undeniable chemistry that sizzles like electricity when he's near. It's both exhilarating and terrifying, a thrilling tightrope walk between what was and what could be.

"Thought you'd bailed on us for good," he adds with a half-smile, trying to lighten the mood. The sharpness in his tone, however, is tempered by a softness in his eyes that betrays his true feelings.

I step closer, absorbing the warmth radiating from his body. "I needed some time," I admit, my voice barely above a whisper. "My mom... she reminded me of what I'm fighting for."

His eyes soften further, understanding washing over his features. "You don't need to justify yourself to me. Just glad you're back."

In an instant, he pulls me into his arms, and the world fades away. It's a moment suspended in time, as if the universe has conspired to bring us together in this perfect bubble of familiarity and longing. The warmth of his body against mine is intoxicating, and for the briefest moment, I forget the doubts that cling to me like shadows. Yet, as I breathe in his scent—citrusy and fresh, mixed with something uniquely him—a tension creeps back in, reminding me of the strings of uncertainty still tied around my heart.

"Let's dance," he says, pulling back slightly to gauge my reaction. There's a glimmer of mischief in his eyes, the kind that makes my pulse quicken.

I nod, excitement bubbling within me, a lightness pushing back against the heaviness of the past week. We move to the center of the studio, the polished floor reflecting our apprehension and anticipation. Rylan takes my hand, his grip firm and reassuring, and I'm reminded of the countless times we've danced together. It's as if our bodies remember the rhythm, a dance we've shared countless times, yet it feels entirely new.

"Just like old times," he murmurs as we sway, the music wrapping around us like a familiar blanket. His touch sends waves of warmth cascading through me, igniting something deep within. I focus on the cadence of the moment, the way our bodies move in sync, flowing seamlessly as if we were born to do this together.

But as the music shifts, the familiar turns to foreign, and I feel the pull of reality crashing in. What if I've changed too much? What if he's still tied to the past I'm desperately trying to escape? The music swells, and I lose myself in the rhythm, every beat pushing my worries aside—if only for a moment.

"See? You've still got it," he says, breaking the tension with a grin that lights up his face. I can't help but smile back, my heart fluttering in response.

"Of course, I do. It's like riding a bike," I tease, trying to mask the inner turmoil brewing beneath the surface.

Rylan raises an eyebrow, the corner of his mouth quirking up in that infuriatingly charming way that always manages to weaken my resolve. "If by 'riding a bike' you mean stumbling and hoping not to fall flat on your face, then sure."

"Hey, I'll have you know I was quite the prodigy!" I retort, a playful glint in my eyes as I spin away from him, feeling the freedom of the dance pulse through me.

He catches up easily, moving with a fluid grace that showcases his natural talent. As we dance, a competitive spark ignites between us, each trying to outdo the other, laughter spilling from our lips like music itself. But even in our playful banter, a part of me remains guarded, aware of the undercurrents pulling us apart.

Just as I'm lost in the moment, a sharp clang echoes through the studio, the door slamming open as a group of dancers burst in, their chatter and laughter filling the space. The interruption jolts me from my reverie, a stark reminder of the reality we both inhabit. I take a step back, the weight of unspoken words settling heavily on my chest.

"Hey, Rylan! You ready for today's rehearsal?" one of the newcomers calls out, her bright smile contrasting sharply with the unease growing between us.

I watch as Rylan shifts, a flicker of hesitation crossing his face before he nods, masking the tension like a seasoned performer. "Yeah, let's do this."

But as he turns back to me, I catch a glimpse of the storm brewing behind his confident facade. The moment hangs between us, fragile and precarious, and I can't shake the feeling that while the dance may flow smoothly, the path ahead is littered with complexities we're not yet ready to confront.

And as the studio fills with energy, laughter, and the promise of another day, I realize that returning to New Orleans means not just reclaiming my passion but also facing the tangled emotions I've tried so hard to avoid. The strings attached are tighter than I thought, and the dance we're doing might just lead us down a path neither of us anticipated.

As the rehearsal progresses, the studio buzzes with energy, the vibrant chatter of dancers echoing off the walls, creating a symphony of excitement that both invigorates and intimidates me. The newcomers—each one a whirlwind of talent and ambition—infuse the room with a frenetic pace. I find myself drifting between them, a ghost at my own revival, soaking in the camaraderie while struggling to reclaim my place in this world that feels so familiar yet strangely foreign.

Rylan moves effortlessly among the group, his confidence radiating like a beacon. He leads warm-ups, his voice cutting through the clamor with a mixture of authority and warmth that makes everyone lean in. I admire how he commands attention without demanding it; he simply is, and that draws people to him. I can't help but wonder if I ever had that same spark, that effortless way of making others feel seen and valued.

"Okay, everyone!" he calls, clapping his hands to gather attention. "Let's pair up for some improv work. I want to see you all play with the music—feel it, don't just dance it!"

The music starts—a rich tapestry of sound, swelling with crescendos that coax the dancers into movement. My heart races as I watch the pairs twirl and leap, their bodies bending in beautiful defiance of gravity, a fluid conversation in motion. I know I should join them, but my feet seem glued to the floor, my mind spinning with doubt. What if my rhythm doesn't match theirs? What if I'm too far behind?

Rylan catches my eye, and there's an understanding between us that transcends words. He gestures me over, his expression shifting from encouraging to a playful challenge. "You with me?"

"Are you sure you want to drag me into the deep end?" I tease, a playful grin breaking the tension that's been creeping in.

"Unless you prefer the shallow end, where the water is lukewarm and the sharks are asleep," he quips, his eyes twinkling with mischief.

With a deep breath, I let go of my reservations and join him, feeling an exhilarating rush. As we start moving together, the world outside the dance studio fades, leaving only the music and the chemistry that crackles between us.

"Remember the last time we did this?" Rylan asks, spinning me out before drawing me back in with a smooth pull that sends my heart racing.

"Are you referring to that disaster at the charity gala where we nearly took out the entire front row?" I laugh, recalling the moment when we misstepped and nearly toppled into a table of desserts.

"Hey, I still maintain that was part of the performance art," he retorts, a glint in his eye. "Unplanned but beautifully executed."

"Right, a modern take on food art. You were the Picasso of cake," I quip, delighting in the familiar banter that makes everything feel just a little less serious.

But beneath our light-hearted exchange, a current of tension thrums, whispering that our playful dance could easily shift into something deeper, more poignant. I can feel the unspoken words hanging between us, heavy like the humidity outside. It's a strange dichotomy—our bodies moving fluidly while our hearts seem to trip over one another.

As we transition into a more intricate sequence, I'm surprised by how easily the movements flow back to me. The dance becomes an extension of my very soul, a way to express the chaos swirling inside. Rylan leads, and I follow, our bodies harmonizing with the rhythm, yet there's a thread of vulnerability weaving through each movement.

After a particularly daring spin, he pulls me close, his breath warm against my ear. "See? I told you the deep end isn't so bad."

"Is that what this is? A lesson in swimming?" I challenge, our faces inches apart, the heat rising between us.

"More like a lesson in trusting the current," he replies, his gaze locking onto mine, holding me captive.

The music shifts to a slower, more intimate tempo, and for a moment, I forget about the other dancers around us. The world fades, leaving just the two of us suspended in this bubble where everything feels right, yet so utterly precarious.

But before I can respond, a loud crash shatters the spell, a dancer stumbling into a nearby stack of props, sending a cascade of practice equipment clattering to the floor. Laughter erupts, and suddenly, the intensity evaporates, replaced by playful teasing and friendly jeers.

"Guess we're not the only ones trying to find our rhythm," Rylan chuckles, pulling away and blending back into the chaos, his laughter infectious.

I stand there, momentarily dazed, torn between the vibrant energy of the studio and the intimacy we had just shared. As the rehearsal resumes, I find myself drawn to the dynamics of the group—the camaraderie and rivalry that sparks creativity. Everyone seems to possess an ease I'm struggling to reclaim, and my heart sinks slightly as I realize how much I've missed.

During a brief water break, I overhear snippets of conversation. Two dancers, their voices laced with laughter, discuss plans for a showcase, a chance for them to shine in the spotlight. My heart leaps at the thought.

"Rylan, are you doing the showcase?" I ask, curiosity bubbling up.

He leans against the wall, his brow furrowed in contemplation. "I'm thinking about it, but I'm also swamped with choreography for the company. It's tough to juggle."

"Isn't that the dance world's mantra? 'Eat, sleep, choreograph, repeat'?" I joke, but the weight of my own aspirations clings to my words.

"Yeah, something like that," he replies, but I catch a flicker of hesitation in his eyes. "You should think about it too. You're a natural."

His encouragement ignites a spark within me, but doubt quickly shadows it. "I don't know. I've been away for a while. What if I'm not ready?"

Rylan's expression softens. "You'll never know until you try. What's the worst that could happen? You trip and fall flat on your face?"

I chuckle, shaking my head, but his words linger. "Or I could surprise myself," I murmur, a realization blooming in my chest.

The thought both thrills and terrifies me. Maybe stepping back into the spotlight, despite the fear, is what I truly need. The challenge beckons, the idea of showcasing not just my dance but the strength I've regained, pulling me like a magnet.

As rehearsal wraps up and the dancers disperse, I linger for a moment, watching Rylan gather his things. He glances over, catching me in a moment of introspection. "What's going through that pretty little head of yours?"

"Just thinking about that showcase," I reply, the spark of ambition igniting into a flame.

He grins, an infectious smile that brightens his entire face. "You know, I think you'd knock it out of the park."

"Now you're just buttering me up," I tease, but inside, my heart flutters at the thought.

"Maybe I just want to see you shine," he counters, his tone serious now, the undercurrents of our earlier conversation resurfacing.

And in that moment, I understand—this isn't just about the dance or the showcase. It's about taking a leap of faith, trusting not just in my abilities but in the connection we share, even amid the uncharted waters ahead.

The next few days in the studio feel like a whirlwind, an exhilarating blend of joy and apprehension that fills the air. Each moment stretches and contracts like a dancer's breath, every rehearsal a step closer to reclaiming not just my technique but also the essence of who I am. Rylan has become my constant, his presence a warm light guiding me through the fog of self-doubt. He pushes me during practice, his encouragement both a balm and a challenge.

"Just like we talked about—feel the music, let it flow through you," he urges one afternoon, the beat pulsing beneath our feet as we navigate a complex sequence. I can feel the anticipation crackling in the air, a shared understanding that what we're doing extends beyond just dance. With every twirl and leap, the weight of our unspoken feelings grows heavier.

But it's during breaks, amid the laughter and banter of our fellow dancers, that I catch glimpses of the deeper threads weaving between Rylan and me. He shares stories from his childhood, little nuggets of his past that reveal the person behind the confident facade. I find myself drawn to him in ways I hadn't anticipated, the magnetic pull between us growing stronger. Yet, lurking beneath my fascination lies an undercurrent of fear—fear of what might happen if I let myself fall too hard.

On a particularly muggy afternoon, the rehearsal wraps up early, and the sun filters through the windows, casting golden rays across the studio floor. Rylan approaches me, his eyes bright with an idea that practically dances on his lips. "How about we take a break? Get some air?"

"Are you suggesting we abandon our rigorous training for something as frivolous as fresh air?" I ask, raising an eyebrow in mock seriousness.

"Absolutely. The outside world exists beyond these walls, you know," he replies, feigning shock as he gestures dramatically toward the door. "Besides, I think we've earned it. The choreography won't escape us in the next hour."

"Alright, fine, but only if you promise not to lead me into any disastrous misadventures. I still have nightmares about that gala," I counter, my voice light but the memories all too vivid.

"Disastrous? I prefer to call it memorable," he retorts, a playful grin spreading across his face as he leads me outside.

Stepping into the vibrant New Orleans afternoon, the heat envelops us like a thick blanket. The streets are alive, teeming with the sounds of distant jazz and the tantalizing scent of beignets wafting from a nearby café. I can't help but smile at the atmosphere, the city's pulse syncing with my own.

"Why did you ever leave?" Rylan asks, breaking into my thoughts as we stroll down Chartres Street, the eclectic architecture and colorful facades surrounding us.

"I needed to find out who I was without all of this," I say, gesturing back toward the studio. "Sometimes it felt like my identity was wrapped up in dance, and when I took a step back, I realized I didn't know what I wanted beyond it."

"Did you find what you were looking for?" His question hangs in the air, filled with curiosity and something deeper that I can't quite place.

"Sort of," I reply, feeling the weight of his gaze. "I found myself, but I think I'm still figuring out how to be both me and a dancer. It's like trying to merge two worlds that feel incompatible."

He nods, his expression contemplative. "You're not alone in that. We all have our dualities—our hopes and our fears. It's what makes us human."

The conversation unfolds easily, like an intricate dance we're both learning together. With each step we take, the barriers I've constructed begin to chip away. I find myself opening up more, sharing stories about my childhood, the pressures of pursuing dance, and the weight of expectations.

"Maybe that's why I'm drawn to the stage—it's where I feel most like myself," I confess, the vulnerability both frightening and liberating.

"And maybe it's where you belong," he replies softly, his gaze locking onto mine, sincerity radiating from him.

A silence falls between us, heavy yet charged. The air is thick with unspoken possibilities, a moment suspended in time. Just as I contemplate how to navigate this new territory, the familiar buzz of my phone disrupts the fragile intimacy, jolting me back to reality.

I pull it out, glancing at the screen, my heart plummeting at the sight of my mother's name flashing across the caller ID. "I should take this," I say, the sudden shift in mood palpable.

"Of course," he replies, stepping back to give me space.

I answer the call, and my mother's voice washes over me, laced with urgency. "Honey, I need to talk to you about something important."

"What is it, Mom?" I ask, trying to mask the anxiety creeping into my voice.

"There's been an incident with the family business. I think you need to come home."

The words hang like a storm cloud over our sunny afternoon, and I feel a knot tighten in my stomach. "What kind of incident?"

"It's complicated. I just—"

Before she can finish, my attention is drawn back to Rylan, who's watching me with a furrowed brow, concern etched across his features. I hold up a hand to indicate I'll be just a moment, but the weight of my mother's words settles heavily on me, suffocating the joyful energy of our day.

"I'll be there as soon as I can," I say, forcing the calm into my tone, but my mind races with questions. What has happened? Why is it urgent?

After hanging up, I turn back to Rylan, who is now wearing an expression that reads both concern and curiosity. "Everything okay?" he asks, the warmth of his voice wrapping around me like a comfort blanket, yet the worry in his eyes betrays the depth of the situation.

"No, I think something's gone wrong back home. I need to go," I reply, the weight of uncertainty crushing down on me.

"Do you want me to come with you?"

The offer catches me off guard, and I hesitate. I can't help but feel the gravity of our moment, the tension still humming between us. "I—"

But before I can answer, a loud crash resonates from across the street, followed by the sound of sirens approaching fast. My heart races as I turn toward the commotion, my gut instinct telling me something is very wrong.

Rylan's grip on my arm tightens, his eyes scanning the scene unfolding just down the block. "What the hell is happening?"

And in that moment, as we stand together, the uncertainty swirling around us thickens, and I know that whatever lies ahead—whether it's a family emergency or something more ominous—we're about to be thrust into a storm neither of us saw coming.

Chapter 13: Shattered Reflections

The moment I step into the studio, the air tinged with the faint scent of sweat and polished wood, I feel a familiar rush of nerves. It's a space that has always offered solace, a retreat from the chaos of life outside, but today it feels different. Today, the light filtering through the tall windows catches Rylan's eyes as he leans against the barre, his silhouette framed by the late afternoon sun. My heart does a peculiar dance, fluttering somewhere between excitement and dread.

"Ready to break a leg?" he teases, his smile warm, yet there's an edge to his voice that sends a shiver down my spine. I can't help but grin back, but beneath the surface, my thoughts spiral. How does he do that? How does he manage to coax joy out of me while I'm drowning in this sea of uncertainty? It's infuriatingly charming.

"I don't think my legs are the problem," I shoot back, folding my arms in a mock display of bravado. "More like the emotional baggage I'm lugging around. You sure you're up for this?" My tone is light, but the gravity of my words hangs in the air between us.

Rylan raises an eyebrow, stepping closer, his presence overwhelming in the best way possible. "You think I'd let a little baggage scare me off? Come on, let's channel that energy into something fierce." He gestures toward the mirrors lining the walls, the reflections revealing more than just our physical selves. They echo the fragmented pieces of who I used to be, the girl who danced with reckless abandon, unburdened by memories that now tug at my heels like persistent shadows.

As the music swells, I can feel the familiar rhythm thrumming beneath my skin, coaxing me to let go. The notes wrap around me, and for a fleeting moment, I forget the weight of my past. Rylan moves with a grace that defies reality, his body a flawless extension of the music, and I find myself drawn to him like a moth to a flame. But every twirl, every leap is underscored by the memories I can't shake—the late-night phone calls, the hollow goodbyes, the broken promises that cling to me like a second skin.

"Focus, Charlie," Rylan chides playfully, snapping me back to the present. His voice is a mixture of amusement and genuine concern, and I can't help but feel that he sees more than I want to reveal. "We're not just here to look pretty. We need to feel it, own it." He's right, of course. But how do I embrace something when I feel so fragmented?

I launch into the routine, my body moving instinctively, but my mind flits between past and present. With every spin, every extension, I can almost hear the echoes of laughter, the ghosts of those who cheered me on, but also the whispers of doubts and insecurities that linger just out of sight. Rylan mirrors my movements, matching my intensity, and in his gaze, I can see the resolve burning bright.

"There you go!" he exclaims after a particularly exhilarating turn. "That was more like it. Where's that fire been hiding?"

"Right behind the pile of old regrets," I quip, but there's truth buried in my humor. Each smile feels like a mask, hiding the fear that tightens around my chest whenever I catch a glimpse of that girl in the mirror. Who am I without the expectations of those who left? I'm caught in a loop, a pendulum swinging between who I am and who I wish to be.

We delve deeper into the choreography, and I can feel Rylan's energy mingling with mine, creating something electric that crackles in the air. He moves closer, guiding my hands as we share space, the warmth radiating from him as we synchronize our steps. The proximity ignites something within me—a spark of hope mingled with fear, a tantalizing reminder that perhaps not all connections lead to heartbreak.

"Do you ever think about the future?" he asks suddenly, breaking the rhythm, his voice soft yet probing. There's a vulnerability in his question that catches me off guard.

"Depends on what future you mean," I reply, attempting to keep the conversation light. But beneath my flippancy, a weight hangs. I can see his brow furrow, the shift in his expression making my heart race. "I mean, I have plans. I want to dance. I want to travel... But then there's reality, you know?"

His gaze never wavers, and I can feel him peeling back the layers, exposing the raw truths I've carefully tucked away. "Reality can be a real pain in the ass, can't it?" he chuckles, but there's a seriousness to his tone that resonates with me.

"I just..." I pause, searching for the right words, feeling a swell of emotions I didn't know I'd unleashed. "I just don't want to let fear dictate my choices anymore. I want to take risks, but..."

"But what?" His voice is steady, encouraging me to continue.

I exhale sharply, the truth tumbling out before I can filter it. "But I don't know how to dance through the shards of my past without cutting myself."

Rylan steps closer, and for a moment, the world around us fades. "You won't. You're stronger than you think. Sometimes, the broken pieces can make the most beautiful mosaic." His words hang in the air, delicate and profound, and I can feel my heart swell with a mixture of gratitude and confusion.

As we resume our routine, I realize that maybe, just maybe, I don't have to hide behind the fragments of my past. With each movement, with each laugh shared between us, I can stitch together a new version of myself, one that embraces vulnerability instead of shying away from it. The music swells, and for the first time in what feels like ages, I'm not just a reflection in the mirror—I'm the woman who dares to dance, even amidst the shards.

The sun dipped lower in the sky, casting long shadows across the dance studio as we took a break. Rylan leaned against the barre, his eyes sparkling with the kind of mischief that reminded me of a boy playing hide-and-seek. I watched him from the corner of my eye, feeling the flush of warmth creep up my neck. It was a feeling I hadn't anticipated when I suggested we practice together, but here we were, tangled in a dance of our own making, where every pirouette held a hint of promise, and every shared laugh echoed deeper feelings.

"Okay, Miss Mystic, what's next?" Rylan asked, brushing a damp lock of hair from his forehead. His breath came out in quick bursts, and the hint of a challenge danced in his voice. "You've got all the moves planned, right? Or are we just winging it?"

I rolled my eyes but couldn't suppress a grin. "Oh, sure, let's just throw caution to the wind and pray we don't break anything—like my dignity." I feigned a dramatic swoon, falling against the barre in mock despair. "The world can't handle a fractured dancer."

Rylan laughed, a deep, infectious sound that resonated through the empty space. "I think the world could use a little more chaos. Dignity is overrated." He straightened up, a mock-serious expression overtaking his features. "Besides, if we're going to shatter some glass, let's make it a good show, right? Go big or go home!"

With a determined nod, I squared my shoulders and assumed a more theatrical pose. "Fine! Just remember, if I fall, you'll need to catch me. It's part of the deal." My tone was teasing, but there was a flicker of sincerity in my words. I didn't just want him to catch me physically; I craved emotional security, the sense that someone was there to support me when I stumbled.

"Deal," he replied, a glimmer of something serious flashing in his eyes. "Just promise me you won't flail like a fish out of water." He punctuated his words with an exaggerated arm gesture, mimicking my earlier mock swoon.

"Only if you promise to keep that charming smile of yours in check. Wouldn't want the whole studio to explode from the sheer intensity of your charisma." I returned his playful jab with a playful grin, feeling the easy banter between us carve a familiar path through my insecurities.

As we resumed our practice, the music shifted to a slower tempo, wrapping around us like a cozy blanket. Rylan stepped closer, our bodies aligning as we glided across the floor. The moment felt electric, charged with possibilities that danced just beyond the edges of our reality. Each movement became an exploration—not just of the choreography, but of the emotions simmering beneath the surface.

"Do you ever wish you could just dance your way through life?" he asked, his voice low, almost conspiratorial. "Like, what if you just followed the music wherever it took you? No inhibitions, no fears."

I thought about it, the notion hanging in the air like a tempting melody. "I used to think that way. Dancing was my escape, my freedom. But life is... complicated." I shifted my weight, contemplating the weight of my words. "You can't always move in perfect rhythm. Sometimes, you step on toes."

His gaze met mine, and I felt the intensity of his attention. "True, but isn't it better to dance anyway? Even if you trip, at least you're moving. It's the stillness that can really get you."

I pondered his perspective, aware of how much his words resonated. "You make it sound so simple. Just dance it out and let the world do its thing. If only it were that easy."

"Maybe it is," he countered, his tone encouraging. "Life's not about perfection, right? It's about finding your groove, even when the music gets a little wild."

With a laugh, I replied, "You make me want to shout, 'Dance like nobody's watching!' but I fear they might be, and I'd end up on a viral video for all the wrong reasons."

Rylan stepped back, a playful smirk lighting up his face. "Oh, I'd pay good money to see that. You tripping and falling in a pile of glitter, making an unforgettable entrance."

"Glitter? Seriously?" I scoffed, raising an eyebrow. "What is this, a high school prom? What's next, a disco ball?"

"Hey, you never know. Maybe we could make it a thing—'Glitter Fridays' in the studio!" He feigned a dramatic pitch, raising his arms as if conducting an orchestra of glittery chaos.

"Why not just throw confetti everywhere while we're at it?" I quipped, unable to suppress my laughter. "At least then I'd have an excuse for looking like a disaster."

As we continued dancing, the lighthearted exchanges carved a comfortable space between us, but I couldn't shake the twinge of something deeper brewing beneath the surface. Rylan was a whirlwind, and I felt myself being pulled into his orbit, each laugh shared a thread weaving us closer. Yet with every shared moment, an undercurrent of fear thrummed in my veins, whispering reminders of my past.

"Okay, let's try something different," he said, his tone shifting back to focused determination. "Let's improvise. Just follow my lead."

I hesitated but nodded, intrigued by the prospect of exploring the unknown. He took my hand, and we fell into a rhythm dictated by the music, moving as one, the dance becoming an unspoken conversation. It was exhilarating and terrifying, a dance of vulnerability and trust.

But as the music swelled, so did the memories I tried to suppress. Faces flickered in my mind—old friends, long-gone lovers, moments of joy intertwined with painful reminders of betrayal and loss. With each turn, I fought against the tide of nostalgia that threatened to pull me under.

"Breathe, Charlie," Rylan's voice cut through the chaos, grounding me. "Just breathe. Feel the moment, not the past."

I met his gaze, and the intensity in his eyes struck a chord deep within me. "How do you do that?" I asked, my voice barely above a whisper, both curious and fearful of the answer. "How do you make it look so effortless?"

"Practice, mostly," he replied, a hint of vulnerability peeking through his bravado. "But it's also about knowing when to let go. The world can throw all kinds of chaos your way. You just have to find your balance and trust that you'll land on your feet."

"Is that how you see the world?" I questioned, intrigued by his perspective. "Like a dance?"

"Absolutely," he said, his confidence infectious. "Each step, each stumble, just part of the choreography. You've got to learn to dance with it."

In that moment, I realized that perhaps he was right. Life wouldn't wait for me to figure everything out. I had to embrace the rhythm, let it guide me. And as we moved together, the weight of my past began to lift, revealing a brighter path ahead.

The music shifted again, this time into a crescendo, and I felt an unyielding urge to lose myself completely. I twirled and leaped, surrendering to the moment, allowing the music to wash over me like a cleansing wave. The world faded away, leaving only Rylan and me—two souls dancing amid a sea of possibilities, forging a connection that felt both exhilarating and terrifying.

And for the first time in ages, I didn't mind if I stumbled; I welcomed it.

The studio's atmosphere hummed with the remnants of our shared energy, still crackling in the air as I twirled and leaped. Each movement became a tiny revolution, a rebellion against the ghosts of my past. Rylan, ever the attentive partner, matched my rhythm, and together we created a tapestry of motion, weaving through the complexities of the moment like dancers on a tightrope, balancing the weight of expectations and the thrill of possibility.

"Okay, now let's add a little flair," he called out, breaking into a playful grin that lit up his face. "Think of it like a movie scene—sweeping gestures, a touch of drama. Channel your inner diva."

"Diva?" I scoffed, my brows furrowing. "I'm more of a 'tripping over my own feet while trying to be graceful' kind of girl."

He rolled his eyes dramatically, feigning exasperation. "You mean to tell me you're not ready to rock a sequined gown and belt out an aria? The world is missing out!"

"Sequins? Please. I'm still trying to untangle myself from the safety net of basic leotards," I shot back, laughing at the absurdity of his vision. "But I suppose I could give it a whirl. Just don't expect a standing ovation."

"Just promise me one thing—no more collapsing against the barre like a deflating balloon. I need you at full energy!" He flashed me a teasing wink, and I could feel the infectious joy radiating off him.

"Alright, alright! But if I end up flailing like a wild animal, it's on your head," I warned, a grin stretching across my face as I prepared to dive into our next sequence. Rylan took my hand, leading me into a series of spins, and for a fleeting moment, it felt as if the rest of the world had faded away. It was just us, two dancers in sync, swirling through the room.

The music shifted to something slower, more sensual, and I could feel the change in our dynamic as our bodies gravitated closer. My heart pounded as I lost myself in the moment, a mix of exhilaration and vulnerability pooling in my chest. I was suddenly aware of the warmth radiating from Rylan, his breath mingling with mine as our movements intertwined.

"See? This is the magic," he said, his voice low, drawing me deeper into the rhythm. "When you let go of the fear and just move."

"Easy for you to say," I murmured, suddenly conscious of every muscle in my body, every sensation coursing through me. "You're not the one who's terrified of everything this could lead to."

"Terrified? Nah," he said, playfully nudging my shoulder. "More like thrillingly excited. Life is too short for 'what ifs.'" He leaned in slightly, his eyes locking onto mine with a depth that sent my heart racing. "I mean, what's the worst that could happen? You try, and it doesn't work out. Or..."

"Or we end up in an epic disaster," I interjected, a teasing smirk on my lips. "I can already picture the headlines: 'Local Dancer Flops on Stage, Leaves Audience in Stitches.'"

"Let them laugh! If they're laughing, you've made an impression," he countered with a playful grin, the teasing lilt in his voice making it impossible for me to stay serious. "But really, I'd rather you be remembered for dancing your heart out than sitting in the back, afraid to try."

His words were like a gentle prod, stirring something deep within me, a longing to break free from the chains of my self-doubt. With a deep breath, I steadied myself and let the music seep into my bones. "Alright, let's do this. I'm ready for my moment of glorious failure," I declared, channeling a sense of playful defiance.

We launched into an intricate combination, our movements growing bolder, each step punctuated with the kind of abandon that had been missing for too long. I let go of the lingering shadows of doubt, losing myself in the dance. Rylan's laughter became the soundtrack to my newfound freedom, and I couldn't help but match his enthusiasm.

As we twirled and leaped, a rush of adrenaline coursed through my veins, pushing me to explore new heights. I was no longer just a reflection in the mirror; I was the dancer, raw and unfiltered, fully immersed in the moment. The studio, with its mirrored walls and wooden floor, transformed into a world of its own—a stage where our fears and dreams collided.

Then, just as I felt the peak of exhilaration, disaster struck. My foot snagged on the edge of the barre, and before I could register what was happening, I was tumbling forward, gravity pulling me down in a spiraling blur.

"Charlie!" Rylan's voice sliced through the air, a mix of concern and instinct as he lunged forward, his arms reaching for me. I braced for impact, fully prepared to make a fool of myself in a spectacular fashion.

But instead of crashing to the ground, I felt his strong arms wrap around me, lifting me as if I weighed nothing at all. The unexpected support sent shockwaves of relief and embarrassment coursing through me. My cheeks flamed as I looked up into his eyes, laughter bubbling between us.

"Maybe we should add 'catching' to our routine," I joked, the air thick with the remnants of my earlier fear, now transformed into something lighter.

"See? You're already improvising like a pro," he replied, his voice laced with amusement. "Though I have to admit, I wasn't planning for the dramatic fall. I'm not sure if that was intentional or just my luck."

"Clearly, I'm a natural," I shot back, rolling my eyes but unable to suppress a grin.

But then, amidst the laughter, something shifted in the air, an unspoken tension building between us. I felt a sudden awareness of the closeness of our bodies, the heat radiating from him, and the unmistakable spark of chemistry that flared to life with each shared glance.

"Maybe... maybe we should take a break," I suggested, the words spilling out before I could fully process them. The sudden rush of emotions left me dizzy, and I needed a moment to regain my balance—figuratively and literally.

"Are you okay?" Rylan asked, his expression softening, the playful spark replaced by genuine concern. "I didn't mean to make you uncomfortable."

"No, it's not that. I just... I don't know, Rylan." I hesitated, the weight of my vulnerability creeping back in. "Things have changed, and I can't quite wrap my head around it all."

"Change can be scary," he said, taking a step back, creating space yet still holding my gaze. "But it can also be... liberating." His voice was steady, calming, but I could see the flicker of worry in his eyes.

"I know," I said, wrestling with the emotions swirling inside me. "But sometimes I feel like I'm just waiting for the other shoe to drop. Like I can't trust that this—" I gestured between us, the intensity of the moment palpable, "—is real."

He searched my eyes, and for a heartbeat, the world around us faded away. "What if we just take it one step at a time?"

Before I could respond, a sudden crash from outside the studio jolted us both. The sound echoed down the hallway, shattering the fragile bubble we had created. A voice shouted—urgent and panicked—cutting through our moment like a jagged knife.

"Rylan! Charlie! You need to come quickly!" The voice belonged to Lily, a fellow dancer and friend, breathless and wide-eyed as she burst through the door. Her expression was frantic, her hair disheveled as if she'd run straight from the chaos outside.

"What happened?" I asked, heart racing as I exchanged a worried glance with Rylan.

"There's been an accident! You need to see this!" Lily's urgency left no room for debate.

In that instant, the weight of my previous thoughts fell away, replaced by a rush of adrenaline. Whatever was happening outside was far more pressing than the turmoil brewing within me.

Rylan and I exchanged a look, a shared understanding that our moment would have to wait. The world we had been creating in the studio faded into the background as we raced toward the door, uncertainty swirling in the air, leaving me to wonder if I would ever get the chance to dance my way into the future I longed for—or if life would shatter my hopes once again.

Chapter 14: Twisting Fate

The rehearsal hall buzzed with a frenetic energy, a palpable hum of anticipation thrumming through the air like a distant drumroll. Sunlight streamed in through the tall windows, casting a warm, golden glow over the polished wooden floor, illuminating dust motes that danced like fairies caught in an endless waltz. I stood in the center, the world fading away as my heart raced in sync with the music that enveloped us. This was my moment, a chance to shed the skin of my past and become something—someone—new.

Rylan moved beside me, his presence a swirling vortex of charisma and intensity. He was the sun in my solar system, and I, a reluctant planet caught in his orbit, unable to resist the gravitational pull. Our bodies glided through the choreography, a blend of passion and precision, each movement a conversation woven from the threads of our shared ambitions. With every leap and turn, I felt the weight of my hidden fears lifting, replaced by a rising tide of exhilaration. Yet beneath that excitement lay a tension, an undercurrent that whispered of uncharted territories in both our lives.

"Let it out, Bailey," Rylan urged, his voice low and insistent, slicing through the rhythm of our routine. "Feel it. You can't just dance your way through it. You have to live it."

I paused, the words hanging in the air like a challenge I wasn't quite ready to face. Rylan's piercing gaze bore into mine, demanding honesty, demanding vulnerability. I wanted to laugh it off, to deflect his earnestness with a clever quip, but something in his eyes rooted me to the spot. He was peeling back the layers I had so carefully constructed, layer by fragile layer, until all that was left was the rawness beneath—a tangled mess of emotions I wasn't prepared to confront.

"Are you saying I should cry in the middle of a pirouette?" I shot back, my voice light, but the tremor of truth lingered beneath the surface. "I can't imagine that would be very graceful."

He chuckled, a sound that ignited a flutter in my chest. "Not crying—more like letting the dance speak for you. You have to show me the part of you that's scared. The part you hide."

Scared. The word reverberated through me like a tolling bell, echoing the truths I'd been avoiding. I could feel the walls I'd built around my heart begin to tremble, and panic bubbled beneath my skin. What if I showed him? What if he didn't like what he saw? It was safer to remain the bright, witty dancer—an enigma wrapped in glittering sequins. But as I stared into his deep brown eyes, a flicker of something else sparked—a desire to be seen for who I truly was.

We resumed our dance, moving through the steps with renewed vigor, but I could sense the shift in the air. Each twirl and leap felt heavier, laden with the weight of my thoughts. Then, in a moment of careless exuberance, I miscalculated a turn, my foot snagging on the edge of the floor. In a heartbeat, I was tumbling down, my body colliding with the ground in a graceless thud. The world spun around me, and for a split second, the room fell silent.

Lying there, staring up at the ceiling, I felt as though I had landed not just on the floor but in the depths of my own reality—a stark reminder of my flaws and failures. The metaphor of my life crystallized in that moment: I kept falling, stumbling over my own insecurities and fears, and it was becoming painfully clear that I had to learn to stand. The taste of the polished wood floor was bitter and cold against my cheek, yet the air above me felt electric, charged with possibilities I had yet to explore.

Rylan's face loomed over me, concern etched into his features. "Bailey, are you okay?" His voice was thick with worry, and for the first time, I saw him not as the dazzling choreographer but as a man who genuinely cared. His presence was like a lifeline thrown into turbulent waters, and in that moment, I felt an overwhelming urge to reach for it.

"I'm fine," I mumbled, my voice barely a whisper as I attempted to sit up, but the truth was the fall had rattled me far more than I wanted to admit. His hand reached out, a warm anchor, and I grasped it, letting him help me to my feet. As I stood, brushing off the remnants of my embarrassment, I caught a glimpse of something in his eyes—an invitation, perhaps. A chance to delve deeper into the raw and unfiltered parts of myself.

"Look, Bailey," he said, his tone shifting, more serious now. "We all fall. It's what we do after that matters. You've got to confront what's holding you back."

I swallowed hard, my heart pounding in my chest like a trapped bird. He was right. It wasn't just about the dance; it was about my life, about the layers of hurt I had encased myself in, hoping to protect the heart that had been bruised one too many times. The weight of his words settled over me, a shroud I wasn't sure I wanted to wear.

Rylan stepped closer, the heat of his body radiating toward me, and suddenly the room felt smaller, the space between us charged with unspoken understanding. "Let's try it again," he suggested, a playful smirk dancing on his lips, as if he knew I was teetering on the edge of a revelation. "But this time, let's break down those walls. Feel the music, and let's dance with all of it—the joy, the pain, everything."

As the music swelled again, I took a deep breath, feeling a newfound sense of determination surge within me. With each movement, I began to shed the protective layers, allowing the rhythm to guide me, to push me. The fear was still there, lurking in the shadows, but so was a flicker of hope—a flicker that told me maybe, just maybe, I could learn to stand tall, no matter how many times I stumbled. Rylan was right beside me, and for the first time in a long time, I felt that I might not have to face my fears alone.

The music swelled around us, and I felt as though I had stepped onto a precipice, balancing between my old self and the promise of something more. Rylan's voice drifted through the notes, urging me forward, and I took a deep breath, inhaling the familiar scent of sweat mingled with the faint, floral fragrance of his cologne. It wrapped around me like a comforting embrace, a reminder that I was not alone in this vulnerable dance. As we launched into the next movement, the adrenaline coursed through my veins, and I let it fuel me, igniting the embers of my spirit.

"Just let it all go," he said, his tone playful yet firm. "Think of this as a therapy session, but with more spinning and fewer couches."

I laughed, a sound that bubbled up from my core, surprising both him and me. "If only therapy were that easy," I replied, matching his rhythm. "Maybe we should add some interpretive dancing to the agenda. 'How to Twirl Away Your Problems 101.'"

"Now that's a course I'd sign up for," he shot back, a grin breaking across his face that momentarily distracted me from the weight of my emotions. His laughter echoed in the vastness of the studio, filling the space with a lightness that hung in the air like confetti.

But as we danced, the jovial atmosphere gradually shifted. I felt myself slipping back into old habits—protective barriers shielding the raw, unfiltered emotions I was so reluctant to share. With every spin, I wrestled with the shadows of my past, each movement a reminder of the fears that had paralyzed me. The music pulsed like a heartbeat, and I fought to keep pace, to break free from the grip of my insecurities.

"Breathe," Rylan instructed, his voice a steady anchor amidst the chaos of my thoughts. "You're not just dancing; you're telling a story. What's yours?"

His question hung in the air, and for a moment, I faltered, the world around us fading into a blur. What was my story? A life punctuated by missed opportunities and heartache, filled with moments of joy that often felt overshadowed by my relentless quest for perfection. I had always been the girl who fell into the background, the one who excelled in dancing but shied away from stepping into the spotlight of my own life.

"I don't know," I admitted, my voice barely above a whisper. "It's messy. It's complicated. I keep waiting for the perfect moment, but it never comes."

Rylan paused mid-step, his brow furrowing as he absorbed my words. "You're waiting for perfection when imperfection is what makes us human. Let it all hang out. Dance your chaos."

With a renewed sense of determination, I plunged into the dance with an unrestrained fervor, the music soaring and enveloping me in its embrace. Each step became a release, a catharsis, as I began to embody the raw emotions I had long kept buried. I twirled, leaped, and spun with abandon, letting the melodies guide me, even if it meant stumbling along the way.

Rylan fell in step beside me, matching my movements as he encouraged me with gestures and smiles, his presence a steady force that made me feel safe in my vulnerability. "There you go! That's it! Let go of the fear. Let the music carry you."

And for the first time in what felt like forever, I felt a surge of hope bubble up inside me, an effervescent sensation that chased away the shadows. I twirled, lost in the rhythm, allowing the music to weave its magic. With every turn, I released fragments of my insecurities, exposing the vulnerable parts of myself that I had hidden for too long.

But just as I was beginning to revel in this newfound freedom, I misjudged a leap. My foot landed awkwardly, and before I could brace myself, I was crashing to the ground again, a startled gasp escaping my lips as I crumpled in an ungraceful heap.

This time, however, I didn't lie there in shock. I sat up quickly, laughter bubbling from my throat, mingling with the music still playing in the background. "Guess I'm more of a 'falling star' than a dancing one!"

Rylan rushed to my side, a mix of concern and amusement dancing in his eyes. "Are you trying to make this a new trend? Because I'm not sure 'plummeting gracefully' is going to catch on."

I chuckled, brushing off the embarrassment that threatened to claw its way back. "If anyone can make it a trend, it would be you," I quipped, rising to my feet with newfound resolve.

"Only if you promise to join me on the journey," he replied, extending his hand to me once more, an unspoken pact forming between us.

I took his hand, our fingers intertwining in a way that felt both electrifying and familiar. "Deal. Just don't expect any pirouettes from me for a while."

As we resumed our positions, the energy shifted. I was acutely aware of the space between us, electric and charged. We were no longer just choreographer and dancer; we were two souls navigating the complexities of vulnerability, inching closer to a shared understanding. I had begun to trust him, to unravel the tightly wound thread of my heart and let it flow freely.

The music shifted, a slow, haunting melody filling the studio, wrapping around us like a tender embrace. Rylan's eyes locked onto mine, and the world faded away. "This is where you really let go," he murmured, his voice low, coaxing me to explore the depths of emotion I had hidden away. "Show me your heart, Bailey."

I took a deep breath, feeling the warmth of his hand still clasping mine, and let the melody seep into my bones. The dance transformed into something more profound—an exploration of not just my fears but the essence of who I was. Every move was deliberate, a reflection of my past, my hopes, and the tangled mess of dreams I had yet to chase.

Rylan matched my rhythm, the intimacy of our connection palpable as we wove together in a delicate tapestry of movement. I surrendered to the moment, pouring every ounce of unfiltered emotion into our dance, unearthing layers I had thought long buried. My heart raced, each beat echoing the exhilaration of finally confronting the fears I had carried for so long.

With every spin, I let the music guide me, and the weight of my hesitations began to lift. I felt lighter, as if the burdens I had shouldered for years were finally being peeled away. I didn't just want to stand; I wanted to dance—not just for others but for myself, for the girl I was becoming.

As we reached the crescendo of the music, I knew that this was more than just a rehearsal. It was a reckoning, a promise to embrace the beautiful chaos of life. I had stumbled, yes, but I was rising again, and for the first time, I was ready to face the world head-on.

The music shifted, flowing from gentle and haunting to a rhythm pulsing with urgency, each note echoing the tumult of emotions stirring within me. As Rylan and I moved together, the air grew thick with tension, an unspoken understanding blossoming between us like wildflowers breaking through concrete. I could feel my heart racing, not from anxiety, but from the thrill of finally stepping into my own light. It was as if the dance floor had transformed into a stage where my soul could shine, unfiltered and raw.

"Okay, let's try something a little different," Rylan said, a mischievous glint in his eye. "How about we add a little drama? Show me the conflict, the yearning." He gestured dramatically, his hands slicing through the air. "I want to see you wrestle with your emotions. Make me feel it."

I tilted my head, raising an eyebrow at him. "Wrestling with my emotions? Are you sure you're not just asking for a dramatic soap opera moment? Maybe I should bring out the heavy eyeliner and start crying on cue."

"Now you're just being theatrical," he shot back, grinning. "But seriously, let it spill over. Dance like your heart is in a tug-of-war, and you're the prize at stake."

The challenge hung between us like the tension in a taut wire, and I took a moment to gather my thoughts. Rylan had a way of pushing me beyond my limits, and I was beginning to realize that maybe, just maybe, he could see a version of me I had long kept hidden. I nodded, letting the energy of the room wash over me, igniting a flame of passion that was as exhilarating as it was terrifying.

As we resumed our dance, I poured everything into it—the longing, the fears, the joy that felt almost foreign. I twisted and turned, my movements a reflection of the emotional tempest brewing within. I thought of all the moments I had held back, the times I had muted my voice, dulled my shine. And in that realization, I found a rhythm that felt true, a pulse that beat in sync with the melody.

"Beautiful! That's it!" Rylan exclaimed, his enthusiasm infectious. "Keep that fire going. I want to see the battle in your eyes, the struggle between hope and despair."

I couldn't help but smile at his unwavering support, the way he seemed to genuinely believe in me, even when I wasn't sure I believed in myself. "So, you want me to look like a fierce warrior then? Just don't expect me to wear a cape."

"Capeless warrior is fine, but you better be ready for a dramatic showdown," he replied, laughing. "We need the audience to feel your stakes."

With his encouragement, I poured everything I had into each move, each leap a testament to my resilience. I could feel the electricity crackling between us, heightening the stakes of our shared performance. As I leapt into the air, I imagined breaking free from my chains, the weight of past failures and fears dissipating like mist in the sun.

But as I landed, the ground seemed to shift beneath my feet. A sudden rush of dizziness took hold, and for a fleeting moment, the world around me spun like the disorienting flurry of a storm. I steadied myself, but a creeping sense of vulnerability tugged at my heart, reminding me of all the times I had fallen before—times when I had felt utterly lost and alone.

"Rylan, wait," I gasped, trying to catch my breath as I fought against the wave of emotions that threatened to overwhelm me. "What if I can't do this? What if I'm not good enough?"

He paused, stepping closer, his expression softening. "You're more than good enough, Bailey. You've got to believe it. It's about the journey, not just the end result."

The sincerity in his eyes pierced through my defenses, igniting a flicker of hope. "But what if I stumble again? What if I fall flat on my face?"

Rylan smiled, an almost boyish grin that made my heart flutter. "Then you get back up. Just like you did before. And I'll be right here, ready to help you rise."

His words wrapped around me like a warm blanket, shielding me from the chill of my doubts. I could feel a shift within me, a growing confidence that urged me to embrace the moment, to fully surrender to the dance. I took a deep breath, letting the music envelop me once more, allowing the rhythm to guide my steps.

"Okay, let's do this," I said, my voice steadier than I felt. "But no more falling, please. I've had my fill of that today."

"Challenge accepted," he replied, his eyes sparkling with mischief. "But if you do fall, I promise I'll catch you."

As we danced, I let the music sweep me away, my body flowing with each note. I became lost in the story we were weaving, feeling the conflict rise and fall like the waves of the ocean. With each pirouette, I released the fear of failure; with each leap, I embraced the thrill of the unknown.

But just as I began to feel invincible, the door to the rehearsal studio swung open, breaking the spell that had enveloped us. In walked a woman, her presence commanding and immediate. She wore an air of authority, her sharp gaze cutting through the haze of our world like a knife through butter.

"Excuse me, but I need to speak with you, Rylan," she said, her voice smooth but laced with urgency.

My heart sank as the moment shattered. Rylan turned to face her, a look of surprise flitting across his features. "Jenna? What are you doing here?"

The tension in the air shifted, and my stomach knotted as I caught the flicker of something unspoken in Rylan's eyes—a history that had just crashed into our carefully crafted present. I felt as if I had stepped onto shaky ground, my heart racing with uncertainty as I sensed the undertow of emotions swirling just beneath the surface.

"Now?" he asked, confusion mingling with concern.

"Yes, now," she replied, glancing between us, her expression unreadable. "It's important. We need to talk about the show."

I stood frozen, the rhythm of my heart pounding in my ears. The vibrant connection I had just begun to forge with Rylan felt threatened, slipping through my fingers like sand. The music faded, leaving an echoing silence that loomed heavy in the air, as if the universe itself was holding its breath, waiting for the next move.

In that suspended moment, I felt the fragile threads of our newfound connection unraveling, the shadows of doubt creeping back in, threatening to engulf everything I had just begun to embrace. What had been a dance of liberation was now overshadowed by the weight of unknown stakes, and I couldn't shake the feeling that everything was about to change.

Chapter 15: Crossroads

The soft hum of cicadas filled the air as the sun dipped low behind the silhouette of the skyline, casting a golden glow over the Mississippi River. I leaned against the cool railing of the balcony, the wooden slats rough against my palms, grounding me in the moment. It was one of those rare evenings when the heat of the day finally surrendered to a gentle breeze, offering a reprieve from the sweltering humidity that had settled like a thick blanket over the city. Below, the river sparkled, reflecting the shimmering lights of New Orleans like a thousand tiny lanterns bobbing in the dark, each one holding a secret I was desperate to uncover.

Rylan stood beside me, his profile etched against the dusky sky. His tousled hair danced lightly with the wind, and I could see the tension in his shoulders, a muscle-bound silhouette of uncertainty and longing. He had always carried the weight of the world with him, his gaze a mixture of determination and shadows. Tonight, however, the energy crackling between us felt different—charged with something unspoken, waiting for the right moment to explode.

"Do you ever think about where you're going?" His voice was low, barely above a whisper, but it cut through the night air with surprising clarity. It wasn't a question I had expected, but as I glanced over at him, I realized it was the perfect entry into the churning chaos of our hearts.

"More often than I'd like to admit," I replied, keeping my gaze on the water, afraid to meet his eyes. "It feels like I'm always searching for a path that leads somewhere, anywhere other than where I am."

The silence stretched between us, thick and heavy, like the muggy summer air. I could sense Rylan's contemplation, the way his brow furrowed as he leaned against the railing, the light from the nearby streetlamp illuminating the sharp angles of his jaw. "I get that," he finally said, his tone tinged with a mixture of vulnerability and resolve. "It's like I'm stuck in this loop, terrified of repeating the mistakes of the past."

He turned to face me, and I was captured by the intensity in his eyes, a deep brown flecked with gold that glinted like sun-kissed leaves. I had seen him wear that same look before, a blend of hope and despair, as if he were searching for something—someone—to anchor him to this moment.

"What mistakes?" The question slipped out before I could hold it back. I had always been curious about the layers he kept guarded behind his façade of confidence and charm. There was a wealth of experience beneath that surface, and I wanted to delve deeper, peel back the layers like the skin of an onion.

"Relationships," he admitted, his voice thick with emotion. "I've had my share of disappointments, you know? There was this girl..." He hesitated, and for a fleeting moment, I wondered if he would reveal the skeleton that lurked in his closet. "I was too wrapped up in my own dreams to see how I was pushing her away. By the time I realized it, it was too late. She was gone, and I was left holding the pieces of what could have been."

I swallowed hard, feeling the weight of his words settle in the pit of my stomach. I had always seen Rylan as the embodiment of success, the kind of guy who had it all figured out, and yet here he was, unravelling before me in the soft glow of twilight. "I didn't know," I murmured, my heart aching for the pain etched in his features.

He chuckled softly, a sound that was both bitter and sweet, like dark chocolate melting on the tongue. "Most people don't. I'm good at hiding it, I guess. But standing on this balcony, looking out at the city, I can't help but think about how easy it is to lose yourself in the chase. The music, the dreams, the spotlight... it all comes with a price."

We stood in silence, the river lapping gently at the shores of our thoughts. I could feel the current of unspoken words swirling between us, and it was intoxicating. "What about you?" he asked, breaking the stillness. "What haunts you?"

I hesitated, the words caught in my throat like a stubborn fish refusing to be reeled in. "I've been afraid of falling," I finally confessed, forcing myself to meet his gaze. "Falling into the wrong relationships, the wrong choices. I lost myself once, and it took years to piece myself back together."

His expression softened, a glimmer of understanding passing between us. "It's a scary thing, isn't it? The idea of giving yourself completely to someone, only to have them shatter you?"

"Exactly," I whispered, the vulnerability of the moment wrapping around us like a cocoon. "But at the same time, I can't help but wonder if the risk is worth it. What if this time is different?"

Our eyes locked, and the air between us shimmered with possibility. I could feel the weight of our unspoken feelings hanging in the balance, a tantalizing mix of hope and fear. Rylan stepped closer, the warmth of his body radiating toward me like the glow of a campfire. "Maybe it is," he said softly, his breath brushing against my skin, igniting a spark deep within my chest.

For a heartbeat, I considered leaning in, closing the distance that had kept us apart for so long. The pulse of the city throbbed around us, a rhythm that seemed to echo my own racing heart. But the shadows of the past loomed large, and I hesitated, caught in the tension of what could be and what might be lost.

Just then, a laugh echoed from somewhere below, pulling me back to reality, shattering the delicate moment we'd woven. It reminded me of the world waiting beyond our bubble, filled with expectations and obligations. I stepped back, the cool night air washing over me, and I could see the flash of disappointment in Rylan's eyes, mirroring my own conflict.

"Maybe we should head back," I suggested, my voice barely steady. I turned away, feeling the gulf between us widen once more, knowing that despite the night's revelations, the distance was still there, looming large and unyielding like the river below.

The weight of unspoken words lingered in the air as we turned back toward the dimly lit interior of the rehearsal space. The sound of laughter from the nearby bar filtered through the open door, each chuckle and clink of glasses reminding us of the vibrant life that buzzed just beyond our secluded balcony. I caught Rylan's gaze one last time before we re-entered the room, a fleeting moment where we seemed suspended in a world of our own making. The air hummed with unsaid possibilities, yet the reality of the situation draped over us like an unwanted shawl.

Inside, the others were still milling about, energy pulsing through the air as they recounted the night's rehearsal. I tried to focus, to engage in the banter, but my mind kept drifting back to the river, to the way Rylan's presence made me feel both electric and terrified. Each laugh echoed, each story told felt like a thread pulling me further away from the tether of my own thoughts.

"Earth to Kira!" Tara's voice broke through my reverie, her eyes sparkling with mischief. "You look like you just saw a ghost. Or worse, a really bad audition tape. You okay?"

I forced a smile, trying to mask the whirlwind of feelings swirling inside me. "Just a bit lost in thought, I guess," I replied, attempting to sound casual, though I knew my tone had betrayed me.

Rylan stepped into the fray, flashing Tara that disarming grin of his, the kind that made the entire room pause. "More like she was lost in the 'I'm crushing on Rylan' dimension," he teased, nudging my shoulder lightly. My stomach fluttered at the casualness of the comment, and Tara's laughter erupted, a peal of sound that drew the attention of others.

"Oh, please, we all saw that. You two are like a romantic comedy waiting to happen!" she exclaimed, waving her hands as if trying to conjure a movie poster above our heads.

The heat rushed to my cheeks, and I was suddenly acutely aware of the weight of Rylan's presence beside me. "Very funny, Tara," I shot back, feigning annoyance while desperately hoping the blush in my cheeks didn't betray me further. "If it's a comedy, I'm definitely not the lead. More like the awkward sidekick who trips over her own feet."

"Trust me, you've got the whole 'will they, won't they' thing down," she winked, throwing her arms around my shoulders. I felt both flattered and mortified, a combination that made my heart race in a way that had nothing to do with stage fright.

Rylan chuckled, a sound that sent a delightful shiver down my spine. "Yeah, but you've got the advantage of charm, Kira. I've seen you pull off awkwardness with style."

"Awkward with style is not exactly what I'm going for here, Rylan," I replied, trying to sound stern while my heart danced to an entirely different rhythm. "I'm aiming for suave, sophisticated, maybe even a little mysterious. Awkward is so last season."

"Good luck with that," he shot back, his grin widening. "Mysterious is just code for 'still figuring it out.'"

We both laughed, but beneath the laughter lay the tender threads of unspoken tension. The playful banter flowed around us, but I couldn't shake the feeling that we were both dancing around a precipice, balancing on the edge of something profound and terrifying.

After a few more rounds of lighthearted teasing, the rehearsal wrapped up for the night. We gathered our belongings, the space slowly emptying as everyone trickled out into the humid night. Rylan walked beside me, his presence warm and grounding, the space between us both inviting and intimidating.

"Want to grab a drink or something?" he asked as we reached the door, the suggestion laced with a casualness that belied the tension we had just shared.

I hesitated. The idea of a quiet corner in a bustling bar sounded appealing, yet terrifying. Would we slip back into playful banter, or would the weight of our earlier conversation resurface, drawing us deeper into territory we both feared to explore? "I—" I began, but the words tangled in my throat.

"Only if you're up for it," he interjected, his tone shifting ever so slightly. "No pressure. Just thought it might be nice to continue the conversation."

I met his gaze, searching for something—reassurance, perhaps. Instead, I found an invitation wrapped in uncertainty. "I could do with a drink," I finally said, the decision hanging in the air like the humid night.

We strolled toward the local pub, the sound of laughter and music spilling into the street, a heartbeat of life that pulsed through the city. The closer we got, the more I could feel the anticipation buzzing between us, an electric current that crackled at our fingertips. As we entered, the dim lights enveloped us, and the scent of spilled beer and warm pretzels greeted us like an old friend.

We settled at a small table in the corner, the noise of the crowd providing a comforting backdrop to our conversation. I ordered a gin and tonic, and Rylan opted for a whiskey, neat. There was something mesmerizing about watching him lean back against the chair, the way the dim light caught the angles of his face, turning him into a living sculpture.

"So," he began, his tone shifting to something more serious, "I know we've danced around it tonight, but I want to know what you think about all this."

I took a sip of my drink, letting the sharpness of the gin ignite my senses. "All what?" I asked, feigning ignorance even though I knew precisely what he meant.

"Us. This..." He gestured between us, a vague but loaded gesture that could mean a million things. "I don't want to rush things, but I also don't want to keep pretending there isn't something here."

My heart thudded in my chest. The moment hung between us, thick and heady, charged with the potential for change. "It's complicated," I finally said, my voice steady despite the storm raging inside me. "I care about you, but I don't want to mess things up. I'm still piecing myself together, you know?"

"Maybe we can piece it together," he suggested, his eyes alight with a mixture of hope and challenge. "I'm not asking for everything right now. Just the chance to see where this could go without the weight of our pasts crushing us."

A flicker of vulnerability crossed his face, and I felt the gravity of our conversation shift, pulling me closer to him. The idea of diving into the unknown with Rylan was terrifying, but the thought of turning away was even more daunting. "I think I'd like that," I replied, my voice barely above a whisper.

His expression softened, and for a moment, the noise of the bar faded into a gentle hum, leaving just the two of us suspended in our own universe. It was then that I realized the path ahead was uncertain, yet full of possibilities, as if the river outside held not only reflections of light but also the promise of new beginnings.

The warmth of the pub enveloped us as we sat across from each other, the low hum of conversation weaving around us like an old, familiar melody. I couldn't shake the feeling that we were on the precipice of something monumental, our words hanging in the air like suspended notes in a song that was both beautiful and haunting. Rylan studied me, his gaze piercing yet gentle, as if trying to unravel the tightly coiled spring of my thoughts.

"Look, I know this might sound a bit bold," he began, his voice steady but low, "but what if we just... took a leap? You and me, no safety net?"

I raised an eyebrow, half-teasing but entirely intrigued. "And if we land in a pile of metaphorical broken glass? You do realize that leaping into relationships has its risks, right? Like, you know, emotional whiplash?"

"Emotional whiplash?" he echoed, a smirk playing on his lips. "I might have to add that to my list of relationship deal-breakers. Right after 'stealing fries off my plate' and 'watching terrible reality TV.'"

I chuckled, my heart racing at his playful banter. "Well, I might have to bring some of those fries into the equation then. Especially if it's fries from that little place down the street. You know, the one that's only open after midnight and serves those giant portions?"

"Perfect. You bring the fries; I'll bring the whiskey. We'll have ourselves a very classy picnic," he quipped, and in that moment, the tension that had clung to us like a shadow eased just a little. It felt good to laugh, to step back from the brink and revel in the lighter side of life, if only for a moment.

"I guess that could be a start," I said, letting the ease of the moment wash over me. "But it's not just about fries and whiskey, is it? There's so much more at stake here."

"Of course," he replied, his tone shifting to something more serious. "But what if we just took it one step at a time? I mean, that's how all great adventures begin, right? A single step into the unknown."

"Okay, but what if I trip on that step?" I challenged, leaning in closer, my heart thumping as I drew nearer to the edge of vulnerability. "What if I end up falling flat on my face?"

"Then I'll be right there to help you up," he said, his eyes sparkling with sincerity. "And we'll laugh about it over those fries. Or I'll let you steal my whiskey."

"Just your whiskey?" I teased, narrowing my eyes playfully. "What's the catch?"

His laughter rang out, and it was infectious. "No catch! Just a promise to make this whole mess less terrifying together."

As the conversation flowed, each moment seemed to pull us closer, the barriers between our hearts fading like the shadows cast by the bar's dim lighting. I found myself leaning in, sharing stories that I hadn't told anyone else, things I thought I had tucked away for good. Rylan listened intently, his gaze unwavering, and I felt an unexpected thrill at the realization that I was beginning to trust him again.

The hours slipped by, laughter and stories melding into a soft, melodic rhythm. But just as I began to feel untethered, blissfully adrift in this new connection, the door swung open with a jarring thud. A group of rowdy patrons burst in, their laughter loud and boisterous, shattering the tender atmosphere we had cultivated. Among them was someone I recognized—a face from the past I had hoped to avoid.

"Great," I muttered, the weight of unease settling heavily in my stomach.

"What's wrong?" Rylan asked, his brow furrowing with concern as he followed my gaze.

"It's nothing," I replied too quickly, but I could feel the tension knotting in my stomach as the newcomer locked eyes with me. It was Claire, my former best friend, and a ghost from a chapter of my life I'd thought I had closed.

"Hey, Kira!" she called out, her voice dripping with faux enthusiasm. "Fancy seeing you here! And with Rylan, no less."

"Yeah, fancy that," I mumbled, wishing for a sudden blackout or perhaps a secret exit. Instead, I forced a smile that felt more like a grimace.

"What a small world, huh?" she continued, her eyes darting between Rylan and me, the tension in the air palpable. "I hear you're doing big things with that musical of yours. How's it coming along?"

"It's... coming," I replied, my throat tight as I glanced back at Rylan, who wore an expression that could only be described as a mixture of amusement and confusion.

"Right, because nothing screams success like three-hour rehearsals and awkward moments on a balcony," Claire said, her tone condescending.

Rylan's eyes narrowed slightly as he straightened in his seat, clearly sensing the shift in the atmosphere. "If you're here to make a scene, I think we'd prefer you do it somewhere else," he said coolly, his protective instincts flaring.

"Oh, don't worry," Claire shot back, a smirk spreading across her lips. "I wouldn't dream of ruining your little moment. Just wanted to say hi to my old friend."

"Old friends don't drop out of your life and then come back like a bad penny," I retorted, unable to help myself. The words spilled out, sharp and unfiltered, fueled by the adrenaline that coursed through me.

Rylan glanced at me, his expression a blend of admiration and surprise, and I could feel the air thickening as our gazes locked. "We're having a private conversation here," he stated firmly, clearly fed up with the disruption.

Claire crossed her arms, the smirk lingering on her face, as if she relished the tension she was creating. "Oh, I see. So, what's the deal? You're really going to try to make this work, then? After everything?"

I could feel Rylan's presence beside me, steady and reassuring, but the shadow of Claire's intrusion darkened the moment, turning our laughter into something unrecognizable. "We're just trying to figure things out," I said, my voice steady despite the churning emotions swirling within.

"Well, good luck with that," she said, dismissive and lightly mocking. "It's a jungle out there. Just remember, not everything that glitters is gold."

With that, she pivoted and sauntered off toward the bar, leaving a trail of tension in her wake. I let out a breath I hadn't realized I was holding, my heart racing not just from the confrontation but from the lingering taste of uncertainty that now flavored the evening.

"Are you okay?" Rylan asked softly, concern etched across his features.

"I will be," I replied, but my voice lacked conviction. The earlier warmth between us felt tenuous, shaken by the unexpected intrusion.

He reached across the table, his hand brushing against mine, and the connection sparked like electricity. "Hey," he said, his tone firm yet gentle. "Don't let her get to you. You've got so much more ahead of you."

Just then, the door swung open again, and I froze, my heart skipping a beat. A man stepped in, his presence commanding and unmistakable. My pulse quickened as recognition struck—Michael, my ex, with a confidence that radiated like the heat of the summer night.

"Just what I needed to see," I whispered, panic flooding my system.

Rylan's hand slipped away as I shifted, the warmth leaving me exposed. "Kira," Michael called out, his voice smooth like velvet, pulling me back into a past I thought I had escaped. "I've been looking for you."

The air felt electric, charged with the intensity of unresolved emotions. I could feel the world around me fade, narrowing into this singular moment. With one foot in the past and another on the precipice of an uncertain future, I was caught between the memories that haunted me and the new beginning that glimmered just out of reach.

Chapter 16: The Pulse of New Orleans

The streets of New Orleans thrummed with a vitality that seemed to pulse through the very cobblestones beneath my feet. A kaleidoscope of colors danced before my eyes, every shade more vivid than the last, as revelers wove in and out of the throngs, their laughter rising above the jazz that spilled from every corner like a sweet, seductive perfume. I felt a giddy exhilaration ripple through me, the kind that ignites when you know you're standing at the edge of something beautiful, something that could change your life if only you let it. Rylan was beside me, and his presence was a warm, intoxicating mixture of comfort and excitement, much like the spicy aroma of jambalaya wafting through the air.

We threaded our way through the jubilant crowd, a tapestry of people wrapped in vibrant costumes and adorned with beads that glittered like jewels in the fading light. The music was alive—an irresistible blend of brass, strings, and percussion that urged our feet to move in time with the rhythm. Rylan caught my eye, and in that moment, the noise faded into the background. It was just the two of us, suspended in a world that felt curated for our joy.

"Do you feel that?" he shouted over the crescendo, his voice brimming with infectious energy. "It's like the city is breathing with us!"

I nodded, laughter bubbling up from somewhere deep inside me. "It's more than breathing; it's dancing! I can practically hear the city singing!"

With a mischievous grin, Rylan took my hand and spun me around, the movement dizzying yet exhilarating. I stumbled slightly, laughter spilling from my lips as I regained my balance. His eyes sparkled with mischief and delight, the very essence of the New Orleans spirit. Every twirl brought me closer to him, and every beat of the music seemed to synchronize with my racing heart.

As we moved through the crowd, the enchanting atmosphere seeped into my bones, momentarily banishing the shadows that had lingered too long. Each face we passed was a mask of joy, strangers united by the magic of the night. I felt like I was part of something larger, a grand celebration that echoed the heartbeat of the city. Yet, beneath the surface of this ecstatic moment, a familiar anxiety flickered in the recesses of my mind. What would happen when the music faded and the lights dimmed?

"Are you okay?" Rylan's voice cut through my thoughts, bringing me back to the now, his brow furrowed with concern. "You look like you've just seen a ghost."

I forced a smile, trying to shake off the creeping doubt. "Just... thinking about how beautiful this is. It feels almost surreal."

Rylan studied me for a moment, his expression softening. "I know what you mean. But let's not worry about tomorrow. Tonight is ours."

His words wrapped around me like a protective cloak, yet I couldn't shake the feeling that this moment—this intoxicating fusion of warmth, laughter, and music—was precarious, like the delicate strands of a spider's web glistening in the moonlight. I clung to his hand, feeling the warmth radiating from his skin, a tether to the happiness of the evening.

As we ventured deeper into the festival, we came upon a stall bursting with vibrant colors—banners and beads cascading down like rainbows. The air was thick with the scent of beignets, sugar dusting the air like tiny, sweet snowflakes. I felt a childlike excitement bubble up inside me, and I tugged Rylan toward the stall, my heart racing with the thrill of simple pleasures.

"Two beignets, please!" I declared to the vendor, my eyes alight with anticipation. The vendor, a jovial man with flour-dusted hands, nodded, preparing our order with the care of a master chef.

"Get ready to have your taste buds dance," Rylan said, leaning closer, the heat of his breath tickling my ear. I shivered, both from the sensation and the gravity of the moment. This wasn't just a festival; this was a revelation, a chance to shed my worries and embrace the unexpected.

When the vendor handed us our powdered treasures, I took a bite, the warm pastry melting in my mouth, enveloped in sweet nostalgia. "Oh my God, this is incredible!" I exclaimed, my voice muffled by sugary delight.

"See? I told you," Rylan replied, taking a bite of his own, a playful smirk forming as the powdered sugar dusted his nose. "You look like a sugar-coated pixie."

"Very funny," I shot back, playfully swatting at his shoulder. But inside, I felt buoyant, each taste and sound weaving a spell that momentarily pushed aside the gnawing uncertainties about the future.

As the night wore on, the firework display began, illuminating the sky with bursts of color that felt like the very essence of life. We found a spot by the river, the cool breeze ruffling my hair as we leaned against the railing. The reflection of the lights danced on the water, creating a beautiful mirror of the festivities above.

"Look at that," Rylan said, gesturing to the sky, his voice low and thoughtful. "It's like the universe is celebrating with us."

I leaned my head against his shoulder, comforted by his presence. "It's breathtaking, isn't it? Almost too beautiful to be real."

Rylan turned to face me, his gaze steady and earnest. "You're real. This moment is real. And I'm here. I promise I'll be here, no matter what."

His words wrapped around me, binding the fleeting joy to something deeper, something more profound. As the fireworks burst overhead, I could feel the warmth of his hand enveloping mine, the promise of connection pulsing through our fingers. I wanted to believe him, to believe that we could carve out our own little piece of happiness amidst the chaos of life.

But as the last firework fizzled and the echoes of applause faded into the night, I felt that familiar chill creep back in. Tomorrow loomed ahead, heavy with expectations and the weight of my insecurities. I squeezed Rylan's hand, hoping to tether myself to this moment, to him, just a little longer.

The last sparks of fireworks faded into the night, leaving behind a sky tinged with darkness, flecked with stars that seemed to twinkle in agreement with the rhythm of my heart. I could still feel the warmth of Rylan's hand wrapped around mine, a tether to this whirlwind of a night. He turned to me, his expression a mix of wonder and mischief, his tousled hair catching the last glimmers of light as he spoke. "So, should we conquer the rest of the festival or head somewhere less... crowded?"

"Conquer? You think you can take on the rest of the festival?" I challenged, arching an eyebrow, unable to suppress the playful smile creeping onto my lips.

"I have it on good authority that I'm quite formidable in the face of beignets and live music," he retorted, a mock-seriousness draping his words. "And don't forget the po'boys. The ultimate challenge!"

Laughter bubbled up between us, a buoyant energy that felt deliciously infectious. My heart swelled, driven by the spontaneity of our adventure. I could see the festival sprawling before us, a vibrant tapestry of people, colors, and sounds. "Alright, then. Let's see what this festival has to offer!"

As we walked back into the heart of the celebration, the music swelled around us again, alive and pulsating like a heartbeat. We made our way through stalls decorated with strings of twinkling lights, each booth a treasure trove of local delights and unique crafts. A woman selling handmade jewelry caught my eye, her table a mosaic of colorful beads and intricate designs.

"Look at that!" I exclaimed, pointing at a necklace adorned with emerald-green stones that glimmered like the bayou at dusk. "It's stunning!"

Rylan paused, his gaze following mine. "It is," he agreed, "but I bet it doesn't compare to the sparkle in your eyes right now."

I rolled my eyes, though the warmth creeping into my cheeks betrayed my amusement. "You're such a charmer, aren't you? Is that your secret weapon in conquering festivals?"

He leaned closer, a conspiratorial grin plastered on his face. "It's either that or an impressive array of food recommendations. What do you think works better?"

Before I could respond, a gust of wind swirled around us, ruffling my hair and carrying the scent of spicy gumbo through the air. The savory aroma clung to the night like a promise of indulgence, and my stomach growled in agreement. "Alright, food it is. Let's find something to eat before I turn into a walking beignet."

We made our way to a nearby food stall, where the vendor was skillfully flipping shrimp in a sizzling pan. The sound of the food frying was like music to my ears, the tantalizing scent drawing me closer. I could hardly contain my excitement as we placed our order, anticipation bubbling like the boiling pot in front of us.

"Two shrimp po'boys and a side of gumbo," Rylan announced confidently, flashing a grin at me. "If you're going to conquer this festival, you need proper fuel."

I couldn't help but laugh. "Are you sure you're not just here for the food? Because I feel like that's the real star of the show."

He raised an eyebrow, leaning in slightly. "Food may be a close second to your sparkling personality. But don't let it go to your head. It might explode."

"Exploding heads would make for quite the festival entertainment," I shot back, my heart soaring with his playful banter.

The banter flowed easily between us, a natural rhythm that felt like an extension of our earlier connection.

When our order was ready, the vendor handed us our steaming treasures, the po'boys overflowing with plump shrimp, lettuce, and a drizzle of spicy sauce that danced on the edge of my taste buds. We found a small table under a string of lights, the glow casting a soft halo around us as we dug into our food.

"This is fantastic," I said between bites, savoring the explosion of flavors. "Who knew you were such a gourmet?"

Rylan chuckled, his mouth full. "Gourmet? Me? Hardly. I just know how to appreciate good food when I taste it."

We continued to trade playful barbs, our conversation weaving effortlessly as the night unfolded. I could feel the weight of my earlier worries lift, replaced by laughter and warmth. Yet, as we finished our meal, a flicker of anxiety returned, an unwelcome reminder of the uncertainty that loomed ahead. Would this night be just a beautiful blip in the passage of time, or the beginning of something more profound?

"Are you ready to explore a little more?" Rylan asked, interrupting my thoughts as he glanced around, excitement bubbling in his voice.

"Absolutely. What's next?" I replied, eager to dive back into the festival's energy.

"Let's check out the live music!" He gestured toward a nearby stage where a band was setting up, their instruments glinting under the lights. The crowd buzzed with anticipation, the air electric with excitement.

As we approached, the band struck up a lively tune, a blend of jazz and rock that had everyone moving. I could feel the rhythm in my bones, a sweet invitation that pulled me into its embrace. Rylan took my hand, leading me closer to the stage.

"Let's dance!" he shouted, and before I could even protest, he twirled me into the throng of swaying bodies.

Laughter erupted as I found my footing, letting the music guide my movements. Rylan mirrored my enthusiasm, our bodies weaving through the crowd as if we were the only two people in the world. Each note struck like a heartbeat, a reminder of life's exhilarating unpredictability.

As we danced, I lost myself in the moment, spinning and twirling, allowing the music to wrap around me like a vibrant shawl. The lights flashed, illuminating Rylan's smile, the way his eyes sparkled as they met mine. He pulled me closer, our laughter mingling with the music, creating a symphony of joy that filled the night air.

"You've got some serious moves!" he shouted, a teasing grin spreading across his face.

"Careful, or I might show you up!" I retorted, thrusting my arms into the air with a flourish that drew a few amused glances from nearby revelers.

"Bring it on!" He challenged, matching my enthusiasm with an exaggerated dance move that sent me into another fit of laughter.

But amid our playful rivalry, a sudden jolt of realization struck me. This moment, this carefree dance under the stars, was something I wanted to hold onto forever. Yet, the shadow of uncertainty loomed over my heart like an unwelcome guest, reminding me that nothing in life was guaranteed.

Before I could dwell on those thoughts, the music shifted to a slower, more sultry melody, enveloping the crowd in a romantic haze. Couples began to draw closer, swaying together, and Rylan caught my eye, his expression shifting from playful to sincere.

"Would you like to?" he asked, his voice dropping to a softer tone that cut through the noise around us.

I nodded, unable to suppress the smile that spread across my face. He pulled me closer, his hand resting gently on the small of my back, guiding me into a gentle sway. The world around us melted away, leaving just the two of us in our own little bubble.

As we moved together, I could feel the warmth radiating from his body, the steadiness of his presence anchoring me amid the swirling uncertainties of life. His gaze held mine, an unspoken promise hovering between us, a fleeting moment filled with both hope and doubt.

"I'm really glad you're here," he said, his voice low, barely above the music.

"Me too," I replied, my heart racing, both from the dance and the weight of what lingered unsaid.

In that moment, I wanted to believe in the possibilities, to grasp the fleeting magic of the night, even as I grappled with the looming questions that hung in the air like the last echoes of the fireworks.

The gentle sway of the music cradled us as we danced under the twinkling lights, a cocoon of warmth and laughter enveloping us in a world that felt like it had been spun just for our enjoyment. Rylan's presence was magnetic, pulling me in, and as I surrendered to the rhythm, I felt the tight coils of uncertainty begin to loosen. The intensity in his eyes held promises that danced tantalizingly on the edge of something deeper, and for a fleeting moment, I dared to believe in it all—the possibilities that stretched before us like the luminous path of the Mississippi.

"Are you always this charming, or is it just the festival magic?" I teased, swaying closer as he twirled me again, our bodies moving in harmony with the vibrant pulse of the music.

"Maybe it's the magic of you being here," he replied, that easy smile of his making my heart flutter like the tiny lights strung above us. "I'm pretty sure I could charm the pants off anyone tonight."

I laughed, caught off guard by the audacity of his words. "You'd have to work a bit harder for that!" I shot back, my playful challenge hanging in the air between us.

As he leaned closer, I could feel the warmth radiating from him, and my breath caught. "Oh, I'm not one to back down from a challenge. What do you say we see how far my charm can take us?" His tone was laced with flirtation, but I sensed an undercurrent of sincerity, a gentle push toward something more intimate.

Before I could respond, a particularly lively beat dropped, and a group of dancers burst into an impromptu routine nearby, their exuberance infectious. I pulled Rylan into the fray, reveling in the spontaneity of the moment. Together, we mimicked their steps, laughing as we fumbled through the choreography, our movements a chaotic blend of clumsy enthusiasm and genuine joy.

"See? Festival magic," he shouted over the music, his grin wide and infectious. "We're basically professional dancers now!"

"Professional dancers who look like they're auditioning for a circus!" I quipped, barely keeping my balance as I tripped over my own feet. Just as I was about to regain my composure, Rylan swept me back into his arms, anchoring me against him.

The proximity was electric, the moment stretching into something sweetly tender. I could feel the warmth of his breath against my skin, and for an instant, it felt like the world around us faded into a hazy blur.

"Maybe we should stick to the two-step," I murmured, my heart racing as I met his gaze, the gravity of the moment urging me to let go of my apprehensions.

"Or we could just stay here, right in the chaos. I like it better that way," he replied, his voice a low rumble that sent a shiver down my spine. The music ebbed and flowed, and as we swayed together, I found myself lost in the depth of his eyes, a world of unspoken things waiting to unfold.

But just as the moment teetered on the edge of something profound, a loud crash echoed through the air, shattering our bubble. I turned to see a group of revelers stumbling into a nearby stall, knocking over an impressive display of trinkets and snacks. The laughter around us transformed into a chorus of gasps and cheers, the festive atmosphere punctured by chaos.

"What just happened?" I exclaimed, pulling back from Rylan's embrace, the jolt of reality jolting me from my dreamy reverie.

"Looks like a little too much festival spirit," Rylan replied, glancing at the commotion with an amused expression. "Should we help them?"

"Definitely," I agreed, the moment of intimacy fading but leaving a warm glow in its wake. We made our way toward the fallen stall, laughing as we joined the crowd to assist in picking up the scattered items, our hands brushing against one another amidst the chaos.

"Your charm really knows no bounds, huh?" I teased as we picked up a particularly colorful set of beads, their sheen catching the flickering light.

Rylan flashed me a cheeky grin, his eyes dancing. "You can't help but shine when you're surrounded by this much chaos. It's like a charm overload."

As we worked, I caught snippets of conversation—people discussing the night's festivities, sharing their excitement about the music, and wondering what the next act would be. But just as I was about to settle back into the lively atmosphere, I felt a sudden chill creep up my spine. The crowd shifted, a murmur spreading through the throngs like a ripple across water. I turned to see a figure weaving through the crowd, eyes scanning intently, and my heart sank as recognition struck.

"Isn't that...?" I began, my voice trailing off as Rylan followed my gaze.

"It can't be," he said, his brow furrowing in confusion. "Who is it?"

The figure moved closer, the shadows of the festival lights revealing a familiar face that sent a chill coursing through me. My heart raced, not out of excitement but sheer panic. The last time I had seen her, it hadn't been a pleasant encounter.

"Cara," I whispered, the name barely escaping my lips as I felt a surge of dread wash over me.

"What's going on?" Rylan asked, concern etching his features as he grasped my arm gently, sensing my sudden tension.

I could barely think straight as memories flooded my mind, tangled and chaotic, a bitter reminder of the fallout from the last time I'd crossed paths with her. "She's... someone from my past. We didn't part on good terms."

Rylan stepped closer, his protective instincts flaring to life. "Are you okay? Do you want to leave?"

"No," I breathed, my voice steadier than I felt. "I can handle this. I just need to..." But my words trailed off as Cara spotted me, a flicker of recognition sparking in her eyes.

She approached with purpose, and the crowd seemed to part for her, as if sensing the tension that followed in her wake. "Well, if it isn't my favorite person," she said, her voice smooth but laced with something I couldn't quite place—sarcasm, perhaps, or a challenge.

Rylan stiffened beside me, and I felt a mix of anger and apprehension churn in my stomach. "What do you want, Cara?" I managed, my tone sharper than I intended.

"Oh, just wanted to see how you're enjoying the festival," she replied, an unsettling smile on her lips that sent an uneasy shiver down my spine. "I hear it's quite the event this year."

"Why do I feel like there's an ulterior motive hidden in those words?" Rylan interjected, stepping slightly in front of me, a protective barrier.

"Relax, sweetheart," Cara purred, her eyes glinting with mischief. "I'm not here to cause trouble. Just curious about what's happening in this little corner of the world."

My pulse quickened, sensing the underlying tension. Rylan glanced at me, gauging my reaction. I didn't know how to respond, but the unease gnawed at me, a sense that the night was about to take a turn I wasn't ready for.

"What do you really want, Cara?" I pressed, unwilling to back down, every instinct screaming at me that this encounter was far from innocent.

"I want what everyone wants," she replied, her voice dipping to a conspiratorial whisper, the crowd around us fading into the background. "I want answers. And I think you hold the key."

As she leaned in closer, the world around us faded into a murmur, and my heart raced with an unsettling mix of dread and anticipation. Rylan's grip on my arm tightened, grounding me as the weight of her words settled heavy in the air.

In that moment, the vibrant festival felt distant, a mere backdrop to the storm brewing at the edge of our newfound connection. I took a deep breath, preparing myself for whatever revelations were about to unfold, my heart pounding with the uncertainty of what was to come.

Chapter 17: Heartbeats Apart

The festival's colors danced vibrantly against the backdrop of twilight, swirling like a painter's palette smeared with joy. Lanterns flickered overhead, their warm glow washing over us, a gentle reminder that life continues in shades of gold and crimson even as shadows loom nearby. I inhaled deeply, letting the sweet, spicy scent of candied apples mingle with the crisp autumn air, attempting to drown out the dread that had nestled in my chest. Laughter erupted from a nearby booth, where children darted in delight, their shrieks echoing the innocent joy that I had somehow forgotten.

Yet, the moment was fragile, as if the very air crackled with unspoken truths. I could sense it in the way Rylan leaned closer, his presence grounding yet disconcerting. His brown eyes, usually brimming with mischief, held an unusual depth, an understanding that pierced through the cheerful veneer of the festival. I stole a glance at him, the corner of his mouth curled slightly, a smile that felt like a fragile truce against the gathering storm within me.

"Let's try that ride," he suggested, gesturing toward the towering Ferris wheel. The colorful cars swayed gently, and for a moment, I could almost convince myself that the ups and downs of the ride mirrored the heartbeats of our own lives. But just as I was about to respond, my phone buzzed, cutting through the moment like a knife through a festive ribbon.

I glanced at the screen, my heart plummeting as I saw my mother's name. The buoyancy of the festival dimmed as I answered, the world around me muffling into a distant hum. Her voice, usually a soothing balm, now trembled with urgency. "Sweetheart, we need to talk. It's about your father..."

The walls of the carnival twisted, contorting around me, suffocating in their embrace. I clutched the phone tighter, grounding myself against the onslaught of dread that threatened to consume me. Rylan's gaze bore into me, a silent inquiry hanging in the air between us. I couldn't meet it; instead, I retreated into the whirlwind of my thoughts, my mother's words echoing like a dirge.

When I finally hung up, the laughter and music of the festival felt like a cruel joke, each sound a reminder of the carefree lives others led. I felt the ground shift beneath my feet, my balance faltering as the reality of my father's health spiraled into a vortex of anxiety. I glanced back at Rylan, whose brows knitted together, concern radiating from him like a heatwave.

"Hey," he began, taking a step closer. "What did she say?" His voice was low, careful, as if he were walking on glass.

"The same," I murmured, my throat tightening. "He's worse, Rylan. They've decided to try something new, but..." I faltered, the words lodged in my throat like stones. "I'm not there. I should be there."

He nodded, the light fading from his expression. "I get it. But you're here too. You can't just..."

"I know! I know!" I snapped, the pent-up fear spilling over. "It's just... It's complicated." My breath came in ragged gasps, and I stepped back, creating distance not just physically, but emotionally. I could feel the walls closing in on me again, the tightrope I had been balancing so carefully fraying at the edges.

"Look, it's okay to feel scared," he said softly, the gentleness of his voice brushing against my frayed nerves. "But shutting me out won't help you. I want to be here for you, you know?"

A surge of anger mingled with guilt, and I turned away, my heart racing with the weight of his words. How could he understand? The intertwining of our lives was a comfort and a burden all at once. "You don't get it, Rylan! This isn't just about me being here. It's about him. I'm... I'm terrified of losing him."

I felt the tears prick at the corners of my eyes, and I blinked them back fiercely, refusing to let the festival's gaiety see my despair. Rylan remained silent, the hurt etched on his face as he wrestled with the frustration of being unable to reach me through the growing chasm of my turmoil.

"I need space," I finally said, my voice barely above a whisper. The words hung in the air, sharp and final. Without waiting for his response, I turned and walked away, each step feeling like an unspooling thread, unraveling the tapestry of what had once felt secure.

The carnival, now a blur of colors and sounds, faded into the background as I navigated through the throngs of people, their laughter a reminder of the life I was desperately trying to escape. I weaved through the crowd, seeking the solitude of a nearby grove, where the trees stood sentinel, their branches heavy with the scent of damp earth and decay.

Here, I let the façade fall away, the mask of bravery crumbling as I pressed my back against the rough bark of a tree. I sank to the ground, drawing my knees to my chest, letting the sobs take hold. The world outside continued to twinkle with joy, but inside me, the storm raged, tossing my heart between hope and despair.

Moments passed, or maybe hours. Time felt like a cruel trickster, bending and twisting as I battled the emotions flooding through me. And in that quiet grove, where nature wrapped its arms around my vulnerability, I realized I didn't just fear losing my father; I feared the fracture it would cause in my world. I feared what it meant for Rylan, for us. How could I let someone in, someone I cared about, witness the wreckage I carried within?

The sound of footsteps broke through the silence, and I looked up to see Rylan approaching, his silhouette framed by the flickering lights of the festival behind him. I wanted to turn away, to shield him from the turmoil that churned inside, but he didn't stop. He knelt beside me, his warmth enveloping me like a comforting blanket.

"I'm here," he said quietly, his voice a soft caress against the raging storm in my heart. In that moment, I felt the first tendrils of hope reach out, daring to intertwine with the shadows that had taken residence within me.

The silence between us swelled like a balloon, threatening to burst with the weight of unspoken words. Rylan remained beside me, his presence both a comfort and an intrusion. I could feel his eyes studying my face, searching for cracks in my carefully constructed façade. The faint glow from the festival illuminated the grove, casting dappled patterns on the ground, yet it couldn't pierce the darkness that had settled in my heart.

"Isn't there a saying about sharing burdens?" he finally said, breaking the stillness. His tone was teasing, yet his eyes remained serious, the warmth in his voice trying to coax me out from behind the wall I had erected. "Or did you miss that lesson in your 'how to be a responsible adult' class?"

I chuckled despite myself, a hollow sound that echoed back at me like a stranger's laugh. "I might have been absent that day. I was busy learning how to be a emotional hermit."

"Ah, yes. The fine art of avoidance." He nudged my shoulder playfully, a spark of mischief flickering in his eyes. "But that's just not my style. I prefer to take the bull by the horns. Or at least poke it with a stick until it notices me."

I couldn't help but smile at his antics, a glimmer of light piercing through the shadows. "If you keep poking that bull, you might end up with more than you bargained for."

"Please," he waved his hand dismissively. "What's life without a little risk? I mean, isn't that why we came to this festival? To live a little?"

"Easy for you to say," I muttered, but the weight of my heart lightened just a fraction. "You're not the one with a family in crisis."

"True," he acknowledged, the humor ebbing from his voice. "But that doesn't mean I can't help you tackle whatever crisis is brewing." His gaze intensified, and I could see a determination flickering in his eyes. "You don't have to carry this all alone, you know."

His words sank in, settling like a pebble in the pit of my stomach. The idea of sharing my burden felt both liberating and terrifying. What if sharing the weight made it heavier instead of lighter? But I couldn't deny that his support was a balm I desperately needed. I looked down, tracing patterns in the fallen leaves, contemplating the path I had taken thus far.

"Sometimes, it feels like I'm living two lives," I confessed, my voice barely above a whisper. "I want to be there for my family, but I also want to be here... with you."

His expression softened, and he shifted closer, brushing his shoulder against mine in a silent gesture of solidarity. "You're allowed to feel torn. It's a big deal, and it's okay to admit that it sucks."

The truth of his words resonated within me, and I felt a rush of emotion I had kept at bay for too long. "I just wish I could split myself in half," I admitted, "one half with my mother, and the other half here, living life and trying to be happy."

"Why not try bringing a piece of home with you?" Rylan suggested, his voice imbued with a gentle firmness. "Talk to your mom, keep that connection alive. Let her know you're still with her, even if you're not physically there."

I pondered his words, an unexpected warmth blossoming in my chest. "It's a nice thought, but how can I help her from so far away?"

"Call her. Text her. You're not leaving her behind just because you're having fun. Besides, you're stronger than you think. I mean, you handled the whole 'not being a hermit' situation pretty well tonight." He gave me a playful grin, and I couldn't help but roll my eyes.

"Okay, okay," I said, waving him off. "I'll think about it."

"Just think about it? Come on! You can't drop a bomb like that and expect me not to want details. I'm not going to let you off that easily."

His persistence was endearing, and I found myself laughing again, the sound ringing out in the otherwise quiet grove. Maybe he was right. Maybe I didn't have to bear this weight alone. Perhaps there was a way to straddle both worlds without losing myself in the process.

"Fine," I relented, the laughter fading into a soft sigh. "I'll call her. But first, I need a moment."

"Absolutely," he agreed, his smile fading into something more serious. "Take all the time you need. Just know I'm right here."

As the sounds of the festival drifted through the trees, I focused on the rhythm of my heartbeat, the pulse of life reminding me that I was still part of this world, still capable of feeling joy amid the pain. I closed my eyes, taking a deep breath, and let the festival's energy wash over me, a vibrant tapestry of color and sound that intertwined with my own tumultuous feelings.

With a sense of newfound resolve, I reached for my phone, the screen lighting up with my mother's contact. Rylan stayed close, his shoulder brushing against mine, grounding me as I prepared to bridge the gap between my two worlds. I hesitated for a heartbeat, the reality of what lay ahead looming before me. But Rylan nudged me with a gentle elbow, offering silent encouragement.

"Hey, Mom," I said when she picked up, trying to infuse my voice with the warmth I felt deep inside.

"Sweetheart! I was just thinking about you!" she exclaimed, and I could hear the tremor in her voice, the strength she clung to like a lifeline.

"Yeah? I figured I'd call since we can't have a full-blown family reunion right now," I replied, attempting to lighten the weight in her tone.

"Smart girl," she chuckled, though it held a hint of sadness. "How's the festival? It sounds so lively."

"It is. They have the best candied apples, and I even tried the Ferris wheel," I said, pulling the words from a place of memory and joy. "But I missed you."

"I miss you too, sweetheart," she replied, her voice softening. "But I'm glad you're enjoying life. That's what I want for you."

Rylan leaned back slightly, giving me the space to connect with my mother, and I sensed the warmth of his support enveloping me like a blanket. "I want to share everything with you, Mom. It's hard being away, and I worry so much."

"I know, and it's okay to worry," she said gently. "But you need to live your life too. We're a family, no matter the distance."

Her words soothed me, weaving through the tumult of emotions I had been grappling with. I felt a weight lift, the knot in my chest loosening, as if her voice had wrapped around my fears and gently pushed them aside.

"I'll always be there with you," she added, a certainty in her voice that pulled me closer, even as we spoke through a phone. "So, promise me you'll enjoy this moment, even if it's hard."

"I promise," I whispered, the sincerity behind the promise illuminating the shadows that had lingered for too long.

"Good. Now, tell me more about the festival. Are there any cute boys?" she teased, her laughter infectious, drawing me back into the warmth of family ties.

"Only the cutest," I replied, a smile breaking free as I exchanged a knowing glance with Rylan, who was watching me with a look that could only be described as playful mischief.

"Give them my best! I expect a full report when you get home," she teased, her voice lightening as we settled into a comfortable rhythm, bridging the miles with laughter and love.

Rylan grinned, and for the first time that evening, I felt a flicker of hope ignite within me. My worlds were not so separate after all; they could intertwine, dance together like the colors of the festival, vibrant and alive.

As I hung up the phone, a peculiar blend of relief and lingering anxiety wrapped around me like a well-worn shawl. The laughter and chatter of the festival filtered through the trees, a cacophony that felt at once comforting and alien. I could hear the distant strains of a band playing upbeat tunes, their notes dancing through the air, yet I stood suspended in my own private world, caught between the vibrant life around me and the weight of my family's turmoil.

Rylan remained by my side, a steady presence even as I felt myself pulling away. "Hey," he said gently, breaking the spell that had settled around us. "You okay?"

"Sure. Just peachy," I replied, trying to muster up a smile that didn't quite reach my eyes. The ache in my heart still pulsed, a reminder that I was far from okay.

"Peachy? Is that what you're calling it now?" He arched an eyebrow, a playful smirk tugging at the corner of his lips. "I'd hate to see what you'd consider 'not okay.'"

I chuckled softly, appreciating his attempt to lighten the mood, but the laughter quickly faded. "You know, it's just hard. I want to be here, enjoying everything, but it feels like I'm wearing a mask."

"Yeah, I get that," he said, his tone shifting slightly. "But it's okay to let the mask slip a little. You don't have to be 'on' all the time."

As I looked into his eyes, I saw a flicker of understanding, as if he could see right through the layers I had built around myself. "Thanks for being here," I murmured, the sincerity of my gratitude warming the space between us.

"Always," he replied, his smile genuine. "But enough about your feelings. Let's get back to this festival. You promised me candied apples!"

"Right! The sacred tradition of sugar-coated guilt," I joked, and for a moment, the shadows receded as we made our way through the throngs of festival-goers, the atmosphere buzzing with excitement.

We navigated through stalls brimming with trinkets and treats. I watched as children darted past, their faces painted with bright colors, laughter spilling from their lips like music. My heart warmed at the sight, a reminder of simpler times when joy felt uncomplicated. We approached a booth selling candied apples, the glossy surface reflecting the lights like little orbs of happiness.

"Two, please!" Rylan said, leaning over the counter with exaggerated enthusiasm.

"Only two?" I teased, arching an eyebrow. "I thought you were the 'let's live a little' guy."

He shrugged, a mock-serious expression crossing his face. "I have to pace myself, you know. Too much sugar and I might just start breakdancing."

"Oh, God, please don't. I can't handle that level of embarrassment." I laughed, the tension in my chest easing as we indulged in the sugary treats. The first bite was heaven—crisp, sweet, and tart all at once—making me forget, if only for a moment, the gravity of my worries.

"Now, this is living!" he exclaimed, his eyes lighting up with genuine delight. I watched him savor the apple, his smile infectious. It felt nice, being able to share this small slice of happiness, and I found myself lost in the moment, letting the flavors drown out the storm inside.

As we wandered further into the festival, the world around us felt almost dreamlike. The sound of laughter, the aroma of fried dough, and the shimmering lights enveloped us, creating a sanctuary where my worries momentarily faded. We ventured toward the game booths, where the excited cheers of players echoed like a chorus.

Rylan's competitive spirit ignited, and he challenged me to a ring toss. "I bet you can't beat me!"

"Challenge accepted!" I laughed, the tension evaporating as we took turns, our playful rivalry drawing us closer. I relished in his antics, the way he dramatically feigned frustration when he missed a ring.

"Next round's on the line!" he declared, his determination making me chuckle. I had to admit, his enthusiasm was contagious.

As we played, a momentary distraction pulled my attention. I noticed a girl standing a few booths away, her smile bright yet distant, her eyes searching the crowd as if she were looking for someone. There was something about her—a familiarity I couldn't place. My heart thudded in my chest, but just as I focused on her, she turned and disappeared into the sea of festival-goers.

"Did you see that?" I asked, nodding toward the spot where she had been.

"See what?" Rylan's focus was entirely on the game, his competitive spirit blinding him to my distraction.

"That girl. She looked... familiar," I murmured, straining to catch another glimpse, but the crowd swallowed her whole.

"Maybe she's a fan of your secret candied apple talent," he quipped, making me roll my eyes.

"Very funny." I couldn't shake the feeling of unease that settled over me like a damp blanket. Why did it feel so important? It nagged at me, a thread unraveling in the back of my mind.

"Okay, focus time!" Rylan said, snapping me out of my reverie. "You're about to witness greatness."

I laughed, shaking off my lingering thoughts, and watched as he prepared for another toss. He took a deep breath, squinted one eye, and threw the ring with all the drama of a Broadway performance.

The ring arced beautifully through the air—then missed spectacularly.

"Wow, that was a dramatic miss," I teased, unable to contain my laughter. "Are you sure you want to keep trying, or should we switch to a less... 'skill-based' activity?"

"Never!" He shot back, feigning offense. "One more try. I can feel it."

Just as he stepped forward for another round, my phone buzzed in my pocket, an unwelcome interruption. I fished it out, glancing at the screen. The caller ID sent a chill down my spine.

"Mom?" I whispered, a wave of unease washing over me.

"Are you going to answer?" Rylan asked, his playful energy dissipating as he sensed the shift in my mood.

I hesitated, the weight of the call pressing heavily on my chest. "Yeah. I just... I didn't expect her to call back so soon."

"Do you want me to go?" he offered, concern knitting his brows together.

"No, stay." I forced a smile, though it felt brittle. I answered the call, hoping to maintain the connection I had just fostered with my mother.

"Hello?"

"Sweetheart, I'm so sorry to bother you again," my mother's voice crackled through the line, tinged with an urgency that sent alarm bells ringing in my head. "There's something important we need to discuss."

My heart raced, the carefree ambiance of the festival fading into a distant memory. "What is it? Is everything okay?"

"Not quite," she replied, her voice shaky. "There's been a development with your father's treatment. I need you to come home."

I felt the ground shift beneath me, as if the very fabric of reality had torn. "What do you mean? I thought he was stable?"

"Things have changed. The doctors found something unexpected."

I clutched my phone, my vision blurring as the weight of her words settled over me like a fog. "Mom, please... What does this mean?"

Rylan, sensing the shift in my demeanor, leaned closer, his eyes searching mine for answers I didn't have.

"There's a possibility he may need to start a different treatment right away, and I want you here. We need to make decisions together," she said, her tone becoming more frantic.

"Okay, okay. I'll come home," I managed to say, feeling the urgency pulse through me like a warning siren.

"Thank you, sweetheart. I love you."

"I love you too," I whispered, even as the reality of her words settled heavily in my stomach.

As I hung up, Rylan's gaze bore into me, the concern etched on his face mirrored the turmoil roiling within me. "What did she say?"

"I need to go home," I said, the gravity of my decision settling over us both.

"Now? Is it that serious?"

"Yeah. It is," I replied, swallowing hard as my mind raced with thoughts of the festival and the warmth of laughter that had felt so close just moments ago.

"Then let's go. I'll drive you," he said, his tone leaving no room for argument.

"Rylan, you don't have to—"

"Stop right there. You think I'm going to let you go alone when your family needs you? Not a chance."

His words struck a chord, and I felt a rush of gratitude mixed with apprehension. The festival lights flickered around us, the laughter and music fading as if the world were holding its breath, waiting for the next twist in the tale.

With a nod, I turned to leave, but just as we made our way through the crowd, I caught a glimpse of that girl again—the one who had faded from view earlier. This time, she stood directly in our path, her eyes wide with recognition as she locked onto mine, a look of fear mingling with urgency.

"Wait!" she called, her voice cutting through the noise, and in that

Chapter 18: Echoes of Love

The studio buzzed with the electric hum of anticipation, the scent of sweat mingling with the faint aroma of lavender that clung to the walls. Mirrors lined the far side, reflecting not just the movements of my body but the swirling chaos in my heart. I was a tempest, and in the center of it all was Rylan, the eye of my storm. His presence, a balm to my frayed edges, made the air around us shimmer with possibilities. Each note from the stereo poured into the space, wrapping around us like a silken ribbon, urging us to move, to connect.

As I glided across the floor, every leap felt like a defiance of gravity, a bold proclamation of joy and sorrow all wrapped into one. Dance had always been my sanctuary, a place where I could drown out the noise of the world. But lately, it had transformed into a bittersweet reflection of my feelings for Rylan, the unspoken words lingering like a mist just out of reach. He was my partner, my confidant, and somehow, my greatest source of pain.

Every twirl brought me closer to him, and yet, it was as if an invisible wall had risen between us. I watched him from the corner of my eye, his body moving with a fluidity that seemed effortless, yet I could see the subtle shifts in his posture—the way his shoulders slumped slightly, a telltale sign of the emotional weight he carried. My heart ached for him, for the distance I had forced between us. And still, I danced, losing myself in the rhythm, praying the music would drown out the doubts that gnawed at my resolve.

As the final notes of our routine echoed into silence, I turned to face him, my chest heaving, each breath a struggle against the tidal wave of emotions crashing over me. Rylan stood still, his eyes deep pools of uncertainty, framed by the tousled waves of his dark hair. The boy who always seemed so invincible now wore an expression of vulnerability that tore at my insides.

"I'm sorry," I whispered, the words barely escaping my lips, laden with the weight of my hesitation.

His brow furrowed, confusion etched across his handsome features. "What for?"

I glanced down, avoiding the intensity of his gaze. "For pushing you away. For not letting you in."

Silence enveloped us, thick and heavy, a shroud that made it difficult to breathe. I could see the cogs turning in his mind, the hesitance in his posture as he took a small step closer. "You don't have to apologize, but it would help if you'd tell me what's going on in that beautiful head of yours."

The compliment was a double-edged sword, one that cut through my defenses while simultaneously shrouding me in warmth. I met his gaze, determination flooding my veins. I could no longer afford to keep him at arm's length. "I'm scared, Rylan. Scared of what we might become, scared of ruining everything we've built."

He stepped closer, closing the gap between us, his hand reaching out to brush against my arm, igniting a spark that traveled straight to my core. "What if what we've built is worth the risk? I don't want to live in a world where you're not a part of it."

His words washed over me like a soothing balm, yet the fear clung stubbornly to my thoughts. "What if it doesn't work? What if we break?"

Rylan's eyes softened, an understanding passing between us that spoke volumes. "We've both felt it—the chemistry, the connection. We wouldn't be the first to navigate the tricky waters of love. But if we don't try, we'll never know."

A shiver ran through me, a mix of excitement and dread. The thought of taking that leap felt like standing at the edge of a precipice, peering down into the unknown. I could see the beauty waiting below, the vibrant colors of love and passion, yet the fear of falling held me captive.

As the tension thickened in the air, he took a small step back, giving me space to breathe, yet his eyes remained locked on mine, unwavering and filled with patience. "Let's just dance, Ellie. Let the music guide us. If we stumble, we'll pick each other up."

With a deep inhale, I nodded, surrendering to the rhythm once more. We moved in tandem, our bodies effortlessly falling into sync. Each step was a reminder of the bond we shared, the undeniable pull that had been building since the first day we met. The melody wove around us, urging us to explore the uncharted territory of our hearts, to dance on the precipice of love.

I felt a surge of warmth as he pulled me into an embrace, our bodies fitting together like puzzle pieces. It was in this moment, surrounded by the echoes of our laughter and the music that enveloped us, that I finally found the courage to confront my feelings. "Rylan," I began, my voice barely a whisper, but the conviction behind it was undeniable, "I think I love you."

His reaction was immediate, a flicker of surprise crossing his features before his expression softened, as if my words had struck a chord deep within him. The room fell away, leaving just the two of us suspended in this fragile moment. His gaze held mine, an unspoken promise lingering between us, and in that silence, I could feel the walls around my heart crumbling.

"I love you too," he finally replied, his voice low and earnest, the truth of his words wrapping around me like a warm embrace. The admission hung in the air, palpable and electric, transforming the space around us into something almost sacred.

In that instant, the tension that had once felt insurmountable melted away, replaced by the warmth of newfound understanding. We were no longer two dancers moving through life, but partners bound by a connection that felt both exhilarating and terrifying. As the music swelled around us, I knew that this was just the beginning of a journey that promised to be filled with laughter, heartache, and everything in between. And somehow, that was enough.

Days blurred into one another, and the dance studio became my refuge, a sacred space where I could unleash my turmoil through every leap and spin. The polished wooden floor gleamed under the soft overhead lights, transforming the room into a stage of emotional release. I channeled my feelings into movement, each choreography a silent plea for understanding and acceptance. With every aching pirouette, the thrill of new love intertwined with the familiar twinge of fear, a delicate balancing act that was as dizzying as it was exhilarating.

Rylan's presence was a magnetic force that pulled me in, even as the walls I had built around my heart began to crack. We danced together, the unspoken tension between us crackling like electricity, a powerful force that both thrilled and terrified me. He was always patient, a rock amidst my swirling emotions, yet I could see the flickers of uncertainty in his eyes. Each time I stumbled, each misstep echoed louder than the last, a reminder of the growing chasm between what I felt and what I allowed myself to express.

One afternoon, as the golden light filtered through the large windows, casting intricate patterns on the floor, I found myself watching him intently. He was practicing a series of intricate footwork, his movements smooth and precise. I couldn't help but admire how his body moved as if it were made of water, each motion flowing seamlessly into the next. In that moment, my heart raced with an urgency that could no longer be contained. I needed to take a leap—not just in dance but in life.

"Rylan," I said, my voice barely above a whisper, yet the tremor carried across the studio. He paused mid-step, his brow furrowing as he turned to face me. "Can we talk?"

The change in his demeanor was palpable; I could see the anticipation flaring in his eyes. "Yeah, of course. What's on your mind?"

His casual demeanor was disarming, yet the weight of my feelings felt monumental, like I was standing on the edge of a cliff. I took a deep breath, fighting against the torrent of emotions surging within me. "It's about us. About what happened last week."

"I'm listening," he said, his voice steady but his gaze searching mine for answers.

I stepped closer, my heart thundering in my chest. "I realized something during our last practice. I've been hiding behind the dance, using it as an escape rather than embracing what's right in front of me."

"What do you mean?" He leaned in slightly, his expression a mix of curiosity and concern, urging me to continue.

"I've been scared, Rylan. Scared of what I feel for you. Scared of how it might change everything between us. But I can't keep pretending that I don't feel this connection. It's real, and it's terrifying."

The moment hung between us, suspended like a dancer caught in midair. His eyes softened, understanding dawning as he took a step closer. "You don't have to be scared. I'm here, and I feel it too. I thought maybe it was just me being foolish."

"Foolish? Not at all! I mean, I've spent more time trying to convince myself that we shouldn't be together than actually enjoying what we have. And it's maddening."

He chuckled, a sound that warmed the air between us. "Maddening? You should've seen me last week. I thought my heart was going to leap out of my chest every time you smiled."

I couldn't help but laugh, the tension easing just a bit. "Well, my heart is apparently very dramatic then. It leaps, twirls, and does its own pirouette when I'm around you."

Rylan's laughter faded into something more serious, a glimmer of something deeper in his eyes. "So, what do we do now? We can't dance around this forever."

"Let's just embrace it," I said, feeling a surge of boldness. "Let's see where this goes. No more hiding. No more second-guessing."

His smile widened, revealing a boyish charm that made my heart flutter. "You mean I finally get to take you on a real date?"

"Only if you promise to keep your feet off my toes this time," I teased, my heart soaring at the thought of exploring this new territory together.

"Oh, I can't make any promises there. My footwork can be questionable," he replied, his voice rich with mischief. "But I'll bring the flowers."

"Just make sure they aren't the ones that wilt after a day."

With a grin, he stepped back, a playful glint in his eyes. "No wilted flowers, then. I'll find the most resilient ones."

As we returned to our routine, the air was charged with a different energy. The music seemed to swell in time with the rhythm of our hearts, transforming our movements into a conversation of their own. Every twirl and dip felt like a new promise, a silent agreement that we would explore the depths of our connection together, step by step.

But just as I began to bask in the warmth of our budding romance, a sudden crash shattered the moment. The studio door swung open, and in walked Cassie, my best friend and the queen of dramatic entrances. Her eyes were wide, her hair flying like a whirlwind. "You guys will not believe what just happened!"

Rylan shot me a look, a mix of amusement and concern, but I felt my heart plummet. Cassie's flair for the dramatic was legendary, and whatever news she brought was bound to shift the ground beneath us. "Cassie, now is not a great time—"

"Don't you 'Cassie' me! This is huge!" She didn't wait for an invitation, her voice rising above the music that still played in the background. "Remember that competition we talked about? The one in New York? Well, I just heard they're adding an amateur category, and you two have to enter!"

Rylan glanced at me, his expression a mix of excitement and caution. "We haven't even been practicing for a competition."

"But think about it! You could show everyone what you've got! I mean, you two are practically the perfect duo!" Cassie beamed, her enthusiasm palpable.

The idea spun through my mind like a tornado, both exhilarating and daunting. A competition meant scrutiny, judgment, and the pressure to perform at our best. It could either solidify our relationship or expose cracks I hadn't yet anticipated.

"Cassie, that's a lot of pressure," I said slowly, trying to process the whirlwind of emotions crashing around me. "What if we fail?"

Her expression shifted to one of unwavering confidence. "But what if you don't? This could be your chance to showcase everything you've been feeling—the passion, the connection. You have to take the leap, Ellie!"

As I looked at Rylan, I could see the excitement in his eyes, his spirit mirroring Cassie's fervor. The competition was a risk, a leap into the unknown, much like my feelings for him. But in that moment, surrounded by my friends and the potential for something more, I realized that perhaps the most beautiful moments were born from stepping beyond our comfort zones.

"Okay," I said, my heart racing with possibility. "Let's do it."

The moment hung in the air, thick with promise and unspoken fears, my confession wrapping around us like the fabric of a dancer's costume. Rylan's eyes glimmered, reflecting a mix of surprise and something deeper, an emotion that seemed to resonate with my own. I felt like a tightrope walker teetering over the abyss, heart racing, but the ground beneath us felt suddenly solid, forged by the intensity of our shared vulnerability.

"I love you," I repeated, the words no longer just an echo but a mantra, each syllable resonating in the depths of my soul. "And I'm ready to explore this with you. Really explore it."

His gaze held mine, unwavering, as a slow smile broke across his face, illuminating the shadows that had danced there moments before. "You have no idea how long I've wanted to hear you say that. I thought I was going to burst from all the waiting."

"Waiting can be torture," I quipped, relief flooding through me, lightening the weight that had settled on my chest. "I didn't know you had it in you to be so patient."

"Or that you'd be this stubborn," he shot back, a teasing glimmer in his eyes that made my stomach flip.

Just as the air between us began to sizzle with the newfound spark of our relationship, Cassie's exuberance crashed in like a rogue wave. "Did I hear someone say 'torture'? Because that's exactly what this competition is going to be—torturous fun!"

"Cassie!" I laughed, the moment momentarily shattered but not diminished. "You really know how to make an entrance."

"I aim to impress," she said, sweeping into the studio with all the grace of a whirlwind. "Now that we've confirmed your love, we need to start planning the choreography for the competition! You know, the one that's just around the corner? Like, really around the corner!"

Rylan's laughter echoed in my ears, a rich sound that filled the room, momentarily pushing aside my nerves. "How do you manage to make everything sound so urgent?"

Cassie placed her hands on her hips, a mock-serious look on her face. "Because it is urgent! You two have potential. The judges will be looking for something unique, something that stands out, and let's face it, you two have a connection that practically screams for attention."

I felt a mix of exhilaration and anxiety at the prospect. This was no longer just about me and Rylan; it was about performing, showcasing our emotions to a panel of strangers. "What do you think we should do?" I asked, glancing at Rylan, who seemed equally torn between excitement and trepidation.

He pondered for a moment, tapping his chin. "We need a story, something that pulls them in and doesn't let go. Something... dramatic."

"Dramatic is my middle name," Cassie chirped, already twirling toward the sound system. "I have just the song! It's the perfect blend of haunting and romantic—like you two!"

"Haunting?" I raised an eyebrow, but deep down, the idea of telling a story through dance thrilled me. "I don't know if that's what we're going for."

"Trust me!" Cassie said as she hit play, and a haunting melody filled the room, weaving around us like mist on a cool morning. The rhythm pulsed with an undercurrent of longing, a yearning that seemed to resonate with everything I felt for Rylan.

"Okay, okay," I conceded, allowing myself to be swept up in the moment. "Let's see where this goes."

Rylan stepped closer, his warmth radiating against me, and together we began to move. The music flowed through us, guiding our bodies as we created shapes and connections, our souls intertwined in the art we loved. I felt free, every ounce of tension slipping away with each graceful turn, lost in the moment and the story we were weaving.

As we danced, Cassie clapped along to the beat, her enthusiasm infectious. "That's it! Keep going! You guys look incredible!"

A surge of confidence bolstered my movements. I spun away from Rylan, feeling the pull of the music wrap around me like a lover's embrace. When I turned back, I found him watching me, a blend of admiration and something deeper in his eyes. In that moment, everything felt possible, the world outside the studio fading into obscurity.

But as the song reached its crescendo, a sharp crack echoed through the air—a sound that sliced through our reverie like a bolt of lightning. The studio door burst open once more, this time revealing a tall figure with an authoritative air, his expression a mix of urgency and concern.

"Ellie! Rylan!" The figure called, and I recognized him immediately—Mr. Cartwright, our dance instructor. The joy that had enveloped us was quickly replaced by a wave of confusion and apprehension.

"What's wrong?" I asked, my heart racing, instincts kicking in as dread began to creep into my veins.

"I just got a call," he said, his voice steady but urgent. "There's been a change in the competition. They've introduced a wildcard round, and it's happening this weekend. You two need to get ready. I know this is short notice, but this could be your chance to shine. A chance to stand out before the big competition!"

"What? A wildcard?" Cassie exclaimed, her eyes wide with excitement. "This is incredible! You two have to enter!"

Rylan and I exchanged a look, a silent conversation passing between us as the implications sank in. We were already preparing for the competition, but now the stakes had skyrocketed. The pressure to perform well had just doubled.

"I—" I began, but Cassie interrupted again, her excitement bubbling over.

"This is your moment! Think of it as your warm-up! You've got to go for it!"

"But we need time," Rylan said, his voice serious now. "We can't just throw something together."

Mr. Cartwright nodded, understanding the dilemma. "I know it's sudden, but sometimes the best performances come from the unexpected. You both have the talent and chemistry to make this work. Trust in yourselves."

My pulse quickened, torn between the thrill of opportunity and the weight of expectation. "When do we have to decide?"

"Now," he said, his gaze piercing. "The deadline is tonight. You'll need to submit your entry by midnight."

"Midnight?" I echoed, my mind racing. The clock was ticking, and I could almost hear it in my ears. This was our chance to truly showcase what we had together, but the thought of rushing into it made my stomach churn.

Rylan's eyes met mine, and in that brief glance, a million unspoken words lingered. I could see the question in his gaze: were we ready for this?

The music had faded into the background, but the rhythm of my heart beat fiercely, matching the pulse of uncertainty thrumming through the room. I took a deep breath, ready to speak my mind, but before I could, a sudden flash of movement caught my eye.

At the studio entrance, a figure loomed in the shadows, watching us intently. A chill raced down my spine. There was something unsettling about the way they stood there, silent and observant, as if they were waiting for the perfect moment to step into the light.

"Do you know who that is?" I whispered to Rylan, my voice barely audible over the sudden tension in the room.

His expression shifted from excitement to concern, and for the first time, I felt an undercurrent of fear creeping in. "No idea, but I don't like it."

As Mr. Cartwright turned to face the figure, the air shifted again, thickening with uncertainty. "Can I help you?" he asked, his tone shifting to one of authority.

The figure stepped forward, the light catching their features, revealing a familiar face—a face I never expected to see here, at this moment.

And with that, everything I thought I knew began to unravel, setting the stage for a confrontation that would change everything.

Chapter 19: The Weight of Truth

The sun hung low in the sky, casting a warm golden hue across the expansive garden, a tapestry of colors bursting forth from every corner. I watched as the petals of the roses unfurled, their delicate fragrances swirling in the warm breeze, teasing memories I tried to keep at bay. Each bloom seemed to dance in time with my racing heart, a vivid reminder of the promise I'd made to myself only days before: to embrace the chaos, to stand firm in the face of uncertainty.

Rylan sat beside me on the wrought-iron bench, the cool metal contrasting sharply with the heat radiating from the ground. He was quiet, his gaze fixed on a point far beyond the garden's hedges, as if searching for answers in the distant treetops that framed the horizon. I could feel the weight of his thoughts pressing down on us, heavy and unyielding, a tangible force in the air between us. I shifted, my fingers brushing against his, a simple gesture laden with significance, grounding us in this moment.

"Do you think we can make it work?" I asked, my voice barely above a whisper. The question hung there, fragile yet insistent, as though the very act of voicing it might shatter the delicate balance we had begun to forge.

His eyes flicked toward me, a mix of vulnerability and resolve flickering within their depths. "I don't know," he admitted, his honesty disarming. "But I want to try. I want to fight for us."

The sincerity of his words settled in my chest, warming me against the chill of doubt that threatened to creep in. Rylan had always possessed a quiet strength, a steadiness that drew me in even when I fought against it. He was a man forged in the fires of his past, the scars visible but not overwhelming, just like the way he wore his worries—almost like armor, but so much more fragile. The ghosts of his experiences hovered around him, but they didn't define him; they shaped him into someone who understood the nuances of love and loss.

"I can't promise it will be easy," I said, the words tumbling out before I could stop them. "I've been broken before, Rylan. I don't know if I'm strong enough to face the truth of it all."

He turned fully toward me, the intensity in his gaze piercing through the walls I had built around my heart. "Neither of us is whole," he said softly, his voice like a balm. "But we can build something new together. Piece by piece."

The concept was both terrifying and exhilarating. I wanted to believe him, to trust that we could forge a future from our fragmented pasts, but uncertainty twisted in my stomach like a coiled serpent. "And what if we can't?" I challenged, my defenses rising like a drawbridge, ready to close off access to my heart.

"Then we'll figure it out," he replied, a hint of a smile tugging at the corners of his mouth. "We'll fall apart and put ourselves back together, over and over again if we have to. Life's not a fairytale, sweetheart. It's messy and unpredictable. But I want to face all of that with you. Even if we stumble along the way."

The wry tone in his voice coaxed a reluctant laugh from my lips, a sound so foreign yet comforting. I hadn't allowed myself to laugh in so long, the weight of my burdens pressing down on me like a leaden cloak. Rylan's presence felt like sunlight breaking through the clouds, illuminating the corners of my heart I thought were forever shrouded in shadow.

"You make it sound so easy," I replied, my tone playful yet earnest. "Like it's just a walk in the park or something."

He chuckled, the sound deep and rich, resonating through me like a warm embrace. "Oh, trust me, it won't be a walk in the park. More like navigating a minefield while juggling flaming swords."

I met his gaze, the seriousness in his eyes making me realize he was only half joking. The past few years had been riddled with obstacles, and we were both scarred survivors of life's tumultuous storms. Yet, amidst the chaos, the thought of standing shoulder to shoulder with him, braving whatever lay ahead, sent a thrill through me.

"I can handle a minefield," I said, emboldened by the conviction in my own words. "Flaming swords? Maybe not so much. But I'm willing to learn."

Rylan smiled, that signature grin that could light up even the darkest corners of my heart. "Then we'll learn together, one step at a time. I promise to be there, ready to catch you when you stumble."

His hand found mine, fingers intertwining in a gesture that felt both new and familiar, a silent promise hanging in the air. It was a connection that transcended the past, reaching toward a future that, while uncertain, shimmered with possibilities.

As the sun dipped lower, painting the sky in hues of orange and purple, I could almost envision our lives unfolding in tandem. With every shared laugh, every moment of vulnerability, we began weaving a tapestry of our own, threads of hope and determination stitching together the remnants of our brokenness. In that moment, the weight of truth began to shift, transforming from a burden into a foundation on which we could build something remarkable.

The air hummed with potential, and for the first time in a long while, I felt ready to embrace it, ready to step into the unknown with Rylan by my side.

As twilight wrapped the garden in its soft embrace, the world around us softened, the vibrant colors of the day fading into gentle shadows. The air was rich with the scent of jasmine and blooming night-blooming cereus, intoxicating and almost surreal. It was as if the universe had conspired to create a moment suspended in time, one that felt both fragile and incredibly potent.

I turned to Rylan, feeling the weight of the evening settle on our shoulders, the unspoken words between us more potent than the fragrant blooms surrounding us. "So, what's the plan?" I asked, breaking the comfortable silence that had draped itself around us like a shawl. "Do we have one, or are we just winging it?"

A smirk danced on his lips, one that hinted at mischief and an underlying seriousness. "Oh, I have a plan," he said, leaning in closer as if to share a secret. "First, we spend the rest of the summer practicing our sword juggling. Then, we throw in a little bit of minefield navigation."

I rolled my eyes, unable to suppress a laugh that bubbled up from somewhere deep inside me. "Right, because that sounds totally sane. Should we add in skydiving for good measure?"

"Why not? Just add a pinch of spontaneity!" His laughter filled the air, and the sound wrapped around me like a warm blanket, instantly banishing the unease I'd felt moments before.

"But seriously," I pressed, my tone shifting to something more earnest. "What happens when the summer ends? We'll still be left with... whatever this is." I gestured between us, trying to capture the swirling mixture of hope and trepidation that filled the space.

Rylan's expression sobered, his brow furrowing slightly as he considered my words. "That's the beauty of it, isn't it? The uncertainty. It means we get to make choices. We can shape what comes next." His gaze locked onto mine, fierce and unwavering, as if daring me to challenge him.

I wanted to believe him. I wanted to throw caution to the wind and embrace whatever came our way, but the shadows of doubt loomed large, whispering of the pain I had endured before. "And what if we make the wrong choices?"

"Then we'll make new ones," he replied, a quiet confidence underpinning his words. "You know, like how you learned to bake. Remember the first time you tried to make that chocolate soufflé?"

A smile broke through my concern, a fond memory surfacing. "How could I forget? It was a disaster. It turned out more like a chocolate pancake than anything remotely soufflé-like."

"Exactly. But you didn't just give up, did you?" His eyes danced with warmth and amusement. "You tried again. You added a little more chocolate, maybe a splash of vanilla, and eventually, you created something amazing. That's life, isn't it? A series of attempts until we get it right."

The analogy struck a chord, weaving its way through my apprehension like a thread of gold. Rylan was right; life was a series of experiments. Each attempt built on the last, and while not every creation would be perfect, every effort had value. "So, I'm just supposed to keep baking?" I teased, attempting to lighten the mood.

"Absolutely," he said, his voice teasing yet sincere. "But with me around, I guarantee there will always be plenty of chocolate."

His easy charm reminded me of the lightness we shared, a connection built on laughter and light-hearted banter. But deep down, beneath the sweet layers, I sensed the gravity of our situation. The path ahead was filled with shadows, both of our pasts looming in the background, ready to trip us up if we weren't careful.

"Okay, so let's say we're willing to keep baking," I mused, tapping my chin as if I were contemplating the most important question of the century. "What's the first recipe?"

He leaned back, fingers intertwined, an amused smile playing on his lips. "Let's start with honesty," he suggested, his tone turning serious once more. "We lay everything out on the table—no sugar-coating, no pretenses. Just us."

I swallowed hard, the idea of absolute transparency stirring something deep within me. "You mean we share our fears, our secrets?"

"Exactly," he affirmed. "You first, or should I go?"

The challenge in his gaze made my heart race. Rylan had this way of peeling back layers, pushing me toward vulnerability even when it felt like I was exposing my very soul. "Fine, I'll go first," I said, steeling myself. "I'm afraid of getting hurt. I'm afraid that I'll wake up one day and realize I've poured everything into this... this us, and it'll crumble like my soufflé."

Rylan's expression softened, his gaze steady and reassuring. "And that's okay," he said gently. "Fear is part of it. But if we're honest with each other, we can navigate those fears together."

I nodded, feeling the strength of his words seep into my bones. "Alright, then. Your turn. What scares you?"

He took a breath, the lightness in his demeanor shifting to something more solemn. "I'm scared of being abandoned again. I've had people walk away from me—people I thought would always be there. I don't want to lose you the way I've lost them."

A pang of empathy shot through me, the weight of his confession settling heavily in the air. "You're not going to lose me," I reassured him, my voice firm. "We're in this together."

"Together," he echoed, the word heavy with promise. It felt as if we had crossed an invisible line, stepping deeper into a realm where trust and honesty could flourish.

In that sacred space, beneath the twilight sky, surrounded by the perfume of flowers and the lingering warmth of the day, I realized that love was more than just a leap of faith. It was the courage to face the uncertainty of life hand in hand, forging a path built on honesty, understanding, and an unyielding commitment to each other. The summer stretched before us, a blank canvas waiting for the colors of our lives to paint it anew.

The air thickened with unspoken promises as Rylan and I leaned into the vulnerability of our confessions. The fading light of day cloaked the garden in an ethereal glow, casting long shadows that seemed to dance around us like lingering ghosts. It felt like a reckoning, a delicate balance of honesty and hope where every word held the power to reshape our futures.

"You know," I said, my voice teasingly light as I tried to diffuse the tension that had settled between us like a heavy quilt, "if we're going to be completely honest, I should admit that I'm also terrified of your cooking."

Rylan's laughter erupted, clear and rich, and I couldn't help but join in. "My cooking? How dare you! I have a culinary prowess that rivals the finest chefs!"

"Oh please," I countered, holding back a grin. "The last time you cooked, I thought I might need a hazmat suit. There were fire alarms involved. I still have the trauma."

"Alright, fair point," he chuckled, shaking his head in mock defeat. "But in my defense, my skills have improved. I could totally whip up a soufflé that won't collapse next time. Just wait and see!"

"Is that a challenge?" I raised an eyebrow, the playful banter igniting a familiar spark between us. "Because I'm all in for a rematch."

"Bring it on, chef!" His eyes twinkled with mischief, the mood lifting as we slipped back into the comfort of our easy rapport.

Yet, beneath the lighthearted exchange, the reality of our situation loomed large. I studied Rylan's face, tracing the gentle lines of his jaw, the way his brow furrowed slightly when he was deep in thought. It was a face that had seen its share of battles, one that bore the weight of a past he was still learning to navigate. I wanted to ask him more about it—the fears that lay beneath his bravado—but something held me back.

The evening deepened, and the first stars began to peek out, twinkling like tiny promises scattered across the indigo sky. "Let's get serious for a moment," I said, settling back into the bench, my fingers brushing against the cool metal. "If we're going to do this—this us—then we need to establish some ground rules. Like, no cooking until we've perfected the basics."

Rylan feigned shock. "You mean to tell me you don't want me to surprise you with breakfast in bed?"

"No, I want to survive my mornings!" I shot back with a laugh, the tension easing further. "And speaking of rules, how about we agree to always communicate? No matter how awkward it gets."

He nodded, his expression sobering. "Absolutely. No more sweeping things under the rug. We face it all, no matter how messy it gets."

"Agreed," I said, my heart pounding in rhythm with the resolve that began to form between us. "And if I ever find myself backsliding, remind me that I promised to let you know instead of hiding in my head."

Rylan's eyes softened, an understanding passing between us. "And I'll promise to keep my past from creeping in and overshadowing our future. No more ghosts."

The warmth of his vow wrapped around me, a shield against the world outside our little cocoon. For a fleeting moment, it felt as if we could conquer anything together. But the tranquility was a double-edged sword; with every promise came the lingering doubt that the past had a way of resurfacing, uninvited.

"I think we should also decide what we'll do when life throws us curveballs," I suggested, feeling a shiver of uncertainty. "Because it will. It always does."

Rylan leaned closer, his voice low and steady. "Then we'll adapt. We'll be like that willow tree in the storm—bending but not breaking. And if one of us gets knocked down, the other will be there to help lift them back up."

I couldn't help but smile at the imagery. "Wow, you really know how to make a girl feel inspired. If we weren't navigating a minefield of feelings, I might think we were writing a self-help book."

"Trust me, if this whole thing falls apart, I'll take the blame," he said, a sly grin forming. "Just remember, it was your idea to juggle those swords."

The banter lightened my heart, but a weight settled back in as I considered the reality lurking just beneath the surface. "So, tell me—what happens when life doesn't give us the option to adapt? What do we do then?"

"Then we get creative," he said, his tone suddenly serious. "We build our own paths, even if that means stumbling a little along the way."

The thought of stumbling together was both reassuring and terrifying. I wanted to believe that we could create something beautiful from our imperfections. Yet, the reality of our pasts loomed like storm clouds on the horizon, threatening to spill over at any moment.

As the last vestiges of daylight faded into twilight, a soft rustle drew my attention to the edge of the garden. A figure emerged from the shadows, lingering just beyond the reach of the warm glow from the patio lights. The unease that had settled in my stomach suddenly twisted into a knot of apprehension.

"Rylan," I said, my voice dropping to a whisper. "Do you see that?"

His eyes followed mine, the playful spark dimming as concern etched across his features. "Yeah. Who is that?"

Before we could piece together what was happening, the figure stepped forward, revealing a familiar face, one I hadn't seen in what felt like ages. "I thought I might find you here," the newcomer said, their voice smooth yet heavy with intention.

Recognition hit me like a wave, and my heart raced as I took in the sight of someone from my past—someone I had hoped would remain a distant memory. I shifted my gaze to Rylan, who was watching me with a mixture of confusion and concern.

"Wren?" I breathed, my pulse quickening. "What are you doing here?"

As the familiar figure stepped closer, I could see the tension etched in their features, the tight grip of secrets spilling over into the night. "We need to talk," Wren insisted, their eyes darting between Rylan and me, revealing more than their lips could speak.

The weight of the moment pressed down on me, a tidal wave of uncertainty crashing over the fragile foundations we had just begun to build. In that moment, I realized we were teetering on the edge of something vast and unpredictable, a truth that could either bind us closer together or rip us apart.

Chapter 20: Unraveled Threads

The dance studio felt like a sanctuary, a cocoon of rhythm and movement where the outside world faded into mere whispers. The polished wooden floor gleamed under the soft, diffused light, casting elongated shadows that danced alongside us. I twirled and leaped, surrendering to the music that wrapped around me like a warm embrace. Each beat reverberated through my bones, urging me to lose myself in the choreography of life. Yet, no matter how I tried to immerse myself in the vibrant world of dance, the incessant ringing of my phone shattered the illusion, each call a reminder that life outside these walls was far from perfect.

Rylan stood by the mirror, a quiet observer and a patient confidant, his brow furrowed slightly as he watched me. His dark hair fell messily over his forehead, framing eyes that always seemed to harbor a glint of mischief and a depth that drew me in like a moth to a flame. He had this way of making the world feel lighter, even when the shadows threatened to encroach. But I could see the concern etched across his face; he knew me well enough to recognize the shift in my spirit.

"Take a break, Elle," he called out, his voice warm and inviting, breaking through my mental fog. "You're dancing like you're trying to outrun something."

I halted mid-pirouette, the world tilting as I landed back on my feet. Rylan had a knack for grounding me, even when I was spinning out of control. He approached, his steps measured, as if he were walking through a field of delicate flowers, afraid to crush anything underfoot.

"Why don't you come sit for a minute?" he suggested, gesturing to the worn-out cushions in the corner of the studio. The fabric was frayed, holding the imprints of countless hours spent in deep conversations, laughter, and sometimes tears. I nodded, feeling the weight of my thoughts pulling me down, and followed him to the corner, where the atmosphere felt more intimate, cocooned away from the echoing walls.

"I'm okay," I tried to insist, forcing a smile that felt brittle on my lips. Rylan arched an eyebrow, skepticism dancing in his expression.

"Right. You're okay in the same way a jigsaw puzzle is whole with missing pieces." He leaned closer, his voice dropping to a conspiratorial whisper, "You can't fool me. What's really going on?"

The floodgates threatened to burst open as I looked into his eyes, those pools of understanding that often made me feel as if he could see straight into my soul. It was maddeningly disarming. With a deep breath, I surrendered to the urge to share the tangled web of my thoughts. "It's my mom," I admitted, the words tumbling out in a rush. "Her health keeps deteriorating. The calls... They never seem to stop. It's like each one is a new chapter in a book I don't want to read."

Rylan's expression softened, and his fingers brushed against mine, grounding me further. "That's heavy, Elle. You don't have to carry it alone."

"I know," I whispered, the lump in my throat constricting as I fought back the sting of tears. "But I need to be strong for her. It's just—sometimes I feel like I'm on this tightrope, trying not to lose my balance. And then there's you..." I trailed off, unsure how to articulate the complex feelings swirling within me.

He tilted his head slightly, a playful smile breaking through the tension. "Me? I'm just the guy who dances with you. Not exactly a weight on your shoulders."

I chuckled, but the laughter felt hollow. "That's just it, Rylan. You're more than that. You're...everything. And the thought of losing you, of losing the joy we have..." My voice faltered as I tried to find the right words, the fear crashing over me like a wave.

His gaze turned serious, his thumb brushing across the back of my hand, a simple gesture that conveyed a universe of understanding. "Hey, I'm not going anywhere. We're a team, remember?"

I nodded, but the weight of uncertainty lingered. "But what if I can't be the partner you deserve? What if I crumble under all this pressure?"

"Then we'll build you back up," he replied, his tone unwavering. "You think I haven't faced my own battles? We all have our demons, Elle. It's what makes us human. And I like you just the way you are, tangled threads and all."

His honesty wrapped around me like a soft blanket, warming the cold edges of my anxiety. The tension in my shoulders eased, if only a fraction, as I leaned into him, the familiar scent of sandalwood and fresh linen enveloping me. "I don't want to lose you. I can't bear the thought," I murmured, vulnerability spilling out in my words.

Rylan chuckled softly, the sound reverberating in the space between us. "You're not going to lose me. Just promise me you won't shut me out when things get tough. I'm here for the long haul, even if that means dancing through the storm."

The metaphor resonated deeply, and I found a flicker of hope igniting within me. I had always loved dancing, but it was in moments like these that I truly understood its significance. It wasn't just about the steps or the music; it was about the connections we forged, the trust we built. And right now, Rylan was my anchor in the tempest, reminding me that even amidst the chaos, there was beauty in sharing burdens, in unraveling threads together.

With a newfound determination, I squeezed his hand, the warmth anchoring me as I began to envision a path forward. The fraying edges of my life didn't have to signify an end. Maybe they were merely a sign of transformation, a call to weave a richer tapestry that embraced both joy and sorrow. As the music swelled in the background, I felt a spark of strength igniting within me, whispering that I could navigate the uncharted waters ahead, as long as I had Rylan by my side.

The air was heavy with the scent of lavender and worn leather as I stepped into my apartment, the familiar chaos greeting me like an old friend. The cluttered living room was a gallery of memories—a stack of books precariously teetering on the coffee table, framed photographs of laughter captured in time, and the ever-present dance shoes strewn haphazardly by the door, remnants of my day-to-day life. It felt like a whirlwind of activity was contained within these four walls, yet a palpable stillness hung in the air, mirroring the tension that had woven itself into the fabric of my existence.

I dropped my bag onto the floor, letting it thud against the wood as I sank onto the couch, the cushions enveloping me like a welcoming embrace. The stillness was suffocating, almost mocking, and I stared blankly at the wall, my thoughts a cacophony of worry and fear. The weight of the day pressed down on my chest like a lead blanket, and I fought the urge to pick up my phone, to scroll through the endless updates about my mother's health. Every time the screen lit up, my heart raced, the fear of bad news coiling tightly within me.

Just as I was about to succumb to the darkness of my thoughts, the door swung open, and Rylan stepped inside, a burst of light in the dimness of my apartment. He had a penchant for arriving unexpectedly, like a comet streaking through my universe. Today, his hair was damp from the rain, and he wore a smirk that was both infuriating and charming, a perfect blend of confidence and mischief.

"Hey there, couch potato. I come bearing gifts," he declared, his voice teasing as he held up a takeout bag from my favorite Thai restaurant. The fragrant aroma wafted through the air, momentarily distracting me from my spiraling thoughts.

I couldn't help but smile, a fleeting reprieve from the heaviness that had settled in my heart. "You always know how to brighten a gloomy day, don't you?" I quipped, leaning back against the couch and watching him move about the kitchen like a man who knew his way around my clutter.

"Only when I'm not too busy rescuing you from your own melodrama," he shot back, his grin widening as he expertly maneuvered through the mess.

"Melodrama? You make it sound like I'm starring in a soap opera," I laughed, but the sound felt brittle.

"More like a tragicomedy," he replied, and I threw a pillow at him, which he dodged with an agility that would have impressed a dancer.

"Okay, Mr. Wise Guy, what makes you think I'm a tragicomedy?" I asked, my voice light yet laced with sincerity.

He paused, placing the food down on the counter, his expression shifting to something more contemplative. "Because you're too strong to be a straight tragedy. You face everything head-on, but you also have this way of turning the mundane into something beautiful—even when it's messy."

His words hung in the air, a bittersweet reminder of the duality of my life. I wanted to believe him, to embrace the beauty amidst the chaos, but the thought of my mother's declining health loomed over me like a storm cloud, threatening to drown out any flicker of hope.

Rylan's voice broke through my reverie. "You should eat something. Trust me, it's hard to conquer the world on an empty stomach."

I sighed, the familiar pull of my appetite finally coaxing me back to the present. "Okay, okay, you win." I moved to the kitchen, where he had already unpacked the fragrant feast—a glorious assortment of Pad Thai, green curry, and spring rolls that promised to ignite my senses.

As we sat down to eat, the atmosphere shifted. With every bite, I could feel the heaviness begin to lift, the flavors igniting sparks of joy amid the shadows. "You really should consider a career as a professional chef," I teased, gesturing to the takeout.

"Only if you promise to be my number one fan," he replied, his gaze piercing yet playful.

"Deal," I shot back, laughter bubbling up as I leaned forward, the momentary connection grounding me. But beneath the laughter was an undercurrent of anxiety, swirling and nagging at the edges of my consciousness.

The conversation flowed easily, a dance of witty banter and shared stories. We reminisced about our first dance class together, the awkwardness that had initially bound us, and how that awkwardness had transformed into a partnership that felt as seamless as breathing. But as we navigated through the lighthearted moments, I found it increasingly difficult to conceal the turmoil roiling inside me.

"Elle," Rylan said, his tone shifting as he leaned back in his chair, his gaze steady. "I know there's something more beneath the surface. You can't keep hiding from it."

I hesitated, the familiar dread creeping back in, threatening to suffocate the moment. "I just... I don't want to drag you into my mess. I can handle it. I've always handled it."

"Handling it doesn't mean carrying the burden alone. Let me help you," he urged, his sincerity striking a chord deep within me.

A heavy silence fell, the walls closing in as my defenses began to crumble. I felt the weight of his gaze, urging me to lay my fears bare. "It's just... it's overwhelming," I admitted, the words spilling out like the floodgates had been opened. "I'm terrified of what's coming. I feel like I'm teetering on the edge of something I can't control."

His brow furrowed, concern etching itself into his features. "You don't have to face it alone. Whatever it is, we'll face it together. Just like we do in dance."

The comparison resonated deeply, and I found myself clinging to it, the rhythm of our lives intertwining in a way that felt both comforting and daunting. I took a breath, my heart racing as I realized how much I wanted to let him in, to share the tangled threads that made up my life.

But just as I was about to reveal the depths of my fears, my phone buzzed on the table, shattering the moment like glass. I glanced down, the screen illuminating my mother's name. A chill ran through me as I picked it up, anxiety knotting in my stomach. "It's my mom," I whispered, the weight of the moment pressing down on me.

"Answer it," Rylan encouraged, his eyes locked onto mine with unwavering support.

Taking a shaky breath, I accepted the call, the familiar voice on the other end a mixture of warmth and worry. "Hey, sweetheart. I wanted to check in."

The conversation unfolded, each word tinged with the fragility of our circumstances. I could hear the tremor in her voice, the fatigue that had seeped into every crevice of her being. As she spoke, I felt the walls closing in again, the reality of her situation crashing over me like an unforgiving tide.

"Everything okay?" Rylan's voice was a gentle murmur beside me, his presence a tether in the storm.

I nodded, even though she couldn't see me, the lie tasting bitter on my tongue. "Yeah, just... catching up. You know how it is."

But as the call progressed, I realized that my carefully crafted facade was beginning to crack. Each "I love you" from my mother felt like a thread being pulled, the fear of loss unraveling the tapestry of my life. And yet, as I glanced at Rylan, his unwavering support grounding me in the chaos, I felt a glimmer of strength begin to flicker within. Perhaps the journey ahead would not be one of solitude but of partnership, two souls navigating the tangled threads together, each step a dance toward an uncertain yet hopeful future.

The call ended, and I placed my phone on the table with a shaky hand, the silence that followed felt heavy and all-consuming. Rylan's gaze held mine, a silent understanding passing between us. The concern in his eyes deepened, shadows of doubt flickering behind his unwavering support. "You okay?" he asked softly, his voice slicing through the tension that had settled in the air.

"Not really," I admitted, swallowing hard as the reality of my mother's condition loomed larger than life. I could still hear her voice echoing in my mind, the way she tried to be brave for me, assuring me that she was fine even as the worry lingered beneath her words like a storm cloud. "She sounds so tired. I hate this helpless feeling."

Rylan shifted in his seat, the intensity of the moment prompting him to lean closer, his elbows resting on his knees. "It's okay to feel that way. It's a lot to carry. But you're not alone in this, Elle. I'm here."

His sincerity was a balm to my frayed nerves, yet the emotional burden still felt insurmountable. "I don't want to drag you into this," I said, frustration creeping into my voice. "You deserve someone who isn't constantly battling a storm."

Rylan shook his head, a fierce determination set in his jaw. "You think I'm going to run because you're facing challenges? You're tough, and that's one of the things I admire most about you. But everyone has their moments. Even you."

"You're sweet. But let's be honest; I'm more like a jumbled mess," I said, attempting to lighten the mood, though the tension still lingered like an unwelcome guest.

He chuckled, the sound warming the space between us. "Yes, but a charming mess. Besides, it's in the jumbled moments that we discover who we really are."

I let out a breath I hadn't realized I was holding, the gravity of his words settling in. There was wisdom in his quirkiness, a truth I desperately needed to cling to. "You make it sound so easy," I replied, a small smile breaking through.

"Only because I have you to inspire me. If you can face the world with grace, I can at least try to keep up."

With every exchange, Rylan was slowly stitching together the frayed edges of my heart, and for the first time in days, I felt a flicker of hope. I stood, moving toward the window, where the city skyline shimmered against the dusk, each light a reminder that life continued despite the chaos. "I just wish I could take the pain away from her," I whispered, more to myself than to him.

"Maybe you can't take it away, but you can be there for her. Sometimes that's all we can do—just show up and be present."

"Yeah, I know," I said, wrapping my arms around myself, feeling both exposed and protected in this moment. "I just... wish I had the strength to face it all head-on. What if I fail her?"

Rylan stood and came up behind me, resting a comforting hand on my shoulder. "Then you learn from it. We all stumble sometimes. You're human, Elle."

The warmth of his touch sent a shiver down my spine, a stark reminder of the intimacy we shared. I turned to face him, our eyes locking, and for a fleeting moment, the world outside faded into oblivion. "What if I'm not strong enough?" I murmured, vulnerability spilling out like an unguarded secret.

"You are strong enough," he affirmed, his voice steady and sincere. "Trust that you've got it in you. Just like you trust yourself on the dance floor, even when you misstep."

The confidence in his words sparked a resolve within me, a flicker of light in the encompassing darkness. I reached out and took his hand, the contact grounding me. "Thank you for believing in me," I said, the words flowing with sincerity.

"Always," he replied, his thumb caressing the back of my hand, igniting a warmth that spread through my veins. "Now, how about we dance? Even if it's just for a few minutes, let's remind ourselves of the joy in movement."

I hesitated, the weight of my worries still clinging to me, but I could see the invitation in his eyes—the promise of freedom and the chance to escape, even for a little while. "Okay," I said, a smile breaking through the uncertainty. "Let's do it."

Rylan stepped back, switching on the speaker, and soon the room filled with a melodic tune that danced through the air like a wisp of smoke. I felt the music wrap around me, urging me to let go, to surrender to the rhythm. Rylan held out his hand, and I took it, allowing him to guide me as we began to sway together, two bodies merging into one harmonious movement.

With every step, I felt the tightness in my chest begin to loosen, the music carrying my worries away like leaves on a gentle stream. We spun and twirled, laughter bubbling up between us as we lost ourselves in the moment. The world outside faded into a blur, and for the first time in what felt like forever, I felt truly alive.

As the song built to a crescendo, Rylan pulled me closer, our bodies moving in sync, breaths mingling in the space between us. "See? This is what it's all about," he said, his voice low and filled with a playful intensity. "Finding joy in the chaos."

I couldn't help but laugh, feeling a rush of warmth flood my cheeks as I gazed up at him. "You're right. This is definitely my favorite kind of chaos."

He grinned, that lopsided smile that always sent butterflies dancing in my stomach. But just as I leaned in closer, the phone buzzed again, slicing through the magic of the moment. Rylan's expression shifted, and I felt the weight of reality settle back in.

"Just ignore it," he urged, but the nagging worry crept back, clawing at my resolve. "It could be important," I replied, already reaching for my phone, unwilling to silence my mother's voice yet again.

I glanced at the screen, my heart dropping as I read the text. "It's my mom. She's in the hospital."

The world around me tilted, the music fading into an unsettling silence. "What? Elle, are you okay?" Rylan's voice was suddenly urgent, his hand gripping my shoulder, anchoring me in this dizzying moment.

I shook my head, panic bubbling up within me. "I don't know. I need to go to her. I need to—"

Before I could finish, the phone rang, and I stared at it, fear racing through my veins. It was my mother. In that instant, the room shrank around me, the walls closing in as I fought to find my breath. Rylan's presence felt distant, even as he remained by my side, his concern palpable.

"Elle," he said, his voice steady. "You can do this. You're strong. Just take it one step at a time."

The ringing continued, and I hesitated, caught in a whirlwind of emotions. The choice loomed before me, the unknown stretching out like a chasm. With shaking hands, I answered the call, and the world around me held its breath.

"Hello?" I managed, my heart pounding, each beat echoing in the silence that enveloped us, the uncertainty of what lay ahead threatening to unravel everything.

Chapter 21: The Storm Within

Every morning, the sun rises, painting the horizon in soft hues of peach and gold, a beautiful illusion that nothing is amiss. Yet, with each daybreak, I feel a shroud of gray draping over my heart, heavy with unspoken fears. My mother's laughter, once the soothing balm of my childhood, is now a distant echo, replaced by sterile hospital sounds and hushed conversations. The news about her impending surgery landed like a brick in my stomach, each detail a fresh wound that refused to heal. I never anticipated this—never wanted to be on the other side of those clinical walls where hope wavered like a candle in a draft.

On a particularly gloomy afternoon, as clouds rolled in from the bayou, Rylan stopped by unannounced, concern etched across his handsome features. His tousled hair caught the flickering light, his shirt clinging just enough to hint at the muscle underneath. My heart did a small flip at the sight of him, but the tumult inside me was louder than any heartbeat, drowning out the warmth that bloomed in my chest. I stood by the window, arms crossed defensively, watching raindrops race down the glass, each one a tiny soldier in my battle against the chaos within.

"I thought you could use some company," he said, voice laced with that familiar mixture of tenderness and urgency. He stepped inside, leaving a trail of warmth that clashed sharply with the chill that had taken root in my bones. I wanted to melt into him, to wrap myself in his arms and forget, even for a moment, the reality waiting just beyond the door.

"I appreciate it, but I really don't feel like talking," I replied, my tone sharper than I intended. The words cut through the air, leaving an uncomfortable silence in their wake. Rylan's brow furrowed, his lips pressing together as if fighting against the tide of emotions swelling between us.

"Okay, but you don't have to go through this alone. I'm here, you know?" His words were a lifeline, yet they felt like chains. The storm within me roared louder, reminding me of everything I didn't want to face.

"Maybe I need to be alone," I shot back, the defensiveness spilling over. I turned away, my gaze focusing on the gray skies beyond, as if they could somehow offer solace. The truth was, I was terrified—terrified of losing her, terrified of the unknown that loomed like a specter. I wanted to shield Rylan from the weight of my grief, to protect him from the darkness that threatened to swallow me whole.

He sighed, a sound heavy with frustration, but also understanding. "You think you're protecting me by pushing me away, but that's not how this works. I care about you, and I want to help." The sincerity in his voice hung in the air, tugging at my heart, but I fortified my resolve. The thought of him seeing me break, of revealing the cracks in my armor, was more than I could bear.

"Help?" I echoed, bitterness tinging the word. "What do you think you can do? You can't fix this. You can't fix her." I took a deep breath, my chest tightening. The storm inside me surged, threatening to spill over. "And I don't want to drag you into my mess."

Rylan stepped closer, bridging the gap between us. "You're not a mess. You're human, and this is hard. It's okay to feel lost, but shutting me out won't help you. It'll only make things worse." His voice was low, coaxing, and a part of me yearned to let him in. But I clung to my walls, stubbornly refusing to crumble.

I forced a smile, though it felt more like a grimace. "I appreciate the sentiment, really. But I need to handle this on my own."

Rylan's expression softened, his eyes searching mine as if trying to peel away the layers I had carefully constructed. "Just promise me you won't disappear. I'll be here when you're ready."

With that, he stepped back, leaving a silence that felt both heavy and liberating. I nodded, even though the promise felt like a fragile thread. As the door closed behind him, a part of me wanted to cry out, to scream that I was breaking. Instead, I returned to the window, staring out at the storm brewing in the distance, the clouds darkening ominously.

Days turned into a blur of waiting rooms and whispered conversations. Each tick of the clock echoed in my mind, amplifying my anxiety. I found myself slipping deeper into avoidance, the vibrant life of New Orleans fading into a muted backdrop. The café on the corner, once my haven filled with laughter and the aroma of freshly brewed coffee, felt foreign without Rylan's easy banter to color my days.

I avoided his calls, convinced that distancing myself was the best way to cope. I busied myself with trivial tasks—cleaning, organizing, anything that could distract me from the gnawing fear that my mother's surgery could lead to something irreversible. I plastered on a smile for visitors, the façade of normalcy becoming a mask that weighed heavier with each passing day.

In the depths of my solitude, the storm raged on. Guilt washed over me, fierce and relentless, like the rain pouring down outside. I should have let Rylan in. I should have leaned on him, let him share the burden instead of isolating myself. The guilt was suffocating, a reminder that love thrives in vulnerability, yet I fought it with every ounce of strength I had left.

And then came the call, the one I had been dreading and simultaneously anticipating. The doctor's voice, steady yet filled with a weighty gravity, shattered the fragile calm I had constructed. I felt the world tilt beneath me, as if the very ground had shifted, and I was teetering on the edge of an abyss. I had to face it now—the storm inside was no longer a choice but a necessity. I needed to confront the turmoil, for my mother's sake, for my own.

The battle within me was far from over, but perhaps it was time to let the tempest rage, to find strength in the chaos and embrace the vulnerability I had fought so hard to avoid.

The days that followed felt like an endless loop, each one blending into the next, with only the drumming rain against the roof to punctuate the monotony. I shuffled through my routines, but nothing held meaning anymore. The vibrant chatter of the café, where Rylan and I had shared countless cups of coffee, now felt like a cruel reminder of what I was pushing away. The barista's cheerful "Good morning!" sounded like a taunt, a reminder of the person I was before this storm descended.

In my cocoon of solitude, I tried to pretend that everything was fine, but inside, I was unraveling. Each time my phone buzzed with a message from Rylan, my chest tightened, a visceral reaction to the guilt that clawed at my insides. I thought about replying—about allowing his words to soothe my fraying edges—but the thought of his concern only amplified my shame. How could I admit that I was drowning when I had promised myself I would stay afloat?

I avoided social media like the plague, knowing full well that Rylan would be sharing snippets of his life, the adventures I was missing out on, the laughter that seemed so far away. It felt like a betrayal to look at those moments without him, a stark contrast to the fog of worry and despair that had settled over my own existence. I longed for connection, yet I recoiled from it, a moth drawn to the flame only to swerve at the last moment.

One afternoon, lost in thought as I scrolled through old photos on my phone, I stumbled upon a picture of my mother and me, arms slung around each other, smiles wide and carefree. The vibrant colors of that day felt like a different lifetime. The warmth of her embrace was palpable, a stark contrast to the sterile coldness of the hospital rooms. I swiped to the next image—Rylan and me, faces alight with laughter at the jazz festival last summer. His laughter was infectious, a melody that wrapped around me like a warm blanket. A small ache settled in my chest, an uncomfortable reminder that I was isolating myself from the very people who wanted to be there for me.

With a sigh, I tossed my phone onto the couch, the soft cushions swallowing it whole, as if even they wanted to shield me from the reality outside. My thoughts turned dark, spiraling down paths I didn't want to travel. I pictured my mother in that hospital bed, surrounded by machines, her spirit dimming like a candle flickering in a storm. The guilt swelled within me, constricting my breath. I should be there. I should be fighting for her, not hiding from the world.

As the storm clouds gathered outside, a sharp knock broke my reverie. The sound reverberated through the quiet room, pulling me from my thoughts. Hesitant, I opened the door, half-expecting to find a delivery person or perhaps a neighbor. Instead, Rylan stood there, a vision of determination and warmth, raindrops clinging to his dark hair, his eyes fierce with concern.

"Hey," he said, voice a mix of relief and frustration. "I was beginning to think you'd turned into a hermit. Can I come in?"

I stood frozen in the doorway, the weight of his presence washing over me like the rain outside. Part of me wanted to slam the door and retreat into my cocoon, but the other part, the part that craved human connection, fought against that impulse. I stepped aside, allowing him entry, the air thickening with unspoken words and emotions that hung like a curtain between us.

"Nice place you've got here," he quipped, glancing around the disheveled living room. "Very... cozy."

"Cozy? More like a tornado hit it." I forced a smile, but it felt brittle, like glass on the verge of shattering.

"I was trying to be polite," he replied, his lips quirking in that lopsided smile that always made my stomach flip. "You could always hire a maid, you know. They're pretty good at making disaster zones look presentable."

I couldn't help but chuckle, a genuine sound that broke the tension, if only slightly. "If only my problems could be solved with a broom and a dustpan."

He stepped closer, his gaze piercing yet gentle. "Your problems might need a bit more than that, but we can start with a good conversation. You've been MIA for too long, and I'm worried about you."

"Worried? Really?" I feigned nonchalance, crossing my arms as if I could block his sincerity with sheer will. "I'm fine. Just taking some time for myself."

"Taking time for yourself?" He echoed, incredulous. "This isn't a spa retreat; it's a personal pity party."

I felt the heat rise to my cheeks, the sharpness of his words cutting deeper than I expected. "It's not like I'm sitting here with a face mask and cucumber slices," I shot back, trying to keep the conversation light, though my heart raced with the truth buried beneath the sarcasm.

Rylan stepped closer, his expression shifting to something softer, more earnest. "I'm not saying you have to be okay all the time, but isolating yourself isn't the answer. You're stronger than that, you know? And you don't have to do this alone."

His words echoed in the room, resonating with the truth I had been avoiding. The vulnerability I tried to shield myself from now felt like a raw nerve, exposed and tingling. I wanted to argue, to cling to my stubbornness, but the honesty in his gaze disarmed me. "I just... I don't want to burden you," I finally admitted, my voice barely a whisper.

"Burden? Please. You're not a burden. You're my friend, and friends help each other, especially when the going gets tough." He paused, running a hand through his hair, frustration evident. "What is it going to take for you to let me in?"

I stared at him, my heart pounding, each beat a reminder of the walls I had erected. The storm inside me waged war against the kindness that radiated from him. "I don't want to drag you into my mess," I murmured, my resolve beginning to crumble.

"Newsflash: Life is messy," he replied, crossing his arms and leaning against the wall, casual yet firm. "If we only stuck around for the good times, what kind of friends would we be?"

His words settled around us, the air thick with an unspoken understanding. I swallowed hard, a lump forming in my throat. Perhaps it was time to let the storm within me spill over, to embrace the vulnerability I had fought so hard to suppress.

"Okay," I said finally, my voice trembling. "But only if you promise to stay."

"Always," he said, and in that moment, the storm within me shifted. The winds calmed, and for the first time in days, I felt the warmth of hope flicker to life, fragile yet persistent, ready to face whatever came next.

The room felt different now, a fragile truce hanging in the air between Rylan and me, as if we were both dancers navigating an intricate routine where one misstep could send us tumbling. The walls that had felt so suffocating just moments ago began to breathe again, the weight of my solitude lifting slightly, like the first hint of sunlight piercing through heavy clouds. I could see the concern etched in his brow, a mixture of empathy and exasperation that made me realize just how much I needed him here—his unwavering presence, the warmth of his laughter, the way he made everything seem just a little more manageable.

"Let's go for a walk," he suggested, his tone light but firm, as though he could sense the tension coiling within me. "I promise I won't make you talk if you don't want to."

I hesitated, my heart fluttering with indecision. Outside, the rain had lightened to a gentle drizzle, the kind that made everything glisten and breathe anew. "Okay," I finally replied, my voice tinged with uncertainty. "But don't blame me if I start spouting poetry about the weather. My muse is currently drowning in angst."

He laughed, the sound rich and genuine, cutting through the remnants of my melancholy. "I'd pay good money to hear that. Lead the way, Emily Dickinson."

As we stepped outside, the fresh scent of damp earth filled my lungs, invigorating and crisp. The streets of New Orleans, usually teeming with life, were quieter today, the occasional splash of a car speeding through puddles punctuating the tranquil stillness. I walked beside Rylan, the rhythm of our footsteps creating a comforting cadence. The city had a way of wrapping its arms around you, the historic buildings standing sentinel, their worn façades whispering stories of resilience and hope.

"Is it me, or does this weather feel like it's straight out of a movie?" I mused, glancing up at the slate-gray sky. "You know, the kind where the protagonist stands in the rain contemplating life choices?"

"Or the part where they realize they're madly in love with their best friend," Rylan added, his gaze flicking toward me, a hint of mischief in his eyes.

"Oh, please. You'd have to be a pretty terrible friend to fall for me."

His laughter rang out, a sweet melody that made my heart flutter. "Have you looked in the mirror lately? You're not giving yourself enough credit. Just because you're currently going through a storm doesn't mean you're not also a rainbow."

I rolled my eyes, but warmth spread through me at his words. "I'm pretty sure rainbows don't come with baggage."

"Everyone's got baggage, Em. It's just a matter of how much you want to carry and who you want to carry it with." He paused, then added, "I'd gladly carry yours, just so you know."

I faltered at that, the vulnerability of his offer threatening to breach the dam I had so carefully constructed. I wanted to lean into it, to surrender to the comfort he offered, but the fear of what that meant gripped me. "That sounds exhausting."

"True, but you're worth the effort." His tone was serious, devoid of the usual levity. The sincerity in his eyes knocked the breath out of me, leaving me momentarily speechless.

In that silence, I felt a flicker of something deeper, a connection that transcended friendship. The wind picked up, carrying with it the smell of rain-soaked streets and the tantalizing hint of beignets from a nearby café. My stomach rumbled, breaking the moment like a bubble bursting.

"Okay, how about we pause this heart-to-heart and grab some food?" I suggested, desperate to lighten the atmosphere. "You can take me to the place that has the best powdered sugar overdose in the city."

Rylan grinned, the sparkle returning to his eyes. "Now you're speaking my language. Let's go before I starve to death from this emotional rollercoaster."

As we made our way to the café, I felt the warmth of his presence beside me, a reminder that I didn't have to face the storm alone. We settled at a small table outside, the air filled with the rich aroma of coffee and fried pastries. I took a moment to absorb the atmosphere—the soft chatter of other patrons, the clinking of cups, the lively jazz music drifting in from nearby.

"Two orders of beignets, please," Rylan called to the waiter, and I couldn't help but smile at the way he commanded the room with his easy confidence.

When the beignets arrived, powdered sugar cascading like snowflakes on the warm pastries, I felt a moment of bliss wash over me. I took a bite, the sweetness exploding on my tongue, and closed my eyes, letting the flavors transport me to happier days.

Rylan watched me, a knowing smile on his face. "You've got a bit of sugar on your cheek," he said, leaning closer, his gaze playful.

"Great. Just what I need—more reasons for you to laugh at me," I replied, wiping at my face with a napkin.

"Who said I was laughing? I'm merely documenting the cuteness for future reference," he quipped, his eyes twinkling. "You're welcome."

The banter flowed easily, and for a moment, the shadows that clung to my heart receded, replaced by the warmth of companionship. Yet, beneath the laughter, a persistent tension lingered—an unaddressed weight that hovered between us.

As we finished our beignets, the conversation turned more serious. "I know it's hard, but have you thought more about your mom's surgery?" Rylan asked, his tone softening. "How are you feeling about it?"

I hesitated, my heart clenching at the thought. "I'm terrified, Rylan. I've never felt so helpless. I just want her to be okay, but I can't shake this feeling that..." I trailed off, unable to voice the fear that gnawed at me.

"That something bad will happen?" he finished for me, his expression sympathetic.

"Exactly. It's like I'm standing on the edge of a cliff, and every time I look down, I see a chasm of uncertainty."

He reached across the table, his hand covering mine, grounding me in the moment. "Whatever happens, you're not alone. I'll be right there with you. We can face the uncertainty together."

His words were a balm, yet I still felt the tension tightening in my chest. "You say that now, but what if—"

"Emily," he interrupted, his voice steady. "Life is full of what-ifs. The only thing we can control is how we choose to face them."

I nodded, though the doubt still simmered beneath the surface. Just as I opened my mouth to respond, my phone buzzed in my pocket, slicing through the moment.

Fishing it out, my heart sank as I saw the caller ID—my father. The apprehension I had felt earlier flooded back, a tidal wave crashing over me. I glanced at Rylan, his expression shifting to concern as I answered.

"Dad?" I said, my voice trembling slightly.

"Emily, we need to talk," he said, his tone serious, a warning embedded in every syllable.

"About what?"

"It's about your mother."

As the words sank in, the world around me faded, the café sounds blurring into a distant hum. Rylan's hand tightened around mine, the connection grounding me in the chaos that threatened to spiral out of control.

"Is she—" I started, but my father cut me off.

"Just come home. We need you here. It's urgent."

The call ended abruptly, leaving me staring at my phone, disbelief and dread crashing together in a tumultuous storm. I looked up at Rylan, my heart racing, his face a mirror of concern.

"What happened?" he asked softly, his voice barely above a whisper.

"I... I don't know," I stammered, my breath quickening as a new wave of anxiety crashed over me. "I have to go."

"Are you sure you want to do this alone?"

"I don't have a choice," I replied, my voice steadier than I felt.

Rylan's expression darkened, the worry etched on his face palpable. "Then at least let me drive you."

With a nod, I stood, the weight of the unknown pressing heavily upon me as I took a step toward the door. The storm within me had transformed into a tempest, and I felt as though I were stepping into an abyss. Whatever awaited me at home loomed like a dark cloud on the horizon, and as I stepped outside, the rain began to fall again, each drop a reminder that the chaos was far from over.

Chapter 22: Bridging the Gap

Days had slipped by, each one dragging its feet like a reluctant child on the first day of school. The silence between Rylan and me had settled like a heavy fog, clinging to everything we once shared—laughter, secrets, plans. I'd avoided his calls, letting them ring out like forgotten echoes, each unanswered chime another reminder of the widening chasm I had inadvertently carved. But the weight of unspoken words had become too much to bear, pressing down on my chest like a stone, threatening to crush me under its relentless pressure.

Determined, I steeled myself for the confrontation. The café where we had spent countless afternoons was alive with the aroma of freshly brewed coffee and the gentle murmur of conversations, each table a small island of intimacy amid the sea of activity. Rylan was seated at our usual spot, his dark hair tousled in a way that made him look both charming and utterly disheveled. He gazed out the window, the golden light of late afternoon casting a warm glow over his sharp features, but the frown that marred his brow pulled my heartstrings taut.

As I approached, my palms were clammy and my throat dry. I could already feel the stares of the baristas, the friendly smiles of other patrons turning into inquisitive glances as they recognized the tension that was about to unfold. I slid into the chair opposite him, the wood cool beneath me, and for a moment, we were two ships passing in the night—each lost in our own thoughts, yet so painfully close.

"Hey," I said, my voice barely a whisper against the backdrop of clinking cups and low laughter.

"Hey," he replied, his eyes still fixed on the street, where pedestrians flowed like water around the obstacles of their day. The energy outside seemed to mock the stillness between us.

I took a deep breath, the scent of roasted coffee beans filling my lungs, grounding me as I attempted to gather my thoughts. "I know it's been a while," I began, the words slipping out like hesitant raindrops. "I've been dealing with... a lot." I let the admission hang between us, hoping he could read the weight of my struggles in my eyes.

Rylan finally turned to face me, his expression shifting from distant irritation to something more tender, yet guarded. "You could have told me," he said, his voice low, a mix of concern and frustration. "You didn't have to go silent."

The guilt churned in my stomach, knotting tighter with each word he spoke. "I didn't want to burden you," I admitted, forcing myself to meet his gaze. "My mother's health... it's been hard. I didn't know how to balance everything. I felt like I was drowning, and the last thing I wanted was to pull you down with me."

"Carter," he said, the softness of my name on his lips making my heart race. "You're not a burden. I'm here because I care about you. You don't have to carry this alone."

His words wrapped around me like a warm blanket, offering a fleeting comfort amidst the storm of my fears. I nodded, a lump forming in my throat. "I'm just torn, you know? I love my mother, and I want to be there for her, but every time I leave her, I feel this weight of guilt. And then there's us, this beautiful thing we have, and I don't know how to fit it all together."

As I spoke, the tension between us began to soften, and I could see Rylan processing my words, his brow furrowing as he contemplated my struggle. The familiar intensity of his gaze ignited a spark of hope in my chest. "We'll figure it out," he said finally, determination lacing his voice. "Together. Just tell me what you need."

I sighed, a breath I didn't realize I had been holding. "I need you," I confessed, the vulnerability of my admission washing over me like a sudden rain shower. "I need your support, your understanding. But I also need to know that you'll be okay with whatever choice I make."

"Do you think I'd ever stop caring about you because of something like this?" he asked, the corner of his mouth twitching in that familiar half-smile that always made my heart flutter. "You're the strongest person I know, Carter. I admire you for trying to navigate this mess, but don't think for a second that I would walk away just because things get complicated."

The sincerity in his voice sent warmth blooming through me, thawing the icy grip of doubt that had wrapped around my heart. I couldn't help but smile, the corners of my lips tugging upwards despite the seriousness of our conversation. "You always know how to make me feel better, don't you?"

He shrugged, a playful glint in his eyes. "It's a gift. Besides, it's easy when you have someone worth fighting for."

The afternoon sun dipped lower, painting the café in hues of gold and amber as we continued to talk. The walls that had built up between us began to crumble, our words weaving a bridge over the uncertainty. We laughed and shared stories, his playful banter lightening the heavy atmosphere. With each laugh, each shared glance, I felt a bit of the weight lift, making space for hope and possibility to grow.

As the evening wore on and shadows lengthened, I could sense the shift in our dynamic—a newfound understanding blossoming in the space between us. I had entered that café with a heart full of trepidation, but as I looked at Rylan, I realized I was no longer alone in this fight. He was my ally, my confidant, and perhaps the one person who could help me navigate the storm that loomed ahead.

But as much as I felt lighter, I also recognized the complexities that lay ahead. My mother's health was a shadow that would follow me, and while I felt buoyed by Rylan's support, the reality of my situation remained. It was a tumultuous path I had to traverse, but at least now, I wouldn't be walking it alone.

The conversation flowed easily, like the coffee we sipped, warm and comforting, chasing away the chill that had lingered for too long between us. Rylan leaned in, his elbow resting casually on the table, the way he always did when he was genuinely invested in what I had to say. His eyes, dark pools of concern and affection, were fixed on me, urging me to share more, to peel back the layers of the tumult I had been hiding. I felt lighter with each word, the heavy burden of silence starting to fade, but deep down, I knew the struggle was far from over.

As I shared stories of my mother's laughter that echoed like distant chimes in my mind, I caught a glimpse of Rylan's hand moving slightly, fingers tapping softly against the table. It was a small, almost subconscious gesture, but it spoke volumes. "You know," he said, his voice warm yet playful, "I've always thought your mom could open a comedy club with the way she tells stories. You definitely inherited that knack for dramatics."

I chuckled, remembering her wild tales of growing up. "Oh, she'd have the audience rolling. Once, she convinced a whole family at the beach that a sea cucumber was a rare type of sea monster. I think they still refer to it as the 'Great Sea Cucumber Incident of 2005.'" I couldn't help but grin, the memory stirring a bubble of joy in my chest.

Rylan laughed, the sound like music, filling the space with warmth. "See? That's the spirit I love. You need to remember that joy even in the hard moments. You're allowed to laugh, Carter. It doesn't mean you care any less about your mom."

His words settled around us, infusing the air with a renewed sense of camaraderie. I nodded, absorbing his wisdom as we sipped our drinks, the conversation shifting to lighter topics, the kind that made us lose track of time. Rylan shared anecdotes from work that had me rolling my eyes at the absurdities of corporate life—his co-worker who mistook a conference call for a karaoke session, belting out 80s pop songs as if the whole company was his audience.

"Honestly, I thought I'd have to mute him," he said, shaking his head, his laughter contagious. "But then I realized, why not let the madness unfold? If you can't laugh at a three-hour meeting turned disco, what's the point?"

"Exactly! If you're going to suffer through work, you might as well add some sparkle to it," I replied, mirroring his laughter. We were lost in our own world, the café around us fading into a blur of chatter and clinking dishes.

But as the clock ticked on, the inevitable reality seeped back in, a reminder of the shadow lurking just beyond our laughter. "So, what's the plan?" Rylan asked, leaning back, the playful tone still there but underpinned with genuine concern. "I mean, with your mom's health and everything. Are you going to stay here longer? You know you have options."

His words hit me like a sudden gust of wind, the fleeting warmth of the café now feeling stifling. "I... I don't know," I admitted, the uncertainty wrapping around me like a suffocating cloak. "Part of me wants to be there for her, but another part of me feels guilty for leaving you behind. It's like I'm juggling two worlds, and any misstep could send everything crashing down."

"You won't drop the ball," Rylan said, his voice steady, an anchor in my tempest. "You're resilient, Carter. You've already faced so much. Just take it one day at a time. You're allowed to feel everything—confusion, guilt, love. They don't cancel each other out."

I looked at him, his unwavering confidence giving me a sense of peace I hadn't realized I needed. "You really believe that?" I asked, a slight tremor in my voice.

"Absolutely," he replied, the corner of his mouth lifting in that infuriatingly charming smile of his. "You're like one of those superhero movies where the protagonist learns to juggle powers without blowing up the city. Only in your case, you'll find a way to save the day without losing yourself. Trust me."

A chuckle escaped my lips, and despite the weight on my shoulders, I felt a flicker of hope ignite within me. "You really have a way with words, you know that? Maybe I should hire you as my motivational speaker."

"I'd charge a hefty fee," he teased, leaning in closer, his eyes dancing with mischief. "But for you? A mere cup of coffee will suffice."

We fell into a comfortable silence, the world outside gradually darkening, streetlights flickering to life, casting a soft glow against the café windows. I was captivated by the way he always found a way to blend humor with sincerity, a rare gift that seemed to draw people in. But just as the warmth of our moment wrapped around me, an unexpected tension sliced through the atmosphere like a sudden chill.

The door swung open, and in walked a figure that made my heart race—a tall man with striking features and an air of confidence that filled the room. It was Derek, my mother's old neighbor, a man who had always harbored an unsettling interest in my family. Our gazes met, and my stomach twisted into knots. He hadn't changed, still wearing that disarming smile that sent shivers down my spine.

"Carter! What a surprise," he called, his voice dripping with feigned delight as he approached our table. "And Rylan! Fancy seeing you here."

"Derek," I said, forcing the word out through a tight throat. I could feel Rylan tense beside me, the air thickening with unspoken questions.

Derek's eyes danced between us, lingering on the way Rylan's hand rested protectively on the table, as if claiming his territory. "I was just in the neighborhood, checking on your mom. She seemed a bit under the weather last I heard. I hope she's doing alright?"

I could hear the edge of concern in his voice, but it felt more like a test than genuine compassion. "She's hanging in there," I replied, my voice steady despite the unease creeping up my spine.

"Good to hear," Derek said, leaning in slightly, his gaze shifting to Rylan. "And it seems you've found a new friend. Hope he's treating you well."

"Rylan's great," I interjected, a fierce protectiveness flaring within me. "He's been incredibly supportive during this time."

Derek's smile didn't waver, but his eyes narrowed just a fraction. "That's good to know. Family is everything, after all."

I sensed a challenge in his words, a reminder of the delicate balance I had been trying to maintain. The lighthearted banter I'd shared with Rylan felt like a distant memory, eclipsed by the sudden weight of Derek's presence.

"I should get back to my mom," I said quickly, the urge to escape the conversation overwhelming. "It was nice seeing you, Derek."

"Oh, don't let me keep you," he replied, the feigned charm still intact. "Just make sure she knows I'm around if she needs anything. I'm always here to help."

The moment felt loaded, the unsaid words hanging thick in the air as I stood up. Rylan followed suit, his protective demeanor returning as we navigated around Derek, the sense of unease lingering long after we'd left the café.

Once outside, I took a deep breath, the cool evening air brushing against my cheeks, refreshing yet filled with uncertainty. "What was that about?" Rylan asked, concern etched on his face.

I shook my head, trying to shake off the remnants of Derek's presence. "I don't know, but I have a bad feeling about it."

"Maybe you need to talk to your mom about him," Rylan suggested, his tone thoughtful. "It could help put your mind at ease."

"Or make things even more complicated," I countered, the weight of Derek's gaze still lingering in my mind.

Rylan paused, looking out at the street, where the vibrant life of the city thrived, oblivious to my turmoil. "Whatever happens, you know I'm here for you. You're not alone in this, Carter."

His words washed over me, a soothing balm against the uncertainty that loomed ahead. The night stretched out before us, full of possibilities and shadows, and I knew that, despite the challenges, I had someone by my side, ready to face whatever came next.

The evening air was alive with the pulse of the city, the sounds of laughter and clinking glasses spilling from nearby restaurants. Rylan and I walked side by side, the shadows of uncertainty still clinging to me like an ill-fitting coat, but his presence felt like a soft light breaking through the gloom. The streetlights cast a gentle glow, illuminating our path as we strolled down a familiar block lined with shops and vibrant storefronts. The comforting scent of freshly baked pastries wafted through the air, drawing me to a small bakery we often frequented.

"Do you want to grab something sweet?" I suggested, feeling a surge of nostalgia. "It might lighten the mood."

"Are you offering to share a brownie or just letting me have the whole thing?" Rylan teased, a twinkle of mischief in his eye.

"Definitely a share, but only because I'm feeling generous today," I replied, bumping my shoulder against his playfully. "You know, one bite for me, one for you. A classic negotiation tactic."

He chuckled, shaking his head. "You drive a hard bargain, Carter. Fine, let's split it. But don't blame me when you end up wanting more."

We made our way into the bakery, the warmth enveloping us like a cozy embrace. The shelves were stocked with an array of pastries that sparkled under the soft lighting. My mouth watered at the sight of decadent brownies topped with a drizzle of caramel and dusted with sea salt. "This place should come with a warning label," I said, eyeing the treats like a kid in a candy store. "Forcing me to choose is just cruel."

Rylan leaned over the glass case, pretending to consider his options seriously. "You could always go for the chocolate chip cookies. Classic, reliable. Like the bread-and-butter of baked goods."

"Don't you dare insult the brownie," I shot back, my hand instinctively reaching for the decadent slice. "This is a gourmet experience, not a snack. I'll have you know that in the hierarchy of desserts, brownies reign supreme."

"Your dessert opinions are as strong as your convictions," he said, laughing. "Alright, fine. One brownie, then we'll compromise and grab a cookie too. The perfect pairing."

As we ordered, the warmth of the bakery seeped into my bones, dispelling the chill that Derek's presence had left behind. I could feel the tension slowly ebbing away, replaced by the comforting routine of choosing treats and sharing jokes. We found a small table in the corner, and as we dug into the rich brownie, the world outside faded into a gentle hum.

"You know," Rylan said, licking a bit of chocolate from his fingers, "I have a theory about the universe. It's just a giant cookie jar, and we're all trying to reach in for the biggest piece while ignoring the crumbs falling all around us."

I laughed, the sound bubbling up from a place I had almost forgotten. "And what happens when we reach for that big piece?" I asked, curiosity sparking.

"Sometimes you get the best bite, but other times, you find a half-eaten cookie that someone thought was still edible," he replied, a smirk dancing on his lips. "Life is all about the risks, isn't it? Do we take the leap and hope for the best, or do we settle for what we think is safe?"

"Sounds like you're trying to get philosophical with your dessert," I said, shaking my head. "Next thing I know, you'll be telling me the meaning of life is in chocolate ganache."

"It might be," he said, a glimmer of mischief in his eyes. "You should try it sometime."

With our sugary feast finished, we stepped back into the cool night air. I felt a renewed sense of purpose, bolstered by the laughter and shared moments. But the ghost of Derek's smile lingered in the back of my mind, a reminder that not all was right in my world.

"Let's take a walk by the park," Rylan suggested, nodding toward the nearby greenery. "I love the way the trees look at night, like they're holding secrets beneath their branches."

"Alright, but only if you promise to keep the philosophical cookie talk to a minimum," I said, playfully nudging him as we walked.

"Deal," he replied, a mock-serious expression on his face. "I'll save my theories for when we're on the verge of a brownie crisis."

As we strolled through the park, the trees swayed gently, their leaves whispering secrets to the night. The moon hung low, casting silvery light over the path, transforming the familiar surroundings into something magical. I took a deep breath, inhaling the earthy scent of the grass mixed with the cool night air. It felt like an escape, a momentary reprieve from the worries that had swarmed around me.

But just as I was beginning to relax, a figure appeared ahead, leaning against a tree, silhouetted against the moonlight. The familiar shape sent a chill racing down my spine. "Carter," Derek called, his voice smooth and oddly inviting. "Fancy seeing you here."

Rylan stiffened beside me, a low growl forming in his throat. "What are you doing here?" he asked, his protective nature flaring.

"Oh, just enjoying a late-night stroll," Derek replied, his tone almost too casual. "I was hoping to catch up with Carter. After all, she has quite a lot on her mind these days."

I felt the tension in the air thicken, sharp and uncomfortable. "What do you want, Derek?" I managed to ask, forcing myself to remain composed.

"I'm here to help, of course," he said, his smile unsettling. "I know things have been rough for you, and I want you to know you can always count on me."

Rylan moved slightly in front of me, his stance protective. "She doesn't need your help. She has me."

Derek chuckled, the sound low and taunting. "Ah, but does she really? You're not the one dealing with the family crisis, are you? I'm just a neighbor trying to look out for her. Besides, sometimes it takes a little bit of distance to see the bigger picture."

The way he spoke sent a shiver racing down my spine. "I appreciate your concern, but I'm fine. I don't need your help," I said, my voice steady even as my heart raced.

"Of course, you think that now," Derek replied, stepping closer, his confidence almost suffocating. "But when the time comes—and it will—you might find yourself regretting the choices you've made. I just want you to know you have options. You don't have to face this alone."

"I'm not alone," I insisted, glancing at Rylan, who remained resolute at my side. "I have support."

Derek's gaze flickered to Rylan, and I could see the calculations racing through his mind. "Let's hope that's enough," he said, his voice dripping with condescension. "But remember, Carter, I'm always just a phone call away. When you need someone who truly understands, you know where to find me."

With that, he turned and melted into the shadows, leaving behind a trail of unease that hung in the air like a dark cloud.

Rylan shifted beside me, tension etched on his face. "What the hell was that?" he asked, his voice low and fierce.

"I don't know, but it didn't feel good," I replied, my heart racing. "He's not the type to just drop by for a casual chat. He has an agenda."

"Do you want me to confront him?" Rylan asked, fists clenching at his sides.

"No," I said quickly, the thought of escalating the situation sending a wave of panic through me. "Let's just forget it. He thrives on drama, and I refuse to give him that satisfaction."

But even as I spoke, I could feel the weight of uncertainty settle back on my shoulders. Derek's words echoed in my mind, twisting and turning, digging into my subconscious. The night felt darker, the shadows longer, and I couldn't shake the feeling that this wasn't over.

With Rylan beside me, I took a step forward, my heart pounding as I sought to regain my footing. But the ominous weight of Derek's presence loomed larger in my thoughts, a reminder that the challenges ahead would test not only my strength but also the bonds I was striving to protect.

Just then, my phone buzzed in my pocket, the unexpected vibration causing my pulse to quicken. I fished it out, the screen lighting up to reveal a message that made my stomach drop—a photo, dark and blurry, but unmistakable. My heart raced as I stared at the image, my breath catching in my throat, the gravity of its implications crashing over me like a tidal wave.

"Carter?" Rylan's voice cut through the haze, but I was already frozen, staring at the screen, the world around me fading as I processed the message that threatened to unravel everything I thought I knew.

Chapter 23: The Dance of Healing

The first touch of dawn slipped through the curtains like a shy lover, casting a golden glow over the wooden floor of the dance studio. I stood at the center, the barre cool beneath my fingertips, as I stretched my limbs in a routine that had become second nature. Rylan had transformed the mundane into the sacred, and as the morning light illuminated the space, I felt it—this palpable energy that swirled around us, a testament to the healing journey we had embarked on together.

"Are you ready?" Rylan's voice broke through the stillness, warm and teasing, pulling me from the haze of concentration. I turned to face him, a playful smile dancing on my lips. He was leaning casually against the wall, arms crossed, that signature grin making my heart do a little leap. "Or do you need another five minutes to fix that hair? It looks like you just woke up."

"Ha, ha, very funny," I shot back, ruffling my tousled locks for effect. "I could say the same about you. That's quite the bedhead you're sporting."

"Hey, it's called artistic dishevelment." He raised an eyebrow, and the way he carried that absurdity made me laugh, breaking the tension that clung to my shoulders. In those moments, I realized how much I had come to depend on his presence, how his lightness could pierce through my heavier thoughts. We were an odd pair, two misfits stitched together by our love for dance and the need for connection.

We began our practice, the floor echoing with the sounds of our movements—the swish of fabric, the soft thud of our feet, the rhythm of breaths. Each step became a dialogue, a conversation without words that spoke volumes about our struggles and triumphs. I had always loved dance, but now it felt like a lifeline, something to cling to amid the chaos swirling around me. Rylan's guidance was firm yet gentle, his touch reassuring as he corrected my form or offered a new perspective on a familiar sequence.

"Try to imagine you're telling a story with your body," he advised one afternoon as we danced through a sequence that had become all too familiar. "Every twist and turn should convey a feeling. You're not just moving; you're living it."

"Living it," I repeated, letting the words linger in the air like a promise. I tried to visualize the emotions I'd buried deep within me, bringing them to the surface with each movement. It was harder than it sounded; some feelings were like shadows, elusive and difficult to grasp. Yet, as I danced, I felt the tension release, like steam escaping a kettle, a sense of liberation swelling within.

As the weeks unfolded, I noticed a shift within myself. My laughter came easier, my steps more confident, a lightness that seemed foreign yet exhilarating. Rylan had a way of encouraging me to push beyond my comfort zone. One day, after a particularly intense rehearsal, he caught me staring blankly into space. "What's going on in that head of yours?" he asked, a knowing look in his eyes.

"It's just... I'm not sure if I'm getting any better," I admitted, a hint of frustration creeping into my voice. "Sometimes, I feel like I'm just dancing in circles."

Rylan's expression softened, and he stepped closer, his warmth enveloping me like a soft blanket. "You're not just dancing; you're evolving. It's not about perfection; it's about growth. Think of it this way: each step you take is a part of your journey. You're learning to embrace the process."

His words settled over me, settling like dust in a sunbeam. I realized I had been too focused on the end goal, on perfecting every move, rather than enjoying the beauty of each moment. I nodded, a newfound determination igniting within me, a flicker of hope that maybe I was exactly where I needed to be.

Then, one evening, after an especially heartfelt session, Rylan suggested we choreograph a piece together. The idea both thrilled and terrified me. "Us? Choreographing?" I stammered, my heart racing. The notion of creating something unique together felt monumental, like jumping off a cliff without knowing where the water would land.

"Why not?" He shrugged, mischief dancing in his eyes. "We've been through a lot together. Let's channel that into something beautiful."

I hesitated, the fear of failure creeping back in. "What if it's terrible? What if we create something that doesn't work?"

Rylan stepped closer, his gaze unwavering. "Then we'll learn from it. Besides, it's not about being perfect; it's about what we create together. Just trust the process."

His confidence was contagious, and I felt myself leaning into it. That evening, we began to weave our experiences into a tapestry of movement, drawing from laughter and shared frustrations, the rhythm of our lives spilling into each step. It felt electric, each beat resonating with a life of its own. I found myself pushing past the fear, allowing creativity to flow like a river bursting through a dam, sweeping away the remnants of my past doubts.

As we worked, we discovered something unexpected. Our dance transcended mere choreography; it became a narrative, a reflection of our struggles and triumphs, a testament to resilience. Every leap echoed the freedom we sought, every spin capturing the dizzying joy of finding our way through the chaos. The studio was no longer just a place of practice; it had transformed into our sanctuary, a cocoon where vulnerability thrived, and healing blossomed like wildflowers breaking through concrete.

In those moments, under the glow of the studio lights, I realized something profound. This was not merely about dance; it was about reclaiming parts of myself I had lost. It was about embracing who I was and who I was becoming, guided by the unwavering belief that I was worthy of every beautiful moment life had to offer. And with Rylan by my side, I was ready to dance through whatever storms lay ahead.

The air in the studio shimmered with the promise of summer, a fragrant mix of freshly polished wood and lingering traces of sweat. Each breath I took felt lighter, a gentle reminder of how far I'd come. Rylan had a knack for turning the ordinary into the extraordinary, and as we began our next rehearsal, I could sense that this day held something special, a spark of inspiration just waiting to ignite.

"Okay, let's start from the top," Rylan called, his voice slicing through the stillness like a knife through soft butter. He assumed his position across from me, his usual boyish grin lighting up his face. "And this time, I want you to really feel it. Let every note pull you into the movement."

"Like this?" I responded, spinning on my heel with an exaggerated flourish, feigning an over-the-top dramatic flair. "Or perhaps I should channel my inner prima ballerina?"

He laughed, the sound warm and inviting. "More like channel your inner tornado, but hey, at least you're in motion."

I shot him a playful glare, but the smile tugging at the corners of my mouth betrayed my attempt at seriousness. It was moments like these that reminded me how vital our partnership had become, how laughter intertwined with our passion for dance. With each step we took, we painted a vivid picture, and I wanted to dive deeper into that canvas, colors swirling in unexpected patterns.

The music started, a haunting melody that wrapped around us like a soft embrace. I closed my eyes for a moment, letting the notes wash over me, transporting me to a place where I felt free—unburdened by past anxieties or fears. As I opened my eyes and moved, I could see Rylan's attentive gaze, a steady anchor amid the tide of emotions threatening to sweep me away.

With every leap and twirl, we communicated, an unspoken dialogue evolving with each graceful movement. The rhythm carried us through the highs and lows, weaving stories of joy, heartache, and healing into our choreography. It was mesmerizing how our bodies spoke to one another; the elegance of our movement reflected not just technique, but a profound connection that transcended words.

Yet, amidst the beauty, a nagging thought lingered in the back of my mind, like a persistent itch I couldn't quite scratch. What if this was all temporary? What if I was only riding a wave of adrenaline that would eventually crash back to reality? The thought darkened my mood, a shadow that hovered just beyond the glow of our shared creativity.

Rylan must have sensed my shift in energy because he stepped closer, tilting his head with that signature inquisitiveness that always made me feel seen. "Hey, what's brewing in that beautiful head of yours?"

"Just wondering how long this is going to last," I admitted, my voice barely above a whisper. "I mean, what if I wake up one morning and realize it was all a dream?"

His brow furrowed slightly, and he shook his head as if trying to dispel my fears. "It's not a dream. This is real. You're real. We're real." He paused, and the intensity of his gaze made my heart race. "I won't let you forget that."

His words hung in the air, heavy yet comforting. They wrapped around me like a warm blanket, igniting a flicker of hope. "Promise?"

"Cross my heart," he replied, making an exaggerated gesture of crossing his heart, which elicited a laugh from me, momentarily chasing away the shadows of doubt.

The rehearsal continued, infused with a renewed sense of purpose. We pushed boundaries, both physically and emotionally, digging deep into our experiences to create something raw and powerful. I had no idea how much time passed as we lost ourselves in our art, the world outside fading into a distant memory.

It was in the middle of one particularly ambitious sequence that it happened. I was attempting a complex turn when my foot slipped on a patch of sweat on the floor. My heart dropped as I felt myself teetering, gravity's cruel hand pulling me down. Rylan lunged forward, his hand catching my arm just in time, but the momentum sent us both sprawling to the ground in a tangled heap of limbs and laughter.

"Wow, what a way to make a dramatic exit," he chuckled, attempting to disentangle himself while still clutching my arm, our faces inches apart. I could feel the warmth radiating off him, and my heart raced—not just from the fall, but from the intensity of our shared moment.

"Dramatic is my middle name," I quipped, feigning nonchalance while the butterflies in my stomach threatened to take flight. As we sat there, the world around us faded, the laughter still hanging in the air like a sweet aftertaste. Something shifted, and I could feel it—a tension that crackled between us, charged and electric.

Rylan's expression softened as he gazed into my eyes. "You know, we could just embrace the chaos. Dance isn't about perfection; it's about the moments that take our breath away."

"Or the moments that send us crashing to the floor," I retorted, a teasing lilt to my voice, though my heart thudded wildly at the unspoken connection lingering in the air.

"True," he replied, his tone serious, but the mischief still danced in his eyes. "But even falling can be beautiful if you make it part of the choreography." He paused, the weight of his words settling in between us, the moment suspended like a breath held too long.

"Let's take a break," I suggested, shifting to sit cross-legged on the floor, attempting to gather my thoughts, my breath. The accidental intimacy of our tumble still buzzed between us. I needed a moment to process the electric tension, to find my footing again.

"Good idea," Rylan agreed, following my lead. He leaned back on his hands, the muscles in his arms flexing effortlessly. "So, how's the journey of self-discovery going? Are you still convinced you'll wake up to find it was all a figment of your imagination?"

"I guess it's a work in progress," I admitted, leaning back and gazing at the ceiling, tracing the pattern of the beams above with my eyes. "Some days feel like a leap of faith, while others are just... well, a little less graceful."

"Grace is overrated," he countered, the warmth of his laughter filling the space. "What matters is that you keep dancing, even when it's messy. Because that's when the real magic happens."

His words resonated deep within me, an echo of truth that felt both liberating and terrifying. I glanced at him, the laughter fading as the reality of my feelings settled in. In that moment, I realized that the dance we were creating together was not just about movement; it was about vulnerability, trust, and the courage to step into the unknown.

As we sat there, the studio filled with the fading notes of our earlier music, I knew that whatever lay ahead, I was ready to embrace it, messy steps and all, with Rylan by my side.

The sun dipped low in the sky, casting a warm, golden hue over the dance studio as the evening progressed. I stood at the barre, watching Rylan in the mirror as he warmed up, his movements fluid and confident. The familiar notes of our latest piece echoed through the air, wrapping around us like an embrace. Each note felt like a promise, a reminder of how far we had come together. The world outside felt like a distant memory, a blurred image that faded more with each passing rehearsal.

"Okay, let's push it today," Rylan said, his eyes sparkling with enthusiasm. "I want to add a little more flair to that ending."

"Flair?" I echoed, raising an eyebrow. "Are we talking feathers and sequins here, or just a little extra jazz?"

"Why not both?" he teased, leaning against the wall with a grin. "I mean, if we're going for dramatic, let's really commit. Maybe a boa too?"

I laughed, shaking my head. "If I end up with feathers stuck in my hair, I'm holding you responsible. You realize that, right?"

"Of course! But just think of the photos. You'd be a dance diva." He spun around, his arms flaring as he mimicked an exaggerated diva pose, and I couldn't help but chuckle at his antics. Rylan had a way of lightening the mood, transforming the pressure of performance into playful creativity.

As we launched into the piece, I poured my heart into every step, feeling the music surge through me like electricity. Rylan mirrored my energy, and for those moments, it was just us—two souls entwined in an expression of passion and resilience. The dance transformed, evolving into a narrative of healing and connection, each movement resonating with our shared journey.

But as we reached the climax of our routine, I noticed something shifting in Rylan's demeanor. He stumbled slightly, a flicker of uncertainty crossing his face. My heart raced as I felt the abrupt change. "You okay?" I asked, my voice cutting through the rhythm like a knife.

He nodded, but there was an unmistakable tension in his shoulders. "Yeah, just... a little off today," he replied, brushing it off with a casual wave of his hand, though the flicker of vulnerability in his eyes betrayed him.

I took a deep breath, instinctively stepping closer. "You don't have to pretend around me, you know. If something's bothering you, we can take a break."

He hesitated, the silence stretching between us like an unbroken chord. Finally, he sighed, running a hand through his hair, the gesture laden with frustration. "It's just... I've been thinking about the upcoming showcase. I know how much it means to you, and I don't want to screw it up."

The admission hung in the air, heavy with unspoken fears. "You won't screw it up, Rylan. You're an amazing dancer. You always bring something special to the stage," I said, hoping to infuse him with some of the confidence I felt blooming within me.

He looked down, a hint of a smile playing on his lips but not quite reaching his eyes. "Thanks. It's just... what if I can't keep up? What if this all falls apart?"

"Then we pick up the pieces and dance our way through it," I replied, my tone more serious now. "But I promise you, I'm not going anywhere. We're in this together."

His gaze met mine, the intensity there almost disarming. "You really mean that, don't you?"

"Of course. I may even bring feathers," I joked, attempting to lighten the mood again.

"Now you've got me intrigued," he said, a glimmer of mischief returning to his eyes. "How about a full-on show-stopping performance with sparkles and all?"

The banter felt good, but beneath the surface, I could feel the weight of Rylan's insecurities lingering. As we resumed our practice, I tried to channel my concern into the dance, pouring every ounce of my energy into creating something beautiful, something that would remind us both of our strength.

As the final notes of our music faded, I sensed a sudden shift in the atmosphere. The door to the studio creaked open, and in stepped a figure I hadn't expected to see—my mother. The surprise caught me off guard, and my heart lurched at the sight of her.

"Mom? What are you doing here?" I asked, wiping my forehead with the back of my hand, the warmth of the rehearsal still lingering in my body.

She looked at me, her expression a mix of pride and concern. "I wanted to see you dance. I've heard so much about your rehearsals with Rylan. Thought I'd finally check it out."

Rylan, sensing the tension, took a step back, allowing me space to navigate this unexpected moment. I could feel the ground shifting beneath me, and the last remnants of my confidence began to waver.

"Uh, well, we were just wrapping up," I stammered, my cheeks flushing with a blend of embarrassment and apprehension. "It's not—"

"Not what?" she interrupted, her tone sharper than I'd anticipated. "Not good enough? Honey, I've seen how hard you've been working. You don't have to downplay it."

Her words struck a nerve. I had always yearned for her approval, and now it felt like a heavy weight on my shoulders. "It's just rehearsal. We're still working on things."

"Rehearsal or not, I'm sure it's beautiful," she said, stepping closer, her voice softening. "I can see how much it means to you. You shine when you dance."

"Thanks," I mumbled, shifting uncomfortably. The warmth of her praise was a double-edged sword, a reminder of my desire for validation mixed with the shadows of our complicated history.

"Why don't you show me?" she asked, her eyes lighting up with enthusiasm. "I'd love to see what you and Rylan have been working on."

I exchanged a glance with Rylan, whose expression mirrored my own uncertainty. "Um, okay," I said, swallowing hard, unsure of what would come next.

As we positioned ourselves for the routine, I felt a new tension, one that seemed to dance on the edges of my focus. With each step, I became acutely aware of my mother's gaze, dissecting every movement, every misstep, like a critical audience member. The pressure mounted, and I fought to maintain my composure.

We began again, the music flooding the space. But as we moved, something felt off—my limbs were heavier, my heart raced in time with the rising notes, and I struggled to breathe through the weight of expectation. It was a dance I had known by heart, yet now it felt like a labyrinth, every turn leading to deeper uncertainty.

And then, just as we reached the climax of our performance, Rylan stumbled again, his foot catching awkwardly as he tried to execute a complicated turn. Time seemed to slow, and I watched helplessly as he lost his balance. I instinctively reached out, but it was too late. He fell, crashing to the floor with a thud that reverberated through the studio like a sudden crack of thunder.

"Rylan!" I shouted, my heart lurching in my chest as I rushed to his side. Panic clawed at my throat, and I knelt beside him, feeling the tension in the air shift to something darker, something heavy.

"Are you okay?" I asked, fear and concern lacing my voice. He winced as he tried to push himself up, and for a moment, the world faded away, leaving only the pulse of my worry echoing in my ears.

But as Rylan opened his mouth to respond, the studio door swung wide, and a new presence entered—someone who felt more like a storm than a blessing. My heart sank as I met the gaze of the figure standing in the doorway, their expression unreadable, cloaked in shadows that threatened to swallow the warmth of our sanctuary.

Chapter 24: Shadows of the Past

The rehearsal studio was a sanctuary, its mirrored walls reflecting the flickering shadows of our exhaustion and passion. The scent of polished wood mingled with the lingering notes of sweat and determination, a heady perfume that had become all too familiar. Rylan and I had been pouring our souls into every pirouette, every leap, crafting a rhythm that felt both exhilarating and intimate. I could almost hear the music echoing in my bones, a haunting melody that danced just beyond my grasp, calling me to embrace the vulnerability that lay entwined in every movement.

As the final notes of our practice faded, Rylan leaned against the wall, his body glistening with sweat, and a satisfied grin spreading across his face. His dark hair fell over his forehead in a way that made my heart flutter—an image so easy to adore. I mirrored his smile, buoyed by the warmth of shared effort, when my phone buzzed with a notification. Distracted, I glanced down, only to find it was just another promotional email about upcoming dance events. I looked back at him, ready to revel in the moment, but my excitement faded as I noticed his expression shifting.

The air turned electric, thick with an unspoken tension as he pulled out his phone. The screen lit up with a name I hadn't heard before: Elise. My stomach twisted. Who was she? The way his brow furrowed and his lips pressed into a thin line sent a wave of unease through me, crashing against the shores of my heart. "Hey, it's just a call from an old friend," he said, attempting to deflect the storm brewing in his gaze. But the slight tremor in his voice betrayed him.

"An old friend?" I echoed, trying to mask my rising anxiety with casualness. "Is that what we're calling her now?" My tone came out sharper than intended, a flash of defensiveness I couldn't quite suppress. Rylan ran a hand through his hair, a gesture I recognized well—a sign of his own turmoil.

"Breathe, Kaylee," he said softly, and I hated how his calm made me feel even more rattled. "She was my partner before I moved here. It's not—"

"Not what? Just a casual call to catch up?" I cut him off, my words spilling like the wine I couldn't bring myself to sip at dinner parties. The thought of him with someone else, sharing intimate moments and stolen laughter, gnawed at me like a hungry wolf.

"Listen, it's complicated," he replied, and my heart sank at the underlying heaviness of those words. "We danced together for years. There were feelings involved, but they're not—"

"Feelings?" I repeated, my voice barely above a whisper, the syllables heavy with disbelief. "You mean, like, romantic feelings?" The very idea felt like a cold hand gripping my throat, squeezing tighter as I struggled to breathe through the tide of jealousy washing over me.

"It was a long time ago," he insisted, frustration creeping into his tone. "We've both moved on. I swear it's not what you think."

But trust is a fragile thing, easily shattered by the weight of uncertainty. I crossed my arms, turning my back to him, the mirrors reflecting not just our shapes but the chasm that seemed to widen between us. "You don't have to explain," I murmured, my voice trembling as I struggled to hold back the tears threatening to spill. "I just... I need to know you're not still attached to that part of your life. I can't compete with ghosts."

"Kaylee," he stepped closer, his presence warm against the chill I felt enveloping me. "You're not competing with anyone. You're everything to me."

His earnest gaze searched mine, the sincerity in his eyes a soft balm to my fraying nerves. But the call continued to loom over us like a dark cloud. I could see it now, the way Rylan's past intertwined with his present, threatening to pull him away from me, as it had done before. The light that once illuminated our shared path flickered as I envisioned him dancing in the arms of someone else, her laughter intertwining with his as they spun under the same bright stage lights that now illuminated our practice space.

"I'm not asking you to choose," I said finally, my voice steadied by a newfound resolve. "But I need you to understand how this makes me feel." I turned to face him, willing my expression to remain firm despite the turmoil inside. "I can't help but wonder if there's still something between you two."

He opened his mouth, likely to offer more reassurances, but I held up a hand. "No, just... let's take a break for tonight. I need some air." The words felt heavy and final, but they were necessary. The warmth that once enveloped me felt suffocating, and I needed to breathe again.

Rylan's shoulders slumped slightly, his disappointment palpable, but I couldn't afford to focus on that now. I stepped outside, the cool night air wrapping around me like a comforting embrace, a stark contrast to the turmoil raging within. I leaned against the brick wall of the studio, staring up at the vast expanse of stars, each one twinkling with its own story, its own past—stories I wished I could ignore, but they clawed at me, relentless in their insistence.

My phone buzzed again, and I glanced down, half-expecting another unwanted email. Instead, it was a text from Mia, my best friend. "Are you okay? You've been quiet." I took a deep breath, unsure of how to articulate the mess swirling inside me.

I typed back quickly, "Just having a moment. I'll call you later." My fingers hovered over the screen as I fought against the urge to spill everything. I didn't want to drag her into this; it felt too messy, too raw. Instead, I closed my eyes, willing the chaos to settle. The night was quiet, save for the distant sound of laughter from a nearby café, and I found myself yearning for simplicity—a time when dancing was all that mattered, when it felt like the world was just Rylan and me.

Yet, as shadows of the past loomed closer, I couldn't help but wonder if I was strong enough to confront the darkness, or if it would swallow me whole, leaving nothing but echoes of what could have been.

The chill of the evening air was a sharp contrast to the heat swirling in my chest as I paced the quiet street outside the studio. My heels clicked against the pavement, a steady rhythm that echoed the erratic beat of my heart. The stars above sparkled like shards of glass against the velvet sky, but their beauty felt distant, detached from the turmoil swirling within me. Each breath I took was laden with the weight of uncertainty, and I wondered if Rylan's shadows were going to consume not just his past but the fragile future I had dared to envision for us.

I leaned against the cool brick wall, the rough texture grounding me as I inhaled deeply, trying to gather my thoughts. Just moments ago, the studio had felt like our haven—a place where we created magic together. Now, it loomed behind me like a fortress of insecurities, its mirrors reflecting not just our bodies but the rift that had opened between us. I could still hear Rylan's voice ringing in my ears, filled with the unintentional tension of someone trying to reassure while wrestling with their own demons.

My phone buzzed again, pulling me from my spiral of thoughts. This time, it was a meme from Mia—a little cat trapped in a cardboard box with the caption: "When you think you're doing fine but then... life." I couldn't help but chuckle, the absurdity of it all breaking through my frayed nerves. If only life were that simple. I quickly typed back a heart emoji, knowing she'd interpret it as my way of saying I needed to talk but wasn't quite ready yet.

Just then, the front door of the studio creaked open, and Rylan stepped out, the warmth of his presence seeping into the chilly night. His face was etched with concern, and for a moment, my heart fluttered at the sight of him. But the shadow of that phone call hung between us, a dark cloud that refused to dissipate. "Kaylee," he began, his voice low and earnest. "I don't want you to think that—"

"Can we not?" I interrupted, shaking my head. I couldn't bear the thought of dissecting his past while trying to salvage our present. "I just need a moment to breathe."

He nodded slowly, the disappointment evident in his eyes, but there was also a flicker of understanding. "Okay. I can do that." He leaned against the wall beside me, the space between us fraught with unspoken words. For a heartbeat, silence enveloped us, wrapping around the night like a soft blanket.

The city hummed around us, the distant sounds of laughter and clinking glasses from the café nearby felt like a reminder of what we were fighting for—normalcy, intimacy, and trust. "You want to grab a drink or something?" Rylan asked after a moment, his voice tentative, as if he were testing the waters.

"Not sure if that would help," I replied, my brow furrowing. "Maybe it would just give us an excuse to pretend everything is okay when it's not."

He let out a sigh, and the sound reverberated with a mix of frustration and concern. "You're right. We can't just gloss over it. But I hate seeing you like this."

"Trust me, I'm not a fan either." I chuckled softly, appreciating his willingness to reach out. "I guess I'm just trying to wrap my head around the fact that there's this whole chapter of your life I knew nothing about. And now it's rearing its ugly head."

"I promise, Elise isn't what you think," he replied, his voice thick with sincerity. "When I left New York, I left her behind too. It was the right decision for my career and my mental health. I don't have any feelings for her. Not anymore."

But I couldn't shake the feeling that there was something unresolved there. The way his eyes flickered when he spoke her name suggested a history that, no matter how much he reassured me, still held weight. "Okay, let's say I believe you. If you two were once close, how do I know she won't come back and stir things up? Or worse, that she still wants something from you?"

Rylan turned to me, his expression earnest yet laced with a hint of frustration. "You don't trust me?"

The question hung in the air, heavy and suffocating. "I want to," I admitted, my voice barely a whisper. "But trust takes time, Rylan. And I'm still learning how to let go of my insecurities."

A moment of silence passed between us, thick with understanding and empathy. "Then let me help you," he said finally, his tone softer now, almost pleading. "I want to show you that I'm not going anywhere. You're the one I want to be with. I just need you to believe that."

His words sank into me, warm and soothing, igniting a flicker of hope that began to chase away the shadows. "You really mean that?" I asked, seeking confirmation in his gaze.

"Absolutely," he affirmed, stepping closer, our bodies almost touching. "You have no idea how much you mean to me."

Before I could respond, a sudden burst of laughter erupted from the café, drawing our attention. A group of friends spilled out onto the street, their voices bright and carefree. One girl, with a cascade of curly hair, pointed toward us. "Hey! Are you guys coming in or what? It's karaoke night!"

Rylan chuckled, shaking his head. "We were just having a serious moment, but sure, let's throw that out the window."

"Why not?" I replied, my heart lightening at the thought. "Sometimes you need a little ridiculousness to reset."

"Then let's embrace the ridiculousness!" Rylan took my hand, his touch warm and grounding as he led me toward the café. The sounds of life enveloped us, laughter and music swirling around like a joyful tapestry.

As we stepped inside, the atmosphere buzzed with energy, the kind of vibrant chaos that could make anyone feel alive. A microphone sat on a small stage, and the crowd erupted in cheers as someone launched into a high-energy pop song. I turned to Rylan, the smile on my face growing wider. "You know I can't sing."

He grinned, mischief dancing in his eyes. "Neither can I, but that's the beauty of karaoke! It's all about confidence. Besides, I'd love to hear your rendition of 'I Will Survive.'"

"Oh, how cliché," I laughed, rolling my eyes. "But, fine. If you sing along, I'll give it a shot."

His face lit up, and just like that, the weight of our earlier conversation lifted. The shadows were still lurking, but for the moment, they were overshadowed by the light radiating from the stage and the laughter around us.

Rylan grabbed a couple of drinks, and as we settled into a booth, the world outside faded into a blur. The energy in the room felt contagious, and soon we found ourselves immersed in the madness of karaoke, the microphone bouncing between us, laughter punctuating our off-key notes.

In that instant, I realized that despite the shadows, despite the lingering whispers of his past, this was where I wanted to be. Here, with him, amidst the music and chaos, I felt a renewed sense of hope, a belief that perhaps we could navigate through this together, one ridiculous song at a time. And maybe, just maybe, we could build a future bright enough to cast those shadows aside.

The karaoke night unfolded like a chaotic masterpiece, each out-of-tune note layering over the last, creating a beautiful cacophony that wrapped around me like a warm hug. Rylan and I took turns belting out lyrics we hardly knew, laughing at our own terrible harmonies while the crowd egged us on. With each song, the earlier tension began to feel like a distant memory, the shadows retreating under the bright lights of the café.

As the night wore on, the air thick with the scent of fried food and spilled drinks, I felt an undeniable thrill coursing through me. Rylan's eyes sparkled with mischief and joy, a side of him I found intoxicating. He caught my gaze and raised his glass, the amber liquid inside catching the glow of the neon lights above us. "To spontaneity!" he declared, his voice a mix of bravado and playfulness.

"To spontaneity and bad singing!" I laughed, clinking my glass against his. Just as I took a sip, the lively beat of a new song echoed through the café, and my gaze shifted toward the stage, where a girl in a sequined top was enthusiastically belting out a ballad. Her voice was surprisingly good, filling the room with a sweetness that contrasted with our earlier attempts at rock anthems. I turned back to Rylan, ready to suggest our next duet when I spotted a familiar figure entering the café.

Elise.

My heart dropped like a stone. She glided in with an effortless grace, her dark hair cascading over her shoulders, and my breath caught as she scanned the room, her eyes finally landing on Rylan. For a moment, everything slowed—time itself seemed to hold its breath, the laughter and music fading into a muffled backdrop. I could see the moment she recognized him, a flicker of surprise transforming into a radiant smile that lit up her face.

Rylan followed my gaze, and his expression changed from delight to apprehension in an instant. "Oh no," he muttered under his breath, an ominous foreboding lacing his words.

I felt my palms grow clammy, my pulse quickening. "What is she doing here?" The question escaped my lips before I could stop it, the bitterness spilling forth like an unexpected tide.

"She probably didn't know I'd be here," Rylan replied, but the way he said it left little room for reassurance. The ease we'd found in each other's company began to unravel, threads of anxiety weaving themselves tightly around us once more.

Before I could articulate my spiraling thoughts, Elise approached our table, her confidence radiating as she slipped into the space beside Rylan. "Rylan! What a surprise!" she exclaimed, her voice bright and lilting, cutting through the heavy tension in the air. "I didn't expect to see you here."

Her presence was magnetic, drawing the eyes of several patrons around us, and my throat tightened with jealousy. "I was just trying to enjoy a little karaoke," Rylan replied, his smile strained, almost forced. "You know, typical Friday night."

"Is that so?" Elise said, her eyes twinkling as she leaned closer to him, her tone playful yet laced with something more insidious. "You always loved a good show. How's your dancing going? I've heard rumors that you're quite the star now."

I could see the tension knotting in Rylan's shoulders, the way he leaned away from her, as if she was a magnet pulling him toward something he was desperate to escape. I clenched my jaw, forcing myself to remain composed. This was supposed to be a fun night, a reset from our earlier conversation, and here she was, invading our space with an allure that felt dangerously familiar.

"I'm just trying to find my rhythm," Rylan replied, his voice steady but lacking warmth. "What about you? Still dancing?"

Elise chuckled softly, a sound that sent prickles down my spine. "Oh, I'm always dancing. You know that." Her eyes sparkled with mischief, as if she was daring him to acknowledge their past. "In fact, I've just landed a role in a new show—maybe we could catch up after?"

I couldn't stay silent any longer. "Maybe he's a bit busy right now," I interjected, forcing a smile that felt brittle against my lips. "We were in the middle of a duet."

"Oh, I didn't mean to interrupt," Elise said, her tone syrupy sweet as she turned her gaze on me. "I'm Elise, by the way."

"I know who you are," I replied, a hint of steel edging my voice. "Rylan's told me about you."

"Ah, the infamous ex," she said, feigning innocence. "It's nice to finally meet you. I hope he's treating you well."

Rylan shifted uncomfortably, the muscles in his jaw tightening as he glanced between us. "We're just having fun, Elise. Like you said, it's a karaoke night. Nothing serious."

Elise smiled, but it didn't reach her eyes. "Of course. Just like old times, right? I didn't mean to bring any drama."

The tension hung heavy, thick enough to slice through, and I felt the creeping sensation of my heart sinking deeper into my chest. I was acutely aware of the shifting dynamics, the way Elise's presence was like a pebble tossed into a calm pond, sending ripples of uncertainty through the space we had built together.

"Maybe you should take the stage, Rylan," she said, her voice low and inviting. "Show us what you've got."

Before he could respond, she took the microphone from the stand and gestured toward him. "Come on! Let's do something fun. I promise not to steal the spotlight... too much."

Rylan hesitated, glancing at me as if seeking my approval. I could see the conflict in his eyes—he wanted to support me, to reassure me, but Elise was a shadow he couldn't entirely shake. "I don't think—"

"Oh, come on! It'll be fun!" Elise pressed, her enthusiasm feigned but persuasive. "You were always the star of the show."

I could feel the heat rising in my cheeks as the laughter from nearby tables grew louder, the group around the stage urging him on. "You should go," I said, forcing the words through clenched teeth. "If it'll make her go away."

Rylan's gaze flickered between me and Elise, the tension palpable. "Are you sure?"

"Yes," I replied firmly, my voice steadier than I felt. "Just... go."

With a reluctant nod, he stepped onto the stage, and the crowd erupted into applause. I watched as he took the microphone, the spotlight illuminating him in a way that made him shine. But I couldn't shake the feeling of dread tightening in my gut. As he began to sing—a mix of confidence and vulnerability—I turned my attention back to Elise, who leaned against the edge of our booth, her eyes glimmering with something dark and possessive.

"Looks like he's still got it," she remarked, her tone dripping with false admiration.

"Yeah, he does," I replied, my voice low. "And he's mine."

Elise arched an eyebrow, her smile widening as she leaned in closer. "Is he, though? Or are you just a temporary distraction until I'm back in town?"

Before I could respond, Rylan glanced back at me, the warmth of his gaze giving me a flicker of hope amid the storm brewing inside. But as he sang, I noticed Elise moving subtly closer, her hand brushing against his arm in a way that felt all too familiar. My heart raced with anxiety as I clenched my fists in my lap, battling the urge to scream or throw something—or both.

I could feel my composure slipping, the earlier laughter and lightness now replaced with a heaviness I couldn't shake. Suddenly, Elise's laughter rang out, sharp and cutting, pulling me from my thoughts. I turned to see her leaning into Rylan, whispering something that made him laugh, the sound echoing in my ears like a cruel taunt.

"Maybe you should just admit it," she said, her voice low enough that I couldn't hear the words but could see the way his expression shifted, his smile faltering.

A flash of insecurity flickered through me, a gut-wrenching twist that left me momentarily breathless. It felt like I was watching a scene unfold that I wasn't a part of, a world where Rylan might slip back into the comfort of his past—one I feared he could still be attached to.

As the song wrapped up, Rylan's eyes found mine once more, but this time, I saw something different—a flicker of confusion mixed with the warmth I had come to love. "Kaylee, are you okay?" he called, his voice cutting through the applause.

Before I could respond, the lights flickered and dimmed. The café fell into a sudden hush, a moment of stillness before chaos erupted as a loud crash rang out from the back, followed by shouts.

I turned, my heart pounding, and saw a figure rushing through the entrance, their silhouette outlined by the harsh streetlights outside. Time slowed as I recognized the familiar face, the wild eyes filled with panic.

"Kaylee! We need to talk!"

The air crackled with tension as I faced the newcomer, my breath hitching in my throat. The shadows from Rylan's past were far from over, and in that instant, I realized just how precarious the balance we had built truly was.

Chapter 25: Echoes of Insecurity

The sun dipped low in the sky, casting a warm, golden glow over the sprawling garden, where vibrant flowers danced in the gentle breeze. I wandered among the rosebushes, their sweet fragrance enveloping me, a bittersweet reminder of the love I sought to nurture but often felt slipping through my fingers. With each petal brushed by my fingers, I recalled the conversations Rylan and I had shared, filled with laughter and dreams, now shadowed by the unwelcome specter of my insecurities. It was maddening how swiftly they had taken root, tangling themselves within my thoughts like the vines creeping up the old stone walls.

As I knelt to inspect a cluster of blossoms, my mind drifted to Rylan's past—the woman whose laughter had once filled our shared spaces. A knot tightened in my stomach. He had been open about his previous relationship, a fact that should have brought me comfort but only fanned the flames of my unease. I had convinced myself that I was strong, that I could navigate this labyrinth of emotions without faltering, yet here I was, ensnared in my own self-doubt.

The whispers of doubt grew louder, echoing in my mind as I recalled the easy familiarity between Rylan and his ex. The way her eyes sparkled when she spoke to him, the gentle touches that lingered just a moment too long. My heart raced with every memory, and I could almost hear the taunting voice of insecurity whispering in my ear, urging me to look closer, to scrutinize every smile, every shared glance. It was a game I couldn't afford to play, yet I felt drawn in, as if the pull of jealousy was a magnetic force, impossible to resist.

I stepped away from the roses, seeking refuge on the patio where the sound of laughter drifted toward me like a siren's call. Rylan was seated at the outdoor table, his animated voice slicing through the evening air. He was engrossed in a conversation with a group of friends, and there she was—the woman whose very presence felt like a flickering flame to my insecurities. My stomach churned as I watched her lean in, her laughter lilting and light. I knew I shouldn't, yet I couldn't help myself; I was like a moth drawn to a flame, too entranced by the fire to recognize the danger.

With every shared story, every burst of laughter, the shadows in my mind grew darker. What was wrong with me? I wanted to be the confident woman Rylan deserved, not the jealous specter lurking in the background. I could feel the walls of my carefully constructed façade starting to crumble. When our eyes met for a brief moment, his expression shifted—concern, perhaps, or maybe just the awareness that I was on the edge of an emotional precipice.

I excused myself, my heart pounding in my chest. I could feel the tension coiling inside me, a tightly wound spring that threatened to snap. I needed to confront this, to lay bare the twisted roots of my doubts before they consumed everything we had built together. I found Rylan later, standing in the kitchen, his back to me as he poured a glass of water. The casual intimacy of the moment was almost unbearable. The sunlight streamed through the window, illuminating the space, but all I could see were the shadows lurking in my mind.

"Can we talk?" My voice was steady, though my heart raced like a hummingbird trapped in a cage.

He turned, the glass pausing mid-air. "Of course. What's up?"

I gestured toward the living room, a battlefield I had not intended to enter. My heart sank as I recalled our laughter echoing through the walls, now replaced with an uneasy silence. We settled on the couch, the space between us feeling like a chasm.

"I—" The words lodged in my throat like stones, heavy and unyielding. "I overheard you talking with your ex today."

Rylan's brow furrowed, a flash of confusion in his eyes. "What do you mean?"

My pulse quickened, and I rushed on, the words tumbling out like a dam bursting. "You two seemed so... comfortable. It's just that I can't help but wonder if there's still something there, something I can't compete with."

The silence that followed was thick, almost tangible. I could see the hurt flicker in his gaze, and it struck me like a blow. "You think I would go back to her?" he asked, his voice a low rumble filled with disbelief. "You think I would choose her over you?"

"I don't know! I just—" I paused, taking a deep breath, struggling against the tide of my emotions. "I feel like I'm always standing in her shadow. You have this history with her, and I'm afraid I'm not enough."

Rylan's expression softened, and he leaned closer, his hands finding mine, grounding me in that moment. "You are more than enough. I chose you. Every single day, I choose you." His thumb brushed over my knuckles, igniting warmth that chased away the chill of my doubts. "But you have to believe that too."

His words hung between us, heavy with meaning. The tension began to dissolve, replaced by the fragile thread of understanding. Yet, as I looked into his eyes, I realized that confronting my insecurities was only part of the battle. I needed to peel back the layers of my own heart, to unravel the twisted vines of jealousy and self-doubt that threatened to choke out the love we were building. I had to find a way to trust not only him but also myself. The journey ahead wouldn't be easy, but perhaps, together, we could cultivate a garden of hope amid the shadows.

The air in the kitchen was thick with the smell of herbs and spices, remnants of the dinner we had hastily prepared. My fingers played nervously with the hem of my shirt as Rylan worked beside me, chopping vegetables with a precision that made my heart flutter, even amid the storm of emotions brewing inside me. I attempted to focus on the sizzling pan in front of me, but my mind was a cacophony of doubt and fear, a relentless drumbeat underscoring our strained conversation from earlier.

"Do you want to add more garlic?" Rylan asked, glancing up from his task, a hint of a smile playing at the corners of his mouth, one that still managed to lighten the atmosphere despite the tension. It was the same smile that had once melted my defenses, but now it felt like a reminder of everything I feared losing.

"Sure, why not?" I replied, forcing a casual tone that didn't quite match the tumult of my thoughts. I fumbled for the garlic, my movements clumsy, as if my fingers were weighted down by uncertainty. Each thud of the knife against the cutting board resonated with the echoes of my insecurities, punctuating the silence that lingered between us.

He continued chopping, the rhythm steady and calming. I watched him, trying to absorb the familiarity of the moment. Rylan was in his element, the kitchen a stage where he effortlessly performed, oblivious to the chaos swirling in my mind. I longed to be that free, to dance around the uncertainties that threatened to hold me captive, yet I felt more like a marionette with tangled strings, unable to break free.

"Hey, do you remember that night we made pasta from scratch?" he asked suddenly, his voice rich with nostalgia. The corners of my mouth turned up involuntarily at the memory.

"Are you talking about the night you declared war on the flour?" I laughed, the sound shaky yet genuine. I could still picture the chaos: flour everywhere, and Rylan attempting to impress me with his culinary skills while utterly failing to keep the mess contained. "You had it in your hair for days."

He chuckled, and the sound warmed me, even as the shadows of doubt still loomed. "I think I still have a little flour in the crevices of my kitchen drawers."

"Good luck finding it," I teased, trying to draw myself back into the light.

But the moment of levity was fleeting, and the dark tendrils of jealousy soon returned, whispering insidiously. I grabbed the garlic, trying to focus, but my thoughts danced around his ex again, her laughter echoing in my mind, a taunting melody that wouldn't fade.

As if sensing my shift in mood, Rylan turned serious. "You know, you can talk to me about anything, right?"

I hesitated, weighing my words. "I just... I want to feel like I'm enough for you," I finally admitted, the confession tumbling out like a whisper caught in the wind. "It's hard when I see you with her."

His expression softened, and he set down his knife, taking a step closer. "You are enough. In every way that matters, you are more than enough for me. You're the one I want to build a future with, not her."

I wanted to believe him. The sincerity in his eyes ignited a flicker of hope within me, but the doubts lingered like shadows in a dimly lit room. "But what if you change your mind? What if she still has a hold on you?"

Rylan took my hands in his, his grip firm yet gentle. "I can't control how you feel, but I can control what I do. You have to trust me. Trust that I'm here, right now, choosing you." His eyes were dark with intensity, holding my gaze like a lifeline.

I swallowed hard, trying to find my voice amid the tangled emotions. "It's just that the way you two interacted... It felt like there was still something there. Something I can't compete with."

"Is this about her, or is it really about us?" he challenged softly, and I flinched at the truth in his words. The reality was hard to face, but I knew he was right. My insecurities were a barrier I had erected, and it was time to dismantle it.

"I don't want to hold you back," I murmured, the weight of vulnerability pressing down on me. "But every time I see you two together, it feels like a mirror reflecting everything I fear about myself. What if I'm not enough for you?"

He sighed, rubbing his thumb over my knuckles. "You're looking in the wrong mirror, then. You should be seeing all the things that make you who you are—your kindness, your strength, your endless ability to care. You are not a shadow; you are the light."

For a moment, I reveled in his words, basking in the warmth of his affection, but the shadows still loomed. "I want to believe that," I admitted, the honesty hanging in the air between us. "But the insecurities are loud, and they're so very convincing."

Rylan stepped back slightly, his expression thoughtful. "How about we confront those shadows together? What if we dig into this—your feelings, your fears—and start building something that feels stronger than those echoes of doubt?"

I searched his face, his resolve igniting a flicker of courage within me. "You're serious?"

"Absolutely. We can set aside time each week—just you and me—where we talk about what's bothering you. No judgment, just honesty. We'll take a magnifying glass to those fears and tackle them one by one."

The idea was terrifying yet exhilarating. "And what if I just end up sounding like a crazy person?"

"Honestly?" He chuckled, the sound warm and reassuring. "You'd fit right in with my family. Crazy is practically a prerequisite for being a member."

I couldn't help but laugh, the tension easing just a little. "Okay, but what if I reveal too much and scare you off?"

"Then I'll be the one making dinner every night for the rest of my life to atone for my fears." He winked, and I couldn't help but feel a little lighter, the shadows retreating just a step.

"Deal," I replied, my heart lifting at the prospect of being vulnerable with him. Perhaps this was the path to healing—not just confronting my insecurities but allowing Rylan to be a part of the journey.

As we resumed cooking, a newfound determination bubbled within me. With each slice of the knife, each stir of the pot, I could feel the edges of my insecurities begin to soften, melting away like the butter sizzling in the pan. The road ahead wouldn't be without its bumps, but with Rylan by my side, I finally felt ready to confront the shadows and carve out a space for the light.

The aroma of garlic and sautéed vegetables lingered in the kitchen, a fragrant reminder of our commitment to each other—and to honesty. The initial tension from our earlier confrontation had receded, replaced by a palpable sense of possibility that hung between us like a fragile thread. As we continued cooking, I caught glimpses of Rylan's playful side, the one that made him utterly charming and impossibly easy to fall for. He tossed in a handful of herbs, his laughter echoing in the cozy space, igniting warmth in my chest that chased away the lingering chill of doubt.

"You know, for someone who claims to be a chef, you're awful at measuring ingredients," I teased, eyeing the way he flung spices into the pan with reckless abandon.

"Cooking is about art, not science," he replied, his eyes glinting mischievously. "Besides, who needs precision when you have passion?"

I rolled my eyes, unable to suppress a smile. "Right, because nothing says romance like a sprinkle of chaos in a pan."

He leaned closer, an exaggerated seriousness in his expression. "Oh, but it's a beautiful chaos. It's like our relationship—wild, unpredictable, but ultimately delicious."

Our laughter filled the room, and I felt the barriers I had built slowly beginning to crumble. This lightness, this spark between us, reminded me of why I was willing to confront my insecurities head-on. But just as I began to settle into this newfound comfort, the phone buzzed on the counter, its shrill tone slicing through our moment like a knife.

I glanced at it, the screen lighting up with a name that sent my heart plummeting—Hannah. Rylan's ex. I felt a rush of anxiety clawing at my chest as I debated whether to say something or ignore it. When I looked up, Rylan was already reaching for it, a frown knitting his brow.

"Should I answer?" he asked, his tone cautious, as if he could sense the storm brewing behind my calm exterior.

"Maybe just text her back?" I suggested, the tension reweaving itself around us.

"Yeah, I could do that," he said, but his finger lingered over the screen. "I should probably clear the air. I don't want you to feel uncomfortable."

A part of me understood the need for openness, yet another part recoiled, the familiar vine of jealousy tightening its grip. "If you think it's necessary." I tried to keep my tone neutral, but I could feel the cracks in my resolve beginning to show.

With a deep breath, Rylan began to type, the silence stretching between us, heavy and fraught with unspoken words. The kitchen, once a haven of comfort, morphed into a stage for this unwanted drama. As I watched him, I felt the familiar thrum of anxiety coursing through me, amplifying every doubt I had tried to shed.

The seconds felt like hours until Rylan finally hit send. He placed the phone down, the tension palpable. "I told her I'm busy, but I'll talk to her later," he said, his voice steady, but I could see the flicker of uncertainty in his eyes.

"Good idea," I replied, but I could feel the skepticism creeping back in. "You know how I feel about this."

He sighed, his shoulders relaxing a fraction. "I know. But I promise, I'm here for you. You're my priority."

Before I could respond, the phone buzzed again, a text from Hannah lighting up the screen. My heart raced as I caught a glimpse of the message: "Can we talk? I need to explain some things."

Rylan frowned, his brows furrowing. "I don't like the sound of that," he muttered. "Why now?"

"Maybe she wants to rekindle something," I blurted out before I could stop myself, my insecurity flaring again like a flame. "Maybe she wants to take you back."

His gaze sharpened, and for a moment, the warmth of our earlier banter felt distant. "You know that's not what I want. We've talked about this."

"Then why does she keep coming back? Why can't she just let you go?" The frustration in my voice surprised even me, the words spilling out like a dam breaking.

"Because she's not ready to let go, but I am," he said firmly. "I've moved on, and I thought you understood that."

"I do, but seeing her name sends me spiraling!" I threw my hands up in exasperation, the whirlwind of emotions too overwhelming to contain. "I thought we were past this, but then she shows up, and it's like I'm right back at square one."

Rylan took a step toward me, his expression softening. "Let's not let her have that power over us. We're building something here, remember? We can't let old ghosts haunt our future."

His words hung in the air, resonating deep within me, and I knew he was right. I wanted to believe in the strength of what we were building.

"Then let's not let this be about her," I said, taking a breath. "How about we plan something fun together to remind ourselves why we're here?"

"Great idea," he said, his eyes lighting up. "What do you have in mind?"

"Let's escape somewhere—an adventure. Just the two of us. A little road trip, maybe?" The suggestion hung between us like a lifeline.

"Road trip it is!" He grinned, the warmth returning to the space as he reached for my hand. But just as our fingers intertwined, the phone buzzed again, this time vibrating aggressively against the countertop. Rylan looked at it, the smile faltering as he read the incoming message.

"Rylan," I said cautiously, sensing the shift in his demeanor. "What is it?"

His expression turned serious, tension radiating from him like static electricity. "It's from Hannah. She... she says she's in town and wants to see me. Now."

The words hung in the air, heavy and fraught with meaning. My breath caught in my throat, and suddenly the warmth of the kitchen felt suffocating. The flickering flame of hope sputtered under the weight of uncertainty, and I felt the shadows creep back, darker than before.

"Right now?" I repeated, the words tasting bitter on my tongue. "What does she want? Does she not understand boundaries?"

"I don't know," he said, running a hand through his hair, frustration etched across his face. "But I have to figure this out. I owe it to her to at least hear her out, don't I?"

The room spun as my heart raced, the thought of him alone with her sending a surge of panic through me. "Rylan, please—"

"Look, I'll set boundaries," he promised, but the conviction in his voice felt thin, like a tightrope stretched over an abyss. "You have to trust me. I'll be back before you know it."

But as he turned away, I couldn't shake the feeling that the echoes of insecurity were rising again, louder than ever. The door creaked open behind him, the promise of confrontation looming like an unwelcome storm on the horizon. Just as he stepped outside, my phone buzzed again, and my heart dropped. It was a message from Hannah: "I need to tell you the truth about us. You deserve to know."

The air grew thick with tension, the weight of uncertainty pressing down on me. I clutched the phone, my mind racing, caught in a maelstrom of emotions as I stood on the precipice of a decision. The shadows had returned, more daunting than before, and as I looked out the door to where Rylan stood, my heart raced with the realization that everything was about to change.

Chapter 26: Unveiling the Truth

The park unfolds before me like a well-kept secret, the kind that wraps you in its embrace just as you step through its gates. Sunlight streams through the leaves overhead, casting a dappled glow on the ground that feels almost magical, as if nature itself is setting the stage for something profound. I take a deep breath, inhaling the scent of blooming jasmine and freshly mowed grass, letting it wash over me like a balm. Rylan walks beside me, his presence a steady anchor in this vibrant world.

We find a bench nestled beneath a sprawling oak tree, its thick branches sheltering us from prying eyes and the chaos of the outside world. I can hear the distant laughter of children playing and the rustling of leaves whispering secrets. Rylan sits, his posture relaxed yet somehow tense, as if he's holding back a storm within. The sunlight catches the angles of his face, illuminating the uncertainty in his deep blue eyes.

"I don't often come here," he starts, his voice low and hesitant, as if the words themselves are afraid of breaking the serene atmosphere. "This place feels different now. It's almost like I've come to understand its beauty only after the storm of my past."

I lean closer, drawn in by the cadence of his words, each one carefully chosen. "What do you mean?" I ask, eager to delve deeper, to peel back the layers of this man who has stirred something within me that I thought long buried.

Rylan takes a moment, gathering his thoughts like a musician tuning his instrument. "When I was younger, I was so naïve. I thought I had it all figured out, you know? The perfect life, the perfect partnership." He glances at me, a flicker of something painful crossing his features. "But life has a way of shattering those illusions. I lost someone I trusted completely, someone who betrayed me when I least expected it."

The sunlight flickers, and a shiver runs down my spine, echoing the coolness of his confession. I feel my heart tighten, recognizing that we all carry scars hidden beneath the surface. "That sounds devastating," I reply softly, wanting to reach out, to comfort him.

"It was," he admits, running a hand through his dark hair, a gesture that reveals both frustration and vulnerability. "I spent years trying to rebuild my self-worth, questioning if I was ever enough. It felt like I was stuck in this loop of rejection, like a record that keeps skipping."

The honesty in his voice resonates within me, amplifying the shadows of my own fears. Rylan's pain is not so distant; I've tasted betrayal, too, and it stings just as sharply. "You are enough, Rylan," I whisper, feeling the weight of the moment pressing down on us like the summer heat. "You deserve to know that."

He looks at me then, those blue eyes piercing through my defenses. "Do I?" His brow furrows, skepticism dancing behind the warmth. "How can you say that when I've been so lost?"

I can feel the tension building between us, a fragile thread that threatens to snap under the weight of our unspoken fears. "Because I see you," I reply, my voice firm yet tender. "You've survived, haven't you? You've pulled through the dark times. That takes strength, and strength is what makes you enough."

Rylan's expression softens, and for a moment, I see a flicker of hope illuminating the shadows that have clung to him for so long. "It's hard to accept that," he murmurs, his vulnerability disarming. "I've built walls to protect myself, but those walls have kept me from experiencing what I truly want."

"Which is?" I probe, leaning forward, the air thick with anticipation.

"Connection," he breathes, the word spilling out like a prayer. "Real connection. I've been so afraid of opening up that I almost missed out on something incredible." He gestures between us, his hand slicing through the air like a decisive declaration. "Like this."

There's a spark of electricity in his words, a promise that ignites something deep within me. My pulse quickens, a rush of emotions swirling in a dizzying dance. "You're not alone in this," I assure him, the words spilling forth as if they've been waiting to be said. "I've held back, too. I've let my fears dictate my actions, pushing away the very thing I wanted most."

The honesty in the moment wraps around us, pulling us closer, revealing a shared tapestry of hurt and healing. "I'm sorry for accusing you," I say, my voice steady yet laced with sincerity. "I was scared. Scared of losing someone I care about before I even really had them."

Rylan's expression shifts, the hardness in his eyes melting into something softer, more vulnerable. "It's okay," he replies, his voice barely above a whisper. "We all have our baggage. I don't want to add to yours; I want to help lighten the load."

A comfortable silence settles between us, filled with the gentle rustle of leaves and the distant sounds of laughter that feels like a soundtrack to our unfolding story. I can feel the walls I've built beginning to crumble, the weight of my past losses lifting as I choose to trust again. The sun shines brighter now, bathing us in warmth, and for the first time in a long while, I feel the stirrings of hope.

"I'm willing to take that chance if you are," I say, my heart racing as I lock eyes with him. "To embrace the unknown together."

His smile is slow, hesitant but genuine, a beacon of light piercing through the remnants of doubt. "Together," he echoes, and with that single word, the promise of a new beginning unfurls between us like the petals of a flower, ready to bloom.

As we linger beneath the sprawling oak, the afternoon light seems to wrap around us, infusing the moment with a warmth that goes beyond the golden rays. I can feel the thrum of potential in the air, an energy that vibrates between us like the strings of a finely tuned guitar. Rylan's presence is a soothing balm to the chaos of my mind, and I revel in the way our shared vulnerability begins to weave an intricate tapestry of understanding.

"I used to think I was the only one struggling to figure things out," I say, breaking the comfortable silence that envelops us like a cozy blanket. "But I guess it's universal, this dance of fear and trust."

He nods, his gaze steady and encouraging. "It's like a tightrope walk. One misstep, and you feel like you're plummeting. But then there are moments when you catch yourself, when you realize you're not as alone as you thought."

His words resonate with me, echoing the sentiments I've carried for too long. "Exactly. It's terrifying and exhilarating all at once." I smile, surprised at how easily the conversation flows now, no longer strained by uncertainty.

Just as I start to relax into this newfound connection, a sudden commotion draws our attention. A group of children races by, their laughter bubbling up like a sweet melody that contrasts sharply with the heaviness of our earlier discussion. One little girl, her hair in pigtails and cheeks flushed with excitement, stumbles and falls, sending a cascade of giggles spiraling into the air. My heart leaps with empathy as I instinctively lean forward.

Rylan chuckles, a rich sound that warms the space between us. "That's the joy of childhood. It's a chaotic mess, but they bounce back so easily."

"Don't I know it," I reply, recalling the countless times I'd faced my own tumbles, both literal and metaphorical. "I mean, I might not have the pigtails, but I've definitely had my share of falls."

"Pigtails or not, we've all got our battles," he replies, his voice playful yet sincere. The banter lightens the air, a refreshing breeze amid the warmth of our earlier revelations. "So, what's your battle, then?"

"Let's see," I muse, leaning back against the bench, the sun filtering through the leaves creating a patchwork of light and shadow on my skin. "I've always been the steady one, you know? The one who keeps everything in line. But there's a storm brewing beneath the surface. I've hidden behind my responsibilities for so long that I've forgotten how to really live. I want to embrace the chaos, but I'm terrified of what that looks like."

Rylan studies me, his expression thoughtful. "What if you found a way to mix the chaos with your steady nature? Like a carefully orchestrated symphony, blending wildness with structure?"

I laugh, appreciating the image. "A symphony of chaos? That sounds like a recipe for disaster—or the start of a very interesting life."

"Exactly," he replies, his smile infectious. "Life isn't meant to be a neatly organized file cabinet. It's messy, it's unpredictable, and sometimes it's downright chaotic. But those moments are what make the best stories."

His words resonate deep within me, and I can't help but feel the walls I've built around my heart begin to crumble. "Okay, Mr. Philosopher, what's your recipe for embracing that chaos?"

Rylan leans in, his eyes sparkling with mischief. "First, you let go of your expectations. Stop trying to control everything. Second, you dive into the mess—maybe try a spontaneous road trip or bake something wildly extravagant. And finally, you don't take yourself too seriously. Embrace the blunders as part of the journey."

"Spontaneous road trip, huh?" I raise an eyebrow, intrigued yet skeptical. "And what do you suggest we take for the ride? A map? A playlist? Or do we just wing it and hope for the best?"

"Who needs a map?" he replies with a grin, his confidence infectious. "The thrill is in the adventure, not the destination. Besides, you can always find your way back."

There's a spark in his eyes that ignites something within me, a flicker of daring that I've suppressed for too long. "Alright then, let's put this theory to the test. What if we just... decided to get lost together?"

His expression shifts, the playfulness giving way to something deeper. "Are you serious?"

I nod, a smile tugging at my lips, emboldened by the potential of spontaneity. "Why not? We've spent enough time dwelling on the past. Let's create some chaos and memories instead."

Rylan's gaze grows intense, his sincerity palpable. "You're really willing to do this? Just... get in the car and drive?"

"Why not? The worst that can happen is we end up in the middle of nowhere, sharing a few ridiculous stories and maybe getting caught in a downpour."

He laughs, the sound rich and melodic. "Okay, then. Let's make a plan. No plan. Just us, the open road, and whatever mischief we can find."

As he speaks, I feel a flutter of excitement in my chest, a thrill that courses through me like electricity. It's a small yet significant leap towards letting go of control and embracing the unknown.

"Alright," I say, my voice steady, masking the whirlwind of emotions beneath. "But we need to make one rule: no looking back. We leave our worries behind."

"Deal."

In that moment, the sun dips lower in the sky, casting a warm glow that wraps around us, illuminating our resolve. I can feel the tension of my past slipping away, replaced by the exhilaration of what lies ahead. With Rylan by my side, the future suddenly seems brimming with possibilities, a canvas awaiting our brushstrokes.

"Let's start with ice cream," I declare, standing up with a newfound sense of purpose. "I've heard that's the perfect fuel for a spontaneous adventure."

Rylan rises, mirroring my enthusiasm. "Ice cream and the open road? Now that's a combination I can get behind."

As we walk hand in hand, I realize that this leap into the unknown feels less like a risk and more like the beginning of something beautiful, a dance of chaos and connection that I never knew I craved. And as the sun begins to set, painting the sky in hues of orange and pink, I can't help but smile, ready to embrace whatever comes next.

The sun dips lower in the sky, casting a golden glow that dances on the surface of the ice cream shop's sign. The air hums with the sweet scent of waffle cones and warm caramel, a siren call that leads us inside. The shop is a charming little nook, filled with the soft laughter of children and the rich, creamy sound of scoops being served.

I scan the menu, my mouth watering at the endless options. "I have to admit, I'm a sucker for the classics," I say, tapping my finger against my chin in mock contemplation. "Chocolate chip cookie dough or a rich mint chocolate chip? I'm torn."

Rylan leans closer, his breath tickling my ear. "You could always go for both. Life is too short for just one flavor."

The warmth of his words sends a delightful shiver down my spine. "You make a compelling argument," I reply, smirking at him. "But I think I'd need to keep my options open. You never know when you'll need a backup plan, right?"

He raises an eyebrow, a glint of mischief in his eyes. "So, are we already strategizing our dessert choices? What's next, an emergency kit in the car for ice cream runs?"

"Absolutely," I say, my laughter ringing out like the tinkling of wind chimes. "You never know when a spontaneous craving might strike. I can see it now: ice packs, extra spoons, napkins—maybe even a small tarp for the inevitable spills."

As we place our orders, I can feel a lightness in my chest, the kind that comes from being truly present. I'm grateful for this moment, for the silliness that makes everything else fade away. When we step back outside, cone in hand, I take a moment to savor the cool, creamy texture as it melts against my tongue.

"This is heavenly," I declare, my eyes widening as I indulge. "I might need to rethink my entire life plan based on this ice cream."

Rylan chuckles, taking a generous lick of his own cone. "I fully support a life plan built around ice cream. If we're going to embrace the chaos, let's do it with dessert."

As we stroll along the park's winding path, laughter bubbling between us, I feel an unfamiliar but welcome sense of freedom. The world around us seems to shimmer, each step filled with possibility. I glance sideways at Rylan, his expression relaxed yet intent, as if he's cataloging each moment to treasure later.

"You know," I say, breaking the comfortable rhythm of our banter, "there's something refreshing about doing something so utterly ridiculous and spontaneous. It makes me feel alive."

"Alive is good," he agrees, a playful glint in his eye. "But I have to warn you, if you keep this up, we might end up on an adventure so outrageous that we'll need a support group."

"Only if there's ice cream involved," I tease back, savoring the last bite of my cone before tossing the empty wrapper into a nearby bin.

We continue walking, our conversation weaving through the air like a gentle breeze, flitting from one topic to the next. The sun sinks lower, painting the sky in shades of pink and orange, and I can feel the pull of dusk as it wraps around us, inviting us to linger a little longer.

"Have you ever considered taking a road trip to somewhere completely unexpected?" Rylan asks, breaking my reverie. "Just packing up and hitting the road with no destination in mind?"

"Actually, I have," I admit, a thrill of excitement bubbling up inside me. "But I've never had the courage to do it. I always thought I needed a plan, a map, some form of direction. But what if I missed out on the experiences that lay off the beaten path?"

He smiles knowingly, as if he can see right through me. "Sometimes the best journeys are the ones that don't follow a map. They're the ones that lead you to places you never knew you needed to be."

A shiver of excitement dances along my spine at his words. "You're right. And who knows what we might discover? New places, new flavors—"

Just then, a sudden gust of wind sweeps through the park, rustling the leaves and sending a shiver through the air. I glance around, momentarily distracted by the change in the atmosphere. My heart skips a beat as I spot a figure lingering by the park entrance, their features obscured by the gathering shadows.

"Hey, do you see that?" I point, my pulse quickening as my instincts scream that something isn't right. Rylan follows my gaze, his playful demeanor instantly replaced with a guarded focus.

"Yeah, I see them," he replies, his voice low and cautious.

The figure shifts slightly, the outline becoming clearer, and a rush of recognition washes over me. "Is that—"

"Let's keep moving," Rylan interrupts, his tone firm, urging me forward.

My heart races, confusion swirling in my chest. "But I think that's someone I know! I need to see—"

"Trust me," he insists, gently tugging my arm to guide me away. "Whatever's happening, it's better if we don't get involved."

I want to protest, to demand answers, but the urgency in his voice makes me hesitate. The figure takes a step forward, and for a brief moment, their face is illuminated by the setting sun. My breath catches in my throat as recognition hits me hard, sending my mind into a frenzy. It's someone from my past, someone I thought I'd left behind.

"Rylan, wait," I whisper, my heart pounding in my ears as the figure moves again, clearly looking for someone. "What if they're here for me?"

His grip tightens around my arm, a fierce protectiveness flaring in his gaze. "I said, let's go. We can talk about this later."

But the weight of the moment lingers in the air, the tension palpable as my instincts clash with my desire to confront the figure. Rylan starts to lead me away, but I can't shake the feeling that whatever is happening is about to change everything.

"Please," I urge, my voice barely above a whisper. "Just give me a moment."

As I turn to glance back one last time, the figure locks eyes with me. A rush of emotions washes over me—fear, confusion, anger, and something that feels like betrayal. They take a step forward, a haunting smile spreading across their face as darkness begins to envelop the park.

And in that fleeting moment, as Rylan pulls me further away, I realize the gravity of the choice I must make. Do I turn back to confront my past, or do I take a leap into the unknown with Rylan, leaving everything behind?

Before I can decide, the air grows thick with tension, and the shadows seem to stretch toward us, cloaking the world in an unsettling chill. The figure speaks, their voice low and chilling, cutting through the night like a knife, and I know, without a doubt, that nothing will ever be the same again.

Chapter 27: The Path Forward

The studio hummed with life, the air thick with the scent of polished wood and the faint hint of lavender from the diffuser in the corner. Sunlight streamed through the tall windows, casting warm golden stripes across the floor, illuminating the dust motes dancing in the light. I stood at the center, barefoot and vulnerable, the smoothness of the polished floor sending shivers up my spine as I adjusted my stance. Rylan was across from me, a mere breath away, his presence grounding yet electrifying.

"Okay, let's try that part again," he said, his voice low and steady, laced with an encouragement that made my heart flutter. I had always admired his ability to transform nervous energy into something beautiful, like turning the mundane into art. The anticipation of performing together was palpable, a spark between us that ignited every time our eyes met.

The melody floated around us, a gentle cascade of notes that seemed to wrap around my limbs, beckoning me to let go of my reservations. I inhaled deeply, filling my lungs with the rhythm that pulsed through the studio. The music was both a refuge and a challenge, a reminder of our journey—a tapestry woven from threads of joy and pain. It was not just about dance; it was about vulnerability, about opening up to the world and each other.

As the music swelled, we moved together, our bodies communicating in ways words could not. Each step was a conversation, a shared breath of unspoken feelings and hidden truths. I could feel Rylan's gaze piercing through me, searching for my soul in the delicate weave of our movements. My heart raced with every twist and turn, every spin igniting a deep connection that resonated within me.

"Remember, it's not just about the steps," he reminded me, a hint of a smile playing at the corners of his lips. "It's about telling our story."

I nodded, knowing full well the weight of his words. I had spent years constructing walls around my heart, believing that keeping people at arm's length would shield me from pain. But in Rylan's presence, those walls began to crumble, and I found myself longing to let him in. This dance was not merely a performance; it was a revelation, a step toward merging our lives in a way that felt exhilaratingly terrifying.

We twirled, our bodies a whirl of motion and intent, and I could feel the warmth radiating from him, enveloping me in a cocoon of security. But beneath that warmth simmered an undercurrent of tension, a subtle reminder of the challenges we faced beyond the studio. Thoughts of past hurts flitted through my mind like shadows, reminding me that our journey was fraught with obstacles. I had learned that love wasn't always enough; it required trust, communication, and a willingness to confront fears head-on.

In that moment, I made a silent vow to embrace the uncertainty. Rylan and I had danced around our feelings long enough; it was time to let the world see the love we were cultivating. I could no longer pretend that everything was perfectly fine, as if our connection was unaffected by the trials we faced. The upcoming showcase was more than just an opportunity; it was a declaration of our commitment to each other, an invitation for others to witness our journey.

As we finished the routine, breathless and euphoric, I looked into Rylan's eyes, the deep pools of sincerity reflecting my own fears and hopes. "What if we really put ourselves out there?" I asked, my voice barely above a whisper.

Rylan grinned, a mischievous light dancing in his eyes. "What if we set the stage on fire?" He reached for my hand, intertwining our fingers, grounding me amidst the swirling emotions. "I mean, we can't let a little fear stop us, right?"

"Right," I agreed, buoyed by his enthusiasm. "But what if we don't set it on fire? What if we bomb?" The thought sent a rush of anxiety through me, but Rylan's grip tightened, his confidence a warm embrace against my doubts.

"We won't bomb," he assured me, laughter lacing his tone. "Even if we do, at least we'll do it together, right? We'll laugh about it later over pizza." His casual mention of pizza made me chuckle, easing the weight pressing down on my chest.

I could picture us, post-performance, collapsing into a booth at our favorite little pizzeria, laughing so hard we'd draw curious glances from other patrons. It was those small moments that had become the fabric of our relationship, and I found comfort in knowing that even if the showcase went awry, we'd still have each other.

With renewed determination, we dove back into our routine, allowing the music to guide us, crafting each movement with intention. I lost myself in the rhythm, surrendering to the dance, and as our bodies flowed together, I realized that this was more than a performance; it was an invitation to embrace all the imperfections that made us beautifully human.

Each step brought us closer, igniting something within me that had long been dormant. The dance was an evolution, a reflection of who we were becoming—not just as individuals but as partners, navigating the delicate balance of love and vulnerability. In those moments, every fear began to dissolve, replaced by a burgeoning hope that perhaps we were stronger together than apart.

The hours slipped away, the sun dipping lower in the sky, painting the studio in hues of orange and gold. We collapsed on the floor, laughter ringing through the air like a sweet melody, the intensity of our rehearsal transforming into a shared joy. As I lay there, breathless and exhilarated, I felt an overwhelming sense of possibility swelling within me. This was just the beginning, and no matter what challenges lay ahead, I knew that with Rylan by my side, we would face them head-on, armed with passion, determination, and a dash of humor.

The next morning dawned crisp and clear, the kind of day that beckons you outside to breathe in the freshness of possibility. I stumbled out of bed, the echoes of last night's rehearsal still dancing in my mind, and poured myself a cup of coffee, watching the steam curl up like tendrils of hope. Each sip was a reminder of the warmth I felt in the studio with Rylan, and the realization that I was on the brink of something profoundly beautiful filled me with nervous excitement.

With the sun streaming through the kitchen window, I pulled on my favorite pair of leggings and a loose-fitting tank top, the fabric soft against my skin. The mirror reflected not just my appearance, but the emotional transformation taking place within me. Gone were the days of feeling invisible; now, I stood taller, fueled by the prospect of sharing my journey—not just through dance, but through life—with someone who genuinely understood the complexity of my heart.

I made my way to the studio, the streets alive with the chatter of morning commuters and the distant hum of traffic. The familiar route felt different today, each step resonating with a newfound sense of purpose. I imagined the audience—friends, family, and perhaps even strangers—gathered to watch our performance, each one witnessing the intimate story of love and growth that we were about to tell. It wasn't just a dance; it was a glimpse into our souls.

Upon entering the studio, I was greeted by the scent of fresh pine from the wooden floors and the subtle notes of lavender lingering in the air. Rylan was already there, stretching and warming up, his silhouette framed by the soft morning light filtering through the windows. He turned as I entered, a grin spreading across his face that sent my heart soaring.

"Look who decided to grace us with her presence," he teased, playful mischief dancing in his eyes. "I was beginning to think you'd slept in."

"Please," I shot back, rolling my eyes with exaggerated flair. "I would never abandon my favorite dance partner. Besides, who else would endure your terrible jokes?"

"Terrible?" He feigned offense, pressing a hand to his chest dramatically. "I'll have you know that my humor is legendary!"

I laughed, the sound bubbling up like champagne, filling the studio with warmth. It was moments like this—light, airy, and full of banter—that made me realize how much I cherished our connection. We fell into our usual routine, a delightful blend of teasing and collaboration as we prepared for the day's rehearsal.

"Let's work on the climax of the duet," Rylan suggested, his tone shifting to something more serious, a hint of excitement threading through his words. "We need it to hit harder, to make it unforgettable."

"Agreed. But how do we make it more powerful?" I pondered, my brow furrowing as I considered our options. "What if we incorporate more of a lift? It'll emphasize the emotional weight of that moment."

He considered my suggestion, nodding slowly. "I like that. It'll not only show the physical connection but also symbolize the support we give each other, lifting each other up."

As we began to work on that section, I could feel the energy shift, our bodies moving in sync like pieces of a puzzle clicking into place. We practiced the lift repeatedly, Rylan's strong arms encircling my waist, his face close to mine, filled with concentration and a hint of mischief.

"Okay, on the count of three," he said, his voice low, a playful smirk playing on his lips. "One...two...three!"

With a surge of strength, he lifted me off the ground, my body soaring for a fleeting moment. I could feel the exhilaration rushing through me, a potent cocktail of trust and adrenaline. But as I came down, the weight of uncertainty crashed over me like a wave, and I faltered, stumbling slightly.

"Whoa there!" Rylan steadied me, laughter bubbling from his lips. "You looked like a bird that forgot how to fly."

"Hey, give me a break! I'm not a professional flyer!" I retorted, shaking off the momentary embarrassment. "Besides, I wasn't ready for my dramatic moment yet."

He chuckled, the sound warm and inviting. "Let's just take it slow. It's okay to feel nervous. That's part of what makes it real."

"Easy for you to say, Mr. Perfect Lift," I replied, my hands on my hips in mock defiance. "You make it look effortless."

"Only because I have a fantastic partner," he shot back, his sincerity softening the air between us. "And it's not just about the dance. It's about how we support each other. If you wobble, I'll catch you. That's the whole point, right?"

His words settled around us, a protective blanket that wrapped me in comfort. The underlying tension in my chest eased, replaced by a growing resolve. "You're right. I just need to trust that we've got this, together."

With renewed determination, we dove back into practice, the music swelling around us like the tide. Each movement became a conversation, a way of expressing our vulnerabilities and strengths. The rehearsal evolved into something more than just steps; it became an exploration of the depths of our connection.

As we worked, I caught glimpses of Rylan's concentration, the way his brow furrowed when he was deep in thought, and the laughter that erupted when we stumbled over a particularly tricky sequence. The moments of frustration morphed into fits of giggles, turning the studio into our personal sanctuary.

But as the hours slipped by, a nagging thought lurked at the edges of my mind. What if we put our hearts out there and the audience didn't respond? What if all of this effort was met with silence? Just as I was about to voice my fears, Rylan caught my gaze.

"Hey," he said softly, his expression shifting to something more earnest. "Whatever happens at the showcase, we're in this together. We're telling our story, and it's already beautiful."

I nodded, grateful for his unwavering support. "You're right. It's about us, not just the performance."

"Exactly," he replied, a flicker of mischief returning to his eyes. "And if we bomb, I promise to buy you the biggest slice of pizza in town. Deal?"

"Deal," I said, laughing as we locked pinky fingers in a childlike gesture of agreement. It felt right, the promise of laughter, companionship, and shared triumphs stretching before us like the sun-drenched studio floor.

With that, we dove back into our routine, the music swelling around us, each note echoing the heartbeat of our connection. I could feel the worries melting away, replaced by the knowledge that, together, we were crafting a story that transcended the stage. We were on the brink of something beautiful, a journey that had only just begun.

The days leading up to the showcase felt like a whirlwind, a beautiful chaos filled with rehearsals that blended into laughter and shared secrets. Each session added another layer to our duet, transforming it into a narrative woven from the threads of our shared experiences. As the date drew closer, the excitement pulsed through me, but so did a nervous tension that I couldn't quite shake. It was as if the air was charged with electricity, and every moment felt both exhilarating and daunting.

One afternoon, as we wrapped up a particularly intense rehearsal, I flopped onto the floor, panting and exhilarated. Rylan sprawled beside me, both of us bathed in the soft glow of the afternoon sun filtering through the studio's large windows. It was peaceful, the world outside momentarily forgotten as we reveled in our little sanctuary.

"Do you think we're ready for this?" I asked, glancing sideways at him, searching for reassurance.

He turned his head to meet my gaze, his expression thoughtful yet playful. "Ready? I think we're more than ready. We're practically professionals at this point," he teased, raising an eyebrow. "But if you want me to throw in some dramatic flair, I could always stage a spontaneous fall during the performance. Just to keep things interesting."

I laughed, the tension in my chest dissipating momentarily. "Please, anything but that. I don't think my heart can take the stress of saving you from a dramatic tumble while trying to keep my own balance!"

"Hey, it would definitely make for a memorable performance," he countered, his grin infectious. "And it would give the audience a story to tell!"

I rolled my eyes, nudging him playfully. "We're trying to tell a beautiful story here, not a slapstick comedy!"

"Is it slapstick if it's unintentional?" he asked, feigning innocence. "Because then it's just art."

We both dissolved into laughter, the sound filling the room, a reminder of how far we had come. There was something about sharing these moments, about the banter that flowed so effortlessly between us, that made me feel invincible. I could feel the bond between us strengthening, each day adding depth to our connection like paint on a canvas.

But as the showcase approached, the reality of performing began to loom larger. Each time we practiced the lift, my heart raced—not just from the thrill of the moment but from the thought of sharing our story with an audience. What if they didn't connect with it? What if they didn't see the beauty in our struggle? My mind spiraled through scenarios, each more nerve-wracking than the last.

"Okay, let's run through the entire thing one more time," Rylan said, interrupting my spiraling thoughts. "And this time, let's make it shine. I want the audience to feel what we feel."

His confidence ignited something within me, a flicker of determination that I clung to as we resumed our practice. We danced through the routine, each movement an expression of unspoken truths, our bodies speaking the language of love, trust, and shared vulnerability. As the final notes of the music swelled, I could feel every emotion pulsing through me, a living testament to our journey together.

But just as we reached the climactic moment of the duet, the lift that was meant to symbolize our strength, a sharp sound echoed through the studio. My heart dropped as I turned to see a figure standing in the doorway, arms crossed, a frown creasing their brow. It was Sarah, the studio owner, her presence suddenly casting a shadow over our joy.

"Can we talk?" she asked, her tone clipped, the weight of her words hanging heavy in the air.

Rylan and I exchanged glances, confusion flaring in his eyes, but I felt an unsettling twist in my stomach. "Uh, sure," I replied hesitantly, pushing myself off the floor. "What's going on?"

Sarah stepped further into the studio, her expression serious. "I just received a call from the venue hosting the showcase. There's been a change in the lineup, and I need to discuss it with you."

A chill ran down my spine. The venue? My heart raced as I anticipated what she might say. "What kind of change?"

"There's been an issue with the sound system. They're concerned about time constraints and have decided to shorten the performance slots for each act. I know how hard you've worked, but..." Her voice trailed off, the implications of her words sinking in like a stone.

"Shorten our performance?" I echoed, my heart thudding in my chest. "But we've planned everything around our duet! We can't just cut it down!"

"I understand," she replied, her tone softening slightly. "But this is out of my control. I'm doing everything I can to advocate for you both, but you might have to adjust the routine or rethink your presentation."

Rylan stepped forward, his brows knit in concern. "What's the new time limit?"

"Three minutes," Sarah replied, her gaze steady but filled with empathy. "You'll need to make quick decisions if you want to keep the essence of your dance."

Three minutes. It felt impossibly short, a cruel twist that threatened to unravel everything we had built. My heart sank, frustration boiling beneath the surface as I exchanged a glance with Rylan. His eyes mirrored my panic, the weight of the challenge settling heavily between us.

"What if we just cut the lift?" he suggested, desperation creeping into his voice. "We could streamline the ending and still make it impactful."

"But that lift is everything!" I protested, panic rising in my chest. "It's the culmination of our journey together. Without it, the dance loses its meaning."

"Then we'll just have to find a way to make it work," he replied, determination flashing in his eyes. "We've faced challenges before. We can't let this stop us now."

Sarah watched us, her expression unreadable. "You have two days. I'm here to help if you need it, but you'll need to work quickly."

As she left the studio, the silence that followed was deafening. I felt as if the ground had shifted beneath my feet, the certainty of our performance suddenly transformed into a tightrope walk between hope and despair.

"Okay, we can do this," Rylan said, breaking the silence as he took my hands in his. "We just need to focus. Let's figure out what we can keep and how we can adapt."

I nodded, though uncertainty gnawed at my insides. "But what if it isn't enough?"

He stepped closer, his gaze unwavering. "Whatever happens, we'll face it together. We've got this, and we'll make it shine."

I took a deep breath, the fire in his determination sparking something within me. "You're right. We just have to trust ourselves and each other. Let's start again."

As we began to map out our new routine, a sense of urgency enveloped us, the clock ticking down on our time together. But just as the music filled the studio once more, the door swung open again, this time revealing someone else entirely.

"Excuse me, are you Rylan and..." The voice was smooth, charming, with an accent that seemed to dance off the words. I turned, my heart racing anew, but it was the sight of the newcomer that sent a jolt through me. A tall figure with an easy smile and an air of confidence leaned against the door frame, watching us intently.

"I hope I'm not interrupting, but I heard about the showcase and thought I'd come by to introduce myself."

In that moment, I felt a familiar pang of insecurity coupled with a flicker of dread. Who was this person, and what did they want? As I exchanged glances with Rylan, my heart thudded louder in my chest. The uncertainty of our performance suddenly felt overshadowed by this unexpected arrival, a new layer of tension coiling tight around us.

"Who are you?" Rylan asked, his tone curious yet cautious.

"Oh, just a dancer looking for a bit of inspiration," the newcomer replied with an enigmatic smile. "And maybe a chance to join you on stage."

Chapter 28: A Leap of Faith

The night of the showcase enveloped the theater in a soft glow, a cascade of lights shimmering against the polished wooden floor. As I stood in the wings, my heart thumped against my ribcage, a frantic drum echoing the anticipation thrumming in the air. The scent of fresh paint mingled with the faint aroma of coffee from the backstage breakroom, a comforting reminder of the countless hours spent rehearsing, laughing, and sometimes crying in this very space. I could hear the murmur of the audience just beyond the curtain, a collective breath held in eager expectation. Each soft rustle of fabric, each whisper of conversation sent another thrill of anxiety darting through me.

"Breathe, Callie," Rylan murmured, his voice a warm balm against my racing thoughts. He stood beside me, tall and confident, his presence both a shield and a spark. With a gentle squeeze of my hand, he anchored me, reminding me that I wasn't alone. "We've got this. Just remember, it's our moment."

His eyes, a striking shade of emerald that gleamed in the dim light, held a confidence that was almost infectious. I nodded, forcing a smile that felt more like a grimace as I glanced out into the vastness of the theater. It was as if the seats were filled with shadows, each one a specter of doubt whispering reminders of my past failures. What if I stumbled? What if the audience saw the tremors in my legs?

"Trust me," Rylan said, his thumb brushing over my knuckles, sending a jolt of reassurance through me. "No one's watching you fail. They're here to watch you shine."

With those words wrapping around me like a silk scarf, I took a deep breath and pushed back against the tide of self-doubt. I focused on the stage, where the spotlight awaited us, a glowing sun illuminating our path. We were about to dance together in front of an audience for the first time since everything changed—the first time since the accident that had taken my brother and had nearly taken my spirit. Tonight wasn't just about showcasing our talent; it was about reclaiming the pieces of myself I had lost in grief.

The stage manager's voice cut through the quiet, announcing us with a flourish that sent a thrill of adrenaline rushing through me. My heartbeat quickened, a staccato rhythm matching the tempo of the music that began to swell from the speakers. As the curtain lifted, revealing the spotlight, I felt as though the world had narrowed to just Rylan and me, the space around us fading into a hazy blur.

We stepped forward, our bodies moving in tandem, each movement a word in an unspoken conversation. The music embraced us, its melodic waves wrapping around our limbs and pulling us into its embrace. Every pirouette, every grand jeté, felt like a bold proclamation of our defiance against the darkness that had once threatened to swallow me whole. I let the music carry me, and as Rylan twirled me under his arm, the gentle whoosh of the air against my skin felt like freedom, like a promise of hope.

The audience erupted in applause, a roaring sea of sound that crashed over me like warm waves on a summer beach. I could see their faces, illuminated by the stage lights, a tapestry of emotions—joy, admiration, and a sprinkle of disbelief, perhaps at how fully we had surrendered to the moment. Their cheers fueled my spirit, replacing the remnants of fear with sheer exhilaration.

"You're incredible!" Rylan whispered as he pulled me closer for a lift, our chemistry electric. The world blurred into a swirl of colors and sounds as he spun us, my heart racing not from anxiety, but from pure, unadulterated joy. The weight of grief, the shackles of past failures, dissolved in the magic of that moment, leaving behind only the thrill of the dance.

As we transitioned into the final act, our movements became more passionate, more urgent. Each leap was a declaration, each turn a revelation. We flowed across the stage, our bodies weaving a story of love and resilience, a story that felt almost larger than life. I found myself grinning, a wide, unfiltered smile that radiated through every pore, and it felt good—no, it felt great—to be alive and fully present, if only for those fleeting moments.

Just as we approached the crescendo, I caught a glimpse of a familiar face in the audience, someone who hadn't been there before. My heart jolted, and for an instant, I lost my rhythm. The unexpected appearance of my mother, dressed in a soft lavender that matched the springtime blooms, struck me like a bolt of lightning. I had almost forgotten what her presence felt like—warm, supportive, yet laced with an undercurrent of tension. Her eyes glistened with unshed tears, and for a heartbeat, I was transported back to childhood days when her applause felt like the highest form of praise.

In that moment of distraction, Rylan caught my eye, his expression questioning but patient. He pulled me back into the dance, wrapping me in the rhythm once more, but the moment lingered at the edges of my mind, a curious mixture of exhilaration and trepidation. Would this performance be enough to mend the rift that had formed between my mother and me?

The final notes soared, and we landed our last pose as the audience erupted into thunderous applause. I could feel their energy wrapping around us, lifting us, and for the first time in a long while, I felt truly free.

The applause echoed in my ears, a symphony of encouragement that wrapped around me like a cherished quilt. The spotlight warmed my skin, but it was Rylan's presence beside me that truly ignited the fire within. We stood in a tableau, our final pose frozen in time, the breathless energy of the performance still coursing through our veins. The audience roared, a wave of sound crashing against the shore of my uncertainty, washing away remnants of self-doubt that had lingered like stubborn fog.

I wanted to bask in this moment, to hold onto it like a lifeline thrown into turbulent waters. Rylan leaned in, his breath brushing against my ear, sending a cascade of shivers down my spine. "You were magnificent," he said, his voice low and intimate, like a secret shared between two lovers. "I think you left them speechless."

I turned to him, my heart fluttering with a mix of adrenaline and something deeper. "And you? I was convinced you'd pull off a double backflip and land straight into the arms of fame," I teased, nudging him playfully. "But I suppose saving me from that missed leap counts as a win, right?"

He laughed, a sound that rang clear as crystal. "I'm just here to keep you from flying off the handle. The last thing we need is a wardrobe malfunction right before the finale." With a playful wink, he straightened, and the two of us took our bows, his hand still firmly in mine.

As we retreated from the stage, the backstage buzz felt like a whirlwind—an array of congratulatory shouts and exuberant laughter filled the air. It was intoxicating, a heady blend of relief and exhilaration, and for a moment, I forgot about everything else: the looming tension with my mother, the darkness of the past, and the uncertainty of what lay ahead. The world outside the theater felt far away, reduced to mere background noise against the vibrant tapestry of the night.

"Hey, superstar!" Elise, my fellow dancer and best friend, rushed over, her wild curls bouncing like a firework display. "That was unreal! Did you see the looks on their faces? I think a few of them might have fainted."

"I did my best not to trip over my own feet," I said, grinning from ear to ear. "But I might have blacked out from the nerves halfway through."

Elise rolled her eyes, her laughter bubbling over. "If blacking out means delivering that level of performance, I might have to hire a personal trainer to scare the daylights out of me every time." She flung an arm around my shoulder, pulling me into a tight embrace that felt like home. "Now come on, let's celebrate. I heard there's cake, and you know how I feel about cake."

"Let me guess—your feelings about cake are as deep as my feelings about dance?" I shot back, and we both chuckled as we made our way through the backstage chaos.

The smell of vanilla and chocolate wafted through the air, drawing us toward a table laden with treats, but my eyes drifted over the crowd. A kaleidoscope of colors—dresses, ties, and smiles—painted the room. I scanned the faces, hoping to catch another glimpse of my mother, that lavender dress standing out like a lighthouse in a storm. But the room swirled with people celebrating, lost in their own happiness, and my heart sank a little. The knot in my stomach twisted again, this time tighter, as the reality of her absence washed over me.

"What's wrong?" Elise asked, her voice a gentle whisper, pulling me back from the edge of my thoughts.

"Nothing. Just... I thought I saw my mom," I admitted, the words tasting bittersweet on my tongue.

Her expression softened, and she squeezed my arm. "You're still waiting for her to see you, aren't you?"

I nodded, the truth raw and exposed. "It's silly, isn't it? I mean, I just performed my heart out, and all I can think about is whether she's proud of me."

"It's not silly. It's human," Elise replied. "You want her to see you as you are now—not just as the little girl who danced in the living room, but as the woman who can light up a stage."

Before I could respond, Rylan joined us, his brow slightly furrowed, a glass of sparkling cider in hand. "What's this? The two most talented dancers in the room feeling sorry for themselves? I thought we were celebrating!"

"Oh, we were just discussing Callie's adoring fans—or lack thereof," Elise said, giving me a playful nudge.

Rylan raised an eyebrow. "You mean the fans who are probably lost in the thrall of your brilliance?" He turned to me, his gaze steady. "Don't let the absence of one person dim your light. You're surrounded by people who love and admire you."

"But what if it's not enough?" I said, the words slipping out before I could stop them. The vulnerability hung in the air, delicate and trembling, and I cursed my inability to keep it at bay.

Rylan regarded me thoughtfully, and in that moment, I saw a flicker of understanding pass between us. "You know, Callie, sometimes it's not about what other people think. It's about what you feel inside. And tonight, you danced like you owned the world. That's what matters."

His words struck a chord deep within, echoing the truth I had been trying to ignore. I was so focused on external validation that I had forgotten to celebrate the journey I had taken to get here—the late nights, the bruised feet, the moments of doubt that I had somehow conquered.

"You're right," I said, a smile creeping onto my face, buoyed by the weight of his reassurance. "It's about owning this moment."

Elise nodded, grinning. "So, can we please indulge in some cake now? I can't celebrate on an empty stomach."

Rylan feigned a gasp, clutching his chest dramatically. "Cake? In the presence of artistry? How dare you suggest such a thing!"

We erupted into laughter, and for a brief, glorious moment, the air shimmered with joy and camaraderie, a delicious distraction from my swirling thoughts. I poured a glass of cider, and as I raised it in a toast, the lights dimmed slightly, drawing attention once again.

A familiar silhouette stepped forward, and my breath caught in my throat. There she was—my mother, standing at the edge of the celebration, her expression a blend of pride and uncertainty. Our eyes locked, and I felt the world shift beneath me. The moment hung in the air, heavy with unspoken words, as the celebration continued around us, oblivious to the quiet storm brewing in that space between us.

The moment stretched, taut with unspoken words and pent-up emotion, as my mother's gaze pierced through the din of celebration. I could see the tentative smile on her lips, a fragile bridge between our past misunderstandings and the hope that flickered in her eyes. It was as if the universe had conspired to thrust her back into my life precisely when I was rediscovering who I was—not just as a daughter, but as a dancer, a survivor, a woman reclaiming her space in the world.

"Mom?" The word slipped out before I could gather my thoughts, my heart racing with a cocktail of nerves and yearning. I felt Rylan's presence beside me shift, a silent anchor in a turbulent sea of emotions.

"Callie, sweetheart." Her voice was soft yet charged with an intensity that drew me in, erasing the chaos around us. "I'm so proud of you. You were extraordinary up there."

Pride. It was a word I had craved for so long, and hearing it slip from her lips was like a balm to the raw edges of my spirit. Yet, lurking beneath that pride was an unease, a question that hung heavy in the air. I could feel the tension creeping back in, a shadow threatening to mar the brilliance of the night.

"Thank you," I said, the words trembling on my tongue. "I didn't know if you'd come. I thought—"

"I know. I should have been here sooner," she interjected, her voice trembling slightly, vulnerability seeping into the air between us. "But I've been trying to figure out how to be a part of your life again without stepping on the past."

"Maybe we could start by just being in the same room?" I offered, a thread of hope woven through my words. I wasn't sure how to navigate this fragile landscape, but the thought of losing her again tightened my chest.

Before she could respond, Elise swooped in, her exuberance a splash of color against the backdrop of our solemn moment. "Callie, I need you! They're cutting the cake, and I can't possibly eat it all by myself!"

"Can't have a celebration without cake!" Rylan chimed in, a playful grin breaking the tension. "After all, it's the best way to win people over."

"Not to mention a key ingredient for getting on my good side," Elise added with mock seriousness, her eyes dancing.

I chuckled, grateful for the reprieve from the weight of the conversation. "Okay, cake first, emotional breakdown later," I said, shooting a look at my mother. "We'll talk more after?"

Her nod was tentative, and I felt a flicker of worry. I wanted to embrace her, to pull her into this moment and shield her from the past, but I also recognized the barriers that still loomed between us. With a deep breath, I turned away from the emotional gravity that tethered us and followed Elise and Rylan toward the table, the chatter of my friends a welcome distraction.

The cake was a towering masterpiece of rich chocolate and fluffy frosting, adorned with bright sprinkles that seemed to wink at us like tiny confetti in the air. I could feel the warmth of celebration seep back into my bones, mingling with the sweetness of the moment. As we dug into the cake, laughter floated around us like music, punctuated by the occasional clang of forks against plates and the joyful clamor of voices.

"Are you going to share that secret recipe with us, or are you going to make us suffer through store-bought cake next time?" Rylan joked, shoving a forkful into his mouth.

Elise rolled her eyes dramatically. "Please, let's be real. You couldn't bake a cookie without setting off the smoke alarm."

Rylan feigned shock. "That was one time! And I'm pretty sure the fire department was overreacting."

Their banter lifted my spirits, and I found myself grinning as I savored the rich chocolate melting on my tongue. But even amidst the laughter, I could feel my mother's presence lingering at the edge of the celebration, a flickering candle in a drafty room. I stole glances her way, watching as she conversed with a few of the other dancers, her posture slightly stiff but her smile genuine.

"Okay, what's going on with you?" Elise asked, her voice low and conspiratorial as she nudged me with her elbow, sensing my distraction.

"Nothing. Just... keeping an eye on my mom," I replied, the words slipping out before I could think them through.

"Still worried about her?" she asked, her gaze shifting toward my mother. "I mean, she's here. That's progress, right?"

"Progress, sure. But I'm not sure what happens next," I confessed, the weight of uncertainty creeping back in. "What if she decides she doesn't want to be a part of my life after all?"

Elise shrugged, her expression thoughtful. "That's a risk you have to take, isn't it? You're opening yourself up again. But maybe she's the one who needs to figure out how to navigate this."

The music shifted, the upbeat melody inviting people to dance, and I felt a pull toward the floor, where laughter and joy intertwined in a vivid tapestry. "Let's dance," I said, grabbing Rylan's hand and tugging him toward the makeshift dance floor.

"Lead the way, my fearless dancer," he said with a grin.

As we twirled and swayed to the rhythm, the worries of the world melted away. I felt free, light, the stress of the evening fading like fog before the sun. Rylan moved effortlessly with me, our bodies synchronizing, the energy between us a palpable current that sparked excitement.

"See? This is what it's all about!" he shouted over the music, his laughter bright and infectious.

I threw my head back, letting the music envelop me, surrendering to the moment. But just as I was lost in the rhythm, my gaze darted to the back of the room. I noticed my mother, standing apart from the crowd, her expression shifting from joy to something darker, an unreadable tension coiling in her shoulders.

And then, in a heartbeat, a stranger stepped into her line of sight. A tall man in a tailored suit, his hair dark and slicked back, approached her with an intensity that made my stomach clench. My heart raced as I watched their interaction unfold, a silent conversation that felt charged with something I couldn't quite grasp.

"Callie?" Rylan's voice broke through my fog, concern lining his features as he followed my gaze. "What's wrong?"

I shook my head, my stomach twisting as I struggled to decipher the scene before me. Something was happening, something that felt both significant and alarming. My mother's smile faltered as the man leaned closer, whispering something that made her expression harden.

I couldn't breathe. "I need to go," I said, the urgency in my voice startling even me.

"Where?" Rylan asked, his brow furrowed, but I was already pushing through the crowd, my heart pounding in my ears. I had to reach her before the moment slipped away, before the weight of the past crushed the delicate thread of hope we had started to weave tonight.

As I approached, I could hear the faintest traces of their conversation, a mix of familiarity and tension that left me cold. "You shouldn't be here," my mother said, her voice tight, and I felt a knot form in my stomach.

"Things are different now, Jennifer. We need to talk," the man replied, his tone low and persuasive.

I took a step closer, the urgency in my chest spurring me on, but as I did, the man turned slightly, and for the first time, I saw his face clearly. Recognition slammed into me like a freight train.

"Nick?" I breathed, the name escaping my lips in a whisper that felt foreign yet familiar.

My mother turned, her eyes wide as she registered my presence, the warmth of our earlier exchange evaporating in an instant.

"Callie," she breathed, panic flickering across her features.

But Nick's gaze was locked onto mine, and in that instant, I knew everything had just shifted once more.

Chapter 29: After the Storm

The stage lights dimmed, their warmth fading into the cool, enveloping darkness that lingered beyond the curtain. My heart raced, a wild drumbeat echoing in my ears as Rylan tightened his grip around me. The scent of his cologne—a hint of cedar and something distinctly him—wrapped around us like a cozy blanket, momentarily shielding us from the chaotic world outside. I leaned into him, feeling the solid strength of his presence. Together, we had navigated this tempestuous sea of rehearsals, expectations, and personal revelations, and now, as the final notes of our performance lingered in the air, I could hardly believe we had made it.

"Can you believe we did it?" I murmured, my voice barely above a whisper, as if speaking too loudly might shatter the magic of the moment.

"Did you see their faces?" Rylan replied, pulling back just enough to look into my eyes. His gaze was a mix of triumph and something deeper, a flicker of vulnerability that momentarily stole my breath away. "We had them wrapped around our fingers. That last scene—"

"Was electrifying," I finished for him, a laugh bubbling up. "I thought the floor was going to crumble under the weight of their applause."

"Or our weight," he countered, grinning like a Cheshire cat. The mischief in his eyes made me smile despite the undercurrents of uncertainty swirling in my mind. What came next? What did it mean for us? The thrill of the night began to fade, revealing the fragility of the future we faced.

We stepped off the stage, the familiar backstage area bustling with crew members and fellow actors still riding the high of performance. I took a deep breath, trying to steady myself, overwhelmed by the rush of emotions. The air was thick with the scent of sweat and stage makeup, yet it felt like home. I glanced around, spotting our friends—the vibrant, chaotic tapestry that made up our little community. They were all there, smiles plastered on their faces, their laughter cutting through the murmur of chatter like a melody.

"Hey, you two!" Jenna, our lead actress, approached us, her wild curls bouncing with each step. "That was incredible! I knew you had it in you, but wow! I'm still getting goosebumps thinking about it." She threw her arms around both of us, her enthusiasm infectious.

"Thanks! I didn't think I'd survive that last monologue without tripping over my own feet," I joked, earning a playful shove from Rylan.

"Just admit you were totally focused on me," he teased, a smirk dancing on his lips.

"Please, I was focused on not dying," I replied, rolling my eyes but unable to suppress the grin that spread across my face. It felt good, this lightness between us. If only it could last.

As the celebration unfolded around us, laughter and shouts of joy harmonizing with the fading echoes of our performance, I noticed a shadow lurking in the corner of my mind. The impending uncertainty loomed, a dark cloud threatening to overshadow the night. What would tomorrow bring? Would our performance be enough to secure the funding we desperately needed for the next production? Would it draw in the audiences we had dreamed of, or would we slip back into the obscurity from which we had fought so hard to escape?

Rylan seemed to sense my shift in mood. He took my hand, his thumb brushing gently over my knuckles, grounding me in the moment. "What's going on in that beautiful head of yours?" he asked softly, his expression turning serious, the playful glint dimming in his eyes.

"Just...thinking about what happens next," I confessed, the weight of my thoughts spilling out. "Tonight was amazing, but it feels like we're standing on the edge of a cliff. What if we fall?"

His grip tightened, a promise held within his touch. "We won't fall. Not if we're together. We've fought through worse, remember? This is just the next chapter."

I wanted to believe him, to let his words wrap around my heart like a safety net, but the nagging doubts refused to fade. "But what if it isn't enough?" I pressed, my voice trembling with uncharacteristic vulnerability. "What if the reviews aren't good, or we can't pull in the audience? What if we're just...fooling ourselves?"

"Then we learn," Rylan said, his voice steady, unwavering. "We adapt, we grow, and we fight. We're not just actors; we're a team. And if I've learned anything from this journey, it's that every storm eventually passes. You taught me that."

His words enveloped me like a warm embrace, yet I still felt that niggling doubt. "But what if I can't carry my weight? What if I'm not good enough?"

"Stop," he interrupted, his eyes fierce, almost pleading. "You are more than enough. You're brilliant, and the way you connect with the audience? That's magic, pure and simple. Don't ever doubt that."

Just then, a loud cheer erupted from the others, breaking the tension. They were gathering for a toast, glasses raised high in celebration. I forced a smile, hoping to push aside my worries, if only for the moment. Rylan winked at me, his confident demeanor rekindling a spark of hope within my heart.

As we joined the group, I allowed myself to be swept away in their excitement. Laughter rang out, a symphony of joy filling the air as we clinked glasses and shared stories of our favorite moments from the performance. The camaraderie enveloped me like a warm blanket, each shared laugh slowly dissolving the shadows in my mind.

Yet, even amidst the celebration, the future loomed large, an unseen force swirling just beyond my grasp. Each joyous toast felt like a countdown, a reminder that the aftermath of this night would soon become reality. The applause might have faded, but the echoes of uncertainty still lingered, whispering that the next storm was always waiting just beyond the horizon.

The laughter of our friends echoed around us, but beneath it, a current of anxiety surged through me like a hidden stream. I attempted to match their exuberance, raising my glass to toast to our success, but the worry simmered beneath the surface, nagging and insistent. I knew I had to shake it off, to embrace the moment fully, yet the specter of uncertainty loomed like a storm cloud waiting to break.

"Here's to the dreamers!" Jenna shouted, her voice ringing out over the collective cheers. "May we always have the courage to chase after our wildest ambitions!"

The glasses clinked, a sweet symphony that resonated with hope. I took a sip of my drink, the tang of citrus mixing with the sparkling fizz, trying to drown out my inner voice. The room was awash in warmth and camaraderie, a kaleidoscope of joyful faces illuminated by the dim, flickering lights. Rylan caught my eye again, a silent reassurance that reminded me I wasn't alone in this whirlwind of emotion.

"Hey, how about a group selfie?" Dave, the ever-enthusiastic lighting technician, suggested, already pulling out his phone and bouncing on the balls of his feet. "We have to capture this moment, the night we finally arrived!"

"Or the night we peaked too soon!" I joked, winking at Rylan, who rolled his eyes playfully.

"I'll take the risk," he said, throwing an arm around my shoulders. "As long as I'm in it with you."

The laughter subsided as we gathered, each of us jostling for position, arms flung around shoulders, some striking exaggerated poses while others simply beamed. I nestled closer to Rylan, our sides pressed together, and just for that moment, the world felt right. The click of the camera echoed through the air, capturing our joy, our triumph, and perhaps, unbeknownst to us, the fleeting nature of this very moment.

Afterward, as we dispersed into smaller clusters, Rylan pulled me aside, a conspiratorial grin dancing on his lips. "I have something to show you," he said, excitement bubbling beneath the surface.

"What is it?" I asked, curiosity piquing my interest.

"It's a surprise," he replied, his eyes sparkling with mischief. He took my hand, leading me toward a quieter corner of the venue, away from the thrumming heart of celebration. The atmosphere shifted from vibrant chaos to intimate stillness, and my heart quickened with anticipation.

We stepped into a small alcove adorned with velvet drapes, dimly lit by flickering fairy lights. Rylan released my hand, turned, and produced a small box from his jacket pocket. My breath caught in my throat as he held it out to me, the soft glow of the lights reflecting off the polished surface.

"What's this?" I asked, my voice trembling with a mixture of excitement and uncertainty.

"Open it," he urged, a glimmer of anticipation dancing in his eyes.

With trembling fingers, I lifted the lid, revealing a delicate silver necklace nestled within the velvet lining. A simple pendant shaped like a star dangled from the chain, its polished surface catching the light in a way that made it seem alive.

"It's beautiful," I breathed, my heart swelling at the thoughtful gift. "But you didn't have to—"

"Of course I did," he interrupted, his tone earnest. "You've poured your heart and soul into this project. I wanted you to have something to remind you of tonight and everything you've accomplished."

I looked up at him, feeling the weight of his words settle deep within me. "You're really something, you know that?" I said, unable to suppress my smile.

"Yeah, I have my moments," he replied, feigning modesty but unable to hide his own delight. "And you know, I thought this would look great on you. It matches your spark."

"Rylan!" I exclaimed, the teasing tone in my voice laced with genuine warmth. "You're going to make me blush."

"That's the plan," he winked, stepping closer, the playful energy crackling between us.

I fastened the necklace around my neck, feeling the cool metal settle against my skin like a talisman of courage. "Thank you. This means so much to me," I said, meeting his gaze. The moment hung between us, thick with unspoken feelings, a palpable connection that buzzed in the air like electricity.

Before I could overthink it, I leaned in and pressed a quick kiss to his cheek. His eyes widened in surprise, a flicker of something—hope?—dancing behind his dark lashes.

"Wow," he said, the breath catching in his throat. "That was unexpected."

"Just wanted to thank you properly," I replied, my voice light, but inside, I felt a deeper truth lingering unacknowledged. We were skirting the edges of something profound, something that could shift the very foundation of our relationship.

Just as the moment settled, a loud crash broke the spell, sending us both spinning toward the source. A table had toppled over in the main area, drinks spilling everywhere, laughter morphing into startled gasps.

"Let's go see if anyone's hurt," I suggested, the reality of the night crashing back like a wave.

Rylan nodded, the earlier intimacy swiftly replaced by the familiar adrenaline of the chaotic world of theater. As we made our way back, I felt the weight of the necklace against my chest, a reminder of our shared triumph, but also the uncertainty that loomed. What would this night mean for us tomorrow? As we rushed into the bustling throng, the laughter and cheers resumed, but my heart raced not just from the chaos but from the realization that the ground beneath us was shifting in ways I was only beginning to comprehend.

The thrill of performance still echoed, but now the stage was set for more than just the next act; it was the backdrop for our lives, intertwined in ways I never anticipated. As Rylan's hand found mine again, our fingers entwining naturally, I couldn't shake the feeling that we were on the cusp of something monumental—a new chapter brimming with the promise of adventure, but also fraught with the shadows of uncertainty waiting to be unveiled.

The chaotic aftermath of the table crash buzzed around us like an angry hornet's nest. Rylan and I maneuvered through the crowd, weaving between scattered chairs and clusters of our castmates, their laughter mingling with shouts of concern. The vibrant energy of the night had transformed into a frenzy of excitement, but the remnants of my earlier doubts still swirled like leaves caught in a storm. I glanced at Rylan, who appeared unfazed, his easy confidence pulling me along in his wake.

"Next time, let's just stick to our dramatic scenes and leave the slapstick comedy to the professionals," I quipped, nudging him playfully.

"Agreed! My talents are wasted on spills and thrills," he shot back, his grin infectious. But even as he spoke, I noticed the flicker of concern in his eyes, the way his brow furrowed just slightly as he scanned the crowd for any signs of trouble.

"Seriously though," I continued, lowering my voice, "do you think everyone's okay?"

"Let's check it out," he said, taking my hand once more, our fingers intertwining effortlessly as we approached the scene. The table lay on its side like a fallen soldier, drinks pooling on the floor and several of our friends kneeling to help right the mess. The atmosphere shifted, the laughter replaced with a newfound camaraderie born from chaos.

"Look, it's a group effort!" Jenna called out, her bright voice rising above the din. "Help me flip this thing back up before it's our turn to perform a rescue mission."

We joined the throng, laughter bubbling up again as the seriousness of the moment faded into the backdrop. With a united effort, we righted the table, and Rylan and I shared a look—one that spoke volumes about the unpredictability of life, both on and off the stage.

"See? Teamwork makes the dream work," he said, nudging me with his shoulder, the playful spirit returning.

"More like teamwork makes a mess," I replied, shaking my head with mock seriousness. "If this is the kind of teamwork we can expect, I might have to reconsider my career choice."

As we stood back, surveying our handiwork, I felt a sense of relief wash over me, mingling with the adrenaline that still coursed through my veins. But as the laughter swelled, the undercurrent of my earlier worries began to rise again, reminding me of the uncharted waters ahead.

Just then, a sharp voice cut through the jubilant noise. "Attention, everyone!" It was Tom, our director, stepping forward with a grave expression that instantly silenced the crowd. "If I could have your attention for just a moment, please."

I exchanged a glance with Rylan, confusion creasing my brow. This was unusual. Tom was typically the life of the party, not the one to bring solemnity to the post-show celebration.

"Unfortunately, I have some news that requires immediate attention," he continued, his tone serious. "I just got off the phone with the theater board. There's been a significant issue with our funding for the next show."

A collective gasp rippled through the crowd, a shockwave of disbelief. I felt Rylan's grip tighten around my fingers, and I instinctively leaned into him.

"Funding issues?" someone shouted from the back, skepticism thick in the air. "What does that mean for us?"

"It means that unless we can secure alternative funding, our next production is in jeopardy," Tom replied, his voice steady yet tinged with worry. "We'll have to meet tomorrow to discuss our options. I know it's late, but this is critical."

The room fell into a tense silence, the reality of the situation settling in like a thick fog. I could hear the faint sound of my heartbeat, a steady reminder of the stakes involved. Rylan's thumb brushed over my hand, a soothing gesture amidst the growing anxiety.

"We've worked too hard to let it slip through our fingers," he whispered, leaning closer. "We can figure this out together, right?"

"Right," I said, though the knot in my stomach tightened. I felt the weight of every sleepless night, every rehearsal, every sacrifice that had brought us to this point. The thought of losing it all made my chest ache.

The conversation around us began to swell, voices rising in both frustration and determination. It was as if a light had been ignited, and now everyone was scrambling to brainstorm solutions, ideas bouncing around like ping-pong balls.

"What if we did a fundraiser?" someone suggested. "We could host a gala or a performance night and charge admission!"

"Or we could partner with local businesses for sponsorship!" Jenna chimed in, her enthusiasm infectious.

Rylan leaned in closer, his breath warm against my ear. "I like the fundraiser idea. We can rally the community and show them what we're capable of. We've got this."

His faith in our group ignited a flicker of hope within me, but doubt still lingered like a shadow, refusing to dissipate completely. "What if it's not enough? What if the board doesn't see it as viable?"

"Then we'll just have to make it so good they can't ignore it," he replied, his eyes gleaming with determination. "We can do this. We won't let it end like this."

As discussions ramped up, I found myself lost in the fervor of ideas and plans, but the underlying tension gnawed at my mind. I couldn't shake the feeling that something deeper was at play, a hidden agenda lurking in the shadows. I leaned closer to Rylan, seeking comfort in his presence, but just as I opened my mouth to share my worries, a sudden commotion at the back of the room caught my attention.

"Wait, everyone!" a voice cried out, cutting through the chaos. It was Max, our stage manager, his face pale and drawn. "There's something else you need to know."

The crowd fell silent once more, and the atmosphere shifted. I felt Rylan tense beside me, his body rigid with anticipation.

"What is it?" Tom asked, his tone sharp, eyes narrowed as he focused on Max.

"There's been a development with the venue," Max said, his voice shaking slightly. "They're considering pulling our lease... for the entire season."

Gasps erupted, panic flashing in the eyes of my friends. The very foundation we had built our dreams upon seemed to tremble beneath us, and I could feel the ground shifting, the uncertainty growing.

"What do you mean?" I heard myself ask, the words spilling out before I could reign them in.

Max ran a hand through his hair, a gesture of frustration and fear. "They've had complaints about noise, about crowds... They're threatening to kick us out if we don't resolve it soon."

My heart raced, the implications crashing over me like a tidal wave. The theater—the heart of our creativity, our home—was at risk.

"Tomorrow's meeting just got a lot more complicated," Rylan said, his voice barely above a whisper, but the intensity in his gaze told me he understood the gravity of the situation as well.

As the murmurs erupted into chaos, my mind spun. How could we possibly face this on top of everything else? The stakes had never felt higher, and yet, I knew that whatever lay ahead, we would have to confront it head-on.

Rylan's hand found mine again, the warmth of his touch anchoring me as we navigated the storm brewing within our group. Together, we faced the uncertain horizon, a tumultuous sea of challenges stretching out before us. But as I looked into Rylan's eyes, I felt a spark of determination igniting within me—a promise that we wouldn't go down without a fight.

And as the reality of our predicament sank in, a shadow flickered at the edge of my mind, an ominous whisper that perhaps the greatest challenges were yet to reveal themselves, lurking in the shadows, waiting for the right moment to strike.

Milton Keynes UK
Ingram Content Group UK Ltd.
UKHW042241011124
450424UK00001BA/148

9 798227 723208